EUGÉNIE—

Beautiful and Tempestuous

Eugénie's wit and charm, and her ability to play her
cards wisely, enabled her to capture the man who became emperor of France. Although her husband—Louis
Napoleon—loved her deeply and allowed her to live in
luxury and fashion, he was fickle and unfaithful.
Eugénie soon became involved in royal intrigue, in
plots and counterplots. She was as clever a politician
as any of the court ministers.

"told in the first person by Eugénie herself . . . she
emerges as a fascinating figure . . . F. W. Kenyon is
dependably authentic in his research and gives stature
to the biographical-historical novel!"
                                    —Virginia Kirkus Service

OTHER BOOKS BY F. W. KENYON

THE EMPEROR'S LADY
EMMA
MARIE ANTOINETTE
MARY OF SCOTLAND
THE GOLDEN YEARS
MISTRESS NELL
THE GLORY AND THE DREAM
THE NAKED SWORD

Our free catalogue is available upon request. Any Tower titles not in your local bookstore can be purchased through the mail. Simply send 15¢ plus the retail price of the book and write Tower Publications, 185 Madison Avenue, New York, New York 10016.

Any titles currently in print are available in quantity for industrial and sales-promotion use at a reduced rate. Address inquiries to our Promotion Dept.

THAT
SPANISH
WOMAN

F. W. Kenyon

A TOWER BOOK

THAT SPANISH WOMAN

Tower Publications, Inc.
185 Madison Avenue
New York, New York 10016

Copyright © MCMLXII by F.W. Kenyon

Library of Congress Catalog Card Number 63-10238

Printed in U.S.A.

Published by special arrangement with Dodd, Mead & Company

Chapter One

WHEN I WAS a girl of sixteen I smoked a cigarette at the bullfight. That, in the year 1842, was outrageous behavior in the daughter of a Spanish grandee. Mama, thinking of her position in Madrid society, was absolutely horrified. So was Queen Victoria when the story reached her ears several years later, though when I was able to tell her my reason she laughed heartily.

Not for many years have I given that particular incident even a passing thought, yet it came up strongly in my mind just now when, humoring the old woman, they bowed me to my desk and placed writing materials within my reach. One of them muttered that the strain would be too great; another, that a whole horde of doctors should be consulted before I attempted to put pen to paper. They spoke respectfully—indeed, they could do no less!—but I sensed disapproval in their voices. Imagine it, an old woman of ninety-two embarking upon the writing of her memoirs! Obviously they think me incapable of looking back from 1918 to 1826. Dolts, the lot of them! Finally, a general move was made to the door, accompanied by the usual little murmurs, "With Your Majesty's permission . . ."; and to my intense satisfaction I was left in peace, to do as I pleased.

Memory is a very peculiar thing. When I was a child, I often startled visitors by talking authoritatively about events which took place before my birth. I believed, you see, that I was acquainted with my parents at the time

5

of their first meeting and I asserted boldly that I could remember not only my own birth but that of my elder sister. Even now, I can still see my heavily pregnant mother resting in the garden when that momentous earthquake shook the land. There she is, poor frightened woman, and there, only a few hours later, am I, Eugenia, future Empress of France, entering the world well before my time. I have a notion, however, that my own impatience was the real cause, not the earthquake. I once told Prosper Mérimée as much and warned him that when I wanted anything strongly enough I knew how to make the earth quake, to say nothing of the unfortunate people on it.

"I must be blind not to have noticed it," the wretch chuckled. "Let us concede, child, that you chose to be born during an earthquake in order to give your birth a spurious, dramatic significance."

"Spurious!" I remember shrieking. "When I become a queen, you'll regret your disrespectful words."

Mérimée bowed deeply. "Ah yes, Your Majesty— the gypsy's prophecy."

I can't be sure now whether there really was such a prophecy, or whether my mother, determined to increase the would-be significance of the earthquake, was quick to invent it. According to the story, she visited a gypsy fortune-teller who predicted that I would become a queen and live for a hundred years.

I was born, then, on the fifth of May in the year 1826 at Granada, and one may find significance—if one wishes—in the fact that it was the fifth anniversary of the death in exile of Napoleon Bonaparte, the first Emperor of France. My father was of noble birth, being none other than Don Cipriano Guzman Palafox y Portocarrero, Count of Teba. As for Mama, she was Maria Manuela Kirkpatrick y Grevignée. What a confusion of names! I was often bewildered by them myself, though strangely attracted by the "Kirkpatrick" which sits so oddly among the rest and is evidence of the Scottish blood which flows in my veins. Important blood, as Mama loved to point out, for it gives me descent from the grandfather of the Scottish king, Robert Bruce.

William Kirkpatrick, my maternal grandfather, migrated to Spain in the eighteenth century. He settled in Malaga and found employment with a merchant who dealt in wine and fruit. In later years Mama's eyes always grew glazed at the mention of such an occupation. Grandfather Kirkpatrick "in trade"! Nevertheless, he possessed an impressive family tree and was a clever businessman. In the course of time, he married his employer's daughter, grew rich and became consul in Malaga for the United States of America.

At my baptismal ceremony I was given the names Maria Eugenia Ignacia Augustina, but I was known from the first as Eugenia.

I made everybody happy this morning by agreeing that the strain really is too great, but that was only to put them off. I pointed to the torn-up writing paper in the wastepaper basket and said, "There you are; that's as far as I got; I promise not to strain my eyes any more." Admittedly there are times when I can see only an indistinct blur on the paper, but after a while it clears and I'm able to continue.

"Never stand still, never retire from the struggle," Mama used to say.

She rarely stood still herself and, as my sister Francisca was apt to remark, was at times a sore trial to poor Papa.

Papa . . . Even after all these years, Don Cipriano stands out in my mind as a romantic figure, possibly because he wore a black patch over one eye, the sight of which he lost when fighting for the French at Salamanca. He was an ardent Bonapartist and played an important but hopeless part in the defense of Paris in 1814. Returning to Spain after the final fall and exile of Napoleon, he took up garrison duty at Malaga. There he met Mama again and fell in love with her. She for her part fell quickly in love with his social position and, in marrying him, gambled on the chance of his elder brother, the Count of Montijo, dying a bachelor.

Uncle Eugenio hated imperialism and had nothing but contempt for "that upstart" Napoleon. He regarded Papa as a renegade and put every possible obstacle in the way of the marriage. Merciful heavens, the Kirkpatrick girl was the daughter of a trader! Thus, for a time, he persuaded King Ferdinand to withhold the royal consent, but urgent messages were sent to Scotland, and presently Mama was in a position to deliver what she called a *coup de grâce*. In other words, a patent from the Office of Heralds in Edinburgh was presented for the King's inspection.

"With Robert Bruce up my sleeve was I not almost too good for a Spanish grandee?" Mama often gloated.

And so Papa and Mama were married, but it was six years before Francisca was born. I made my appearance a year later. Finally, there was my brother who died while still a child.

Mama was clever as well as restless and ambitious. When Uncle Eugenio married suddenly, she hid her disappointment, made a friend of the new bride and, through her, gained a larger allowance for Papa and a fine house in the Calle del Sordo at Granada. Happily for Mama, Uncle Eugenio died without issue and Papa became Count of Montijo.

"But your father was cheeseparing," Mama often brooded. "Instead of loosening the pursestrings, he tightened them."

Even so, Mama succeeded in setting up a *salon* which was frequented by artists, writers, musicians and all the important foreign visitors she could gather together. Papa took an interest in only one of these visitors, the French writer Prosper Mérimée. At that time, we had moved to Madrid, Papa having become a senator, and our house in the Plaza del Angel was often the meeting place of diplomats and Spanish politicians. Yet for all that, Mama was consumed by a growing yearning for Paris. A *salon* in the French capital, how wonderful *that* would be! But Papa, counting the cost, was adamant.

"So! You can't afford it!" Mama raged. "How preposterous!"

Papa removed the black patch, a disconcerting habit of his when involved in an argument, and looked at her plaintively with his one good eye.

"Mérimée has deprived you of your senses with his stories of life in Paris."

Mama chuckled unexpectedly. "Say rather that I have deprived him of his with my plans for a Bohemian *salon*."

Mérimée had fallen instantly under Mama's spell, and he regarded her as the cleverest conversationalist a writer was ever likely to meet. He was deeply indebted to her, also, for a marvelous story about a gypsy girl. Later he wrote it in his own words, and later still Bizet used it for his now famous opera, *Carmen*.

Papa remained adamant, Mérimée departed and Mama sulked. Even the outbreak of the Carlist War left Papa unmoved. People died in the streets; there was massacre after massacre. Papa caused a strong guard to be placed on the house and whenever he slipped out by a side door, we wondered fearfully if we would ever see him again.

"Escape is now impossible," Mama wept. "Paris is the dead dream of a woman all but dead herself."

And then came that dreadful cholera epidemic, a disaster far worse than civil war, but Papa still hesitated.

"Let your wife and daughters die of cholera, but what of your son and heir?" Mama flung at him.

In a way, her words were another *coup de grâce*.

"You shall take the children to Italy," Papa decided.

"Italy? An unhealthy climate. The water alone would kill us."

Papa was defeated and knew it. "Very well—
France."

And so, at the age of eight, I set foot on French soil
for the first time in my life. A cholera epidemic, and . . .
voilà! It's an ill wind, a very ill wind indeed, as Mama
was fond of saying, that blows nobody good.

Flowers, you must agree, is a delightful name for a
governess, particularly an English governess. Mama, attracted by the name even more than by Miss Flowers'
undoubted qualifications, engaged her soon after we
reached Paris. From the Continental point of view,
Flowers was a typical English "Miss," a born old maid.
She knew her place and kept it with the silent understanding that we would do so, too. We assumed that she
was the unmarriageable daughter of an impoverished
clergyman, for such English females—or so Mama asserted—always sought employment abroad as govern-
esses. She dressed plainly, as befitted her station, and
smelled faintly of lavender, little linen bags of which she
concealed among her cothing.

Flowers taught us English while Prosper Mérimée, a
constant visitor, taught us French. The English lessons
were tedious but the French a sheer delight. How well I
remember the latter! They consisted to a great extent of
stories which Mérimée invented on the spot. There
were pens and aunts in them, for sure, and cats also—
such sportive little cats, tearing about with the wind in
their tails. Even so, we looked forward to the occasional
serious lesson—oh, those impossible irregular verbs!—
for Mérimée never failed to reward our efforts with the
most delicious French confectionery.

"But not a word to Miss Flowers. You know what
she would say."

"We do! We do!"

"Put it in English, I beg of you. It carries a greater
sense of doom in that language."

"Sweets are very bad for the teeth!"

Later, after the death of my poor little brother, Francisca and I were sent to the Convent of the Sacred Heart in the Rue de Varennes. Flowers pursed her lips, the closest she ever came to revealing emotion. We imagined, Paca and I, that this daughter of an English clergyman was shuddering in private horror. I almost always called my sister "Paca," except when displeased with her. Then, of course, it was a very stern "Francisca." Mama herself preferred the full "Paquita."

Because of Mérimée and his friends, our Paris *salon* had an amateur political flavor. The heated political arguments were well above my head, but I was entranced by the stories I heard of the rise and fall of Napoleon Bonaparte. Already the dead Emperor was a legend. Ah, the romance of it all! Small wonder I became as ardent a Bonapartist as dear Papa.

Mérimée carefully explained the French political situation and I wrote it all down painstakingly on ruled paper, scratching away in my childish script about the great Napoleon's Bourbon successors, Louis XVIII and Charles X, and how the latter, insisting upon the divine right of the Bourbons, brought about the revolution of 1830. Then, somewhat bored, I drew a picture of a large umbrella, since Louis-Philippe, the new King, always carried one rain or shine—his way of showing everybody, said Mérimée that he was willing to be a good little middle-class monarch.

Soon after that, Paca and I went with Mama to visit one of her friends, Madame Delessert, the wife of the Prefect of Paris. It was our habit, Paca's and mine, to play with the Delessert children while Mama gossiped with Madame, but there was no gossiping for Mama that day. We knew something was amiss the moment we reached the Prefecture, for the street was crowded with shouting, gesticulating people.

"Is it another revolution?" I asked hopefully.

Entering, we came upon a young man in civilian

clothes and two stern members of the National Guard. The young man—we later learned he was actually twenty-eight—stood apart from the soldiers, but was obviously their prisoner. Madame Delessert appeared suddenly and, looking like a flustered hen who had found her straying chickens, tried to hurry us away.

"Who is he?" I whispered hoarsely.

"The Bonaparte Pretender!"

He bowed courteously, a bow intended for me, I told myself proudly, and not for the Prefect's agitated wife.

It was Mérimée who told me later that Louis-Napoleon, nephew of the Emperor, had planned a *coup d'état* at Strasbourg, but had failed miserably. Captured, he had been brought to Paris before being sent into exile in America. One must be grateful to "King Umbrella" for his clemency. Had he executed his rival, there would never have been the Empress Eugénie.

In my dreams, for I dreamed of Louis-Napoleon many a night, I saw the Bonaparte Pretender as a brave, romantic figure standing apart from his captors, while I, kneeling before him, swore passionately that rather than marry any other man I'd enter a convent.

We had been in Paris for five whole years when alarming news reached us from Madrid. Papa was gravely ill; it was imperative that we should return at once. Mama departed hurriedly with her maid Pepa, leaving Paca and me to follow with the lavender-scented Flowers.

Poor Papa was dead when we reached Madrid. Mama herself had arrived only just in time for a dramatic death-bed scene. We found her in deep mourning, pale beneath the black veil and seemingly distracted with grief. She clutched us to her bosom, wept with us and moaned that she really had been a bad wife to stay away from home so long. Then a faint smile, a smile which disappeared almost before I recognized it, crossed her face.

12

"Before the end came, I made your dear father a solemn promise, a promise I'm determined to keep."

She sighed dreamily. "I promised to do everything in my power to find suitable husbands for you two poor little waifs."

The "two poor little waifs" glanced at each other again. What an exciting thought! Then we felt ashamed of ourselves. Mama's veil was quite saturated with tears. She gathered us to her bosom again and for a moment, a fleeting moment, I saw that faint smile once more.

"Children, your dear, good Papa made adequate provision for his bereaved family. We are rich, quite rich."

Riches and real freedom for the Countess of Montijo! I waited, looking up at her expectantly. She heaved another sigh.

"It's an ill wind that blows nobody good."

Chapter Two

MAMA FOUND THE period of mourning irksome. She would have dispensed with it altogether had it not been for the "proprieties." Even so, she compromised with "the look of things" during visits to our country house at Carbanchel. That is to say, we entertained ourselves privately with amateur theatricals and behind locked doors continued our dancing lessons.

Toward the end of that period, I was sent to England to spend a few months at an English school, there to polish up my English among the native English. Flowers accompanied me and after a private visit to a small provincial town—one assumed she stayed with her clergyman father—she reappeared to take me back to Spain. I remember very little of my experiences at that English school, but I do recall the smell of those English girls. Oh, a very clean, respectable smell, a smell strongly suggestive of carbolic. The thought of it still revolts me. I remember, too, their inane chatter about boys and their quarrels about the sports mistress. During the journey back to Spain, Flowers made a surprising pronouncement.

"Dona Eugenia, you have acquired an upper-class English accent. Admirable, yes, but I urge you to employ it sparingly."

"Indeed?"

"In time, Dona Eugenia, it would spoil the shape of your lovely mouth."

Arriving in Madrid, I found that Mama had emerged

fully from her period of mourning. She said she knew how the butterfly felt when escaping from the chrysalis and added joyfully that she had now burst like a meteor upon Madrid society. She had her weather eye cocked, as the English say, for suitable husbands for her two beautiful daughters. There were lavish, dignified entertainments at our town house and gay, less restrained weekend parties in the country where my passion for riding was given full rein. And, of course, most exciting of all, there was a succession of magnificent balls.

I can see us now, Paca and me, drawing all eyes in our direction at our first ball. Tears spring to my old eyes at the memory, the all too vivid memory. Is it possible that this ancient creature who sits here dreaming of the past was ever that lovely young woman, Eugenia Palafox? There she stands at her sister's side, the taller of the two and fair, where Paca, a truly Spanish beauty, is dark. That red-gold hair—Titian would have loved it, Mérimée always said, those blue eyes—a Scottish inheritance, the proud tilt of the little head, the perfect neck, the graceful sweep of those creamy-white shoulders. . . .

But it was Paca, not I, who was sought out that night by the most handsome young man at the ball. How I shook with indignation! Having gained Mama's gracious permission, he danced again and again with my sister and glanced not once in my direction, or so I imagined at the time.

"Who is the wretch?" I asked Mama furiously.

"Come, come, child, were you deaf when I presented you?"

In truth I'd heard not a syllable of his name. Deaf, yes. Speechless, also, and in a sense quite flustered. How intense one can be at sixteen!

"You feel drawn to him already," Mama was saying wisely.

"On the contrary, his rudeness repels me."

"Rudeness, Genia? His manners are beyond reproach."

The young man, she went on to inform me, was a duke twice over, one dukedom being English, the other Spanish. In short, he was the eighth Duke of Berwick and the fourteenth Duke of Alba.

"On the English side he is the descendant of a king," Mama exulted.

I thought instantly of the gypsy's prediction. "Is he likely to become King of England?"

Mama sighed regretfully. "His illustrious ancestor, the first Duke of Berwick, was born on the wrong side of the blanket."

"Illegitimate," I said contemptuously.

"Not the present duke, darling."

"Nevertheless—"

"Illegitimacy brought about by a king is very different from illegitimacy brought about by a nobody."

"In the sight of God, Mama?"

My virtuous mother turned up her eyes to heaven. "Even in the sight of God, by Whose grace kings mount their thrones."

Alba, as we came to call the "double" duke, was James Stuart FitzJames. The original FitzJames was the son of King James II of England and one of his many mistresses, a certain Arabella Churchill. I met one of the present-day Churchills recently and when I reminded him of Arabella's looseness, he wasn't in the least amused. It was a simple, if somewhat shocking, thing in those far-off days, you see, for a king to ennoble his natural children.

After the last dance, Alba came back to Mama with Paca on his arm. Naturally I'd danced many times myself, the pangs of love notwithstanding. In a way, that special way known only to women, it pleased me enormously to think that while Paca had been sought by only one man, a dozen had danced with me and many more had been turned away. Alba kissed Mama's hand

—he could do no less since she thrust it beneath his aristocratic nose—gave Paca a ceremonious bow, glanced unseeingly in my direction and disappeared.

Paca's dark eyes flashed angrily. "A repulsive creature. I loathe the sight of him!"

"You danced with him the whole time," I pointed out.

Paca stamped her foot. *"Qué fastidio!"*

"You appear to be on the point of tears," Mama remarked.

"Why did you find it a bore?" I asked curiously.

Paca stamped her foot again. "Is my dress attractive? Indeed it is, but he made no mention of it. Are my eyes soulful? They are, but he spared them not a glance!"

Mama looked quite bewildered. "I observed him many times in earnest conversation with you."

"He had only one subject, Mama. You may not believe it but that subject was Eugenia." Paca turned on me with a wild sweep of her fan. "Your creamy skin and lovely neck reminded him of a swan."

My heart was suddenly singing within me. "What else did he say, Paca?"

"The rest of you made him think of a Viking goddess. I told him that such creatures were large, muscular and frightening, but he refused to believe me and laughed dreamily. Dreamily, please note!"

"Then why didn't he ask me to dance with him?"

"He was much too diffident. You're a deity as well as a swan. He stood back in awe."

I went to bed that night the happiest girl in Madrid.

"My task is lightened considerably," Mama remarked, lingering in my room when she came to bid me goodnight. "Without a doubt, the match will make itself."

The second ball took place a few weeks later. Alba, whom we hadn't seen meanwhile, set our hearts fluttering—Paca's in despair, mine in hopeful anticipation—when he wasted no time in approaching Mama. How tall and dark and desirable he was! Oh, the grace of his bearing as he bent over Mama's hand, kissing it.

"My dear Duke!"

"My dear Dona Manuela!"

A moment later, the beautiful, unattainable swan was in Alba's arms. He danced with me the whole evening and matronly heads nodded wisely. Gratifying progress, you say? Nothing of the kind! When Alba spoke at all, he dwelt at length of Paca's charms. Those rich, full lips —he also called them generous, that lovely skin, deeper than the shade of ivory! Never had he seen a more entrancing example of Spanish beauty. And her eyes! Not challenging, not coquettish, as one might have expected, but gentle, infinitely gentle.

It was absolutely infuriating.

At the next ball, Alba, as if striving to be scrupulously fair, divided his time equally between Paca and me. But a pattern had been set. While with me, he talked only of Paca; while with Paca, only of me.

"Perhaps he'd like both of us," Paca pondered.

"Not being a Turkish sultan—"

"Obviously he cannot make up his mind between you," Mama cut me short. "My children are now in competition, one with the other."

Regarding this as a challenge, I was the first to take it up and achieve a measure of success. After all, steady progress with a man is always possible if he can be induced first to talk about himself. One listens, one interjects a flattering phrase, and—*voilà!* Nevertheless, being the sort of person I am, I shunned the flattering phrase and rested content with an occasional, intelligent remark. In no time at all, the dear fellow was telling me earnestly that I possessed a remarkably clever brain.

Paca eventually took up the challenge herself and we compared careful, rather cautious notes.

"I don't think I know men as well as you do, Genia,

and I'm by no means as clever as you are. All I could do was utter little gasps of wonder and pretend to know nothing whatever about the worldly things he discussed."

"Little gasps of wonder! I could never bring myself to that, Paca."

"Ah, but you're a much stronger character than I. So much more independent." She smiled quite innocently.

I glowed with pleasure. I'd always known it and here was my sister admitting it freely.

"The Duke said he feared I was abysmally ignorant," she sighed.

I could but smile my satisfaction. "You regard that as progress, darling?"

"But of course, Genia."

"Poor Paca, what a goose you are!"

My sister and I in competition, one with the other? Not as far as *I* was concerned. In no time at all the man who admired both my beauty and my brains would ask Mama for my hand in marriage. Mama was inclined to agree and, to help things along, invited Alba to join one of our week-end parties at Carbanchel. He accepted gratefully and after the first country jaunt became, as they say, one of the family. Even so, he showed less sign than ever of declaring himself.

"The Duke is a very great gentleman," Paca asserted. "He realizes that it would be unseemly to speak to either of us of love before first approaching Mama."

"It's possible to do unseemly things in a seemly manner," Mama murmured.

"It really is?" Paca exclaimed thoughtfully.

"Action must be taken before this pretty friendship becomes unshakably established," said our anxious mother.

"You mean to force him to declare himself?"

"I fear I must."

"Unseemly action in a seemly manner?"

"Naturally!"

Mama was frankly unseemly when she summoned Alba to her presence one momentous afternoon. Actually summoned him, as if she were a queen and he a noble of the lowest rank. I heard almost everything that passed between them, for I concealed myself behind a heavy curtain with an inner door held open should sudden flight be necessary.

Mama began without preamble. "The whole of Madrid is talking, and talk of that sort is injurious to my daughters' reputations."

Alba was instantly contrite. "My dear Dona Manuela, you overwhelm me with confusion."

I wanted very much to see his face, but the tone of his voice seemed sufficient. Mama, with that quick, merciless thrust, had surely gained the upper hand. Her next move was to laugh gently, understandingly.

"My poor Alba, you appear to have brought yourself to a pretty pass. Rest assured, dear boy, you have my heartfelt sympathy. After all, the fault was mine."

"Yours, Dona Manuela?"

"It was unreasonable of me giving birth to two beautiful daughters."

There was a moment's silence, then he said earnestly: "Were there but one and she Eugenia, I should be obliged, despite all I have observed, to ask for her hand in marriage."

All he had observed? *Despite* all he had observed? I came close to clutching at the curtain in an agony of incredible doubt.

Mama laughed softly. "Come, come, do you still regard Eugenia with awe at a time like this? *Really,* my dear Alba!"

"Awe?" I heard him ponder.

"Understandable perhaps," Mama conceded.

I felt happier instantly. Married to Alba I would indeed have the upper hand.

"I can but regard with awe her remarkable spirit of independence," he went on, his voice rising strongly.

"Likewise her amazing intelligence. Both attributes are admirable, but I ask you, Dona Manuela, would any self-respecting man seek such distressing traits in a wife?"

Admirable, yet distressing? Alba was speaking of me, Maria Eugenia Ignacia Augustina! Only by the greatest effort of will did I prevent myself from tearing aside the curtain and flinging myself between him and Mama. Despair followed anger. Oh, that tight burning feeling in my breast! I turned away with a stifled sob. Melodrama, yes, but at that time it seemed tragedy, sheer tragedy. In a word, my own especial grand opera.

Alba was speaking again, softly, lingeringly, lovingly.

"Francisca . . . Paquita . . . Paca . . ."

"Paquita, then, is your choice?"

"My dear Dona Manuela, how could you possibly doubt it?"

I could bear no more. Flying to my room, I flung myself face down on the bed. I wanted to weep but found myself incapable of tears. Real living tears, that is, but there were tears, bitter and scalding, in my heart.

After an age during which I grew older by many years, Paca stole softly into the room. A mouse, I thought, a mouse which, by means best known to itself, had swallowed a double duke. Oh, her manner was apologetic but her eyes were radiant.

"Genia, darling . . ."

"Why *you?*" I demanded furiously.

She glanced away demurely. "I think perhaps because my only ambition is to be a good wife and mother."

"You actually told him that?"

"Yes, Genia."

"How utterly shameless of you!"

"Yes indeed. I hung my head the moment the words were out of my mouth and apologized."

"What did he say?"

"Not a word. He took me gently in his arms and kissed me."

"Francisca!"

"Now you're very angry with me."

"With Alba more than you. What an idiot to be deceived so easily!"

It takes a woman to see through a woman, but I realized that ancient truth much too late.

Paca touched my shoulder hesitantly. "Genia, I'm sorry."

"You'll be sorrier still in a few minutes. I took poison just before you came. Wait a little while and you'll have the satisfaction of watching me die in agony."

Paca screamed and ran for Mama. In a moment the whole house was in confusion with servants running wildly hither and thither, all of them screaming, too. Paca returned. Tears were streaming down her cheeks. The family physician, she said, had been sent for. But strangely, as I waited and wondered how best to brazen out my lie, neither Mama nor the doctor appeared. Uneasily I made the most of the situation by groaning and clutching my stomach. Paca flung herself upon me, sobbing hysterically. I was at all events making her suffer a little longer.

Mama strolled into the room at last. Yes, she actually strolled!

"Emetics are both disgusting and painful," she said gaily.

I sat up at once. "Emetics?"

"You would prefer to die, Genia?"

"But I want to die, Mama!"

"Very well, I shall sit with you and wait calmly for the end."

Paca, no longer deceived by my play-acting, was sent to her room. Mama seated herself in a chair, took up a book and began to read. Oh, that steady, deliberate turning of the pages! I sustained it and her silent presence for an hour before admitting defeat.

"Mama, I'm hungry."

Mama turned another page. "Poison makes one hungry? Remarkable!"

"You wanted Alba for me. Why have you given him Paca?"

Mama closed the book. "Be sensible, Genia. I admit my disappointment. I even believe that your heart is broken—for the time being. But would you have me say 'no' to the Duke of Berwick and Alba and be left with two unmarried daughters on my hands? A mother must be ready at all times to compromise with circumstances. I have at least achieved a brilliant match for one of you."

"That's all you think about, the brilliance of the match."

"But of course, child. In making a marriage, the man himself is of small account in comparison with the position he holds. No male creature is worth breaking one's heart over. Remember that always, Countess."

"Countess, Mama?"

"With Paquita about to become a duchess, it is only fitting that you should assume the family title of Teba."

"Dona Eugenia, Countess of Teba . . ." I said dully.

"Precisely."

"It means less than nothing to me."

"Come, darling, look on the bright side. Have you forgotten the gypsy's prediction? Greater things are in store for my favorite daughter."

Chapter Three

HAVE YOU EVER observed the blank, bright smile
on the painted face of a china doll? Just such a smile
was mine at Paca's marriage ceremony and the feasting
and merrymaking which followed it. I even managed to
maintain the smile when my new brother-in-law embraced me, but I know I trembled violently at his brief,
unemotional touch. He noticed it, too, and had the
grace to look momentarily confused.

Gradually, however, I grew ashamed of myself, of the
sisterly resentment which Paca's radiant happiness was
creating in me, and the coolness that had sprung up between us melted quickly away.

"We must now have a brilliant match for you also,"
Paca declared happily. "Mama will see to it."

"Dear heaven she will! Her loins are tightly girded
for the fray."

Paca looked at me seriously. "You must make a radi-
cal change in your tactics, Genia. Goodness, child, if
you continue to behave as you did with Alba, you'll
turn all your suitors away."

Actually it was Mama who turned away the first
three suitors. One was rich, but his riches came from a
grandfather who had been "in trade," and, moreover,
he possessed no title. The next was a nobleman but lamentably poor. The third would inherit both an ancient
title and a considerable fortune if a cousin obliged by
dying, but the cousin was disgustingly healthy.

24

"Eagerness must be tempered by caution," Mama pronounced.

Presently she brought forward an eligible suitor of her own. I can't remember his name, but I know he was a grandee three or four times over and as rich as an American millionaire.

"Eminently suitable," I said diplomatically.

Mama kissed my cheek. "I knew my little Genia would be sensible."

She was hurrying things along much too rapidly. I began to fear that the young man had actually asked for my hand after meeting me only once and that Mama had secretly given her consent. Fortunately, he had merely asked permission to pay me court and, having gained it, invited me to accompany him to a bullfight.

"Unchaperoned?" I asked Mama, knowing she would agree if I appeared to disapprove.

Her nose twitched slightly. "I see no harm in it, providing you behave in a seemly manner."

A seemly manner! An American millionaire, one—say—whose fortune came from canned meat, would have enjoyed my outrageous conduct that day and would have pressed his suit with renewed vigor. But the unknown one—*l'Inconnu,* as I'll call him—was a Spanish grandee.

Ah, the Countess of Teba, what a spectacle she made of herself!

Let us look at her closely. Demurely cloaked, she allows *l'Inconnu* to lead her out to his coach. There she throws the cloak aside, revealing a peasant costume. The tight bodice is cut much too low even for a peasant girl, and the many-colored skirt flares out provocatively as she spins round on her heels. *L'Inconnu* grows pale. He makes to speak but remains chokingly silent as his eyes pass from the riding whip she carries to the wicked little dagger in her belt.

"Dismiss the carriage!" she orders imperiously.

"My dear Dona Eugenia—"

"I prefer to go to the bullfight on horseback."

The horses are brought from the stables, two of the most spirited Andalusians in the whole of Madrid.

"But where are the saddles?" *l'Inconnu* stammers.

"Riding bareback is greater fun!"

"The—the Countess of Teba bareback?"

"*And* astride!"

And so they reach the arena, Dona Eugenia outpacing her escort. What a sensation in the streets of Madrid! And at the crowded bullfight itself! How the shameless creature loves it all! She struts about; she chats with the toreadors, tapping them on the shoulder with her whip. She even strolls forward, as if the right is hers alone, to present the prizes. And *l'Inconnu?* Stony-eyed, he lags behind, further and further behind, causing this Carmen of Carmens to laugh delightedly. Surely she should receive a prize herself, having vanquished her own particular bull.

Well, well, there it is, one of my precious memories of a naughty, willful girl.

Untiringly Mama filled our house in the Plaza del Angel with a steady stream of eligible young men, but the word had got about. They were either distantly polite or cast upon me many a speculative glance. I grew hot with shame but stubbornly persisted in a reckless public display. Nevertheless, three dukes emerged, bolder than the rest, but before they could ask for my hand, singly or collectively, I disposed of them in one stroke, *en bloc,* as it were. I'm sure I wasn't the first female to smoke a *pepelete,* as the cigarette was then called, at the bullfight, but obviously a countess so lacking in self-respect was no wife for a duke. That cigarette, rolled for me reluctantly by one of the dukes, was my first and my last. It nauseated me so much that I was very nearly sick in the horrified grandee's lap.

"Your wings must be clipped," Mama fretted, "but in heaven's name how?"

There had been much unrest in Spain since the fall of the Emperor Napoleon. Don Carlos, King Ferdinand VII's brother, was known to be at the back of at least one revolt. King Ferdinand had married again, for the fourth time, his new bride being also his niece, Maria-Cristina of Naples. This niece-wife bore him a daughter, the Princess Isabella. And when Ferdinand died three years later, Don Carlos made a bid to take the throne from the baby Queen and her mother, the Regent. In the end, however, General Narvaez gained control for the Moderate Liberals a year before Paca's marriage and Queen Isabella, then thirteen, was declared of age. General Narvaez, her Prime Minister, became one of our most frequent visitors. It was through this association that Mama achieved her ambition and became the leading hostess in Madrid. Furthermore, it led to the clipping of my wings. The temporary clipping, at all events.

"A court appointment, that is the solution," said Mama. "Impeccable behavior will then be obligatory."

She gained appointments for both of us. Mama was duly installed as *camerara mayor* to her Majesty and I as one of the maids-of-honor.

"Strict decorum is absolutely essential now," Mama gloated.

After a week at court I knew that it would not be long before the ghastly etiquette, the deadly ceremonial, would stifle me. Strangely enough, it was Mama herself who provided a means of escape.

Paca came to me one day, her manner mysterious. I wondered if she was going to have a baby and, wanting to tell me, was held back by the conviction that such things must not be discussed with a young unmarried woman. Having talked vaguely about this and that, she finally took courage and blurted out one short, quivering sentence.

"Genia, have you noticed a change in Mama lately?"

"She's taken to blushing suddenly, and for no apparent reason."

"Blushing!" Paca looked embarrassed and lowered her voice to a whisper. "She may well blush!"

"But at what, Paca?"

"Her own guilty thoughts, Genia. I've every reason to believe that she's conducting a secret love affair."

"Mama? Ridiculous!"

"She's been seen leaving the palace late at night. Also, she's been seen returning much later—from the palace gardens.

"Are you sure, Paca?"

"Alba had it from a court official. I spoke to her about it but she laughed in my face. Please talk to her, Genia. Discovery and an open scandal would be dreadful. The Queen would dismiss her instantly."

Ah! I thought, gripped by a lively interest, a breath-catching hope.

"Is the man known to you?"

Paca looked heavenward. "General Narvaez has been seen leaving the palace at the same time, by another door."

Mama left the palace late that very night, I following at a cautious distance. It was a clear night, no romantic moon, but the stars very bright. Even so I almost lost her when, with remarkable agility, she disappeared into the depths of a small plantation of mimosa. A light laugh—Mama's—and a deeper laugh—Narvaez?—guided me to the trysting place.

Now! I thought, and uttered a piercing scream. Then I waited for the approaching thud of feet before uttering another. Mama was the first to emerge.

"Eugenia?"

"Mama, what a surprise! I was taking a quiet walk when a great shadow loomed up and frightened me."

Mama's friend joined us. One glance showed me that he wasn't the general. I saw a smooth young face, a wisp of a mustache and no hair whatever on the chin. I recognized him then, a minor court official, the younger, babyish son of an impoverished but highly regarded count.

The first palace guard was now within earshot. In a moment we'd be surrounded. Mama would certainly be disgraced and dismissed, but what of the entirely innocent Dona Eugenia? The thought of being retained in the Queen's service was more than I could bear.

"Hide, Mama!" I hissed, and flung myself upon the boy's chest.

It so happened that the Queen herself was out walking with two of her ladies. All three appeared on the heels of the guard, and there I still was, not in the boy's arms but he—forcibly—in mine. Her youthful Majesty was incensed. The boy and I were dismissed on the spot; he was taken away under guard and I sent home in a carriage to the Plaza del Angel.

Mama, very shamefaced, joined me the next morning. Nevertheless, she tried to hide her embarrassment beneath a show of vast indignation. More irritating still, she made no attempt to think of me.

"The Queen is nothing but a hypocrite. She has engaged in more than one secret love affair herself."

"At her age, Mama?"

"Age has nothing to do with it when a female is born that way."

"As you were, Mama?"

"Really, child . . ." Mama faltered. Then she sighed tragically. "Thirty-nine comes upon a woman so suddenly."

How incorrigible she was! If she were admitting to thirty-nine, that would have meant that she was ten on her wedding day!

"The question is what to do next," she went on briskly. "With the court closed to us, our position in society is considerably weakened. I was growing bored with court life in any case. Travel abroad is clearly indicated.

We shall go to London to begin with. This new scandal has deprived me of all hope of finding you a Spanish husband. Even the French would look at you askance—for the time being, at least."

"And the English?"

"They, darling, are not so finicky."

Chapter Four

TODAY OUR FLIGHT to London, as Mama called it, is very clear in my mind. But what a different place it was in 1848 from London today. No motorcars in the streets, no aeroplanes in the sky, not a single telephone to alarm the timid and no phonographs blaring out their popular music. Stagecoaches were fighting a losing battle with the new railway lines, to be sure, but the locomotive was still regarded with suspicion and fear even though Queen Victoria had expressed her approval after her first train journey six years earlier.

It was an eventful enough year in the world at large, with revolution in the air in many parts of Europe. King Louis-Philippe, he of the large umbrella, was forced to flee France, and from the safety of exile stand helplessly by while a new French Republic was proclaimed. Further afield, on the far-off American Continent, the Mexican War came to an end with the United States gaining new territory vaster in area than the whole of France and Germany. There, too, in California, a part of the new territory, gold was discovered. But Dona Manuela, Countess of Montijo, was busily searching for another sort of gold, an eligible English husband for her favorite, but still unmarried daughter. She failed lamentably, chiefly because the English mothers, mindful of their sons' welfare, regarded dear Mama as just a little too "pushing." I could hear the unspoken thoughts behind their frozen, well-bred smiles: Like mother, like daughter. I returned their frozen smiles and came close to ruining the shape of my mouth by outdoing them in respect of the upper-class accent. It was joyous fun, really.

We were well received—politely, at all events—by the great ladies of Belgravia. Notice simply had to be taken of us, for soon after our arrival our presence was commanded at a reception—a very dull affair, in all conscience—at Buckingham Palace. There was the appealing little figure Mama called Queen Victoria, not dreaming that, in the course of time, Her Majesty and I would become close friends.

"Many doors are now open to us, Genia!"

Nevertheless, Mama soon grew to feel as stifled in the very proper atmosphere of upper-class English society as I had felt at the court of Queen Isabella. I refer, naturally, to the respectable ranks of that society—the closely guarded preserves of early Victorianism. In desperation, then, she sought the company of those who were somewhat beyond the pale but still very much of the upper-class.

The widowed Countess of Blessington stands out in my mind as a typical example. She was over fifty and still amazingly beautiful. Many stories were told of her early love affairs and the countless scandals attached to her name. Her *salon* was thronged with cosmopolitan society, writers and painters of every nationality and a constant flow of foreign political exiles.

I well remember our first evening at Lady Blessington's. Mama quickly gathered a group of people about her and once again I listened with resignation to the greatly exaggerated story of our "flight." Political intrigue of the highest order, that was the specific cause!

Elsewhere this story had been received with well-bred, long-suffering stares. At Lady Blessington's, Mama expected a livelier reception. Even an incredulous laugh would have spurred her on to greater efforts. Extraordinarily enough, people began to drift away before she was in full voice, and soon we were left entirely alone.

"Such rudeness, Genia!"

Competition was the real cause. Mama's audience had joined a larger group at the other side of the room and all of them were now listening in complete silence as a man's voice droned on and on.

"Probably one of those hysterical Chartists," Mama decided. "Let us at least catch a glimpse of him."

The silent crowd moved slightly to make way for us, but even so, a full glimpse was impossible. I first saw his feet, then a pair of tightly trousered legs. The man was evidently reclining in a deep armchair. I listened for a moment to his voice, not taking in the sense of the words. It was rather harsh, the accent German.

"And there it is, the story of my escape from Ham," he concluded.

"Ham!" Mama whispered. "He must be Prince Louis-Napoleon."

We knew, of course, that the Bonaparte Pretender was living in exile in London, just as we knew the main details of his exciting career since that day twelve years ago at the Prefecture in Paris. Returning from the American exile, he had attempted another *coup* at Boulogne. Failure and arrest were followed by the sentence of perpetual imprisonment in the grim fortress of Ham. Yet here he was in England, planning another *coup,* or so people said.

I moved closer and studied the Prince's face with interest. It was oval and pale-complexioned. He wore a drooping mustache, much fuller than I remembered, and he'd grown a beard—the style later known as the "imperial." His hair was vaguely chestnut in color, the beard much darker, while the mustache, in strange contrast, was almost fair. His grey eyes were disappointingly small. His age at that time was forty.

Mama, having curtsied, was attempting to hold him

in conversation, he leaning back in his chair and looking up at her broodingly.

"We met once before, Your Highness."

"Indeed, Madame?"

"At the Prefecture in Paris."

"Forgive me, but I have no recollection whatever."

"Oh, the briefest of meetings and of course no introduction. Pray forgive me for reminding Your Highness of that unhappy incident. I am, I earnestly assure you, an ardent Bonapartist, as was my late dear husband."

"Admirable."

"The late count was decorated by your uncle, the Emperor himself."

Louis-Napoleon looked at Mama with greater interest. "I failed to catch your name, Madame."

"Montijo, the Countess of Montijo. My husband, then the Count of Teba, fought at the gates of Paris. Permit me, Your Highness, to present my daughter, Dona Eugenia, Countess of Teba. She, too, was at the Prefecture that day, that most unhappy day."

I curtsied. I felt faintly affronted that Louis-Napoleon, prince though he was, should still remain seated. He was not yet a ruling monarch, I told myself indignantly, and contented myself with the thought that I was paying tribute to the legend, not the man. The brooding look was now gone from his face. Indeed, he was staring at me in frank appraisal, the small grey eyes full of a lively interest.

"The beautiful daughter of a beautiful mother," he said and dismissed us with a slight inclination of his head.

"Insufferable!" I told Mama angrily. "One would think he was emperor of the world, not a penniless exile."

"Penniless, yes," Mama murmured reflectively, "and yet . . ."

I knew what she had in mind, and to me at that time it seemed preposterous. Later she summed up the pros and cons, giving me the impression that she was a book-keeper engaged in the dull but important task of double entry.

"The sight of you aroused his interest, but ought we take steps to cultivate it? A title there, but no money. My daughter a princess! Imagine it! Her Highness, the Princess Eugenia!" Her face fell as she turned to the debit side of the account. "A title created by Napoleon Bonaparte. A poor sort of title in the world today. Let us be frank and admit it. Yet on the other hand, if he succeeds in restoring the Empire . . ."

"As Emperor, he'd seek a wife of royal blood."

"The Empress Josephine was not of royal blood. She married Napoleon long before he became Emperor. A gamble, Genia, but I do believe we should take it."

"How easy you make it sound. A flick of my fan and Louis-Napoleon is mine."

"No, no, that in itself would be insufficient. The Prince is a man of the world, not a callow youth. Those little lines of dissipation beneath his eyes, for instance. Louis-Napoleon, the bachelor Prince with many mistresses to his credit. He has the Empress's blood in his veins as well as Bonaparte blood, and you know what Josephine was."

I'd forgotten that Louis-Napoleon was the son of Josephine's daughter by her first husband.

"Mama, if you're suggesting that to attract him I must—"

"No, not that," she said hurriedly, "though Josephine was Napoleon's mistress before she became his wife. She . . ."

"Mama!"

"Forgive me," she said huffily, and then a beatific smile crossed her face. "Louis-Napoleon has reached the age when many men look upon innocence in wonder and pursue it as desperately as a poor wretch stranded on the sands of the desert pursues the mirage of water."

Laughter bubbled up in me. There was Louis-Napoleon crawling on the hot sand in rags and there was I, a sheet of nonexistent water. The purest of pure water, too.

"Genia, be sensible."

"Dear Mama," I said contritely, "it would give me much pleasure to make you the mother-in-law of an emperor."

She looked at me suspiciously. Was I joking? In part I was. But it had occurred to me that if I did pursue the Prince or induced him to pursue me—a nice distinction there, as any woman knows—and success was mine, I'd be free forever of Mama's matchmaking.

"Genia, darling . . ."

"If the Prince is really interested, if that interest can be cultivated and *if* he pays me court, I shall listen at least attentively."

A month passed before our second meeting with Louis-Napoleon, again at Lady Blessington's. By that time, the members of the Blessington set were even more boring to me than the dull, respectable Victorians of court circles. It was boredom, then, as much as Mama's appealing glances that pushed me forward in a preliminary attempt to throw my cap at His Highness's feet. I say "feet" advisedly, for once again they were the first glimpse I caught of him and once again, a little wearily, he was telling the story of his escape from Ham.

When the story ended, I observed Mama at the Prince's side, talking and laughing with an archness that sickened me. Presently she was replaced by a young woman of arresting gracefulness, taller than I and darker. The expression on her face, a pretty enough face, was so impassive I was reminded of a Grecian head. The Prince caught sight of me, smiled and beckoned. I approached slowly, anger stabbing at my heart. To be *beckoned*—even by a prince!

"The Countess of Teba—Miss Howard," he said, with a wave of his hand.

Miss Howard and I inclined our heads guardedly.

Another wave of the princely hand and one of us was dismissed. The Countess of Teba, or Miss Howard? Apparently the latter, for she gave me that blank smile of instinctive female hostility and withdrew from the Presence.

Louis-Napoleon patted the seat of the chair next to his. An Imperial concession. Delightful! I was on the point of thanking him ironically when suddenly I remembered Paca's warning. I doubted if I could convincingly gasp in wonder, but I could at least try. I also remembered Alba's words to Mama about my remarkable spirit of independence, also my amazing intelligence. A show of either in the presence of His would-be imperial Majesty could well lead to quick defeat. Therefore, simulated gasps of wonder, an air of dejected female submissiveness. Nauseating, but necessary.

"Your mother informs me that you were born on an important anniversary," the Prince remarked.

"I was?" I asked, and achieved a giggle.

"The fifth anniversary of my uncle's death."

"Ah yes. I'd quite forgotten." I made my eyes grow big and round; the gasp of wonder followed almost automatically. "Think of it, just think of it!"

"I myself was eighteen at the time," he went on, his eyes taking on a glazed look, though I failed to notice this quickly enough. "My father was still alive but I was already dreaming of doing what he, apparently, was incapable of doing."

"And what was that, Your Highness?"

"Need you ask, Countess—you, an ardent Bonapartist?"

"The Bonaparte cause is ever in my heart," I lisped, "but I know nothing of politics. Politics were never a woman's business."

"As you wish," he shrugged.

I ought to have known then that I was making a series of ridiculous mistakes, but I ran on heedlessly. I was Paca talking to Alba about the domestic duties of a woman. When at last I fell silent, Louis-Napoleon was staring at me fixedly. I tried again, for the silence between us was really disquieting.

"And your dear mother, was she still alive when you were eighteen?" I asked desperately.

A grim smile crossed his face. "Alive and as great a matchmaker as your own dear mother."

He started to rise, but fell back as if exhausted. Weakly he waved his hand, weakly he inclined his head. Clearly he was dismissing me. I was so mortified that I ignored him until he waved his hand again.

"The flies are very troublesome," I said, with a final giggle.

I was still within earshot of Louis-Napoleon when Lady Blessington approached him.

"My dear Madame," Louis-Napoleon said feelingly, "I have never been able to bear a stupid woman."

Dear Paca! I could cheerfully have wrung her neck!

Mama and I were just taking our leave of Lady Blessington when I saw that Miss Howard was at the Prince's side again. She had the look of a governess watching serenely over her young charge.

"Who is she?" I asked.

"The Prince's landlady," Lady Blessington replied, with a smile which Mama later described as lewd.

"Landlady?"

"She possesses a pleasant little house in Berkeley Street. His Highness has been—er—boarding there for quite some time."

I glanced at Miss Howard again. No, not a governess but a woman of doubtful reputation holding her pet dog on an invisible leash.

"One hears she has every intention of marrying him," Lady Blessington added.

The leash was no longer invisible; I could see it distinctly.

"The Bonapartes were never renowned for good taste," I chirped brightly.

And that, as you may well imagine, made me feel a little happier.

We spent only a few months in London during which I had no further meeting with Louis-Napoleon. Mama herself met him briefly in the Park. He paused, bowed distantly and passed on without a word. His "landlady" was with him, the leash tightly held—that most effective of all leashes, for it was made of gold.

"Miss Howard," said Mama, having gathered together all the information she could, "is the daughter of a brewer. A very respectable brewer, if brewers can ever be called respectable. He disowned his daughter when she ran away from home at the age of fifteen to live with a wealthy young man in London. Later, she met Lord Blessington's cousin, a certain very wealthy Mr. Martyn who settled an income upon her and gave her a fortune in property. Then she deserted him for Prince Louis-Napoleon and has lent His Highness at least thirty thousand pounds."

"The Prince must be an amazing spendthrift."

"No, Genia. The money is to be spent in another bid to re-establish the Empire. Miss Howard insisted on it. Repayment, in kind, will never be demanded. Marriage is her sole aim. What a disgusting thought, a brewer's daughter the Empress of France! The Bonapartists are horrified."

Presently we learned that Louis-Napoleon had left suddenly for Paris, not to attempt a third *coup d'état* by force of arms, but at the invitation of four French departments. They had chosen him, you see, to represent them in the Constituent Assembly of the Second Republic.

"The gravediggers are busily at work," Mama pronounced. "To place the Prince in the Assembly is the first turn of the spade. If he's half the man his uncle was, he'll seize the spade himself. A few deft turns on his own account and the Second Republic will fall headlong into the grave."

Miss Howard was quick to follow the Prince to France. We caught a glimpse of her at the Hotel Meurice when we passed through Paris on our way to Spa. The matchmaking fever was upon Mama again and though she complained of rheumatism I knew the mineral waters of Spa were not her aim.

"European princelings are often seen at Spa," she said.

It was while we were at that fashionable watering place that news of Louis-Napoleon's next move reached us. Overnight he had become the First Magistrate of the Second Republic. He was to hold office for a term of four years. President of the Second Republic, yes, but he chose to style himself Prince-President, a broad enough hint in all conscience.

How many watering places did we visit during the next two years? I no longer care to remember. At last we returned to Spain and were well received—even in court circles. Mama threw herself feverishly into a round of social activities and another bout of matchmaking. The gentleman concerned was Don Jose Hidalgo, a Spaniard with many interests in Mexico. He was a handsome man, lavish in the compliments he paid both Mama and me, and much in demand at the great houses of Madrid. I'd no desire whatever to marry him, but to avoid recriminations—and for the fun of the thing, too—I flirted with him outrageously.

"Your conduct is disgusting," Mama said, surprisingly.

"I thought you wanted me to encourage him."

"Do you realize how old he is?"

"Thirty-five? Forty, perhaps?"

Mama nodded thoughtfully. "Even if he is thirty-five, the difference is not too great."

She should have said "even if forty," I thought, but clearly her mind was on other things. Her eyes narrowed speculatively.

"Don Jose is only a secretary at the Mexican legation, but he has held other responsible posts in London and Paris. I had a long talk with him about Mexican affairs. He's an ambitious man and is working for the creation of a separate kingdom in Mexico. A kingmaker, you see. If he succeeds, he will have the highest position possible at the Mexican court. Ah, the New World! The possibilities in Mexico for an ambitious woman are infinite. And that, of course, is what Don Jose seeks in a wife—an ambitious, fearless woman."

"An unhealthy climate, Mama. Assassins' bullets on the one hand, yellow fever on the other."

Mama laughed airily. "Don Jose has yet to ask for your hand in marriage."

"True."

"As your dear sister remarked only last night, it is impossible to tell from his charming conduct whether he is paying court to you or—to me."

"Mama!"

Another matchmaking bout? Yes indeed, but the match Mama seemed intent on making this time was her own, not mine. Her "even if thirty-five" was amply explained, as was her reference to my "disgusting" conduct.

Thereafter, she monopolized Don Jose whenever she could and by a ruse succeeded in spending hours alone with him. She had no head for business, she told him. The family lawyers were dolts. Her affairs were in confusion. If only Don Jose, to whom such matters were surely child's play, would come to her rescue! Don Jose did. Meanwhile, I'd ceased flirting with him, and when he spoke of this one day, I thought I saw an opportunity of bringing the ridiculous situation to a head.

41

"Flirting isn't always an end in itself," I said demurely. "The time sometimes comes when seriousness must take its place."

He looked at me gravely. "I think I understand."

Don Jose was closeted with Mama for an hour, helping once more to straighten out her affairs, and I was left to wonder if I had made a mistake. Had he really been paying court to Mama? It seemed ludicrous, but . . . *had he?*

I saw him before he left the house.

"Thank you," he said enigmatically.

Just that and no more!

Mama remained in the library for quite some time, then she sent for Pepa, ordered her to begin packing at once and sent for me too. She'd been weeping; that was obvious in spite of the over-generous layer of powder on her face.

"Mexico?" I asked.

She stirred herself briskly. "Certainly not! What a foolish suggestion. The country is suffering from the after-effects of war. Conditions are even more chaotic than before. That is one reason why I refused the offer he made. The unhealthiness of the climate is another. I refused him for both our sakes."

Clearly he had asked for *my* hand in marriage, but I thought it kinder not to pursue the subject further. Yet why then had he thanked me?

"Do we go to Spa again, Mama?" I asked.

"Spa? That is even worse than your inane suggestion of Mexico. We go to London, Genia. London is the only really civilized city in the world. And by the way, your own affairs are in need of straightening out. The best thing you can do is consult with Don Jose before we leave. A steady friendship is developing there. I regard dear Jose as our very special family adviser."

My own affairs were in no need of straightening out, but I pretended that they were. After all, there was a question I was dying to ask Don Jose Hidalgo.

"Why did you thank me?" I said, when we were poring over my personal accounts together.

"You want me to speak frankly, Dona Eugenia?"

"If a diplomat can ever do that—yes."

"Very well! I was in a difficult position. You gave me a way of extricating myself. Your tone of voice told me that you were no more anxious to marry me than I was to marry you. You wanted to free your mother of what —to me, also—was becoming an embarrassing infatuation. Therefore I asked for your hand in marriage, knowing that I would not be trapped by her acceptance of it on your behalf."

"You are much too clever, Don Jose."

"As clever as yourself, would you say?"

"Surely!" I said smugly.

"I can see an interesting future for you, Dona Eugenia, providing you marry the right man."

"You appeared to pay court both to Mama and myself. Why?"

"I sought a close association with your family because of the influence of the Duke of Alba at Queen Isabel's court."

London, inevitably, was a disappointment to Mama.

"Is the whole male population in mourning?" she asked, during a Sunday stroll in the park. "Just look at the men in their black frock coats! It's quite impossible these days to distinguish between a gentleman and an office slave. The gentlemen set a ghastly example and the slaves copy it slavishly. Social progress, Genia! Queen Victoria's husband is responsible, I fear. He sanctioned the depressing black frock coat and, as a result, they are seen everywhere! When I was a girl, gentlemen looked like gentlemen. No, London is not the city I thought it. Paris, not London, is the only civilized city in the world. The new Paris. Bear that well in mind. The Paris of the Prince-President."

"He, too, has sanctioned the black frock coat, Mama."

She ignored this. "The Prince, dear Genia, has not yet married his landlady."

Chapter Five

IT WAS Mérimée who found us an apartment in the Place Vendôme. The rooms were large and airy. There was ample accommodation for our little household: Mama and myself, Mama's maid-companion Pepa, my own newly engaged French maid and a cook with the highest references.

I loved the situation of our new home, even the crazy chimney pots seen from the back windows, but especially the Emperor Napoleon remote on his tall column which we looked out on from the windows at the front. France was a Republic, for sure, but the President was another Bonaparte. We saw him often from our front windows as he rode through the Place Vendôme. He had taken possession of the Élysée Palace and had installed Miss Howard in a fine house well within walking distance. We thought him a commanding figure on horseback, much more impressive than when seen lounging in an armchair.

"Paris is in flux," Mama brooded one day. "I can see very little progress. A new government, a new republic, a Prince-President, yes. But where, I ask you, is all that getting us? Asphalt on some of the streets, a little more of that revolting gas lighting, some new sewers, a few new railways and the cancan at the Jardin Mabille. The age of elegance is passing. I have even observed a growing number of black frock coats."

We were driving along the Champs Élysées with Mérimée. Winter had come upon Paris, but the day was bright and sunny and many gay parasols were in evidence.

"I think I prefer London after all," Mama went on darkly. "There we had no difficulty in meeting the Prince-President socially."

That, then, was the core of her dissatisfaction.

"Perhaps I can do something about it," Mérimée suggested.

"You, Mérimée?"

"Princess Mathilde and I are old friends."

"Ha!" said Mama, her eyes gleaming brightly.

Princess Mathilde was the supreme dictator of Paris society. Moreover, she was the Prince-President's cousin. A few days later, after Mérimée had approached her, we received an invitation to join an informal party at her hotel in the Rue de Courcelles. It was almost certain that the Prince-President would be the guest of honor.

I experienced then a moment of panic. The thought of facing again the man who had described me as a stupid woman was more than I could bear, but soon an idea began to form in my mind. The Prince had seen me only twice. If I dressed differently, if I arranged my hair in a different style, would he recognize me? All I needed was a few moments of conversation with him to convince him that I was anything but a fool. There was still the question of my name, but that difficulty I overcame at the last moment.

Princess Mathilde's *salon* was crowded when we arrived with Mérimée. The Princess gave poor Mama only a passing glance, but her eyes held mine with obvious interest.

"Dona Eugenia de Montijo, Countess of Teba," she repeated. "A pretty name. You are very welcome, my dear."

Princess Mathilde was thirty-one at that time. Her eyes were alert, perhaps a little cunning, I thought, and her voice was inclined to boom as if she were the commander of an army marching into battle. Oscar Wilde, though not yet born, would most certainly have used her as a model for one of his English dowagers. She was the daughter of the Prince-President's uncle, old King Jerome. Everybody knew that Louis-Napoleon had once been in love with her, but she had married a Russian, Prince Demidoff, was separated from him and lived openly with a certain Count de Nieuwerkerke. She was a passionate, quick-tempered woman, a law unto herself.

After a few words with Her Highness, I moved away on Mérimée's arm. Mama herself was lost in the crowd. There was no sign of the Prince-President but Mérimée assured me he was expected at any moment.

"And Miss Howard?"

"My dear Eugenia, she has never been received by Princess Mathilde. The poor creature is kept firmly in the background of the Prince-President's life."

His Highness arrived at that moment, accompanied by Princess Mathilde's brother, Prince Napoleon-Jerome. There was a slight lull in the general chatter and somebody cried, *"Vive l'Empereur!"*

"Premature, but one sees how the wind is blowing," Mérimée murmured. "Wherever he appears in the country, whenever he opens a new railway, little cries like that are heard."

Louis-Napoleon strode past us with a nod for Mérimée and a casual glance at me, no hint of recognition in his eyes.

"I'll present you at the first opportunity," Mérimée said.

"Wait!" I begged.

"My dear?"

Mama had decided some time ago that I should be known by the surname "Montijo," hence Mérimée's form of presenting me to the Princess. In London, Louis-Napoleon had known me as Dona Eugenia,

Countess of Teba. The name, Palafox, was entirely strange to him.

"Present me simply as M'm'selle Palafox," I decided.

Mérimée's eyes twinkled. "Between us, we are plotting a new story."

I looked at him stonily. "Writers are the most unscrupulous people in the world. If ever you dare to write it—!"

His eyes twinkled again.

An orchestra was playing at the far end of the crowded *salon* but not, at that moment, for dancing. Princess Mathilde had ordered the conductor, Daniel Auber, to give a special rendering of his latest composition. No one showed the slightest interest. Far from listening attentively, everybody talked all the louder. It was, I fear, the fashion in those days, even in high society. Auber was a temperamental fellow. He leaped angrily up and down, waving his baton frantically. The music rose in volume, so did the chatter, and soon a deafening duel was in violent progress. Louis-Napoleon, either out of good manners or because his ears were splitting, called for silence. The chatter ceased; so did the music.

"Proceed, Monsieur Auber!"

Auber bowed, cast a smile of triumph upon the subdued gathering and raised his baton. I realized then that the chatter was preferable to the music; I myself have never cared much for Auber's compositions. Louis-Napoleon stood a little apart from everyone else, arms folded, eyes half-closed, face impassive. Only once had I seen him standing, but I was a child that day at the Prefecture and had thought him tall. I saw now in disappointment that he was really short, little more than five feet six inches. He wore a tail coat which made him look even shorter, as did his mustache, the ends of which were now fiercely waxed.

In the heavenly silence which followed Auber's last violent crescendo, Mérimée brought me face to face with the important little man and begged permission to present me. Louis-Napoleon looked at me vaguely. Impassivity had given place to bewilderment. The poor fellow had yet to recover from the frightening impact of Auber's music.

"But of course," he said at last.

Mérimée bowed. "M'm'selle Palafox, Your Highness."

I curtsied neatly. "Your Highness."

"A lady writer, perhaps? My cousin's *salon* is crammed with writers these days."

"A student of the arts," I responded, "but possessing no artistic pretensions."

"Music being one of the arts, M'm'selle, I take it you have a definite opinion of Monsieur Auber's work?"

"Very definite."

"You—like it?"

"No," I said frankly, "but I, too, hate rudeness, especially fashionable rudeness."

"Fashionable rudeness?" He looked at me quizzically. "Ah yes, I think I understand, M'm'selle."

"Even bad music must be listened to politely."

"I quite agree."

"The same, unfortunately, applies to bad conversation."

His eyes more blue than grey in the candlelight, held mine provocatively. He offered me his arm and we began to stroll among the crowd unobserved, as it happened, by dear Mama. Daniel Auber! How I blessed him and his bad music! We discussed music a little longer, then painting and writing. He appeared to be growing impressed and for that reason I refrained carefully from contradicting him. There was one awkward moment.

"That story of Mérimée's—*Carmen,* isn't it?" he said thoughtfully. "I'm told he got the original idea from the Countess of Montijo. Is that correct?"

"I believe so," I said faintly.

"In that case, an interesting woman. I remember meeting her in London and thinking her a fool."

"One can be misled by first impressions," I said, still more faintly and hurriedly changed the subject. "I'm told Your Highness is more interested in science than the arts."

"I certainly dabbled in science of a sort while at Ham. My small laboratory there . . ."

He talked with enthusiasm, a surprisingly boyish enthusiasm that appealed to me, about his experiments while a prisoner at Ham. At times we had to raise our voices to a shout, for there was music again and people were dancing.

"But of all the sciences, that of politics is now your deepest interest," I said.

"Ah yes, political science, M'm'selle!"

"A small but important part of which concerns the activities of paid agents."

His eyes clouded. "Indeed?"

"The theatrical claque, as it were."

Thereupon he took me up quite sharply. "One cannot establish an Empire merely by paying people to shout 'Vive l'Empereur!' " He appeared on the point of turning from me abruptly, but paused for a moment to call Prince Napoleon-Jerome to his side. "Be a good fellow and dance with the Countess."

"Countess?" I gasped, thunderstruck.

He took my hand and placed it in his cousin's. "Dona Eugenia, Countess of Teba. Spanish, I believe. Ask Auber to play a fandango."

It was then that he turned abruptly away. A moment later I saw him taking leave of Princess Mathilde. Napoleon-Jerome was still holding my hand.

"One has the distinct impression," he drawled, "that the Prince-President was making me a little present."

"It was deliberate, quite deliberate," Mama complained. "The Prince-President arrived, the Prince-President departed. I never caught a glimpse of him. Because you were unwilling to meet him yourself, you took steps to prevent my *forcing* a meeting."

This was the morning after Princess Mathilde's party. We were sipping our chocolate, though more of Mama's was slopping over into the saucer than entering her mouth. It was most amusing that the story of my meeting and talking with Louis-Napoleon hadn't yet reached Mama's ears.

"Prince Napoleon-Jerome was very entertaining," I said, unwisely, as it turned out.

"Napoleon-Jerome?"

"I danced with him."

"I saw you with a large, dark individual, but I never suspected—" She broke off, poured the chocolate from the saucer into the cup and drank it at a gulp. "How many times did you dance with him?"

"Twice, and we talked for at least an hour."

Mama nodded her head thoughtfully. "Prince Napoleon-Jerome, son of ex-king Jerome of Westphalia . . . Royal blood there, Genia, on his mother's side. Whereas the Prince-President, when all is said and done . . ."

She was incorrigible, that mother of mine, absolutely incorrigible!

Within a week we were summoned to another evening party at Princess Mathilde's. Mama was beside herself with joy and spent hours selecting just the right evening gown to show off my beauty to full advantage. In those precrinoline days of high necklines, it was cut, I remember, a trifle lower than modesty would normally have permitted, but a single strand of pearls round my neck brought it within the range of provocative decency. Small pearl earrings and a gold bracelet in the shape of a snake completed my array of jewelry. I penciled my eyebrows darkly and put rouge on my cheeks, a light touch only. I carried a fan, ivory and exquisitely carved.

Napoleon-Jerome came to our side the moment we entered the *salon* and stayed with us after we had paid our respects to his sister. Mama all but crowed with pleasure. This particular Bonaparte prince was well known for his imperious manner, the way he had of brushing everyone from his path; yet here he was, affable without the slightest hint of condescension. Even at twenty-nine, he had a massive body which more than matched his large head; altogether an unlovely sight, the more so since his beak-like nose made me think of a bird of prey, one far too heavy to take the air. The way he had of holding me when he danced with me should have warned me of his intentions, but I flirted with him unheedingly, and when the Prince-President appeared, I laughed immoderately in his hearing.

Naturally, I chose not to see him. Very few people did see him—Mama herself was once more unaware of his presence—for he left within a few moments of his arrival, a Bonaparte scowl on his face.

"A pity you chose to ignore my cousin," Princess Mathilde remarked toward the end of the evening. "It was he who commanded your presence this evening."

"Our story is going somewhat awry," Mérimée said when I confided in him. "A villain not of our own seeking has made his appearance. Be warned about Prince Napoleon-Jerome. He is a man of very little honor."

"I found him possessive but gallant, Monsieur."

"Gallant? He has the reputation of absolute brutality where women are concerned, as Rachel could tell you."

"Rachel the actress?"

Mérimée nodded. "His present mistress. Not for nothing has he been called the uncouth Corsican."

Napoleon-Jerome called at our apartment the following afternoon with flowers for me and a basket of imported fruit for Mama. Two nights later he took us to the Comédie-Française to see his celebrated mistress and we met her afterward in her dressing-room. I looked in vain for signs of bruises on her arms and laughed to myself at the way she imitated the Prince's walk behind his back. The following week, it was a box at the Théâtre des Variétés. We also met several times at his sister's, but Louis-Napoleon was never present.

"Things are coming to a head," said Mama. "The dear man has let slip more than one broad hint. He will declare himself very soon."

And he did, the gallant Napoleon-Jerome. We were at the Théâtre des Variétés once more. Mama, making a great show of having spied a friend I knew to be imaginary, had bustled from the box. He bent forward and kissed my shoulder.

"Tomorrow evening, you and I alone."

"The chaperon dismissed at last?" I said uneasily.

"Would you have us followed to the bedroom?"

I rose instantly.

"Wait!" he commanded. "What else had you expected? A proposal of marriage perhaps?"

"From an uncouth Corsican, Prince?"

That infuriated him. The jibe had obviously been flung at him more than once in spite of the royal blood on his mother's side. He seized my arm roughly.

"When I marry, Countess, I want a real mother for my legitimate children. You, by God, could never be that."

I tore my arm free and slapped him on the face. Finally, my hand tingling not unpleasantly, I left the box, a dignified figure, I hoped, and went home alone.

Princess Mathilde received us graciously when next we were summoned to her *salon,* and I caught a distant glimpse of Louis-Napoleon. To my intense annoyance, however, Napoleon-Jerome was also present. He joined me at once and offered me his arm in apparent friendliness. Before I could turn from him, Louis-Napoleon came between us suddenly and I found my arm in his. Silently he led me from the *salon,* on through the vast hall and down the wide steps to a waiting carriage. A moment later, we were rolling along the Rue de Courcelles. His continued silence, grim and lowering, was more than I could bear. I burst out laughing.

"You find this abduction amusing, Countess?"

"More frightening than amusing, Monsieur. I've heard so many stories about your late uncle—the Bonaparte forcefulness where women are concerned."

"You think I resemble him strongly?" His voice was suddenly eager.

"Not having known him, Your Highness—"

"Or do you mock me?" Now, surprisingly, there was sadness in his voice.

So that was it, I thought. He wanted to model himself in all things on the late Emperor. I was touched. In that moment I recognized the weakness which he strove to keep hidden within himself, or rather, the fear of weakness, which is possibly more dangerous than weakness itself. In that moment also, I began to feel affection for him.

"The Bonaparte strain is a strong one," I said diplomatically. "It would be strange if you failed in many ways to resemble the Emperor."

"Napoleon-Jerome!" he burst out. "That cousin of mine and you! Is that a display of the intelligence I had come to believe you possessed?"

"You thought me stupid in the first place."

"Answer my question, Countess!"

"You presented me to your cousin. You placed my hand in his."

"I was angry with you."

"*And* you showed it."

"That was remiss of me."

"Were you angry because I'd tricked you?"

He laughed smugly. "I recognized you the moment I saw you."

"What about my reference to the theatrical claque then?"

"Yes," he admitted, "it was very touchy of me. Naturally I pay my agents to cry 'Vive l'Empereur!' just as my enemies pay theirs to cry 'Vive la République!' "

He lit a cigar and smoked for a while in brooding silence. He had much on his mind that night. A *coup d'état* was being painstakingly planned, though neither I nor the general public was aware of it then, and many political obstacles still stood in his path. Naively I thought him merely nervous in my presence.

"I thought you stupid in the first place," he went on presently, "but later I had reason to doubt it. Your remark about the flies being troublesome—your later remark which naturally reached my ears, about the Bonapartes never having been renowned for good taste . . ." He laughed shortly. "Even sarcasm requires a certain amount of intelligence. I deserved it. My rudeness provoked you."

"Rudeness, Monsieur?"

"You thought me rude not rising from my chair. Even today, Prince-President though I am, my short stature still embarrasses me." He laughed woefully.

"You look magnificent on horseback."

"A fact well known to me."

"And you take full advantage of it."

"Full advantage."

His mood changed quickly. He became remote, withdrawn, and he issued a sharp command to the coachman. We were back in the Rue de Courcelles before he spoke again.

"It was indiscreet of me to carry you off. One must think of your reputation. The gossips will be busy already. Go in and face them alone. I have work to do. Please make my excuses to Mathilde."

Princess Mathilde sent for me one afternoon a week later and received me alone in her boudoir. Her manner was very affable. We chatted about the theatre and clothes until tea was brought in. Then she looked at me lingeringly.

"Since I've grown to consider you one of my friends, I shall call you 'Eugenia.' "

I inclined my head and waited.

"Have you seen my cousin again since he carried you off so possessively?"

"No, Madame."

"He spoke of you yesterday in glowing terms."

"Then he spent the evening with Miss Howard at the Comédie!"

"A ridiculous indiscretion," Mathilde said angrily. "At this critical stage he should tread with the utmost caution—" She broke off with a laugh. "I had thought that his growing interest in a young lady of irreproachable character would bring an end to the Howard influence. How clever are you, Eugenia? Do you aim, as your mother does, at marriage?"

"Marriage with the Prince-President? An impossibility surely!"

"The other thing?"

"Never!"

Mathilde took up a marzipan confection in the shape of a tiny gondola and popped it into her mouth. "Because of the Howard scandal, the people would accept you with relief." She swallowed the gondola greedily and reached for another. "Now, tell me everything. Begin at the beginning. Every meeting, every word that passed between you."

She laughed uproariously at the story of my lamentable failure in London, but her eyes narrowed when I told her that Louis-Napoleon had not been completely deceived by my imitation of a brainless beauty.

"Louis was deeply attracted from the first. Only Miss Howard keeps him from you now. We shall begin our campaign at the Élysée Palace."

Our campaign? Mathilde was taking it for granted that I was a willing recruit, as indeed I must have been.

The invitation to our first reception at the Presidential Palace came from Princess Mathilde, not from Louis-Napoleon himself. The Princess, I knew, was always the official hostess at the Élysée whenever the bachelor Prince-President entertained. But even so, I feared that Louis-Napoleon, having done nothing of his own accord to further our acquaintance, might receive me coldly and order my name to be struck from any future lists of guests. Judge, then, my relief when his eyes lit up with pleasure at the sight of me. His lips lingered longer than strictly necessary when he kissed my hand, and it seemed to me that he turned from me reluctantly to greet other guests.

It was a glittering gathering that night at the Élysée. Several ambassadors were present, including Lord Normanby, Queen Victoria's representative. His wife, mindful no doubt of Victoria's conservativeness in dress, had a dowdy look. I myself wore an innocently plain blue silk long enough to conceal my ankles, and the heels of my shoes—my aim being to inspire Louis-Napoleon with confidence—were the lowest obtainable. Mathilde was very complimentary. I should be taking her part, she murmured, my look of "belonging" being so much more pronounced than hers. I could not agree. It was pleasing to stand at her side and let everybody observe the contrast: myself so slim, elegant and dignified; the Princess shorter than I, the expanse of her bosom too vast, the pad of flesh between her shoulders fully exposed, the short sleeves of her dress on the point of bursting. Marzipan gondolas, I thought, and resolved never to eat them again myself.

I could see that Louis-Napoleon was anxious to talk with me, for he was casting many a glance in my direction as he moved among his guests. I was touched at seeing him try to increase his height by balancing on his toes. A little wave of affection, love of a protective kind, was growing within me. He joined me at last, a decorous figure in that august gathering, but his eyes faintly distrait.

"My uncle should be here tonight to prompt me," he said.

But he was looking with barely disguised hostility at Lord Normanby, his thoughts clearly on some diplomatic wrangle rather than on amorous exploits.

"What would the Emperor have done," he asked intensely, "if warned to beware of dynastic tyranny?"

I recalled one incident from my study of the life of the Emperor Napoleon. "Monsieur, do you remember an historic occasion in which another British ambassador, Lord Whitworth, was involved?"

"Ah, yes! Whitworth suffered a violent trouncing in the presence of the entire diplomatic corps. My uncle was at his rudest."

"A calculated rudeness."

"You advise me to follow suit?"

"The Whitworth incident was followed by war. That would be unfortunate now."

He appeared satisfied with my reply. "We must have peace with England, a lasting friendship . . . Tyranny!" he burst out. "Have I the look of a tyrant?"

"*I* tremble at the sight of you!"

He relaxed with a laugh, led me back to Mathilde, whispered in her ear for a moment and left me with her.

"Congratulations, Eugenia," she said. "He wants you to remain when the rest go."

"And my mother?"

Mathilde's bosom heaved and bounced. "She's to be occupied with a tour of the palace."

I experienced a moment of apprehension when Louis-Napoleon later led me to his study. Normally, or so gossip had it, he went at night from the Élysée directly to Miss Howard's house. Gossip also insisted that

58

if she were not "immediately available," he went casually elsewhere or brought a cancan dancer to the Élysée. Now I, by no means a cancan dancer, had been brought to the palace. Nevertheless, I took courage from the fact that Mama had not been sent away.

A servant entered the study on our heels, placed a silver tray on the desk and withdrew. There were two small goblets on the tray and a crystal decanter. Louis-Napoleon filled the goblets and handed one to me.

"Marsala. Your favorite wine. How do I know? I asked your mother."

"That was thoughtful of you, Monsieur."

"Her late Majesty, my mother, was fond of Marsala."

"You must have loved her dearly."

"I adored her, M'm'selle. Poor Mother! I don't think she was ever really happy with my father. The marriage was arranged by the Emperor and the Empress. You can imagine how odd I thought it when I was very young that my grandmother should also be my aunt. As you know, my mother was Hortense de Beauharnais, the Empress Josephine's daughter by her first husband. Unable to bear the Emperor children, the Empress tried to hold him by marrying her daughter to his favorite brother Louis. She failed, though she had the satisfaction of seeing my mother become Queen of Holland. Am I boring you, Eugenie?"

It was the first time he had addressed me thus, striving to give my name its French pronunciation, but the German accent came through so thickly that it sounded like Oo-gay-nee." It was strange that the man who wanted to be Emperor of France should speak French with a German accent, but that wasn't his fault. He had been brought up in Germany after his uncle's fall.

"Apparently I *am* boring you," he said, and lit a cigar.

"I was merely thinking that your story was a sad one."

"A story that would never have happened if the Empress Josephine's first husband had not gone to the guillotine during the Revolution. Do you believe in fate?"

"I do, but I like to think that one can push it along at times according to one's own desires."

"Even that is fate. But enough! Tell me about yourself. Have you ever been in love?"

"Countless times."

"Seriously?"

I regretted the lie and the coquettishness of its utterance. "Truly, Louis, I've been in love only once. And yes, it was serious. He married my sister. I thought the world had come to an end."

"First love! How painful it is! I wept—I actually wept when my uncle, King Jerome, refused to let me marry Mathilde . . . Eugenie, let me see your feet. Come now, quickly!"

"Monsieur!"

He leaped at me and dragged my skirt above my ankles. "As I suspected! Low heels and most unfashionable. What a sacrifice—what a kindly sacrifice." He kissed me briefly on the cheek. "Dear Eugenie."

"I prefer the comfort of low heels."

"As you wish!" He became aloof, instantly impersonal. "Come, the hour is late. We must find your mother at once."

Did he regret having betrayed a sudden upsurge of sentimentality, or was he angry with me for seeming to deny any thought of "a kindly sacrifice"?

Mama and Mathilde were waiting in the reception hall, their heads together, both talking at once. They sprang apart at our approach and looked above and around us with a casualness that was ludicrous.

Louis-Napoleon held me back for a moment. "I think you may tell them that considerable progress has been made."

There was laughter in his voice, but beneath it a brooding, serious undertone.

Chapter Six

AFTER THAT FIRST reception Mama and I were often at the Élysée, and now and again I had a talk with the Prince-President in private. I was making a point of learning all that could possibly be learned from the newspapers, little as that was, and occasionally, though Louis-Napoleon never really confided in me at that time, I gained a glimpse of the moves he seemed to have in mind.

"What if I were to aim only at becoming President for life?" he asked me one day, when we were driving in the country.

"I wouldn't be hoodwinked myself," I laughed. "Your uncle first became Consul for life."

"And within five years was Emperor, yes."

"Your present term of office expires in a year's time. I say your present term. Actually I mean your only term. According to law, you're denied the right of re-election. I realize that something must be done. Do you propose to wait until the end of next year?"

He left my question unanswered for a few moments and seemed engrossed in a careful study of the leafless trees which lined the road. Mama, the constant chaperon, had been left behind for the first time. She was absolutely sure that Louis-Napoleon was on the point of asking me to marry him, and I must say I was inclined to agree with her.

"Grim sentinels, those trees," he said at length. "The end of next year, Eugenie? Not even till the end of this year. December second is the anniversary of two important events: the Battle of Austerlitz and my uncle's coronation. We shall live, I hope and pray, to know that date as an even more important anniversary."

"Only a few days from now, Louis!"

He took my hand in his. "Please get the habit of calling me Napoleon."

"If you wish it . . . Napoleon." It was difficult to keep my mind on politics, but I tried valiantly. "Why not a cautious move—re-election, say, for ten years?"

He released my hand. "Others have already suggested that. Re-election for ten years and by the will of the people."

He went on to say that money was his greatest need. The presidential allowance was insufficient for his plans, and the Assembly had refused either to increase it or extend his term of office. It would be a different matter if the Bonapartists were in the majority, but there were the Legitimists, the Republicans and the Orleanists, often at loggerheads yet of one voice in this. Accordingly, he'd turned to three or four financiers for help and they had lent him money secretly. Apart from this, he was largely indebted to a certain good friend. She had made a big sacrifice in pawning her jewelry, taking out heavy mortgages on her London property, and even selling her valuable stable. He made no mention of the good friend's name, but I knew that he referred to Miss Howard. Mathilde and her mission! The Howard hold was surely even greater now.

"I'm not without money myself," I said quickly.

"Nothing would induce me to ask such a sacrifice of you, Eugenie."

"Why not, Napoleon? The cause is very important to me. Everything I have is yours."

"All I ask of you is you yourself. For the rest—the material things—I want to give, once I am able to do so, not receive."

The man, as distinct from the cause, if the two could

really be separated. "All I ask of you is you yourself." Clearly he was stating a fact, not posing a question. I fell silent, my heart troubled by the increasing bruskness of his tone.

"Neglected, but soon to be set in order," he said.

At this moment, the carriage had turned unexpectedly into a weed-covered drive. The trees which lined it were so overgrown their naked branches brushed eerily against the carriage windows.

"The house itself is in better shape than the grounds but in need of new paint. The furniture is old and shabby but that can be remedied easily enough. I want you to choose everything for yourself. That's why I left things as they are."

We drove on in silence. First Napoleon-Jerome, now Louis-Napoleon. Or was I wrong? The truth seemed to stare me brutally in the face, and yet . . .

A moment later I was being helped from the carriage. I can remember very little of that country house. A massive front door, a lofty entrance hall, a few sticks of furniture in the only room we entered. That and no more.

"Yours, if you care to accept it."

"An inconvenient distance from Paris."

"But a pleasant enough retreat, Eugenie. Naturally, you shall have an apartment in the city also."

"Why not the top floor of Miss Howard's house? You could climb the stairs on alternate nights."

Heavy-handed as my sarcasm was, he looked at me amazed. "Is it possible that I've been misled?"

"Misled? By me?"

"By Mathilde, then."

"Mathilde!" I exclaimed.

"She gave me to understand . . . She . . ." He was fumbling for words. "You talked together at length. Discreetly, of course." And again, ridiculously, a look of confusion on his face, he said, "She gave me to understand—"

"That I was eager to become your mistress?"

"You sound in a devil of a temper," he complained. "Apparently I have been misled."

"Your wretched cousin actually did say that I—that I . . . !"

"Not in so many words, but the inference was clear enough. I loved you less—that is to say, I respected you less when Mathilde approached me on your behalf, but the need which was growing within me day by day remained."

"The physical need!"

"The need of everything that you are. Please understand that, Eugenie."

His abject pleading made pleasant enough music, but his refusal to ask the one question which could make me his caused tears to spring to my eyes. He ignored them by turning his back on me.

"I was shocked at the suggestion," he went on. "It had never occurred to me that you of all women . . ." He swung round and faced me again. "It is perhaps a morsel of comfort to discover that I was right, that all the respect I'd felt for you is fully recovered. I can only hope that the respect you felt for me . . ."

"If I ever felt any at all!" I raged, the tears streaming down my cheeks.

". . . is fully recovered also," he finished lamely.

"I still feel respect for the future Emperor."

His poor face cleared. "Ah!"

"If not for the man," I added quickly.

"How unjust you are! I was misled, Eugenie—misled!"

"As you wish."

"Let us at least remain friends," he said stiffly. "Anything I can do to make amends . . ."

"Anything, Monsieur?"

"Within reason," he said harshly, and strode across the room. "In actual fact, it is Mathilde who should be forced to make amends. Please do me the kindness of telling me all that passed between you. Your honesty has always done you credit. I'm ready to believe you, whatever Mathilde may say in her own defense."

I told him everything, thus being obliged to utter what appeared to him to be the dread word—marriage.

"Dastardly conduct!" he exclaimed.

Melodrama rather than tragedy, you see.

"Punish her," I urged quickly, "by dismissing her from the position of official hostess at the Élysée."

He looked at me somberly. "Neither she nor I may have entree there after December second. I go either to the grave or to the Tuileries."

"I'm sure you count on the Tuileries, that place of kings," I said. I bobbed my head and added, "Sire."

His eyes sparkled. "True, true. And by God, the Tuileries it shall be!" He paused for a moment. "But—dismiss Mathilde? I fear I have a family obligation."

The Bonaparte clan! The Empress Josephine had good reason many times to rage against the compulsive grip it had on the Emperor Napoleon, the way the family tie survived all the family quarrels. Often in the future, I was to feel that the ghost of Josephine was at my side, weeping and raging with me.

"Mathilde remains, then?"

"As she would, even if you accepted my offer."

"You insult me by even speaking of that again!"

"There's no hope for me? No hope whatever?" he asked plaintively.

"None!"

"Who knows? I might grow to respect you even more."

Of a sudden, he was being very charming. His face shone beatifically. It was that of a choir boy, but I remembered the devilry that possesses choir boys out of church.

"What if I agreed to dismiss Miss Howard?"

"You would really do that?"

He shook his head. "I am under a very great obligation to Miss Howard. And neither you nor Mathilde can make me forget it. Mathilde! Her aim is clear, now."

"To replace one mistress with another, thus retaining her own position at the Élysée. But can she keep you a bachelor forever?"

"She would marry me herself if she could. Unfortunately for her, divorce has been abolished. She remains tied to Demidoff, hoping meanwhile that, as Emperor, I'll restore divorce. Knowing that, as Emperor, I must marry and beget an heir. *Not* knowing that I am negotiating in another direction."

"A royal princess?"

"Of course," he said simply.

Not Princess Mathilde, not Miss Howard, not the Countess of Teba, but a *royal* princess. Stupidly I had chosen to ignore the very thing I had always known.

"Shall we go?" he asked abruptly.

In the carriage, I remembered Miss Howard's sacrifice and made a bid—a subtle one, I thought—to outdo the woman.

"We seem to have reached a better understanding," I began.

"How noble of you to say that, Eugenie!"

"Everything I have is still yours, but only if you fail."

"Why that condition?"

"You won't need it if you succeed, but if you fail ... !"

"Failure would be the end of me. You know that as well as I do, so you have nothing to gain by making your offer. You would have a broken man upon your hands. I'm deeply impressed, Eugenie, deeply touched."

During the evening of December first, I received a short letter from Louis-Napoleon:

"I am vitally concerned that no harm should come to you. Remain in your apartment tomorrow, the next day and the next. The second day of a revolution is more dangerous than the first, the third more critical than either the first or the second. Destroy this letter at once."

I destroyed it and remained indoors simply because two special policemen, dressed to look like gentlemen of leisure, were stationed at the door. Revolution, I remember thinking . . . Was Paris to be torn by bloody revolution in order that Louis-Napoleon might extend his term of office?

Not having been taken fully into his confidence, I, like the general public, was left to speculate and await the outcome of his secret political moves. On the morning of the second, he gained control of the Army in Paris and issued a number of proclamations. Dubbing the Assembly a reactionary one, he brought about its dissolution by force. Clearly, he had taken the law into his own hands in a bold attempt to change that law, but he assured the people that the whole nation would be given the opportunity to choose freely, for or against him, at a plebiscite which would soon take place. And he promised to resign if the voting went against him.

Bloody revolution? Paris, on the whole, took the not entirely unexpected coup calmly enough. True, during the second day there was a disturbance in the Rue du Faubourg Saint-Antoine and three people were killed, but on the third day all active opposition was crushed. The plebiscite took place on December twentieth, and by the end of the month the full result was known. More than seven million people had voted yea; scarcely a tenth of that number, nay. By the will of the people, Louis-Napoleon was President of the Second Republic for a period of ten years and possessed the power to draw up a new constitution. By his own will, he regarded himself Emperor-elect. Would he, I wondered, achieve this final aim?

Early in the new year, I met Louis-Napoleon again for the first time since that December day in the country. We were commanded, Mama and I, to grace one of his receptions with our presence. It took place at the Élysée, for he had decided against a too eager occupation of the Tuileries, and there once more I rubbed shoulders with diplomats, army generals and ministers of state.

Louis-Napoleon was surrounded by a little group of privileged admirers—the King holding court. My two enemies were with him, Napoleon-Jerome on his right, Mathilde on his left. It is always wise to disarm one's enemies with a ready smile. Accordingly, on that occasion I smiled sweetly when Napoleon-Jerome kissed my hand, and I paid tribute to Mathilde's rank by curtsying when that wretched woman boomed a greeting. Louis-Napoleon looked on approvingly.

"As I suspected," he said, drawing me aside for a moment, "the Countess of Teba is wearing the highest heels in Paris tonight."

"I procured them deliberately, Monsieur."

"You thought to tower over me, to intimidate me? How foolish of you! Never again will I find embarrassment in my short stature. Henceforth I shall stand erect before all men."

"All women also, Napoleon?"

"You have a particular one in mind, Eugenie?"

"I was thinking of the princess you propose to marry."

"Ah yes! Adelaide of Hohenlohe, niece of the Queen of England. Well, we shall see."

"A splendid match."

"I'd marry for love if it were possible. Confound you, M'm'selle, I *want* to marry for love."

"Who knows? You may grow to love Princess Adelaide."

"How can I, loving you as I do?"

"And—Miss Howard?"

"You are permitted to meet me in public; she is not. That should be your answer."

"I recognize no answer there."

"*I* do, Eugenie."

"Sacred and profane love?"

His eyes grew opaque. "You possess a waspish tongue, Countess."

"Miss Howard meets you in private," I said, "and that I'll never do again."

"Never?"

"Not while she holds you on that golden leash of hers."

I regretted the words before they were fully uttered. How stupid to overplay my hand, to place myself in a position from which, my pride being what it was, retreat was out of the question.

"An ultimatum," Louis-Napoleon said harshly. He had grown suddenly pale. Perhaps it was a family characteristic. His uncle, it was said, never flushed with anger, but always grew pale.

"*If* I am never to see you in private, only in public—"

"Well?"

"It would be better if you went away."

"Ah, you dismiss me!"

"In doing so, I dismiss a part of myself, the better part."

I studied him closely. He looked as sincere as he sounded. He was actually suffering!

"Would to God I'd failed," he said intensely, "and was in a position now to accept your offer."

"You expect me to believe that of the tallest man in the world?"

He had the grace to look sheepish. "Obviously I cannot have everything."

"Am I to be sent to the border under guard?"

"You actually mean to obey me?"

"You issued what amounts to a royal command. What else can I do but obey? I, a foreigner in your country?"

I curtsied and withdrew. That is to say, I backed mockingly from the royal presence, but I must admit to feeling a little stab of panic. Having overplayed my hand, I'd been forced into accepting dismissal. Through my own stupidity I was leaving the country. How many men's hearts really do grow fonder because of absence? In any case, Louis-Napoleon was bent on marrying Queen Victoria's niece. If his heart really burst with fondness, what then? Oh, the tumult of my thoughts that night.

During our round of farewell visits, Mama insisted on calling at all the embassies even though we were known only slightly at most of them. It was infuriating to hear her tell everybody that we were going to Spain, yes, but only in the certainty of a quick recall to France. Oh dear—that hint of mystery in her voice, that wise nod of her head, that glint in her astigmatic eyes! Mastering her disappointment at the turn of events, she was putting what she called a brave face on things.

When it came to the point, I left Paris in a black mood, but at the border a courier overtook us with a letter from Louis-Napoleon. "When I can bear it no more, when all obstacles have been removed, I shall order you back," he wrote.

"There!" Mama cried triumphantly, "what have I been telling everybody!"

Chapter Seven

"MY DAUGHTER is bespoken."

That delightful phrase of Mama's rings out to me across the years. She first uttered it to Paca and Alba, saying no more yet swearing them to absolute secrecy. Out it popped again when an elderly Spanish count asked for my hand in marriage.

"My daughter is bespoken."

Three other suitors approached her during the few months we spent in Madrid and were dismissed in the same way. It was a pleasant enough change: Mama no longer playing the eager matchmaker.

One thing troubled me vaguely at that time. My suitors were all elderly and one was really quite old. They were searching for a wife of mature years and settled disposition; at least the Old One was indiscreet enough to admit as much. I was twenty-six. The years were slipping by far too quickly. Was that how they regarded me in Madrid—as a woman of mature years and settled disposition? Worse, some of my girlhood friends, all long since married, were inclined to look upon me as a maiden aunt for their children. Bespoken? They smiled knowingly. Having failed in all our travels to find me a husband, Mama had now brought me back to Spain in despair.

Meanwhile Louis-Napoleon and I were exchanging letters. He wrote that he missed me desperately; I replied that a desperate situation called for desperate

71

action, implying, since I mentioned the Old One's proposal, that I myself was contemplating very desperate action indeed. He replied smoothly that even a man of his own age was a little too old for me. That letter I refrained from answering, at which he wrote and asked if he had offended me in any way. It was his intention, he added, to raise me to the position I deserved. His intention, merely. Plainly he was still refusing to commit himself in any definite way, so in reply I quoted one of Mama's "apt" phrases: The road to hell is paved with good intentions. That letter he refrained from answering.

Nevertheless, I was beginning to wonder if the Princess Adelaide negotiations were proving difficult and likely to collapse.

Louis-Napoleon's next letter contained a reference to the prediction made by the gypsy when I was born; Mama, impossible woman, admitted to having told him about it before we left Paris. So I was to become a Queen, he wrote, and live to a great age, perhaps a hundred! *"Eh bien,* I may yet live to see you mount a throne but surely not to follow so ancient a lady to her grave." Heartening? Judge for yourself! He added a postscript: "I hear that one of the minor rulers of Europe is searching for a wife; the Countess of Montijo and her daughter had better start their travels again."

Ignoring that comment, I wrote that I had no faith in predictions, only in fate, inescapable fate. And tongue in cheek, I added a postscript of my own: "That I should live to see you on a throne is all I ask of life."

And then it came, the summons to return to Paris. The letter reading like a telegram, contained only three brief sentences.

"Come back. The golden leash is broken. No other obstacle remains."

A command unmistakably, but naturally I obeyed it, confident in my heart that the Princess Adelaide negotiations had collapsed at last.

It was winter again when Mother and I took up residence once more in the Place Vendôme. Mérimée was the first friend to greet us and he quickly gave us the latest news.

"Louis-Napoleon," he said, "has the quaint idea that God has chosen him, a Bonaparte, to give France lasting peace and to restore the glory which was shattered by the treaties forced upon her after the fall of his uncle. He now resides at the Tuileries and the servants wear the same livery that his uncle's servants wore. The flagstaffs no longer have pikes on top but imperial eagles. The civil code has been given its old name again, the Code Napoleon. New coins are in circulation. The reverse side bears the inscription *République Française,* certainly, but on the obverse side we have the bearded President and the inscription: Louis Bonaparte. The audacity of it, Eugenia! Even in America a president must be in his grave before appearing on the coins."

On the afternoon of our return, I found the whole apartment filled with flowers and a note of welcome in which Mama and I were invited to a reception at the Tuileries. It took place in the Salle des Maréchaux, and again, as at the Élysée, Mathilde was the official hostess, a smiling Mathilde who whispered that I must remain when the others departed. Louis-Napoleon was stouter than I remembered him and in consequence looked shorter. Nevertheless, there was something impressive and commanding in his bearing now. Everybody noticed it and listened respectfully when he talked. And how he talked! As I listened and watched, I became aware of a characteristic which had eluded me before. The Prince-President never gesticulated, and that, in the presence of many Frenchmen, set him apart from the rest.

When at last the guests began to take their leave, General Emil Fleury, one of the aides, approached me and led me discreetly to Louis-Napoleon's study which overlooked the gardens and had once been used by the ill-fated Louis XVI. The Prince-President, he said, would join me as soon as possible. Meanwhile, if I cared to partake of a little refreshment . . . I smiled at the sight of the Marsala, my favorite wine, thoughtfully provided once again.

A few moments after Fleury withdrew and before I could begin an inspection of the study, the tapestry covering an inner door was flung aside and there, to my amazement, stood a woman I recognized instantly as Miss Howard. She approached me languidly, remarking that there were many secret entrances to the Tuileries, all of which were well known to her, especially the most secret of all, that which gave access to the Prince-President's bedchamber. Then she poured a glass of wine for herself and shrugged imperceptibly when I refused to take any myself.

"Dona Eugenia, Countess of Teba, or am I mistaken?"

"You're not mistaken, M'm'selle."

She inclined her lovely head. "The virtuous virgin. Do you really expect to win him that way, Countess? How foolish of you. I have the better of both you and Princess Adelaide. He took a holy oath to marry me and, more important still, gave me his written promise."

"I don't believe you," I said faintly.

"As you wish." From the neck of her gown she took a folded sheet of paper, unfolded it and placed it in my hand. "A copy only. Read it and go back to Spain."

I stared stupidly at the writing on the paper. When I looked up again, Miss Howard was gone and, sinking into a chair, I began to read what was clearly a love letter. If I felt any shame at what I was doing, I remember nothing of it now. Louis-Napoleon rushed into the room a few moments later, dragged me to my feet and embraced me.

"Eugenie! At last!"

I pushed him away, thrust the letter into his hand and turned my back on him. First I heard his gasp of surprise, then I felt his hands on my shoulders.

"How did you come by this?" he demanded, swinging me round to face him.

I told him, glancing from the half-empty glass of Marsala to the tapestry.

"Is nothing sacred to a woman?" he asked idiotically. "Love letters should be cherished and guarded."

"A love letter, Monsieur, but a promise of marriage also."

"Place it in the hands of a lawyer and he'll tell you that marriage is by no means promised."

"Did you write to Princess Adelaide in the same legally cautious vein?"

"I wrote to her father, not to the girl herself. I stated my intention clearly, incontrovertibly. In plain, simple language, I asked for his daughter's hand in marriage. I still have high hopes of success."

I ran to the door and flung it violently open.

"Wait, Eugenie! I want to marry you. Please let me explain."

"You brought me back by a trick! The 'golden leash broken, no other obstacle between us.' What utter rubbish!"

"The golden leash *is* broken," he insisted. "Miss Howard is to be repaid in full." He tried to take me in his arms again. "Let me explain your own position, the plan I have in mind for you."

"You explained it clearly long ago," I said, and ran from the room.

Mama was waiting in the Salle des Maréchaux with General Fleury. I ignored their curious glances and marched past them as only a strictly moral young woman knows how to march when morally affronted. Mama called after me feebly but I went on, only to get lost for a time in a maze of ill-lit passages and antechambers. When finally I extricated myself and reached the carriage, Mama was sitting in it, with her hands clasped tightly in her lap.

"So! You quarreled with the Prince-President."

"One quarrel in one night is more than enough, Mama."

"Surely you were impressed by the offer he made?"

"You know my views on that sort of offer!"

Mama sighed deeply. "I think you must have misunderstood him, darling. After all, the precedent set by Mrs. Fitzherbert—"

"Mrs. Fitzherbert? Who, pray, is she?"

"Was, Genia. She died some years ago. Obviously you gave the Prince no time to explain himself fully."

It turned out that General Fleury had talked earnestly with Mama on Louis-Napoleon's behalf. Mrs. Fitzherbert, it seemed, had married George IV of England, one of Queen Victoria's wicked uncles, while that future King was still Prince Regent. Fleury had drawn a parallel between Mrs. Fitzherbert and me, hoping, still on Louis-Napoleon's behalf, that I would gladly follow her precedent.

"A morganatic union," Mama stressed. "You understand what that means?"

Vaguely I did, but Mama in her eagerness hastened to make the meaning abundantly clear. Morganatic marriages took place between kings, princes and nobles, and women of inferior rank. They were also known as "left-handed" marriages, since the left hand was given, not the right. Children of such marriages were legitimate but could not inherit the rank or possessions of their male parents.

"Am *I* of inferior rank to Louis-Napoleon?" I raged, addressing the absent Prince-President rather than Mama. "The Bonapartes were Corsican nobodies before Napoleon made his way in the world. Louis-Napoleon himself hasn't the smallest drop of royal blood in his veins. His father was Napoleon's brother, his mother Josephine's daughter. He had aristocratic blood from his mother, but certainly not *royal* blood." I was working myself up to greater heights of indignation and quite enjoying it. "Inferior rank! But for the Emperior Napoleon, our precious Prince-President would be selling oranges or fish or some such thing on the quay at Ajaccio."

Mama hesitated for a moment, then said reluctantly, "Your Grandfather Kirkpatrick sold fruit and wine. Try to be sensible, *Countess*. The Prince-President is not yet married to the Princess Adelaide. If he marries you first, even morganatically, the time may come when your own marriage can be represented as the only legal union. French law is most peculiar and is always being changed."

"He would marry me first? General Fleury said that?"

"Not in so many words," Mama was obliged to admit, "but the poor man is so infatuated. It behooves you to listen to him sympathetically, not make terrible scenes."

Mama was right, I admitted grudgingly to myself. I'd absence in Spain. It was no fault of his that he must missed Louis-Napoleon more than I believed during my form a royal alliance. Had he not said that he would marry for love if he could? A morganatic marriage would be marrying for love. I believed in his cause, I trusted his ambition, I saw him as the benevolent father of a new and glorious France.

"Mrs. Fitzherbert was as moral a woman as you are," Mama went on quickly. "As good a Catholic, too. She knew she was doing nothing wrong."

"I was hasty," I said contritely. "I should listen, as you say, with sympathy."

Mama heaved a deep sign of relief. "Darling, we're invited to a hunt at Fontainebleau," she laughed.

"Accept, then."

She laughed again. "I've accepted already."

Louis-Napoleon's guest traveled from Paris to Fontainebleau by special train, and from the railway station made the short journey to the château in an imposing cavalcade of richy furnished carriages. Princess Mathilde was standing at her cousin's side when the majordomo announced our arrival. She must have resented my presence but she smiled on me charmingly and I smiled back. Louis-Napoleon had time for only a few brief words with me, for other guests were being quickly announced.

"I was still naive enough to expect you to come," he whispered.

"And I to do so," I whispered back.

The unspeakable Napoleon-Jerome appeared and escorted me to my apartment which, by some mischance, he said, was quite some distance from my mother's. He, too, smiled charmingly.

"You resisted my advances," he said thoughtfully. "Do you hope to gain a crown by resisting my cousin's?"

"France is a Republic, Monsier. Surely it's treason to speak of crowns."

"But not to think of them, Countess. Are you really what you seem—a truly frigid woman? I begin to pity the poor fellow who may have to share with you the marriage bed."

Frigidity and morality—I wonder how often the two have been confused?

The next morning we were told that Louis-Napoleon was free to join the hunt. The December air was crisp and clear, a perfect day for hunting. I was dressed and ready well before the others, but I hung back, making sure of being the last to appear in the courtyard. The little gasp of admiration at the sight of me was pleasing. My riding habit was new, close-fitting but not too tight, and beneath the long skirt, I wore little grey trousers. The highly-polished spurs on my high-heeled boots flashed in the sunlight, while the ostrich feather in my hat made me look taller than ever.

"No woman has a right to possess such a figure," Mathilde complained in mock despair.

Louis-Napoleon, his eyes devouring me, brought up my horse, a handsome chestnut and one of the finest in the Fontainebleau stable. I glanced pointedly from the side-saddle to my spurs as he stooped to help me mount.

"The saddle must be changed," I said, tapping it with my pearl-handled riding whip.

The saddle was hurriedly changed. Miss Howard always rode astride. She was one of the finest horsewomen of Louis-Napoleon's acquaintance. Very well, then, the time had come for him to admire the greater skill of the Countess of Teba. Once again he started to help me mount, but I leaped up unaided and, while he mounted his own horse, sat drinking in the beauty of the scene. There were splashes of brilliant color everywhere: the green costumes of the Fontainebleau hunt, the red of Lord Cowley and his secretary, the yellow of yet another foreign diplomat—it was almost as if a rainbow had fallen from the sky and disintegrated in the courtyard.

Louis-Napoleon glanced at me, not at Mathilde, plumply wedged into her side-saddle. Were we all ready to start? I waited no longer, but dug in my spurs and galloped from the courtyard. Behind me, I heard the signal from the hunting horn, the barking of the dogs and the pounding of a single horse's hoofs. Louis-Napoleon's, of course! The hunt within the hunt was in hectic progress.

I was sure I could outpace him but discretion held

me back. He drew level, streaked past and quickly reined in his horse.

"Come, Countess, you can do better than that!"

"You over-estimate my skill, Monsieur."

He shook his head and laughed knowingly. "Are you afraid of offending my male dignity?"

Afraid! I dug in my spurs again. Louis-Napoleon gave me a lengthy start before racing after me, but soon drew level, outstripped me and remained well ahead until I was forced to admit myself beaten.

"Shall we dismount and rest for a while?" he asked innocently.

For answer, I gave his mount a sharp cut across the flanks with my whip and rode off in the opposite direction to rejoin the hunt. Louis-Napoleon followed me presently, a look of admiration on his face, not the scowl I was expecting.

That night he dined alone with the ministers who had come out from Paris to confer with him and it was midnight before he sent the message which released us and allowed us to go to bed. Scarcely had I closed my door when I heard a tinkling noise at the window. It was repeated almost immediately. I stepped cautiously onto the balcony. Louis-Napoleon was busily throwing pebbles from the garden below. I could see his eager smile quite clearly in the moonlight.

"Come down, Eugenie. I want to talk to you."

"At this hour of night? Certainly not."

"As you wish. I can reach you easily enough. There's a secret passage by way of the old royal chapel."

"Ah yes," I said, the opportunity being too good to resist. "The chapel. That way but no other."

Louis-Napoleon disappeared at once. I ran to the door and waited. Had he grasped the real meaning of my words? A few moments later, there was a light tap on the door, then another a great deal louder.

"Let me in, Eugenie, or I'll make such a row everybody will come running to see the fun."

I opened the door. "Fun, Monsieur?"

"Ah, another scene," he said, in mock despair.

"Not unless you make it yourself."

He flung himself into a chair and grasped the arms tensely. After a few moments of silence, he relaxed and stared at me blankly. He had the appearance of a man in a trance. Alarming as it was then, I grew accustomed in the years that followed to seeing him in that condition. It was a habit of his when deep in thought.

"I have a number of things on my mind," he said at last.

"So have I, Napoleon."

He smiled faintly. "One only, Eugenie. The chapel. Nevertheless, the ceremony will take place in the privacy of my study."

"You seem sure I'm ready to accept a left-handed marriage."

"I can offer you no other sort."

I held out my left hand. "When do you propose to take it? Tomorrow?"

"You'd marry me tomorrow?"

"Gladly."

He came fully out of his trance. *"Mon dieu,* Eugenie, do you think me a fool? My marriage with Princess Adelaide must take place first."

"Then it's either a right-handed marriage or nothing, Napoleon."

"An ultimatum?"

"Or nothing," I repeated, "and with that you will have to be satisfied."

"I refuse to believe you," he said, "and with that, you will have to be satisfied."

Stalemate. The two of us facing each other across an imaginary chessboard.

A few days after our return to Paris, a second plebiscite took place, the all-important plebiscite at which the nation was asked to vote for or against the setting up of the Second Empire with Louis-Napoleon as Emperor.

The ground had been carefully prepared. Even before a single vote was cast, everybody—friend and enemy alike—regarded the result as a foregone conclusion. The only interesting question left to be answered was whether Louis-Napoleon would choose to call himself Napoleon II or Napoleon III. The first Napoleon's son by Marie Louise had never reigned, but the Bonapartists had thought of him and spoken of him as Napoleon II until the day he died. Louis-Napoleon scarcely hesitated; a new Bonaparte Emperor must do all in his power to please the Bonapartists.

The second plebiscite gave him a greater majority than the first. He was proclaimed the Emperor Napoleon III on December second, a nicely calculated piece of showmanship. Was it not the anniversary of the *coup d'état,* the Battle of Austerlitz and the coronation of the first Napoleon? His uncle, ex-King Jerome, and his cousin Napoleon-Jerome, now styled the Prince Napoleon, were named his immediate heirs until such a time as marriage gave him a son.

Meanwhile, Napoleon III and I still faced each other across that imaginary chessboard. We had not met again since the hunting party at Fontainebleau, but I accepted an invitation to be present at his first imperial review, chaperoned, of course, by Mama, and had a prominent position at one of the palace windows. We were present at the reception that night and at the succession of dinner parties, balls and fetes which followed. In no time at all, the whole of Paris was gossiping. Why was it, people asked each other on the boulevards, that not since the first day of his reign had the Emperor considered an imperial gathering complete without the presence of the Countess of Montijo and her daughter?

Before Christmas there was another hunting party, this time at Compiègne, and there a half dozen of us were commanded to take an early morning walk with the Emperor. All but I had been given an additional command and one by one, on some ridiculous pretext or other, they begged to be excused during the saunter.

"I admit to being out-generaled, Sire," I laughed, as the last of our companions disappeared from sight.

"May I take your arm?" he asked, hugely pleased with himself.

He was walking on my left. I fell back a pace, skipped behind him and caught up with him on my right.

"The thought is always in your mind," he said wryly, but took my right arm firmly in his. "This deadlock is growing intolerable."

Deadlock, stalemate—the meaning was the same, so I told him about the imaginary chessboard which lay between us.

"Any sensible chess player would sweep the pieces from the board and engage in a new contest," he said eagerly.

"The result would be the same."

"Meaning you would make the same moves?"

"Certainly." I freed my arm and to hide my agitation stooped in pretended admiration of a dew-covered clover leaf sparkling in the sunlight.

"Pretty," said Napoleon, bending at my side.

"Yes."

"One of my moves would be different. It would place my king, that is to say, myself, the Emperor, at your immediate disposal now, not after the marriage with Adelaide."

I was strongly tempted, but a new thought, flashing suddenly into my mind, held me back. "If I bore you a son, he would never be your heir."

Napoleon looked at me searchingly. "You would care more for your son's future than your own? Come, Eugenie, answer me!"

"Than my own or his father's."

His face clouded. "We'll say no more about it."

Later that morning Count Bacciocchi, aide to the Emperor, left hurriedly for Paris. On his return the following afternoon, he bowed ostensibly before me and presented a small package wrapped in tissue paper.

"With His Majesty's compliments, Countess."

Tearing off the wrapping, I discovered a velvet-covered jewel box and within it an exquisitely wrought silver clover leaf studded with three tiny but superb diamonds. The accompanying card bore the words: "I beg you to wear this trinket when you come to my New Year's Eve ball at the Tuileries." The signature was the single Imperial N.

My dress for that ball—to me the most important ball of my life—came from Madame Vignon's, then the most fashionable house. She and her girls sat up all night in order to have it ready in time. The most cunningly designed piece of extravagant simplicity in white satin—that was how Madame Vignon described it. M'm'selle Palmyre, her most serious rival, would throw a dozen fits if she saw it and put up the shutters.

It was a magnificent, glittering gathering at the Tuileries that night, but as far as I could see not a single royalist aristocrat was present. The legitimists hated Napoleon even more than did the extreme republicans and had either departed for their country estates or disdainfully ignored the Emperor's invitations. Nevertheless, it was a most formal occasion; that ugly word "protocol" was on everybody's lips.

Napoleon occupied a throne-like chair set upon a dais and looked most impressive in his full court regalia. Mama curtsied with a gesture that was nothing if not imperious; then I curtsied myself, much more decorously. Napoleon's eyes flashed briefly at the sight of the clover leaf on my breast and again as he saw the tiny earrings which I'd ordered to match it. With that, Mama and I moved to the seats which had been assigned to us at the left of the dais and were about to seat ourselves among the wives of the ministers of state when Madame Drouyn de Lhuys, wife of the Foreign Minister, rose majestically and waved us back.

"Dear me, are we in the wrong place?" Mama fussed.

"Indeed you are, Madame. Would you presume to take the seats set apart for really important people?"

There was a momentary silence, then Napoleon rose and stepped down from the dais.

"Madame . . . M'm'selle . . ."

Thereupon he ushered us to the seats at the *right* of the dais and placed us with ex-King Jerome, Princess Mathilde and Prince Napoleon-Jerome, behind whom sat the more distant members of the Bonaparte family.

"Did you put the silly woman up to it?" I asked Mathilde, sweetly.

"Knowing the Emperor as I do, would I be so stupid?" she replied, just as sweetly.

There were more insults to come. Napoleon-Jerome, assuming a troubled air, asked his old father if there were any truth in the story which suggested that the Countess of Teba's real father was that amusing writer, Prosper Mérimée. A further insult followed quickly, for just as we were going in to dinner I heard a snort of anger behind me and turning saw Madame Fortoul, wife of the new Minister of Education.

"So! The Spanish adventuress takes precedence over us all!"

Quickly I stood aside for her. "One adventuress at a time is more than enough for the Emperor."

But my rage was a pain which I knew would soon become unendurable. I can remember very little about the banquet—my vis-à-vis at table, I think, was Baron de Rothschild, our banker—but I do remember dancing later with an infatuated colonel whose hands, despite his gloves, were revoltingly clammy. And the Emperor? I refused even to look at him when he approached me.

"Dance with Madame Fortoul, providing she finds your Imperial Majesty acceptable."

"Eugenie—"

"You brought me here to be insulted!"

He took me firmly by the arm. "Come to my study."

Once there, my rage boiled over in a torrent of words. Napoleon listened patiently until, having stigmatized all the Bonapartes as opportunists, adventurers and Corsican bandits, I fell into a chair exhausted.

"Have you the strength to repeat it all in French?" Napoleon asked, "or even in English?"

Unconsciously I'd raged at him in my native tongue!

"So fortunate for my peace of mind I know only a few words of Spanish," he added, trying to make me laugh.

"That wretched cousin of yours!"

"It was wrong of him to repeat the gossip but—"

"*Repeat* it! He invented it—*invented* it!"

"No, Eugenie. It reached Fleury's ears before his."

"Paris is a hateful city, the new court a disgusting place populated by ill-bred upstarts. I shall leave France at once."

Napoleon bowed stiffly. "I cannot hold you by force any more than I can take you by force. I can only hope that the force of your affection, if not your love, will hold you here, come what may."

"Come what may . . ."

Those words gained an increasingly unpleasant significance during the next few days. Other unsavory stories were added to the one heard by Fleury and repeated by Prince "Plonplon."—Napoleon-Jerome had not yet gained his derisive nickname, but I always think of him as Plonplon and cannot resist using it now as I write.—It seemed as if the whole of Paris was talking and speculating about me and avidly believing every new and scandalous lie. Nothing of this appeared in the newspapers, but pamphlets were printed privately and passed surreptitiously from hand to hand on the boulevards.

Meanwhile Mama and I were superintending our packing. A splendid start for the new year, she complained, but agreed that we could no longer remain in France.

"And why indeed should we, Genia? A poor sort of court when the people across the Seine stand contemptuously aloof."

She was referring to the impregnable royalists of the Faubourg Saint-Germain, and they, she added, were in reality our own aristocratic counterpart in France.

"Remain and we shall become hopelessly *déclassé!*"

Our preparations were almost completed when we heard a rumor that the newspapers would soon announce the betrothal of the Emperor and the Princess Adelaide. Count Walewski, French Ambassador in London, had arrived suddenly at the Tuileries where he had been observed in earnest conversation with Lord Cowley. Later, the two had been observed in earnest conversation with the Emperor, after which all three had smiled and shown every sign of deep satisfaction.

The next morning Napoleon came to our apartment unattended. He spoke hesitantly to Mama—indeed, his manner was surprisingly diffident—and asked permission to spend a few moments alone with me.

"A last farewell before you take her away, Madame."

Mama curtsied. "Your Majesty's will is law."

"In this instance, yes," he agreed, diffident still.

He had brought with him a small portfolio and from it, the moment we were alone, he took out a sheaf of crumpled papers.

"There is only one answer to the lies that are being told about you, Countess. I have here an announcement for the newspapers. It will appear first in *La Patrie*. Please read it and tell me if you consider it suitably worded. Then you shall hear me run through a new speech. I worked all night on both."

I took the single sheet he offered me and began to read with the utmost curiosity.

"Aloud, please!" he commanded.

I cleared my throat: "It is reported that a happy event is soon to take place, one which will strengthen his Majesty's government and ensure the future of his dynasty. The Emperor is on the point of marrying Mlle. de Montijo, Countess of Teba and . . ."

The paper slipped from my fingers; Napoleon picked it up and gave it back to me.

"Continue!" he said sternly.

". . . and the official notification will be made to the Legislative Body by the Emperor himself on Saturday. The Countess, whose sister is the Duchess of Alba, is a member of one of the noblest families in Spain. . . ."

"Indeed she is," Napoleon interrupted. "You have among your collateral ancestors a Queen of Portugal, a King of Galicia and a Doge of Genoa."

"You seem to know more about my family tree than I do myself," I said weakly.

"I ordered a painstaking research some time ago."

So stunned was I by Napoleon's amazing *volte-face* that I found difficulty in putting two clear thoughts together in my mind.

"The Princess Adelaide—" I stammered.

"Her family tree is of no interest to me. Nor is the girl herself. I was always afraid that on meeting her I might dislike her intensely. As far as *I* am concerned, she has ceased to exist."

I was still groping for words. "To—to jilt a princess for *me*? I can't believe it, Napoleon. I must have misread your announcement."

Then I began to read it again as carefully as I could.

"Are you searching for the word morganatic?" Napoleon asked. "How silly if you are! Would such a marriage take place in Notre Dame?"

The paper slipped from my fingers once more. "Please tell me why you changed your mind."

He took me in his arms. "Dear Eugenie, it was something you said yourself. Those touching words of yours about your son's welfare. You would care more for *his* future than your own or his father's. I knew then that you must be the mother of the future Emperor."

I was close to tears. Napoleon kissed me tenderly, released me reluctantly and set about reading his speech. It was a rough draft only, he said, and I was to suggest any alterations that might occur to me as "proper." I listened, still in a daze:

"Gentlemen, I accede to the wish so often expressed by the nation . . . I am here before you to announce my impending marriage. The union is not in accordance with ancient royal tradition, and therein lies its advantage. The lady of my choice is of lofty birth, Spanish, but by education French, by instinct French and by the blood of her father shed for the Empire, French also. She asks nothing of France but that she may be permitted as Empress to serve the nation. She is gracious and good, kind and gentle, as was the wife of General Bonaparte who was not herself of royal blood . . . As the third Empress of France, I can but believe that she will bring to life again all the virtues of the first one, the Empress Josephine . . ."

My balance was much recovered. I looked at Napoleon in amazement. "Josephine a virtuous woman? People will laugh at you."

"She became a faithful wife long before she mounted the throne with my uncle," he said primly. "In any case she was my grandmother. I never knew her to be anything but kind and gentle. I honor her memory."

"No more need be said," I conceded, wiping that amendment from my mind.

Napoleon took up another sheet of paper and went on sternly: "I am here now, gentlemen, to say to you, to *France,* that I prefer a woman I love and respect to a royal alliance with a stranger. In scorning calculated ambition through dynastic prejudice and placing family happiness first, I shall grow stronger in my duty, not weaker." His tone was becoming dogmatic and in consequence, the German accent more pronounced. "When I go to Notre Dame I shall present my Empress to the people whose trust in me will grant me their sympathy, understanding and love—" He broke off abruptly. "Have you any additions to suggest?"

"A complimentary reference to your uncle's second wife would please the Royalists."

"True, since *that* royal alliance was an important event, out of duty to my uncle's name I must recognize it as such. Are you clever enough to think of a way of pleasing the Republicans also?"

"There are many parvenus among the Republicans," I said reflectively, "and you yourself have often been called a parvenu."

"You think I should admit it, take pride in it?"

"Yes."

Napoleon asked for pen and ink and we set to work together on this new idea, this brilliant idea—as we thought it at the time. Alas, it was a serious mistake. Many of his supporters were shocked, others were tolerantly amused, while the far-seeing ones regarded it rightly as a diplomatic *gaffe*. At that moment, of course, the future was unknown to us. I'd ventured into the political arena for the first time and was mightily proud of my imagined astuteness, heaven forgive me. Heaven forgive me? Why should I say that? In my ignorance of political insincerity, I was entirely sincere myself—poor innocent Empress-to-be.

"We've quite forgotten your mother," Napoleon said suddenly. "I came here humbly to ask for her daughter's hand in marriage. It would be an unkindness to ignore her altogether."

Mama was truly magnificent. She bottled up her excited feeling of triumph by an effort of will that was scarcely human and looked at the Emperor of France in cold appraisal.

"This is a grave situation, Sire. My duty as a mother is plainly to weigh the pros and cons both deeply and carefully."

Napoleon tried not to laugh. "You fear I may not be entirely acceptable, Madame?"

"Sire, there is a vast difference in station between my daughter and you."

"You also fear that I may not be as serious as I appear to sound?"

Mama inclined her head. "The announcement has yet to be printed in the newspapers."

"The only delay is caused by you, Madame."

Mama came to the point at once. "By the time I receive your Majesty's offer in writing, I shall have made up my mind one way or the other."

Napoleon's eyes twinkled. "Had your son lived, Madame, he would surely have become a lawyer."

His letter reached Mama the next morning, and the announcement duly appeared in *La Patrie*. Napoleon made his speech on the twenty-second of the month and followed it by asserting that the civil marriage would take place on the twenty-ninth, the religious ceremony on the thirtieth.

"A week only!" Mama gasped. "What a frantic rush!"

We moved that day to the Élysée Palace, there to be received by a solemn group of Napoleon's lawyers on the one hand, and on the other by Madame Fould, wife of the Minister of State. The lawyers informed me that His Majesty had made immediately available to me an income of a quarter of a million francs, and Madame Fould added that nothing now stood between her and the purchasing of a suitable trousseau.

And with that the frantic rush began.

Chapter Eight

IN LOOKING BACK over the years to that brief, exciting period during which Mama and I held court at the Élysée Palace, I can remember as vividly as anything else something Napoleon said about the newspaper world. If fate hadn't made him Emperor of France, he said, he would have been inclined to choose the career of a newspaper editor. When I asked him why, he smiled and explained that editors had the power to castigate even an Emperor. In later years he agreed with me that it went further than that, since editors seem to take upon themselves the guise of the Almighty. They advise, they scold, they reproach, sometimes they even stoop to praise a little, and all in the most pontifical language imaginable. One can but feel sorry for them. Nobody ever listens quite attentively enough. Silly people continue to do silly things in spite of editorial fury, contempt and rudeness. The Kingdom of Heaven remains in its proper place. Not even the God-editor and his Archangel editorial writers can tear it down and set it up on earth.

"You would hardly relish an editorial chair in France," I told Napoleon. "Remember the censorship."

"I was thinking of the free press of England, *chérie*."

I sensed that he was anxious on his own account. Would the British press, seeking to shape public opinion, scold him because of his choice of bride? I was a little anxious myself, for I knew how much he counted upon strengthening the ties of peace and friendship with

Great Britain. I need not have worried. The British newspapers expressed much astonishment but on the whole treated me gently enough.

Because of the French censorship, our own press was much more circumspect. Editors were permitted just two "indiscretions" before placing their newspapers in danger of suspension. Happily, no indiscretions were leveled against the future Empress. Indeed, little hymns of praise appeared daily in honor of my beauty, my piety and my generosity. I admit that I was growing vain about the position which would soon be mine, but even so journalistic exaggeration was a little too much for my sense of proportion. I considered it less than generous when I refused six hundred thousand francs with which the City of Paris wanted me to buy diamonds and directed that the money should be used instead for the establishment of a school for girls of poor parents. Napoleon was deeply touched, but Plonplon remarked in my hearing that I was carefully playing to the gallery.

"The poor are as much entitled to education as you are," Napoleon took him up sharply. "May they make more of it than you, Monsieur."

Callers came daily to the Élysée to offer their congratulations, and the British newspaper correspondents were ever to the fore. One of them, winning Mama's heart unconditionally, concerned himself diligently with a detailed description of my mounting trousseau.

"Am I to understand, Excellency, that your trousseau comes from the two great fashion houses of Paris, Madame Vignon's and M'm'selle Palmyre's?"

"In the main, yes, but Madame Barenne's services have also been called upon."

"Let us begin, Excellency, with the creations from the House of Vignon."

"Up to the present moment," Mama interposed, "there are thirty gowns from Vignon but many more yet to be delivered. One doesn't expect a man to understand these things, but since you are busily writing everything down, you may as well tell your readers that the Mechlin and Valenciennes lace on the three morning peignoirs is absolutely exquisite, and the color of the silk linings rose, blue and white respectively. As for the *robes de chambre*—one is of black velvet with sky-blue facings, while the others . . ."

And so it went on, an interminable list—satins, silks, velvets; brocade with flowers of silk and gold; silk watered with gold and silver; velvet with flounces of Brussels lace and a decking of bees and crowned eagles. Not even the Empress Josephine had possessed so magnificent a wardrobe, Mama claimed with more enthusiasm than accuracy.

"Your paper will actually publish a description?" I asked the young man.

"I assure you, Excellency!"

"How remarkable. I thought British newspapers were a man's exclusive preserve."

"Certain female inroads are being made. I venture to predict that in the not too distant future the ladies, God bless them, will have special pages printed for them."

Napoleon appeared at that moment, laden with a huge bouquet. To his embarrassment, the young newspaper gentleman wrote an immediate description of the flowers and, to his further embarrassment, asked him boldly if there was any truth in the report that a certain Miss Howard had been sent to London on a government mission.

Napoleon called his aide. "Escort this too inquisitive gentleman from the palace."

"Miss Howard . . . ?" I questioned lightly, when Napoleon and I were alone together.

"I sent her to London, yes," he said stiffly. "My secretary, Moquard, went with her, his task being to see that she actually crossed the Channel. Her mission is of small importance, a mere pretext in order—well—"

"In order to remove her at this important time in our lives?"

"Yes. She would be capable of making an unpleasant scene. I promise you I shall never see her again."

He told me then what I had really understood all the time, that his reason for announcing so early a marriage date was an attempt to forestall the opposition his family was endeavoring frantically to organize. Mathilde had wept and gone down on her knees imploringly— how I'd have loved to witness such a spectacle!—and Plonplon, cursing him for a fool, had called meeting after meeting of those ministers who still hoped for a royal alliance. Fortunately, Napoleon added, my generous action in declining the gift of the City of Paris had removed the bulk of ministerial opposition.

Two days before the civil ceremony, Napoleon and I received Holy Communion together in the chapel at the Tuileries. I wanted it as much as Napoleon himself, even though we knew that cousin Plonplon and certain extreme republicans would sneer that our only aim was to appeal to the religious sentiments of the people.

Napoleon was in a very solemn frame of mind when he came to the Élysée to take me to the chapel and said at once that he wanted me to be absolutely sure of the rightness of the step I had taken when agreeing to marry him.

"The rightness as far as you yourself are concerned," he stressed. "There have been many sorry changes in France since my uncle fell from power. In marrying you, in making you Empress, I may be exposing you to many grave dangers. The throne I am so intent on your sharing with me is not yet secure. If you want to draw back, Eugenie, please say so before we kneel together at the altar. If I loved you less, it would not have occurred to me to warn you like this."

I was so deeply touched that speech became difficult. "I don't want to draw back," I managed to say.

Napoleon embraced me gently. "I'm well satisfied, *chérie*."

In the carriage during the drive to the Tuileries, he laughed lightly, spoke of the need for a clear conscience now that we were to take Holy Communion together and murmured just a little mischievously that he had a confession to make.

"Only a very small one, Eugenie. It concerns the Princess Adelaide marriage negotiations. I asked you to marry me after receiving her answer, not before, as I permitted you to believe."

"Her answer was 'yes' and you really did jilt her?"

"Conceited woman! Her answer was 'no.' I deceived you in order to make you happy."

Having been deeply touched only a few moments ago, I was now raging with indignation and, yes, a vastly injured pride. That, you see, was the diabolical thing Napoleon was able to do to me—a sign, some would say, that I really was in love with him.

"A clear conscience indeed! You tell me now only because the truth will soon become public property. A very small confession—you call it *that?*"

"Eugenie!"

"What if her answer had been yes? Come, Sire, the truth!"

"I would have jilted her," he said stoutly.

"The truth, *the truth!*"

"It would have broken my heart, but—yes, I would have been obliged to marry her."

"There!"

"How unkind you are," he said woefully. "Adelaide's refusal was the thing I prayed for. The relief was so intense I all but wept for joy. Unbelievably I was able to please myself. I was able to marry for love, Eugenie."

My anger was disappearing rapidly. As a very great concession, I allowed him to take my hand in his.

"I was sure the answer was yes, Napoleon. There was obvious good news from London. Walewski, Cowley and you were all so delighted."

He dwelt on my words for a moment. "Ah yes! Queen Victoria had expressed approval of my assuming the title of Napoleon III."

"Merely of your assuming the title?"

"Indeed no. Approval, full approval, of my becoming Emperor. Her Majesty is the ruler of a country swayed by liberalism. British liberalism was horrified at my *coup d'état* but not at my becoming Emperor by the will of the people. A fine distinction, but an important one, according to British logic."

"Does Queen Victoria approve of me as Empress?"

"She has no right to express an opinion, but if she does disapprove, you yourself will be given an opportunity of winning her over. A state visit to England—that is what I shall work for, *chérie.*"

To be received by the Queen of England, not as the Countess of Teba, but as a reigning Empress, an equal—! A dizzying thought indeed!

Two days later, at eight o'clock in the evening, Mama and I left the Élysée for the civil marriage ceremony at the Tuileries. With us in the carriage were the Imperial Master of Ceremonies and the Spanish Ambassador, while in the carriage which rolled ahead were my newly appointed Ladies-in-Waiting. In spite of the bitter coldness of that January night, the crowd in the Rue du Faubourg St. Honoré was so dense that our progress was impeded again and again. There was a constant cry of "Vive l'Impératrice!" along the entire route to the Tuileries. Mama, determined to be gloomy of a sudden, shook her head and reminded me that the people had first cheered Marie Antoinette before they became an unruly mob and hooted her.

The Grand Chamberlain received us in the courtyard

of the palace and escorted us to the grand stairway at the top of which Prince "Plonplon" Napoleon and his sister Mathilde took charge of us.

"So kind of you, cousins," I murmured.

"We are not yet related," Plonplon glowered.

Nevertheless, they ushered us stoically into what was known as the family *salon* where the Emperor himself was waiting to receive us. His involuntary exclamation of admiration was very pleasing. My white silk gown was extremely simple in appearance but covered in Alençon lace far more costly than anyone would have guessed. Round my waist was Marie Louise's diamond and sapphire belt which, along with other State jewelry, Napoleon had succeeded at last in prizing from the grasp of the Senate. He himself wore his general's uniform, the Collar of the Legion of Honor which had belonged to his uncle, and the Collar of the Golden Fleece, worn haughtily in the past by Charles V, Emperor of Germany and King of Spain, but acquired by the first Napoleon as his own by right of conquest.

At a curt nod from Napoleon, the Master of Ceremonies led the way to the Salle des Maréchaux where a large gathering awaited us. The church, the state, the army and the navy—all were represented. The color of the spectacle was dazzling—the cardinals' red robes, the operatic dress uniforms of the officers, the be-jeweled, be-ribboned orders of the ambassadors.

"The Emperor!" the Master of Ceremonies intoned reverently.

Everybody sprang to attention. Napoleon and I mounted the dais and the Minister of State placed himself solemnly between us. Uncle Jerome gave me an encouraging little nod. He was a kindly old man, often much embarrassed by Plonplon's rudeness.

"Your Imperial Majesty!" the Minister of State intoned. "Sire! Does Your Majesty declare that you take in marriage Her Excellency, Mademoiselle Eugenie de Montijo, Comtesse de Teba, here present?"

It has been written that Napoleon grew pale, trembled and after a horrible moment of hesitation uttered an indistinct "I do." In actual fact, he squared his shoulders and spoke up loudly, though I must admit that his German accent was thicker than ever before.

"I declare that I take in marriage Her Excellency, Mademoiselle Eugenie de Montijo, Comtesse de Teba, here present."

Then it was my turn.

"Mademoiselle Eugenie de Montijo, Comtesse de Teba, does Your Excellency declare that you take in marriage His Majesty, the Emperor Napoleon III, here present?"

I held my head high and tried not to sound as eager as I suddenly felt. But nervousness still plagued me. My own accent betrayed it as Napoleon's had betrayed his.

"I declare that I take in marriage His Majesty, the Emperor Napoleon III, here present."

I could but wonder at the shortness of the civil ceremony. Even the Minister of State's final words left me unconvinced that I really was the Empress of France.

"In the name of the Emperor, in the name of the Constitution and in the name of the law, I declare that His Majesty Napoleon III, Emperor of France by the grace of God and the will of the nation, and Her Excellency Mademoiselle Eugenie de Montijo, Comtesse de Teba, are united in marriage."

By the grace of God, I remember thinking. As if God had any part in a civil marriage. I was still unmarried, I told myself, and would remain so until Napoleon and I were joined together, truly by the grace of God, in holy matrimony at Notre Dame.

Uncle Jerome was the first to bow before me, kiss my hand and call me Empress. Plonplon was the next.

"A German accent, a Spanish accent," he muttered nastily. "And this is France!"

"You have a German accent yourself," I reminded

him. "Fortunately, the Emperor's heir will grow up to speak French in all its purity."

"You go straight from here to your confinement, Madame? How remarkable!"

Napoleon was busying himself with the register which lay on a gilt table in the centre of the dais. It was Napoleon I's own family register. The first entry recorded his adoption of Josephine's son, Eugene de Beauharnais; the last, the birth of his own son by Marie Louise. Now there was a new entry—the first since 1811.

I was staggered by all the family names ascribed to me in that register. Mama and Mérimée had worked for hours assembling them and had even called upon the services of the College of Heralds. Every possible title from every possible branch of the family had been brought into use. On Mama's side, they had delved back and back to the days before Christ—who could say them nay?—and through Grandfather Kirkpatrick, I appeared as the descendant of a Fenian king. If it was Mama's object to out-ancestor the Emperor, she certainly succeeded, but if it was also her object to look down on the parvenu from a lofty height she failed lamentably. Napoleon claimed not a single ancestor. He was described merely as the Emperor Napoleon III. The dignified simplicity of it made me hot with shame.

While I was signing the register, I felt a slight movement beneath my feet, and by the time the last witness had appended his signature, the dais, hurriedly constructed for the occasion, was swaying perilously.

"An earthquake!" Mama shrieked. "Born during an earthquake, married during another."

Actually, too many people had crowded upon the slender platform. They scattered now from all sides of it Plonplon himself offered me his arm and as he guided me down to safety remarked that the weight of my ancestors had obviously been too great. The joke of an enemy, if it appeals to me, has always been acceptable.

"The Fenian king was a massive gentleman," I laughed.

Plonplon nodded. "Massive enough to shake the Empire to its foundations."

Amazingly enough, I managed another laugh. "I thought it was *your* weight, Cousin."

My ladies then led me away to change into a less formal gown. Later, when I reappeared in the Salle des Maréchaux, feeling lighter and happier in rose-colored satin, five hundred guests bowed before me, and presently we all trouped to the Flora Pavilion to hear a cantata. The composer and once again the conductor was Auber.

"Oh, *no!*" I protested privately to Napoleon.

How I suffered! How we all suffered! The cantata itself was short enough, but the irrepressible Auber had arranged what he was misguided enough to call a "musical entertainment" of two hours' duration.

"Were he not so privileged—!" I said crossly.

Auber was more than privileged, for through the years the successive rulers of France had come to attach a certain superstitious importance to his name. Governments fell, kings fell, republics fell. But always, as if enduring forever himself, he sprang up to celebrate a new era or a new event with an endless flow of cantatas, marches and heaven knows what besides. To have refused his services now would have been tantamount to throwing down the gauntlet to fate.

By eleven o'clock my head was spinning and my temper vile. That army of ancestors in the register, that dais that almost collapsed, and now Auber—Daniel François Esprit Auber! Small wonder I still regard that civil ceremony as an *opéra-bouffe*.

A dazed-looking Emperor escorted Mama and me to our carriage. Plonplon and the rest of the court followed, all looking equally bewildered.

"Tomorrow, *ma petite femme,*" said Napoleon, kissing my hand.

Plonplon rallied instantly. "The first Napoleon would have said tonight. He was ever impatient, romantically."

Napoleon's eyes glinted in sudden anger. "We revere our uncle's memory, we honor his name, we thank him for all he did for France . . ."

"This is a speech, Sire?"

"Silence! The first Napoleon, we can but admit, used religion—even his Holiness the Pope—solely to serve his own ends. I, the third Napoleon, place God before myself. I have given you an Empress tonight, but in the eyes of God I have not yet taken a wife."

And so, more happily than I expected, I went home with Mama for the last time.

And now, what do I remember of my real wedding day?

Paris was already *en fête* when I drove once again from the Élysée to the Tuileries. That was at midday. The morning mist had vanished, leaving the winter sky clear and blue. Military bands were playing in all parts of the city and since ten o'clock, processions of tradesmen, banners flying in the light breeze, had been winding through the streets. Mama was with me again and at her side in the carriage the newly appointed Grand Master of my own separate household.

"Merciful heavens!" Mama exclaimed, and leaning forward tore aside my veil. "Pearls! Pearls on Your Majesty's wedding day!" She shrank back in horror. "Remember the Spanish proverb. Pearls on a wedding day are a symbol of tears to come. Take them off, I beg of you!"

I shook my head. "Can I expect to go tearless through all the years of my reign?"

She dropped her voice and hissed in Spanish, "You're tempting fate. Your husband will betray you with another woman."

"Because of the pearls? How ridiculous, Mama!"

At the Tuileries, Napoleon led me at once to a balcony and there we stood bowing like marionettes while an artillery salute and the cheering of the crowd below rang in our ears.

My wedding gown was of white velvet. A wreath of orange blossoms held my long lace veil in place. Marie Louise's diamond and sapphire belt was round my waist again, and the diamond coronet on my brow had once been worn by Josephine. Napoleon, determined to re-create the imperial glories of the past if only by inference, wore the full dress uniform of a general, the top boots highly varnished, the white breeches immaculate.

The long procession to Notre Dame was led by regimental bands and flanked by haughty cavalry officers. The Emperor and Empress sat in the state coach which had carried Napoleon and Josephine to their coronation and, six years later, Napoleon and Marie Louise to their wedding. I kept thinking about that. Poor Josephine divorced; Marie Louise set imperiously in her place. Were their two ghostly figures with us in the carriage they had known so well? I shuddered involuntarily at the thought.

"Why have we stopped?" I heard Napoleon ask sharply.

I emerged from my daydreaming. We had progressed no further than the triumphal arch outside the palace.

"Well?" Napoleon demanded of a nearby staff officer.

There were a few whispered words which I failed to catch.

"Have it replaced!" Napoleon snapped.

"How angry you sound," I ventured.

"I have no more faith in bad omens than I have in good ones," he asserted grimly and untruthfully. "The Imperial Crown fell from the carriage roof. The same thing happened when my uncle and Marie Louise drove to Notre Dame. I beg you to ignore the superstitious people who will remind you of it later."

In the newly constructed Rue de Rivoli, there was another delay. The crowd was thicker there than anywhere else, and for several minutes—the cordon of soldiers broken—people swarmed about the carriage. There were banners fluttering everywhere, some depicting the Imperial Eagle, others the tricolor. Children were held up by their parents to stare at me in my gilded glass cage, a cage suspended in the midst of a shouting throng. Terrifying indeed had everybody been crying "Down with . . ." instead of "Long live . . ." Then I laughed crazily at the sight of a poodle scampering in front of the black horses, a poodle with a tricolor bobbing on its head.

"Paris always loves a spectacle," Napoleon remarked cynically. "I'm more conscious of curiosity than the warmth of a loving people."

"The enthusiasm is surely genuine," I said weakly.

"Genuine? The spectacle, aided by a fine day, is a magnificent success. I recognize approval of that rather than approval of *us*."

I felt utterly miserable. "So our life together must be one long skillfully contrived spectacle."

Napoleon took my hand in his. "Dear Eugenie, you have much to learn. Beneath the spectacle we shall build, God willing, a great and enduring dynasty."

Inspiring and heartening words. The misery of a moment ago was replaced by a steady confidence, not only in Napoleon but in myself. "The two of us together," I said.

We reached Notre Dame at last.

The Archbishop of Paris received us in the grand portico with cardinals, bishops and priests behind him. The Archbishop was "second best." What a triumph if His Holiness the Pope could have been induced to come to Paris to marry us! Napoleon would have delayed the wedding indefinitely had there been any chance at all.

Earlier, even before the plebiscite, he had been negotiating with His Holiness about a coronation. Pope Pius VII had crowned Napoleon I in Notre Dame; therefore, Pope Pius IX should be the one to crown Napoleon III and later marry him.

Alas, it was an entirely different situation. Pius VII had been dragged to Paris unwillingly by the then all-powerful Emperor, whereas Pius IX was in a position to demand certain concessions. The negotiations broke down. Napoleon III was never crowned, one of the strangest aspects of a strange story, and it was Sibour, Archbishop of Paris, who married us.

Fifteen thousand candles lit the whole interior of Notre Dame, their flickering light caught and reflected by the rows of lustres in the aisles. A rainbow of streamers trailed down from the roof; cloth-of-gold and crimson velvet covered the gallery and shields bearing the arms of France and Spain separated each compartment. Magically the Montijo arms had achieved twenty-five quarterings and now all but obliterated the humble Bonaparte arms displayed with them on the pillars. One would have thought that Dona Eugenia was a high-born Spanish princess condescending to marry the parvenu Emperor.

It was a long and tiring service, even though Napoleon and I, sitting on our thrones for at least an hour, took but little part in it. Once again the music, described by the newspaper gentlemen as "divine," was not to my liking. Auber had composed it hurriedly, and with the assistance of a nameless hack. Berlioz, whose work I liked, had submitted a few pieces, but Auber swept them aside in a frenzy of contempt and hatred. Imagine, if you can, the dignity of Notre Dame shattered by an Auber orchestra of five hundred musicians! Another touch of the *opéra-bouffe,* but there was organ music, too, and with the chants and fugues I was well satisfied.

After the traditional blessing of the wedding ring and

the pieces of silver, we rose from our thrones and knelt at the high altar beneath a canopy of ermine-lined crimson velvet. There the intrusion of *opéra-bouffe* was forgotten. I was aware only of the solemnity of the occasion—the Archbishop's words which truly made us man and wife, the softly spoken benediction, the presentation of the holy water and the first stirring words of the *Te Deum*. No memory of Auber, however irritating, can take from me the greater memory of those sublime and holy moments.

We left Notre Dame by the western door and returned in procession to the Tuileries. And there, in the gardens, a band of children descended upon us from all sides and pelted us with flowers. It was a touching scene. Many of the onlookers wept. Quick tears sprang to my own eyes, too.

"Not another skillful contrivance?" I asked Napoleon fearfully.

"Spontaneous and unrehearsed," he assured me, beaming with pleasure. "See! They're all wearing our medal!"

Thousands of medals had been struck for the occasion. I have one still among my souvenirs of the past. The Emperor's head is on one side with the inscription: *Heureux mariage de S.M. Napoléon III;* mine on the other with the inscription: *Impératrice des Françis, 30 janvier 1853.*

Chapter Nine

WE SPENT our honeymoon at Villeneuve-l'Étang.

Ah, but to call it a honeymoon—that is really absurd. We were surrounded by court officials and a number of Napoleon's close friends, to say nothing of Mathilde and Plonplon. Mama, too, might as well have been present.

Villeneuve-l'Étang, the small country house which stood grimly in the Park of Saint-Cloud, was a gloomy place of dark rooms and damp walls. Everybody was surprised that Napoleon should take me there in spite of his claim that it possessed a more intimate atmosphere than the château at Saint-Cloud. When the real reason became known, there was much laughter at our expense (behind our backs, of course) and many ribald jokes were told along the boulevards.

"Miss Howard planned a surprise for the honeymooners," Plonplon was quick to inform me. "She's in residence at the château. A charming scene, Your Majesty! The mistress waiting to receive the newlyweds. Fortunately—some would say *un*fortunately—the Emperor learned of her presence in the nick of time. She's been ordered to remove herself but seems in no hurry to obey."

"A fabrication, the whole story. Miss Howard is in England."

Plonplon smiled sardonically. "She got no further than Le Havre. A storm delayed the Southampton packet, thus enabling her to read a newspaper report of the Emperor's announcement, and back she came to Paris in a fearful rage. Fortunately—again some would say *un*fortunately—Mocquard was able to pacify her sufficiently to prevent a scene at Notre Dame. Now she is no doubt wondering, as we all are, if Your Majesty has discovered in your Imperial husband a good and satisfying lover."

The next day I came face to face with Miss Howard and, with Plonplon's words still hotly in my mind, I blushed uncontrollably. Napoleon had taken me driving in a little phaeton as a means of temporary escape from the crowd at Villeneuve-l'Étang. The weather was delightful, with signs of an early spring all about us in the avenues of the park and the country roads nearby. We ventured as far as Versailles since I wanted to see the dairy established by Marie Antoinette at the Trianon and there, entirely by chance, we came upon Miss Howard. Napoleon saw her first and tried to hurry me away, but she stood squarely in our path, curtsied and wished us all possible happiness. Sarcasm? It must have been, softly spoken though her words were.

"I return to Paris today," she added, addressing Napoleon in English, assuming perhaps that I knew no English. "Saint-Cloud is free of my presence. You may move there with your bride if it pleases you." She sighed faintly. "Had your marriage been a political necessity I would gladly have sacrificed myself to so pressing an expediency, but I shall never resign myself to this personal whim on your part."

Flustered, Napoleon made no reply.

She then turned to me and addressed me in French: "I trust Your Majesty will call on me in Paris. We could, perhaps, become friends. I even look forward to your husband, should you yourself permit it, regarding me in future as a friend." Her glance strayed to Napoleon and again she spoke in English. "Or do you take the view, Sire, that you could be my lover but never my friend? Very well! The former capacity, if you desire it."

I was about to tell her warmly that I spoke English even better than French, but, remembering the dignity of my position, I held, oh—so slenderly, my Imperial peace.

"Look upon me, Sire, as a second Josephine," she went on. "The first, when cast aside, took with her your uncle's star." She curtsied as if dismissed. "Your Majesty . . ."

"Countess . . ." Napoleon mumbled, and bowed stiffly.

Countess! The only word he'd uttered the whole time. Miss Howard, though I was unaware of it then, had just been created Countess of Beauregard.

"A whim!" I broke out when we were in the phaeton again. "So I am your wife only because of a whim!"

"No, no," Napoleon said earnestly, "because of the greatest love of my life."

During the drive back to Villeneuve-l'Étang, we discussed the organization of my personal household. Many appointments had already been made, but I was still in need of a secretary. I thought at once of Mérimée and put forward his name, expecting Napoleon to agree without hesitation.

"Mérimée? Admirable in many respects, but aren't you forgetting the gossip? Your mother and he . . ."

"A libel and you know it!"

"*I* know it, but others are ready enough to believe the worst. If you gave Mérimée a position at court, it would be said that you wanted close at hand the man who is supposed to be your father. It would be assumed that you were tacitly acknowledging him."

"As you wish, *Sire.*"

"How displeased you sound! Let me risk your greater displeasure by discussing your mother's future. It would be better if she returned to Spain without delay."

"Because of the scandal?"

"Not altogether. She has a capacity for intrigue. Was she not dismissed from Queen Isabella's service because of political intrigue?"

I laughed and told him the true story of the dismissal. Napoleon laughed, too, and agreed that Mama should be allowed to remain in Paris, but not at the Élysée Palace. He would lease a house for her in the Champs Élysées and permit her to savor to her heart's content the social importance of being the Emperor's mother-in-law.

"Are you missing her?" he asked.

I dwelt on the question thoughtfully. Mama and I had been together for so many years I surely ought to be missing her, perhaps even tearfully, but incredibly it came upon me that, if I was missing her at all, it was with a certain amount of relief. Hedged in as I was by encroaching court etiquette, I knew a new freedom and rejoiced in it. The maternal limitations were gone forever.

"I think she must be missing me more than I am missing her," I said truthfully.

But Mama showed little sign of missing me when she presented herself at the Tuileries the moment the court returned to Paris. Her manner was both brisk and airy as she inspected my apartments which were situated on the floor above Napoleon's. Everything was in appalling taste, she declared. I must do something about it at once. No changes had been made in the palace since Louis-Philippe's day and everybody knew how plebeian his taste was.

"The Emperor has given me a free hand," I said patiently, and told her about the plan for her to live in the Champs Élysées.

"Ah! I'm to be marched out of the Élysée!"

"Mama!"

"Pooh! As if I wanted to remain in that ghastly mausoleum! You may not believe this, Eugenia, but when I returned there from Notre Dame, the whole place was deserted. I ran from room to room, I hurried down to the kitchens—how hungry I was!—but not a single cook was on duty to provide for my modest needs. The whole staff was out watching the fireworks. The desertion was deliberate, a warning of the dismissal to come."

"The Emperor is not dismissing you, Mama."

She sighed dramatically. "Loneliness is something I must get used to. Oh, I intend to be reasonable about it. A woman must leave her parents and follow her husband. That is clearly stated in Holy Writ."

"I think you're going to miss the matchmaking," I laughed.

"*Miss* it, Eugenia? I'm only too thankful I was able to make so good a match for you. Believe me, I was near the end of my tether. I could see no future for you but that of a disgruntled old maid. Now, tell me about this house in the Champs Élysées. Is it large enough for my needs? Will I be able to entertain as adequately as my position demands? Will my *salon* be graced on occasion by the presence of my daughter, the Empress?"

I hesitated for a moment, thinking of Mama's bohemian leanings. Napoleon had warned me that, as Empress, I must choose my friends with the utmost care. I had ceased to be a private individual. Government policy, the trend of political affairs, must be considered at all times.

"I shall visit you privately as often as possible," I said.

So while Mama was setting up her *salon* in the Champs Élysées, I myself was very busy at the Tuileries making the changes which had been in my mind from the first. Accompanied by the Grand Master of my household, I poked my inquisitive nose into countless storerooms and attics, there to discover many priceless treasures collected by Napoleon I. A careful selection was made and the interior of the palace entirely transformed.

111

My ladies' drawing room, the chamber where two of them were always on duty, was particularly offensive in its drabness. The ladies were young and gay and must, I decided, have gay and colorful surroundings. This achieved, I gave my attention to my private drawing room and the small *salon* which stood between it and my ladies' drawing room. Because of the choice of colors they came to be known as the Blue Drawing Room and the Pink *Salon*.

Meanwhile, from a social point of view, there was the problem of the aloof aristocrats of the Faubourg Saint-Germain. If we could induce only two or three of them to accept court appointments, Napoleon said, their "desertion" might lead to a steadily increasing stream of other desertions across the Seine.

"What of our Imperial dignity?" I asked solemnly. "Surely they should pay their respects before we approach a single one of them."

"Imperial dignity must be set aside in the face of political expediency, *chérie*."

After careful inquiry we decided that I should invite two highborn ladies to take tea with me privately and discuss appointments which, in their own opinion, might be considered acceptable. One pleaded illness; the secretary of the other regretted that his mistress was out of town. Both, as we well knew, were in excellent health and still resident in Paris.

Immediately after this flat refusal, it reached Napoleon's ears that Mama had already invited the same two ladies to visit her *salon* and that they had declined with frigid politeness. Thereupon he summoned Mama to the Tuileries and asked her coldly why she had issued the invitations. Mama laughed knowingly.

"Sire, I am fully aware of the difficulties which face you. It was in my mind to help by breaking the ice. First my *salon,* then the Empress's drawing room. After all, Sire, the Empress is the daughter of one whose rank is equal to theirs."

"Were you aware that Her Majesty was on the point of inviting them to the Tuileries?"

"Dear heaven!" Mama gasped.

"My mother knew nothing of our plan," I told Napoleon. "Naturally I confided in no one."

"A remarkable coincidence," Mama tinkled.

"Certainly an unfortunate one," Napoleon said heavily. "I know the temper of my royalist aristocrats. They were insulted at being invited first by the mother. But for that, Madame . . ."

A rebellious look crossed Mama's face. "I humbly beg Your Majesty's pardon for displeasing you unwittingly."

Napoleon bowed stiffly. "In future, Madame, you must submit your guest lists to the Empress before issuing invitations."

"Hamstrung!" Mama muttered, and backed haughtily from our Imperial presence.

Napoleon laughed lightly. "I may be wrong, Eugenie, but I suspect that your doughty mother has declared war on me."

And war it was. Guest list after guest list was submitted to me, but other names were added after I gave my approval. On one occasion, I visited Mama privately for a quiet little tête-à-tête only to find myself the guest of honor at a large informal party at which, horror of horrors, one Republican and two notorious communists were present. I withdrew at once—a little reluctantly, I must admit—and was able to keep the story from reaching Napoleon's ears. The climax, however, came suddenly.

"Your mother gave a large party last night," Napoleon informed me one morning, a stony look in his eyes. "Was the guest list submitted to you first?"

"Yes, but—"

"You approved, then, of Turkish, Russian and English diplomats rubbing shoulders with each other in your mother's *salon?*"

113

"They do precisely that at the Tuileries."

"With the exception that political agitators are never invited here. Two were present at your mother's last night. They provoked a heated discussion of possible Russian aims toward certain Turkish territories."

"I'm sure Mama wasn't deliberately meddling in politics."

"Deliberately or not, her presence in Paris is becoming far too dangerous. Many people will assume that she has the ear of her son-in-law, the Emperor, and are likely to regard her *salon* as a sounding board of Imperial policy."

"Russian aims—" I said, more to sidetrack him than anything else.

"If Russia moves against Turkey, war—the one thing I want to avoid—will become inevitable. The Tsar is a despot. I doubt if one-fifth of his subjects are free people. He's a dictator rather than an emperor, a dictator politically and religiously. Moreover, he looks beyond his own realm and dreams of world conquest. As far as I am personally concerned, he regards me as a dangerous rival. Dangerous, that is, if I succeed in forming a strong alliance with England . . ." Napoleon broke off with a laugh. "I'm not inviting you to meddle in politics, Eugenie, merely putting you *au fait* with the present situation in Europe. You understand, I hope, how necessary it is for your mother to be sent back to Spain."

"Yes, I think I do."

"There's a domestic aspect also. You were unaware of it, but on the eve of our marriage, one of the dressmakers issued a writ. My lawyers took care of the matter and avoided a scandal. Now they must do the same thing again. Make it clear to your mother, please, that she must leave France within a week."

That incorrigible mother of mine, living beyond her quite ample means simply because her son-in-law was the Emperor! She denied it at first, then admitted with a laugh which suggested pride in the fact that she had indeed lived beyond her means since my marriage.

"But not before, darling," Mama insisted. "Madame Barenne overcharged me grossly. That was my only reason for refusing to make a settlement."

"I don't think I quite believe you, Mama."

She gave me a haughty look. "Are you hinting that I delayed payment in the hope that His Majesty would settle the debt?"

"The suggestion is yours, not mine."

"So it is," she admitted, with a telltale giggle. "And now it appears that I've cooked my goose. Or do I mean I've killed it?"

"Whatever you mean, Mama, there'll be no more Imperial golden eggs."

"Poor Eugenia, your husband is as mean in money matters as your dear lamented father. I leave for Spain more in sorrow than in anger. If you come to feel the pinch too severely, I shall help you as best I can."

"Thank you, Mama," I said ironically.

"One thing I insist upon. I must be permitted to return for your confinement."

"The Emperor will not object to that."

"Are you expecting a baby already?" she asked hopefully.

"No, Mama."

"How disappointing for His Majesty. The poor man will soon grow impatient. Oh, not with you, darling, but with himself. Miss Howard bore a child by another man but none by the Emperor. He has led a life of reckless dissipation and may now be paying for his sins. Until you bear him a child, the poor man will be plagued by horrible doubts about himself and the fate of his dynasty."

On the eve of her departure, Mama wept a little. She was torn, she said, between two great fears. What if my fate were that of Marie Antoinette? Or, yet again, that of Josephine who was set aside because of her failure to give the first Napoleon a child?

"Just which fate would be the worst I find it hard to decide," she concluded.

The Emperor's mother-in-law left Paris gaily and importantly. Mérimée accompanied her as far as Poitiers, and she told him "in strict confidence" that she was not going into exile, as one might suspect, but to pursue with all the skill at her command a secret mission on her son-in-law's behalf. A few days later, a final unpaid account reached the Tuileries. At the last moment Mama had acquired an extensive wardrobe of new traveling clothes. Neither I nor the Emperor, she wrote in an unapologetic letter of explanation, would have wanted her to reach Madrid in *rags*.

Chapter Ten

HOW WELL DID I know the Emperor Napoleon III when I married him? I prided myself that I knew him very well indeed, but that was vain and silly. You must live with a man really to come to know him, I grew fond of saying, just as if I alone had made that obvious discovery. Nevertheless, living with a man who is also a ruler hedged in by court etiquette makes the "knowing" a protracted business. We were alone together but rarely, except, of course, during the hours of night and they, Napoleon said romantically, were made for love. What, I ask you, can you discover about a man through physical love alone?

To come to the point, I soon discovered that my husband's stubbornness was the most outstanding trait of his whole character.

"You think it a bad trait?" he asked, when I charged him with it during an argument about the actress, Rachel.

"When you know yourself to be in the wrong and still remain stubborn, yes."

"Only rarely do I know myself to be in the wrong, *chérie*."

"But then you fall into one of your trances until the subject is changed, and by that time you've convinced yourself that you're right."

He would appear to listen reasonably enough, even in a trance, and then, if bored or in flat disagreement, would spring up with that veiled expression in his eyes and—*voilà!*—you found yourself dismissed unceremoniously. On the other hand, if he were pleased and in full agreement, he would burst into a flow of talk, an impressive, bewildering monologue, at the end of which you left his presence ready to believe that your own so right idea was his alone. Napoleon was as great a spellbinder as the most skillful of religious fanatics.

"Day by day my ministers come to me with the most contradictory advice," he said. "Confusion would result if I did not follow the dictates of my own reason."

"We were discussing a personal matter, not state affairs," I pointed out.

"I thought we were discussing my alleged stubbornness."

"An example of which is all too evident in your insistence that Rachel should give me lessons in deportment."

"The suggestion was yours," he said mildly.

"Mine!"

"You remarked that her gracefulness exceeded even your own."

"What of it?"

"And now when I agree that Rachel must give you lessons—"

"You judge me in need of them, *Sire?*"

Napoleon sighed patiently. "Come, Eugenie, you suffer often from what might be called stage fright. You look very sure of yourself at all times, but I know and *you* know, that you often feel anything but that. Take, for instance, the way you sometimes stand in front of a mirror practicing in secret as if at a reception."

"Scarcely in secret," I said, badly nettled. "You appear to have spies everywhere."

"Goose!" he laughed. "I happened to catch you at it and withdrew before you saw me. Rachel shall pay you a visit tomorrow afternoon."

"I won't receive her."

"Wait," he said, flinging himself into a chair and settling himself in a simulated trance. "Proceed, *chérie*."

I knew the futility of it but I proceeded as valiantly as I could. Did he think me, I asked, a poor relation from the provinces, even an ill-clad, stammering Bonaparte from Corsica? Was he aware that I had moved in the highest society in Madrid, London, Paris, Brussels and many other cities? Had I not been maid of-honor at the Spanish court? In need of lessons in deportment indeed! Oh, I knew his game only too well. Rachel was once his mistress. He was taking an interest in her again. His aim was to bring Rachel to court, let it be known that the Empress had received her and keep her at court.

"I expect apartments have been prepared for her already," I concluded breathlessly.

Napoleon lit a cigar. "Rachel will visit you informally. The guards will admit her on a special pass. She will not at any time be received at court." He rose briskly. "Tomorrow afternoon, then, at three o'clock. My thanks, Eugenie, for an excellent suggestion." He kissed my cheek. "How beautiful you are! Hebe or Psyche—I wonder which? Only when anger shakes you, do I see any trace of ugliness. Never be angry with me, *chérie*."

Rachel duly arrived. She was discreetly dressed and heavily veiled, Pepa reported, and had brought with her another woman, tall, slender and also heavily veiled.

"Shall I send them away?" Pepa asked.

I hid a smile. Pepa behaved at all times as if she were my chief lady-in-waiting and she bossed me shamelessly. Pepa, remember, was Mama's maid-companion and had insisted on remaining in my service when Mama went home to Spain. I allowed her many liberties. After all, I'd known her all my life and it was a joy to talk to her in Spanish, she being the only Spanish woman in my household.

"Let them wait for an hour," I decided.

However, I capitulated within half an hour. Rachel's

acting had always held me entranced and had she not made me laugh when imitating Plonplon's walk?

"I took the liberty of bringing an assistant," she announced.

The "assistant" curtsied and removed her veil.

"Incarnation!" I exclaimed in astonishment. How silly it must sound, but that was actually the "assistant's" name.

Incarnation, Paca and I had played together as children in Madrid and later had been together at the convent in Paris. Now she was married to a French gentleman notorious for his many love affairs and, because of that, Napoleon had forbidden Incarnation to appear even privately at the Tuileries.

"I'm well acquainted with many disreputable people," Rachel chuckled. "With all the latest scandals, too. Who knows, we may spend many a happy hour, the three of us, gossiping merrily."

A cunning creature, Rachel. She had won me over at once by bringing Incarnation secretly to see me. As for gossip, I'd never cared much about it until suddenly deprived of it. And how we gossiped, the three of us! Rachel came three times a week and each time I felt like a child released from too much study. Now and again Rachel minced about the Blue Drawing Room, a caricature of an Empress waving her hand to the invisible crowd, inclining her head to the invisible Royalists, growing ridiculously solemn in the presence of the invisible Queen Victoria. Recklessly I provided additional special passes for Rachel, so that our number had grown to a baker's dozen by the time Napoleon caught us gossiping. Rachel, I remember, was telling us how she had locked Plonplon in her dressing-room one night, thus causing him to spend hours in solitary confinement, when suddenly she broke off in mid-sentence and stared fixedly at a mirror on the wall. We all followed her gaze.

"The Emperor!" Incarnation whispered in horror.

Napoleon's reflection remained immovable. We sprang hurriedly to our feet and turned to face him. The others, with the exception of Rachel, had quickly lowered their veils.

"Charming," said Napoleon, his face pale with anger.

"Is it Your Majesty's wish that I should present my friends?" I asked, trying to brave it out.

Appearing not to have heard, he moved into our little group and lifted a veil here, another there.

"Ah, Vivienne of the *Comédie*," he said, "and unless I am much mistaken—yes, Gabrielle, also." He came at last to Incarnation. "And this lady, Your Majesty?"

My head shot up defiantly. "Madame Manuel."

Napoleon bowed, turned his back on poor Incarnation and strode to the window. A moment later Rachel hurried her friends from the room and I was left alone, or so I thought, with the outraged Emperor.

"Rachel has come to the Tuileries for the last time," he said, without turning away from the window.

"But it was such *fun*, Napoleon!"

He grasped suddenly at the long velvet curtain and tore it aside, thus revealing yet another veiled young woman.

"Sire," she said demurely, and curtsied deeply.

Then she removed her veil and gave me a lovely smile. "Your Majesty has been very kind and hospitable. I shall come again, if I may, entirely as myself, not in the guise of a dancer. Gaiety such as I never expected can be found at the Tuileries."

"Entirely as yourself?" I asked faintly.

She laughed pleasantly. "I'm a spy from the enemy camp, Madame, and how dull and lifeless it is, that camp on the other side of the river."

"May we know your name?" Napoleon asked gruffly.

"Angelique de Granville," she said, and was gone.

"By heaven, the daughter of the Duc de Granville!" Napoleon exclaimed softly.

"She curtsied and called you 'Sire'!"

"And she asked if she may come again!"

"Entirely as herself, Napoleon!"

His face clouded. "Was there a hint of mockery in her voice? Nevertheless, we shall risk one more rebuff. Send her a formal invitation to your next ball."

The invitation was accepted; others were issued later at Angelique's suggestion, and a steady stream of desertions began until only the Comte de Chambord and his more faithful followers remained aloof. He, however, was the Orléans Pretender and according to his own way of looking at things could do no less.

"I'm well satisfied," Napoleon said, when taking chocolate with me one morning in my boudoir. "You've performed a miracle."

"We should really thank Rachel."

"Nonsense! Angelique de Granville found you charming. But for that, there'd have been no miracle."

"I still think we ought to feel a little grateful to Rachel."

"You want to continue the lessons in deportment?"

"We-ell—" Oh, he was clever, that Emperor of mine!

"You think rather of the doubtful joy of a gossip with Rachel."

"A gossip with my old friend Incarnation would be joyful, too. A little private liberty in that direction would help me to feel less like a caged animal."

"You walked into the cage of your own accord, *chérie.*"

"No, Napoleon, I was dragged into it, and then you slammed the door and locked it."

"We appear to be quarreling," he said mildly. "I, the Emperor, have made it a rule never to want what I know I cannot have. You, the Empress, must do the same."

"You've wanted and got many things which to others have seemed impossible."

"Only because I've known I myself, that I could get them."

"In a word, the rule is no rule at all, as far as you are concerned. There's nothing you know you cannot get. You think *you* can get everything."

He looked at me patiently. "Precisely what I've been trying to tell you."

"Then the rule, as you interpret it, shall certainly be mine also. I'll meet Rachel at her own house, Incarnation at hers."

"I absolutely forbid it."

"So speaks the Emperor of Emperors!" I cried, and ran from the room.

"Wait!" he called after me.

But I took no notice and behaved quite shamefully. My mood was much the same as the day I rode bareback to the bullfight, though my revolt now was against the whole tiresome etiquette of the Imperial court, not against a would-be suitor. Nor was I wearing the costume of a Spanish peasant, but the negligee of an Empress. Splendid! I remember thinking as I marched from my apartments and turned deliberately to face the guard who stood like a statue in the vestibule. Irritatingly enough he appeared not to have seen me.

"Are you shocked?" I asked.

He neither spoke nor moved. He was one of that fine body of soldiers, the *cent-gardes,* carefully and sternly schooled in the art of absolute immobility. Far from admiring him then, I regarded him as the sole representative of court etiquette and longed with all my heart to break down his devotion to discipline.

"Do you know who I am?" I demanded.

There was no response. He was a figure in wax, not a living guard at all.

"Imbecile!" I screamed, and slapped his face.

Instantly ashamed of myself, I returned to my apartments. The outer door was still open and there stood

Napoleon, blocking my way. He stepped aside and followed me in.

"You appear to be in need of further help from Rachel," he said coldly. "She shall pay you three private visits. I myself will be present at each."

Rachel visited me twice only. Her third visit was canceled because of sudden illness on my part. I thought at first I was catching a feverish cold. I felt hot and cold, all at the same time. Accordingly, I took a very hot bath prior to going to bed early and during it a violent stab of pain heralded an alarming hemorrhage. There were shrieks of horror from the two ladies present—as Empress I wasn't even allowed the privilege of a bath in private—and for a moment, horrified myself, I stared at the spreading tinge of pink, then deeper pink, in the water.

Dr. Conneau, Napoleon's old friend and chief physician, and Mr. Dubois, later my accoucheur, were instantly summoned. I was lifted from the bath, dried hastily by my ladies and carried to my bed by the two doctors. Later, Conneau and Dubois questioned me carefully, even persistently. I saw this as a sort of inquisition and grew more angry than indignant until I realized the veiled reason for it all.

"The Emperor immediately assumed that a miscarriage had taken place," said Dubois.

"Had Your Majesty confided in us earlier—" Conneau added.

"We would be in a position to state definitely," Dubois interposed, "that Your Majesty was in the second month of pregnancy when the hemorrhage occurred."

"If Your Majesty were ready to confide in us now—" said Conneau.

"A definite statement could indeed be made," Dubois concluded.

I knew then what was in their minds possibly because lightheadedness sometimes gives one second sight, but chiefly because of Mama's remarks before leaving for

Madrid. They were thinking, then, that a declared—one might almost say, a medically certified—miscarriage would restore Napoleon's confidence in himself.

"Your questions embarrass me," I said.

"Madame, this is a serious matter, an affair of state."

"Gentlemen, I'm just as shy now as I was then."

"Then?" Dubois asked excitedly.

"Your Majesty means two months ago?" Conneau pressed.

"Yes," I said faintly.

"Ha!" said Dubois.

"Splendid!" said Conneau.

"We quite understand," Dubois added.

"Quite!" Conneau agreed.

No more was asked of me. The worthy doctors withdrew well pleased with me and themselves, and presently a very jaunty Emperor came to see me.

"So I was right, Eugenie! A sad disappointment to both of us, indeed to the whole nation, but after all we will have the pleasure of trying again. A happy thought, *chérie!* Duty in this instance is a pleasure also. As soon as you're well enough, we will have a second and quieter honeymoon at Saint-Cloud."

"The château, not Villeneuve-l'Étang?"

"The château, naturally." But my oblique reference to Miss Howard wasn't lost on him and he changed the subject hurriedly. "By the way, Mathilde has made constant inquiries. She's very distressed. I think it would be a kindness to receive her."

"Your cousin comes frequently to the Tuileries. I've never yet refused to receive her."

Napoleon inclined his head. "What I ask is that you receive her privately here in your bedroom. It would please me very much if you and Mathilde became real friends. I assure you she no longer resents an Empress having taken her place at court."

I doubted it as much as his claim that she was very distressed on my behalf. Mathilde loved her brother,

Plonplon, and would be no more pleased than he if I bore Napoleon a son and thus deprived him of any chance of mounting the throne. Nevertheless, Napoleon's request would become a command in the end and I was still too ill to engage in yet another revolt. Finally I agreed—ungraciously—to receive Mathilde. She sailed into the room with a large bouquet of flowers in one hand and a large box of bonbons in the other, while beneath one plump arm was a newspaper.

"I trust all possible care is being taken of you," she boomed.

"Oh yes," I said tartly, "or at least of the body whose duty it is to produce an heir to the throne."

She flourished the newspaper in my face. "I'm furious, absolutely furious!"

Then she spread it before me on the bed and I saw the announcement which she had encircled heavily in red crayon. Her Imperial Majesty, I read, had suffered a miscarriage in the second month of her pregnancy. The paper, the *Moniteur,* was Napoleon's official organ and the announcement had been inserted on his behalf by the Grand Master of Ceremonies. Of *ceremonies,* mark you!

I flung the newspaper from the bed. "How embarrassing to have intimate details published like this!"

"An Empress is deprived of all privacy. You should be used to that by now. My quarrel with Napoleon is this complete defiance of tradition. Pregnancy is never announced officially, never recognized officially, until after the fourth month. Many queens have had miscarriages before the fourth month, but they've never been announced."

"Then why was Napoleon so hasty?"

Mathilde's eyes glinted shrewdly. "He wants the world to know that he's fully a man."

So there it was again. My husband's doubts about himself as they had already been made abundantly clear to me by the doctors.

Mathilde laughed hoarsely. "A Prince, this cousin of mine, a mighty Emperor but also a man, a real bull of a man. Am I shocking you, my dear?"

"No," I said, laughing in my weak condition.

"What a joy it is for women to be able to talk frankly with each other," she ran on, "to laugh about the vanity of those ridiculous creatures—men. What an idiot Napoleon is! The announcement has stirred up immediate public gossip. Idlers in the boulevards are chuckling and asserting that you became pregnant much earlier, before the marriage, in fact—"

"Mathilde! How horrible!"

"No really sensible person will believe it, of course. Everybody knows that your resistance brought the Emperor finally to heel."

She laughed when she saw that I was ready to laugh myself. Mother of God, what a fool I was! Laughing with her, trusting her.

"I'm tiring you," she said. "May I call again tomorrow?"

I went to Saint-Cloud a week later accompanied by a solicitous Mathilde but not by Napoleon. Her friendliness seemed faultless, yet all the time I had a queer feeling that I was allowing her in some way to make a fool of me. Napoleon wrote daily. They were tenderly worded letters. Deeply as he was immersed in state affairs, he missed me every minute of every hour of every day, but he was stoically holding his impatience in check and would join me for our second honeymoon only when the doctors gave their permission.

After a week at Saint-Cloud, we heard that the Emperor had gone to Versailles to review the troops, as he often did, at the nearby military camp.

"Why not drive over and surprise him?" Mathilde suggested.

I agreed readily enough. A military review was always exciting and I had yet to visit the camp at Satory. We were late starting since Mathilde took longer than usual over her toilette, and as a result, we missed the review itself. We were even too late to speak to Napoleon and caught only a brief glimpse of him, resplendent in his favorite uniform, as he stepped into a waiting carriage. Unsuspicious as I was, I thought it a strange procedure. Why a closed carriage when the streets of Versailles would be crammed with people waiting to see the Emperor as he so enjoyed being seen, magnificent on horseback?

"Let's try and overtake him," Mathilde suggested.

For a time we lost sight of Napoleon's carriage, but on turning a bend came upon it again, stationary at the side of a tree-lined road. To my surprise, Napoleon was striding across to another carriage, an open one, beneath the trees on the other side. What an extraordinary sight he was! He'd made a partial change of clothing and, still wearing his red uniform trousers and polished boots, had replaced his military cap and tunic with a top hat and a frock coat. A moment later, he was seated in the little open carriage, the upper part of his body alone visible.

"A disguise of some sort?" Mathilde wondered. "Here we have a private gentleman out for a drive with —good heavens, yes!—a lady friend."

The lady friend was Miss Howard. I recognized her instantly as our carriage drew level.

"Whip up the horses," I instructed the coachman hurriedly.

Then I fell back against the cushions, momentarily stunned by shock.

"You knew the Emperor was seeing her again," I said furiously.

"I thought everybody did," Mathilde answered sweetly.

"You brought me here intent on hurting me!"

"My dear Eugenie, I was sure you knew the whole amusing story."

Amusing!

"You're speaking to the Empress of France," I said pettishly.

Mathilde bobbed her head. "Your Majesty . . ."

After that we drove back to Saint-Cloud in silence, and just as I was alighting from the carriage, Napoleon rode up on horseback. The top hat and the frock coat had disappeared. He was in full military uniform once more.

"I was at Satory," he said, "and found the temptation to visit you irresistible."

I turned on my heels. "A formal visit, Sire? Why not a top hat and a frock coat?"

That held him back while I ran up the steps, but he was close on my heels when I reached my private drawing room. You may imagine how ready I was to despise him if he offered an apology, but he did no such thing and that, naturally, left me feeling badly cheated.

"Apparently you caught me red-handed, *chérie.* Do you propose to make a scene? If so, I shall sit at ease and wait till the storm blows itself out." He flung himself into a chair. "Proceed, Eugenie."

Determined not to make a scene, I rang for Pepa and instructed her as calmly as I could to prepare for a long journey.

"Madrid?" Napoleon asked, when Pepa had bustled away.

"Possibly."

"Your delectable mother will be fascinated."

It was impossible then to keep my temper in check. Impossible for any wife in the face of such an insufferable attitude. Oh, the shocking things I said, but I'd raged at Napoleon for fully five minutes before realizing that the words tumbling from my mouth were Spanish.

"This happened once before," he reminded me, "but I can well imagine what you have in mind. You think it horrible of me that I was unable to wait until you were well again. How unreasonable of you! You think I no longer love you. That is stupid. I love and honor you above all other women. Didn't I marry you? Didn't I decide that you should be the mother of my son? Your beauty drives me insane with longing even when I'm with other women. You go on a journey, yes. A short one. You go back with me to Paris."

"Never!"

"It's gratifying to know you love me enough to be jealous."

"I *hate* you!"

"As you wish."

"You keep me in a cage. There's no escape, but I can at least keep the door locked against the man who calls himself my husband."

"Have you forgotten that you were determined to think only of your son's welfare?" Napoleon asked dreamily. "Or was it a clever trick to trap me and make yourself Empress?"

"I spoke the truth," I said hotly. "I gave no thought to your ridiculous sentimentality."

He sprang up then, deeply hurt, deeply shocked and—in his own naive way—deeply indignant. For a few moments he paced the room struggling to control himself and at last looked at me pleadingly.

"I beg you to remember your duty, Eugenie."

"Duty!"

"To the Empire if not to me."

"The Empire of which I'm a mere slave!"

"Do you seek divorce?" he asked suddenly.

Divorce! Angry and hurt as I was, the very suggestion appalled me. I fretted often under the restraint which my position demanded of me, I longed for the privacy I knew I would never have, I wanted a faithful husband rather than a man concerned chiefly with dynastic yearnings. Yet I liked being Empress and enjoyed the adulation of the people, the subservience of court officials, the apparent loyalty of the old aristocracy. Empty reasons, in all conscience, but beneath them, struggling for full recognition, was a sincere desire to work for the good of my new country, if only Napoleon would permit it in a political sense.

"The fate of Josephine, but not for the same reason," he mused. "My grandmother accepted her husband's infidelities."

"Are you threatening *me* with divorce?"

"I adore you too much to set you aside," he said simply. "I asked, remember, if *you* sought divorce."

"My religion would never permit it," I said promptly.

"Very well then! Refuse me your bed if you must, but I'll never divorce you."

"Thank you, Napoleon. On those terms, those terms alone, I'll return with you to the Tuileries."

He smiled broadly. "I accept, of course. My personal charm, to say nothing of your devotion to duty, will get the better of you in the end."

And now, a word about Napoleon-Jerome, the "Prince Napoleon," and how he got the nickname "Plonplon." It came about because of the Crimean War which broke out during the summer of my second year of marriage. The trouble began as early as May 1853 with the withdrawal from Constantinople of the Russian ambassador. Napoleon was still determined that I shouldn't "meddle" in politics; my personal task was to charm both friends and enemies alike. But he continued to keep me *au fait* with political events and confided in me his hopes and fears. He was sworn to peace; he had promised France both continued peace and increasing prosperity. Now these aims were threatened by Russia whose obvious plan was to swallow up Turkey and thereby become a menace to French interests in Syria and Egypt.

"War stares us in the face," Napoleon said, when

Russian troops marched into Rumania and down to the Black Sea.

He still hoped that diplomatic negotiations would solve the Russo-Turkish quarrel, but Turkey had no faith in this and soon Russia and Turkey were openly at war. Finally England and France reached an agreement and jointly declared war on Russia.

"This is a holy war," Napoleon announced, having agreed to it reluctantly, "a war to preserve peace in Europe."

The French nation as a whole began to show a certain guarded enthusiasm. War at so great a distance was mildly exciting. Paris itself was unaffected by it. Most Parisians resented the change which Napoleon was making in their city far more than the declaration of war. That new Ministry of Public Works, for example, and that unspeakable Haussmann whom Napoleon had placed at the head of it. New buildings in the place of slums? New, wide streets in the place of dark stinking alleys? New parks for the people? An outrage, the whole thing. The assertion that cholera and typhoid would disappear overnight was a mere excuse for the squandering of public money. Haussmann was a maniac, an iconoclast. Once he'd finished, Paris as one knew it would have gone forever. And gas—if you please—gas to be piped through the whole city! Better to run the risk of disease than the certainty of gas poisoning.

Ah well, change is often resented. But in time the grumblers grew proud of the city Napoleon gave them. After all, it brought in foreign visitors by the thousand and that, while giving one a secret laugh at their antics, meant more money in one's pocket.

Napoleon was anxious to go to the Crimea himself, but his ministers persuaded him against it and Napoleon-Jerome, created a general of division, went instead. His behavior there was really disgusting. He was not a coward, he insisted in his letters of complaint, but the mud was more than any fastidious prince should be expected to sustain. There was also the risk of death from cholera against which one as close as he to the throne should take every precaution. It soon became evident that the French officers placed little trust in his military ability, and one of them, a certain colonel who shall remain nameless, returned to Paris with the story that the Russians were laughing contemptuously at the Emperor's mighty cousin.

"Sire, they call him 'Plonplon.' "

"How peculiar," said Napoleon. "What does it mean?"

"Sire, the Russians are using a new lead bullet. On being fired it makes the sound 'plon-plon.' "

"So?"

"Sire, the Prince Napoleon is said to take hasty cover every time he hears that sound. Sometimes, I fear, he's said to run from it in a most undignified manner."

Napoleon's face grew horribly impassive. "Prince Plonplon shall be recalled at once."

And sure enough he was—the dear, fastidious Plonplon.

Meanwhile, my husband the Emperor was courting me with all the diffidence of a young man in love for the first time in his life. He brought me presents of the most priceless jewelry, filled my apartments with flowers and wrote touching little love letters. He was grateful, he said, that I had refrained from locking the door at the top of the private stairway which led up from his bedroom to mine. I replied promptly that, apart from wanting to avoid an open scandal, I trusted him implicitly. His tactics weakened me, I admit, but I told myself that whatever he did or said, I'd never capitulate.

I weakened even more when I learned that Miss Howard had been sent to Italy and would not be permitted to return. But even that was not sufficient. In the end I was won over by my own arguments. It seemed clear to me that I was playing Mathilde's game for her, and Plonplon's as well. A childless Empress, *that* was what they wanted. There was also the little word "duty." My conscience troubled me sorely. I'd always prided myself on my honesty and now, even though the fault was Napoleon's—not mine, I was behaving dishonestly.

And so I capitulated, but it was never quite the same again for me, whatever Napoleon himself might have felt. I tried constantly to rid my mind of the nagging thought that we were committing an act of duty, not an act of love, but I failed miserably. In consequence, I tried also to act the role of an enraptured partner, but in that too I failed, and Napoleon, being Napoleon, was quick to notice.

"This frigidity, *chérie,* am I really the cause of it?"

"No," I told him sadly, "something within myself is responsible, something beyond my control, beyond my own choosing."

Napoleon lit a cigarette and smoked in silence for several moments. How strange to reflect that but for the Crimean War cigarette smoking might never have become popular in France and England. It was in the Crimea that our soldiers discovered the habit, and that same colonel who told us the story of Napoleon-Jerome's nickname brought Napoleon a box of specially prepared Turkish cigarettes. They were very similar to the *pepeletes* of my own country and Napoleon, liking this new form of smoking, had quickly become an addict. A supply of cigarettes was rolled for him each morning by his valet, and heaven help the poor fellow if he failed to roll enough.

"It was never merely duty on my part," Napoleon went on. "I married for love. Please remember that."

"I love and respect you in all other things," I said desperately.

"Thank you," he said humbly. "Love and respect are of greater importance to me than passion alone. I can promise you this, Eugenie: once you give me an heir, I'll make no further demands on your sense of duty. It will be sufficient for me then to feast upon your beauty and hear people exclaim in wonder 'How lovely the Empress is!' "

That, of course, was love-making of a very subtle order, but instead of melting my physical coldness, it merely tickled my vanity.

It is sometimes said, quite wrongly of course, that frigidity prevents conception, and as time went by I began to believe in that old wives' tale. Napoleon began to believe in it, too, though he made only an oblique reference to it.

"Perhaps if I were to put a love potion in your Marsala . . ." he tried to joke.

"Was I frigid before the miscarriage?" I challenged.

"No," he admitted.

"If it *was* a miscarriage," I found myself taunting him.

"Eugenie!" His quick alarm was pitiful. "But Conneau and Dubois, they—"

"They forced me in shyness to agree that conception had taken place."

"Forced you?"

"Because of—"

"I quite understand," he cut me short. *"Mon dieu,* the fault is mine, not yours?"

Specialists were called to the Tuileries from several countries and I was obliged to submit to embarrassing examinations, but with a result that remained embarrassing only to Napoleon. There was no reason, they told us, why I should not in time conceive and bear a healthy child. Frigidity a handicap? The very suggestion was laughable. Countless frigid women had found themselves pregnant. It was one of the blessings of nature.

"So the fault *could* be mine," the agitated Emperor muttered.

They hesitated, those learned specialists. Being foreigners, they owed Napoleon III no allegiance, but after all he was an Emperor; one must think of his Imperial dignity, his manly pride and, last but not least, the very large fee which had been stipulated in advance.

Napoleon scowled darkly. "Come, gentlemen, you are men of science. I myself have always been interested in scientific experiments. Concoct as many new tonics as you like. I'll gladly take the lot. But remember, I want no records kept. You're sworn to secrecy, absolute secrecy."

One doctor prescribed a mustard-colored mixture which stank to high heaven. Napoleon took it bravely—for his rather troublesome cough. Another suggested that he should give up smoking those endless cigarettes. Napoleon complied, again because of the Imperial cough, but for three days only, days of sheer hell for all of us at court. Finally both he and I were advised to take a course of sea bathing and we went south to the lovely privacy of little known Biarritz where later we built a fine villa.

It was during the Biarritz holiday that Napoleon went to Boulogne to meet Queen Victoria's consort, Prince Albert. We had our British alliance but had not yet been invited to meet Queen Victoria. Did she still regard the Emperor of France as a dangerous adventurer and for that reason wish to abstain from personal contact? Much to Napoleon's delight, Prince Albert addressed him as *"Sire et mon frère."* A promising sign, surely!

For, supreme as our court was in France, we were not yet on equal terms with other European courts. A state visit to England would lift us, as it were, from the butler's pantry to the drawing room upstairs. We waited anxiously and at last, eight months after the Boulogne meeting, the invitation arrived.

I often laugh at the circumstances of that formal invitation. In plain words, we learned that we would be made welcome in England if first we asked to be asked. The Queen of the most exclusive court in the world was always cautious about issuing invitations to out-and-out strangers. Imagine, then, the picture which was being created in my mind of a haughty, unbending Victoria, a martinet of martinets!

"Your task," said Napoleon, "is to charm her thoroughly."

Oh dear, how frightened I suddenly felt.

Chapter Eleven

NEVER TO THIS day do I experience an English fog without recalling our arrival at Dover in the Imperial steam-yacht *Pelican,* nor the anxious way we paced the deck and peered toward the mist-shrouded shore while awaiting an opportunity to step on English soil.

Drouyn de Lhuys, our Foreign Minister at that time, was rowed out to the *Pelican* as soon as the fog began to lift, for he had traveled earlier to London to discuss the possibility of peace in the Crimea and to make final arrangements for our arrival. He told us at once that Prince Albert was waiting at the landing stage to greet us. Then he looked approvingly at the plain grey cloak I was wearing as a protection against the weather.

"Eminently suitable, Madame!"

Napoleon studied the cloak seriously. "Drab enough for the unstylish Queen of England, you mean?"

"One can scarcely call Her Majesty drab," Drouyn de Lhuys said appraisingly, "but her taste in clothes is certainly—hum—"

"Uninspired?" I asked.

"Let us say conservative, Madame."

"Then she'll frown on my own taste immediately," I said, and removed the cloak.

"Mon dieu!" Napoleon exclaimed, staring in horror at a dress he had previously admired. "Surely you're dressed for a fete."

With Drouyn de Lhuys to advise us, Napoleon himself went through my wardrobe. Dress after dress was examined and thrown aside in deepening despair. The situation, or so it seemed, was as desperate as if the Russians were at the gates of Paris.

"I can't find a single suitable garment," Napoleon complained.

It was the clever but scornful Pepa who came to his rescue, holding at arm's length a tartan dress of modest design. I explained that it was a new one, but that on occasion I wore such dresses in honor of my Scottish ancestors.

"Queen Victoria has Scottish ancestors also," Drouyn de Lhuys exulted.

Napoleon sighed in relief and lit another cigarette, though the one he had placed on the dressing-table was still burning.

"Does the Queen approve of smoking?" I asked innocently.

"Indeed no," Drouyn de Lhuys groaned. "She hates it in every form. It disgusts her to come upon a man who reeks of tobacco smoke."

And so it came to pass that the Emperor of France promised to refrain from smoking in Queen Victoria's presence and the Empress stepped from the Imperial yacht wearing a tartan dress and a plain straw bonnet. What a fright I must have looked! But Prince Albert smiled his approval and remarked that the Queen was much drawn to all Scottish associations.

During the train journey to London, he and Napoleon spent most of the time discussing the works of Schiller and Rousseau, but from Napoleon's voice I could tell that he was very nervous. Feeling just as nervous myself, I gazed out of the window and wondered what Queen Victoria would say to me and what I would find to say in reply. Napoleon had instructed me not to address her until she first spoke herself, just as if I were a little girl at her first adult party.

The fog had lifted and there, flashing past the window, was the green of the English countryside. I had forgotten that soft, beneficent green which is England's alone. I felt a lump in my throat, just as if I were an exile returning after a long absence.

"Is this Your Majesty's first experience of train travel?" Prince Albert asked.

"Indeed no, Monsieur."

Albert smiled reflectively. "I shall never forget our own first experience twelve or thirteen years ago. The Great Western Line had just been opened and the Queen decided we must give it our blessing. Of course, we looked upon the locomotive as a fearful monster belching smoke and sulphur and were rather fearful about the whole thing. Court etiquette presented a disturbing difficulty. The Master of the Horse was shocked, since he was always in charge of the arrangements when the Queen traveled. He, poor man, knew nothing about driving a locomotive. Etiquette was shattered for once, and the job—quite rightly—was left to the conductor. We boarded the train at Windsor and actually reached Paddington within half an hour. The Queen was delighted but I myself was somewhat alarmed. The children, you may be sure, found the velocity thrilling and told him to drive faster."

We all laughed heartily and began to feel more at ease, as the thoughtful Albert had intended I should. I took heart, too, from the fact that court etiquette could be shattered on occasion, even by the fearsome Victoria.

From Charing Cross Station, we drove in procession to Paddington Station where the royal train was waiting to take us to Windsor. It was to be Windsor Castle first instead of Buckingham Palace, just in case our reception by the people of London proved unfavorable. The sun was shining brilliantly—the Queen's weather, Albert called it—and the route from Charing Cross to Paddington was thronged with sightseers. Much to our satisfaction, a satisfaction clearly shared by Albert, there was a great deal of cheering.

"I have a great affection for England," Napoleon said emotionally. "But for her generous hospitality, I—an exile—would have been completely homeless."

It was still the Queen's weather when we reached Windsor. The Queen herself was waiting at the castle entrance to receive us. The thirteen-year-old "Bertie," who later became Edward VII, stood at her side; the other royal children were grouped prettily about them and farther back stood a semicircle of courtiers.

"Your heels are too high," Napoleon whispered. "We should have thought of that."

Victoria was even shorter than I remembered from my brief glimpse of her several years earlier, but her queenly dignity, as I saw at a glance, made one forget that instantly. She was thirty-six at that time and had been on the throne for eighteen years. She wore a drooping straw bonnet that made my own plain bonnet look rakish, and a nondescript dress of grey silk. Dowdy attire, you say? Possibly, but certainly not dowdily worn. Even now, after so many years, that horrible cliché "every inch a queen" springs to mind. Had I been on stilts, like a circus performer, no one would have noticed. Indeed, after feeling only frightened and nervous, I was now plainly terrified.

The Queen of England advanced upon the Emperor of France. He bent and kissed her hand; she, standing upon her toes without appearing to do so, saluted him first on one cheek, then on the other. A French form of greeting, I thought in wonder. Was she simply putting a French guest at ease, or was she reminding him that the rulers of England had once claimed France as a dominion? Then she turned to me, embraced me briefly, glanced at the tartan dress beneath my open cloak, and embraced me again, almost lingeringly.

"You appear to tremble, Madame," she said. "Are you frightened?"

"Yes," I said frankly.

"Of *me?* How peculiar. Do I look like an ogre?"

I glanced at the smiling, adoring Prince Albert and from him to the royal children who were trying not to be the eager, friendly boys and girls they so obviously were.

"You look like a very happy wife and mother," I blurted out.

The faintest of blushes touched Victoria's cheeks; her eyes sparkled with pleasure.

"The Emperor appears to be frightened, also. He keeps fumbling in his pockets. Something must be done to stop him; otherwise he will spoil the appearance of a very handsome uniform."

Napoleon, as if hearing her words, removed his right hand from his pocket. Then he stared at the cigarette he was grasping, remembered his promise and replaced it hurriedly.

"Ah, I quite understand," said Victoria, her nostrils flaring slightly. "We must send him to the House of Commons."

"Madame?"

"Much to my dismay, they now have a smoking-room there." She smiled faintly. "On the other hand, my dear, the fireplaces of your apartments here would give him quicker relief."

"Fireplaces, Madame?"

"The Queen's wishes are often circumvented that way. The fireplaces are large enough to stand in."

And so it was that the Emperor of France, joined on occasion by Prince Albert, smoked to his heart's content from inside one or another of the Windsor Castle fireplaces. Dear Victoria! She was often a great deal more amused than history records.

Our suite at the castle was spacious and beautifully furnished; but, during those first moments, I was unable to share the interest Napoleon was showing in the Rubens and Vandyke paintings on the walls. Somebody had made a catastrophic blunder. The trunks containing my entire wardrobe had not yet arrived. I possessed only the clothes I was wearing and within an hour we were to take dinner with the Queen in St. George's Hall.

"Ha!" said Napoleon when I told him.

"Make my apologies—tell the Queen I have a dreadful migraine."

"Ha!" he said again.

"You *want* me to go to bed? You fear I may embarrass you at dinner?"

For answer he strode to my bedchamber and returned a moment later with a blue silk evening gown hanging over his arm. I recognized it instantly, for it belonged to one of my ladies.

"A close enough fit, *chérie*."

"And plain enough to be acceptable to the Queen of England?"

"Indubitably."

"You planned this, Napoleon! My trunks were delayed deliberately."

"Ha!" he said most irritatingly for the third time.

Victoria herself was resplendent in the most formal of evening gowns and was covered with diamonds, whereas I, since my jewel case had also gone astray, wore only the flowers from a vase in our drawing room. Some were in my hair, the rest at my waist to hide the poor fit of my borrowed dress. To my surprise, Victoria admired the flowers at once.

"A touch of appealing simplicity. I can well believe, as Prince Albert says, that you are the leader of fashion in France. I could never be a leader of fashion myself, but I was at least responsible for one innovation. *Unwittingly* responsible. I injured my foot some time ago and, hating the sight of the bandage as I lay on a couch receiving my ministers, I pulled down my skirt to cover it. It wasn't queenly modesty, I *assure* you. And would you believe it? Within a matter of days the dress designers brought out the extremely long skirts that are still inflicted upon us today. How silly to think that because I injured my foot, it became immodest to reveal our ankles!"

The conversation during dinner was concerned almost entirely with the Crimea. Peace, as we had hoped, was not in sight. The Allies had gained some great victories, it was true—Alva, Balaclava, Inkerman—but our losses were frightful and now, after a harsh winter, cholera was wreaking greater havoc than the mortal enemy.

"As a result," Albert summed up, "we have something akin to panic among the high command, as well as jealousy and intrigue."

"Sufficient reason for my going out to the Crimea and placing myself in supreme command," Napoleon said eagerly.

Victoria exchanged a quick glance with her husband.

"In England we consider that the distance is too great," said Albert smoothly, "and that it would be unwise for the Emperor of France to be so far removed from his capital."

"The danger is my own most serious objection," Victoria added.

"There's danger everywhere, Madame."

With that, Napoleon fell silent and Albert quickly changed the subject.

The next morning my trunks arrived and the Queen insisted on inspecting my entire wardrobe. With her was her eldest daughter, Princess Victoria, who flung her arms around my neck and begged permission to see "all the lovely clothes from Paris." They looked on in silence as I displayed dress after dress, wondering meanwhile if the Queen disapproved as Napoleon was sure she would.

"I could never wear any of them," the Queen said at last in regretful tones, "but *you,* Madame—Come! Vicky and I shall select the prettiest for tonight's ball."

They chose an ivory brocade decorated with silver

tassels. You can imagine what I said to the mighty Emperor afterwards. One word, heavily charged with sarcasm, was sufficient.

"Men!"

From that moment on, young Vicky, fifteen at the time, became my shadow, while little Prince Arthur, the Queen's youngest son, became Napoleon's. Even the royal dogs seemed friendlier than any other dogs in the world.

"Most promising," Napoleon acknowledged, with a seriousness that made me want to laugh. "The English are always ready to like you if their children and their animals—*especially* their animals—show full approval."

Arthur told Napoleon very gravely that his sister Vicky had fallen in love with me and the girl herself, much less gravely, begged me to send her a pretty dress from Paris. She was close at my side that afternoon during a review of the household troops in Windsor Park. Lord Cardigan, the leader of the famous charge of the Light Brigade, was presented to us and later rode with Napoleon and Albert during the inspection.

"The Emperor rides very well," Victoria remarked, "but Phillips is much too fiery and that makes me nervous."

"Phillips, Madame?"

"The horse Prince Albert gave him. Ah, but look! The Emperor has him well in hand. Phillips has never been mastered so perfectly before."

Apparently Phillips, as well as the children and the dogs, approved of the parvenu Emperor.

The festivities that night took place in what Victoria described as the Picture Gallery, and there she and Napoleon opened the ball by leading a quadrille.

"Until today this was known as the Waterloo Room," Napoleon said, as he danced with me later. "Very tactful of the Queen to change the name. My uncle, her grandfather's greatest enemy, suffered final defeat at Waterloo."

At Vicky's urgent request, I left the ball for a few moments to bid her goodnight and she confided in a pleased whisper that her mother liked me almost as much as she herself did. The Queen had actually written in her diary that I was full of courage and spirits while at the same time possessing the prettiest and most modest manner. It was really unbelievable.

"And this evening," Vicky went on, "Arthur heard her tell Papa that she was beginning to like the Emperor too. One simply *must* like people Phillips likes. He has good manners, Mama said—the Emperor, I mean!— and is quiet and easy and—and *dignified*. One could almost believe he was born a King's son. Mama said that, too."

A backhanded compliment, the last bit, but the whole report was promising enough.

The next day, the third of our visit, was the Day of the Investiture: the day, one might say, when Victoria fully accepted Napoleon into the company of ancient royal families, for on that day he became a Knight of the Garter. The investiture was preceded by a council of war from which the Queen and I, at Her Majesty's own wish, were excluded. Let the men resolve all the difficulties themselves, she said, but she knew and I knew that the only real difficulty was Albert's task of persuading Napoleon against going out to the Crimea. At midday they were still in the council chamber and lunch was sent in to them while Victoria and I lunched alone.

"Dare we disturb them?" she asked at two o'clock.

"They'll be late for the investiture if we don't, Madame."

"You have greater courage than I," she smiled.

Accordingly I knocked peremptorily at the door. Prince Albert was the first to emerge, his cheeks pink, his eyes dazed. I could well believe that Napoleon, de-

146

termined to get his own way, had treated him to a very long dissertation indeed.

"The Emperor has a very good German accent," he said wearily, "and his knowledge of Schiller is formidable. What an amazing memory! He recited passage after passage faultlessly."

"Schiller!" Victoria said blankly. "How very interesting."

The investiture in the throne room was a very impressive ceremony. The Prince of Wales wearing a kilt stood at attention near my chair and little Prince Arthur edged his way through the legs of the gentlemen until he was as close to Napoleon as he could get. Not having quite known what to expect, I was amazed to hear the Emperor of France swearing a number of oaths of fidelity and knightly service. Later, as the Queen walked with us to our suite, he smiled slyly.

"Your Majesty will be well served by your newest knight—on the battlefield."

Victoria pressed my arm lightly. "The Emperor is just as stubborn a person as I am. Is it possible that I have met my match at last?"

There was admiration, not anger, in her voice.

That night at the state ball Victoria kept my husband constantly at her side. Napoleon had lost his earlier nervousness and talked lengthily now while Victoria listened as if she were a young girl entranced by the splendor and erudition of her first *beau*.

"The Emperor is a most *remarkable* man," she told me, "a most extraordinary man." She paused, as if busy with her diary and heavily underlining the flattering adjectives. "He possesses *indomitable courage, unflinching* firmness and *great secrecy*. Do you ever really know what is in his mind?"

"Only rarely," I avowed, truthfully enough.

Napoleon and I traveled to London the next morning with the royal family and were given splendid apartments at Buckingham Palace. That day there was a state luncheon in our honor at the Guildhall. The luncheon was a pleasing triumph for Napoleon. Once an exile in London and unrecognized by the Queen, he was now being feted as the Emperor of a powerful nation, a sincere ally and Her Majesty's friend. His speech was roundly applauded since the sentiments he expressed were acceptable to all. We, the two great Western Powers, he said, were not allies merely through the accident of war, but we were also firm comrades in the pursuits of peace.

The last two days of our visit kept us busily occupied. We went to Covent Garden to hear Beethoven's only opera, *Fidelio,* and spent hours at the newly opened Crystal Palace where, after viewing the many exhibitions, Napoleon decided privately that our own coming Industrial Exhibition would be of greater importance. On the last evening there was a final ball, but before it there was also a final council of war.

"While the men talk and argue," said Victoria, inviting me to her private drawing room, "let us have a pleasant little talk all by ourselves."

"You hope to have more success with me than we can expect Prince Albert to have with the Emperor," I laughed.

"Knowing that a wife may succeed when all other wise counsel fails, yes."

"Why are you so set against the Emperor going out to the Crimea?" I asked frankly.

"It would cause trouble with the British general staff," Victoria replied, just as frankly, "if the Emperor of France assumed command of the allied armies as he would rightly expect to do. His presence would also stir up unhappy memories in the whole of Europe of the military aims of his late uncle. We know, you and I, that the Emperor's aim is really for peace, but others are still in doubt. His ministers, as well as mine, are much against his going. He himself is our only obstacle. Let me make a confession, Madame. I agreed to this state visit for one reason only and knowing that the Emperor would remain in Paris until a date was announced or the idea rejected, I delayed again and again."

"In order to keep him from the Crimea."

Victoria nodded. "But now that we have become good friends I wish with all my heart that personal regard rather than political expediency had prompted me to make you welcome."

"And if I fail to keep the Emperor from the Crimea, personal regard will suffer in no way, Madame?"

"In no way at all. I admire and respect both you and the Emperor."

"Because of Phillips, the children and the dogs?"

Victoria laughed merrily. "I think I know what you mean, but you must not be led astray by a popular misconception about the English. Children and animals are often much taken with the most impossible people. We in England are not as gullible as some believe. And speaking of misconception in another sense," she touched my arm gently, "you have been married over two years and are still childless."

I blushed hotly. Victoria's remark was as unexpected as it was bewildering. The Queen of England, conservative England, speaking of such things? Nevertheless, as I came firmly to believe and still believe, Victoria wasn't really a Victorian.

"I seem to have embarrassed you," she went on in surprise. "How peculiar. I see nothing against my talking to you frankly as one wife to another. And am I not the mother of eight children? You look healthy and you appear to have the right sort of figure for child-bearing. I believe a miscarriage was announced?"

"We-ell—"

"How very unfortunate. You must take better care of yourself next time. No tight lacing, no riding—certainly not bareback, no dancing, much as you love it, no running up and down the stairs as I've seen you do. The condition which we so nicely call 'interesting' is also a critical one. Women are by no means as delicate as men believe, but even so, my dear . . . !"

"I shall take all possible care of myself next time," I promised solemnly.

She touched my arm again. "Let us pray that you will have good news for me by the time I am able to visit Paris." She smiled mischievously. "I take it I shall be quite well received if I ask to come?"

"It would be difficult for me to receive Your Majesty in France as well as I have been received in England. But are you in a position to make an official announcement at once?"

"What have you in mind, Madame?" Victoria asked curiously. "Your eyes have narrowed alarmingly."

I laughed guiltily. "If you were to promise to visit Paris, yet withhold a definite date . . ."

"Ah yes!" she broke in. "That might keep the Emperor from rushing off to the Crimea."

"Shall I tell him, too, that you will come only if he forgets the Crimea?"

"If you judge it expedient, yes."

A smile of complete understanding passed between us.

"Of course," she added, "Prince Albert may still succeed with the Emperor."

A few moments later Napoleon and Albert emerged from the council chamber. Napoleon was smiling blandly and Albert was mopping his brow heavily.

"Schiller again?" Victoria asked brightly.

"Rousseau," said Albert, "Jean Jacques Rousseau."

"We also discussed Your Majesty's impending visit to France," said Napoleon. "Our own industrial exhibition is something which you must make a point of seeing."

"I should like to come to Paris," Victoria sighed. "Indeed, I *want* to come, but if the Prince has actually committed me—"

"Informally only," Albert put in hurriedly.

150

"Splendid! Let us say, *informally,* that when the time is opportune a visit will certainly be made."

And again she and I exchanged a smile of complete understanding.

At the leave-taking the next morning, young Vicky burst into tears and had to be dragged from my arms. Little Prince Arthur gave me a small bouquet of violets and was in tears also. Tears are such infectious things. I began to weep myself while Napoleon cleared his throat suspiciously and Albert turned sternly away to hide his own emotion. Victoria saluted Napoleon on both cheeks and seemed incapable of withdrawing her hand when he kissed it.

"Dear me, I seem to have taken a cold," she said.

"Paris in May is just the place for one's convalescence," Napoleon murmured persuasively. "Today is April twenty-first. The *Exposition Industrielle* opens on May fifteenth."

"So short a time," Victoria protested, still struggling with her "cold." "Unstylish as I am, it would be impossible for me to acquire anything suitable to wear by that date."

"Paris is full of dressmakers," Napoleon laughed.

Victoria pretended to sneeze. "Alas, the Queen of England must remain patriotic in all things."

"Do you always have the last word, Madame?" Napoleon teased.

"Always!" she said firmly.

Chapter Twelve

A FEW DAYS after our return from England, I went driving in Napoleon's new park, the Bois de Boulogne, to inspect the progress being made there by Haussmann's workmen. Napoleon was to join me later on horseback, as if by accident, thus making a semi-state occasion of the inspection.

I remember having been very cross with him before leaving the Tuileries, for we had argued once again about the Crimea and he had refused steadily to believe that Victoria would only come to Paris if he promised not to go out to the battlefield. I was still feeling cross when he failed to appear in the Bois at the appointed time, so I told General Fleury, who arrived hurriedly and alone, that I would wait no longer.

"Madame," Fleury gasped, when at last I permitted him to speak, "your presence is required urgently at the Tuileries. An attempt has just been made on the Emperor's life."

"Still another plot?" I cried in horror, for several had been exposed already. "Is the Emperor seriously injured?"

"Happily, no. The attack was made in the Champs Élysées. Two shots were fired but neither reached its mark. His Majesty behaved magnificently."

However, Napoleon appeared just as my carriage was leaving the Bois and reprimanded Fleury for alarming me and calling me back to the Tuileries.

"Not even a dozen assassins could prevent me from

joining the Empress," he said, addressing the crowd that had gathered.

Inevitably there were cheers. If bravery and fine speeches were all that the people wanted, the Second Empire would still be flourishing today.

Plonplon was waiting at the Tuileries and offered Napoleon his "heartfelt" congratulations on a miraculous escape. The police had arrested the would-be assassin, an Italian fanatic who had come close to success because he possessed no accomplices. Plots hatched by a single individual were always difficult to detect.

"My popularity with the people has been vastly increased," Napoleon said, after receiving a tremendous ovation at the opera that night. "I have nothing to fear from any man who is misguided enough to try and kill me. Providence placed me on the throne, and as an instrument of Providence, my mission is a holy one. Nor is it yet completed. For that reason alone I run no danger—neither in Paris nor on the battlefield." He then announced that he would leave for the Crimea immediately after the official opening of the *Exposition Industrielle*.

Happily, his departure was delayed by affairs of state and councils of war and finally canceled by what I can only regard as a blessed miracle.

"If I have good news for you this month," I said one morning, "will you return from the Crimea at once?"

"Eugenie!"

"Tomorrow will be the fourth day," I said. I will admit I was excited myself.

His face fell. "We've had irregularities before, sometimes as long as a week."

"I feel different this time," I said.

A week passed; then a second week. The physicians held lengthy consultations and equally lengthy arguments. Finally the accoucheur Dubois, son of that other Dubois who delivered Marie Louise's son, announced that as far as he was personally concerned no doubt remained. I wept in relief. So did the Emperor of France.

"I have decided to remain in Paris until my son is born," he said pompously.

"And afterward?"

"I shall have little time for a visit farther afield than the nursery. It is pleasing to know that everybody now feels exactly as I myself have felt all along. In short, a visit to the Crimea would be unwise from every point of view."

His words of wisdom were communicated to Queen Victoria and Her Majesty, while writing me a private letter of congratulation, announced that she would make a state visit to Paris during the month of August.

Napoleon went to Boulogne to meet the royal party and later that same day was in Paris again with Queen Victoria, Prince Albert, the Prince of Wales—Bertie, and the Princess Royal, the young Vicky. They drove down the newly constructed Boulevard de Strasbourg, on through the Bois de Boulogne and out to Saint-Cloud where the court was in residence. Victoria wore a ridiculous straw bonnet designed more for the rigors of a Channel crossing than the importance of a state occasion. At least, it would have looked ridiculous on any other woman, but she, being Queen Victoria, wore it regally.

The news of her impending visit had raised many old memories and grievances. She was the first reigning English sovereign to come to Paris since the English king Henry VI was crowned there over four hundred years ago. The French remembered the many wars that had taken place since then, the battles that had been fought on land and sea. Was it possible, Paris asked itself, that France and England, allies now in the Crimea, would never be enemies again? A French victory, that of Tehernaya, was announced the day before Victoria arrived. This put everybody in a good mood, even those who suspected that England was using France as a tool in the war.

So the Queen of England was given a tumultuous welcome in Paris and bands played "God Save the Queen." Very nicely stage-managed, of course, but soon it was seen that the welcome was absolutely genuine. Indeed it was! The hat shops did a thriving trade in bonnets *à la reine Victoire*.

Victoria loved Saint-Cloud. So did I, even though the château reminded me of Miss Howard who had since married an Englishman by the name of Trelawny and troubled me no more.

"Everything is in excellent taste," the Queen observed while we were taking our first breakfast together. "Magnificent, yes, but also very quiet and becomingly royal."

"No revolting parvenu display?" Napoleon teased her.

"None whatever," she smiled.

The "parvenu" Emperor had certainly come up in the world.

At Victoria's insistence, I was spared every possible exertion in the task of entertaining her. At the state balls I was permitted to dance only once or twice; she slowed down her pace to a crawl when we walked abroad together; and at the state dinners she instructed me, just a little bossily, to eat only the plainest of food.

"I will not have it said that the excitement of my visit was the cause of another miscarriage," she told me sternly. "Nor do I subscribe to the fallacy that a mother-to-be must eat enough for two."

In the point of fact, the food was so plain that I had little appetite for it. Napoleon, you see, had taken note of the plainness of the meals served at the royal table in England and a special edict—nothing elaborate, certainly no garlic whatever!—had gone to the Imperial kitchen, much to the despair and the near revolt of the cleverest chefs in the world.

"The coffee is very nice," Victoria remarked, "and the food surprisingly and gratifyingly English in flavor."

Flavor, indeed!

At one of the balls I wore my first crinoline. I say "my" advisedly, for the crinoline was my own invention, a resurrection in part of the early Spanish farthingale. It was a simple, modest affair, that first crinoline, but even so Victoria found it fascinating.

"May I ask how many yards of silk were needed for the dress?"

"Only ten, Madame."

"What of the actual crinoline? Some very stiff material, perhaps?"

"A petticoat of horsehair."

"Dear me, does it scratch?"

"I'm wearing a thin silk petticoat beneath it."

Victoria laughed softly. "Pray don't think me rude, but is this innovation designed to hide your pregnancy?"

"It is indeed, Madame."

"Ah, then the crinoline will grow larger as you yourself grow larger."

"Surely!"

At the next ball, several crinolines were worn, and before the royal visit ended every fashion-conscious woman in high society possessed one. Victoria bought a crinoline herself and showed it to me proudly before her maid packed it.

"For my next pregnancy, Madame!"

The climax of the visit was a solemn procession to the Hôtel des Invalides. We went by a torchlight in a dramatic thunderstorm. One could almost believe that the nephew of Napoleon, the Thunderer, had commanded the storm in addition to the torchlight and the organ music. It was an emotion-stirring scene, the Queen of England and the Emperor of France standing together at the great Napoleon's tomb while the organist played "God Save the Queen." The nephew knew well what he was about in choosing an organ for so solemn an occasion instead of the martial note of a military band.

We stood in a row—Victoria, Napoleon, Albert and myself—with the royal children just in front of Victoria and me. She wore a preposterously large white silk hat which from time to time caused me to edge slightly away from her. It troubled the young Prince of Wales too, tickling the back of his neck when she bent forward to whisper in his ear. Her command was obeyed instantly and the boy, a charming, touching sight in his Scottish kilt, knelt at the tomb. The generals and the colonels wept unashamedly, as only Frenchmen can, but I wondered uneasily if the London newspaper gentlemen, noting this royal gesture, would suggest that Her Majesty had gone further than strictly necessary to please the French.

"Do you think it was a mistake, a really bad mistake?" Victoria whispered, her head bowed.

"No, Madame," I whispered back, "but perhaps your newspapers . . ."

"They have never been known to comment unfavorably on my hats," she declared.

"I like it very much myself," I said, finding it hard not to laugh at how falsely I had judged her meaning.

Just as there were tears when we left London, so there were tears again when the royal family left Paris. Victoria embraced me lingeringly and bade me once more to take the greatest possible care of myself.

"This visit is the happiest I have ever experienced," she said. "The Emperor has been amazingly kind and thoughtful. He appears to know all my likes and dislikes. He possesses the art of being familiar without any of the offensiveness of familiarity. I am very grateful—to *both* of you," she added, including me somewhat hurriedly. "And just fancy, we have become intimate friends, you and I, the Emperor and my husband."

Her final words, uttered after she had once again saluted Napoleon on both cheeks, expressed fully my own deep feelings.

"We must pray for two things—the safe delivery of an Imperial child and peace in the Crimea."

My last state appearance before my confinement was at a reception in honor of another royal visitor, King Victor Emmanuel of Sardinia. It so happened that Napoleon wanted secret talks with him, talks of which I, to say nothing of the government, remained in ignorance for quite some time. As far as most of us knew, Victor Emmanuel was in Paris in search of pleasure. I disliked him at first sight but it was my duty to receive him graciously if not warmly. He was thirty-five at that time, a large, strong man, a ladykiller and quite terrifying in that respect—or so people said. His manner was brusk and his conversation, even in my presence, disgustingly unrefined.

"I love all pretty women," he told Napoleon, after kissing my hand, "but here in a city crammed with pretty women we have an Empress who is even more than beautiful."

Nothing disgustingly unrefined in that, you say? Ah, but he spoke with a leer in his voice that made my flesh crawl.

"Much is told me of the women of Paris," he went on. "Is it true, Sire, that they do not wear drawers?"

Napoleon ignored my frown of distaste and laughed pleasantly. I should have guessed then that Victor Emmanuel was essential to his political plans.

"Not in winter even?" the lecherous Sardinian asked. "But how wonderful!"

"Your Majesty maligns the ladies of Paris," Napoleon chuckled.

"I am misinformed by my ministers, yes?"

"About the *ladies,* certainly. But some of the women, the professional dancers, for example—"

"Those of the cancan? That is more than wonderful!"

There was worse to come when Napoleon took him to the Opéra Comique. The story, greatly exaggerated in its passage through the boulevards, reached the Tuileries even before Napoleon returned from the theatre. Victor Emmanuel, Pepa told me, became instantly entranced at the sight of one of the ballet girls.

"I must have her," he said, digging the Emperor in the ribs. "She is readily available, yes?"

"One would imagine so—at a price."

"So! I am careful of my money. How much would she demand?"

Napoleon's chamberlain sought out the girl and returned with the news that her price was five thousand francs for a king.

"Impossible!" Victor Emmanuel roared.

"My privy purse is available," said Napoleon.

"A present, eh? Then I accept!"

Naturally I reproached Napoleon hotly, telling him that I blushed for him and the part he had played in what amounted to a public transaction conducted there in the theatre.

"It is necessary always to accommodate one's guests," he said equably. "I want Victor Emmanuel's daughter Clothilde for Plonplon."

Then he changed the subject smoothly, thus keeping the deeper implication of his plans carefully to himself. He went on to tell me that the peace negotiations would be conducted in Paris. The war, you see, had come to an end with the fall of the Russian naval base at Sevastopol, but the allied troops would remain in the Crimea until a peace treaty was drawn up and signed.

"A peace congress in Paris is a personal triumph for me," he said. "It will be an additional triumph if the signing of the treaty coincides with the birth of my son."

"How sure you are that the child will be a boy!"

"We are in the hands of Providence and Providence will not disappoint us."

He spoke, I could but note, as if Providence were in *his* hands and would meet with *his* wishes without the slightest hesitation.

The official announcement of the Imperial pregnancy had appeared in the *Moniteur* after the fourth month. It was now the fifth month. The remaining four months which followed my last state appearance were irksome and rather dreary. Napoleon permitted me to appear but rarely, even at private functions, so that I took very little part in the festivities which marked the presence in Paris of the peacemakers. I did, however, attend a fancy dress ball given, I seem to remember, by our Foreign Minister. But the most I could do was sit among my ladies, an onlooker only, watching enviously and holding a sort of court as Lord Cowley and others came to pay their respects. Cowley himself was standing at my side when Count Cavour, Victor Emmanuel's Prime Minister, approached. He was said to be a clever man and was taking a part in the peace negotiations, this because a Sardinian army had fought with French and English troops in the Crimea. The Count was short and bulky and wore spectacles through which he peered with his head on one side as if deaf as well as shortsighted. With him was one of the most beautiful young women I had ever seen, and her slimness, despite my enlarged crinoline, made me acutely conscious of my own pregnant condition.

Cavour bowed. "Your Majesty . . ."

Then he made the presentation. The girl—she was little more than sixteen—was his niece Virginia, the wife of the Count Castiglione, one of Victor Emmanuel's equerries to whom the King had married her a year ago. Even at fifteen, said Cavour whose manners were no more refined than his master's, she was a fully matured woman and more experienced—there was no

How do your cigarette's tar and nicotine numbers compare with True?

Place your pack here.

Compare
your cigarette's
tar and nicotine
numbers
with True.

No numbers on the front of your pack? True puts its numbers right out front. Because True, regular and menthol, is lower in both tar and nicotine than 99% of all other cigarettes sold. Think about it.

LATEST U.S. GOVERNMENT TESTS:
12 MGS. TAR, 0.6 MGS. NICOTINE

Warning: The Surgeon General Has Determined That Cigarette Smoking Is Dangerous to Your Health

© Lorillard 1971

Regular or menthol.
Doesn't it all add up to True?

doubt what he meant by "experienced"—than her husband.

"You must present the Count also," I said faintly.

"Alas, Madame, *he* is not in Paris."

Napoleon appeared at that moment. The girl curtsied but in such a manner as to suggest that no curtsy was called for. Napoleon kissed her hand. No words were spoken. Clearly it was not the first meeting of the Emperor of France and La Belle Castiglione as everyone in Paris was soon calling her. The orchestra that night was conducted by Johann Strauss whose lovely waltz, the "Blue Danube" was all the rage. Strauss raised his baton at a nod from the Imperial chamberlain, the girl slipped her arm through Napoleon's and away they waltzed.

"Delightful," said Cavour.

"Her costume, Monsieur?"

"That also, Your Majesty."

Castiglione, as I shall call her henceforth, was dressed as the Queen of Hearts, a deliberate choice, I feel sure, to be flaunted deliberately before my eyes. The actual heart was a heart-shaped purse and hung from the belt round her waist.

"Not a heart of gold," I murmured, "but rather a heart made for gold."

"No one can doubt it," Cavour chuckled, "nor the means by which she would fill it."

At that moment, much to my relief, Lord Cowley engaged Cavour in conversation and led him away.

Later that evening, Lady Cowley informed me that Castiglione was lodged at the Élysée Palace with Victor Emmanuel and his suite, and that Napoleon went there often and not always to discuss the peace negotiations with the King. She assumed, did Lady Cowley, that I knew all about the intrigue, otherwise she would not have spoken.

"We look to Your Majesty to bring the *affaire* to a quick conclusion," she said confidently.

"*We,* Lady Cowley?"

"My husband, the Ambassador, and the Foreign Office in London."

"I fail to see why your Foreign Office should be in the least concerned."

"We are concerned with the result, Madame, not the *affaire* itself. For several days now, my husband has failed to gain a private audience with the Emperor, so engrossed is he with the pretty little countess. It will do his nerves no good—no good at all."

"Your husband's?"

"No, *no,* Your Majesty! The *Emperor's.* Think of his age. Think of his responsibilities at the peace conference. A frolicsome young woman like that. Quite a man-eater, or so I'm told. Even King Victor Emmanuel was obliged to send her packing. His doctors warned him—"

"Madame!"

"I am very, very serious, Your Majesty."

I was forced to believe her. Lady Cowley might well have been discussing a sudden disastrous fall on the London Stock Exchange or the Paris Bourse. Indeed, her seriousness, getting the better of her normal English reserve, made me want to laugh crazily.

"I shall ask the Emperor to receive Lord Cowley tomorrow," I promised.

But she lingered a few moments longer, grimly serious still. "How dreadful if the peace of Europe is at stake, Your Majesty. The Emperor grows old before his time. Further excesses may lead to complete apathy, or irritation, or—or infirmity of purpose. With Your Majesty's permission, I would advise a consultation with the Emperor's physicians."

I was shocked and hurt. "Further excesses" suggested that there had been others before Castiglione and that others would follow her.

The next morning I summoned Dr. Conneau and asked him to speak in strict confidence. To my surprise

162

he confirmed everything Lady Cowley had said, though naturally he evaded the intimate side of the matter, as I myself did. Hard work, longer hours of it than a younger man could be expected to sustain, these were the causes of the Emperor's debility. I was urged to restrain him, to persuade him, if possible, to delegate a number of duties which his ministers could well perform. This I attempted at the first opportunity, and as a result Napoleon looked at me balefully.

"I quite understand, Madame."

"You really do, Sire?"

"Interference. Inexcusable interference!"

I laughed sarcastically. "Naturally there are certain activities which you would hardly relish delegating to your ministers, unless a special new ministry is created."

"I beg you not to interfere in state affairs," he said irritably.

"State affairs?" I jeered. "My impression is that King Victor Emmanuel has given you a present at no cost to himself, in return for the costly present you gave him."

Napoleon laughed dryly. "Bait for the trap, but while enjoying the bait, I shall enter the trap only if it suits me."

"Bait? A bait which in some way concerns the unification of the Italian states?"

I was deeply interested in this question and later was to become frantically involved in it, heaven help me, but Napoleon seemed not to have heard my words.

"Thank you for not making me a scene," he said roughly. "I love and honor you above all other women. I've said it before. I say it again. For the rest, I am what I am and nothing will ever change me."

I studied him carefully. There was a weary look in his eyes. His face was drawn and paler than usual. There was more grey in his hair than I'd noticed before. At forty-eight he looked older than his years physically, but was he old before his time mentally? I held my peace. Useless for me to urge him once again to rest.

"Lord Cowley would appreciate a private audience," I ventured.

"I received him an hour ago. Lady Cowley's interference was unnecessary and presumptuous."

That in itself set my mind at rest. Napoleon had seen Lady Cowley in conversation with me at the ball and had drawn the right conclusion. He was as mentally alert as ever.

During the last weeks of my pregnancy I scarcely left my apartments at the Tuileries, but I took quiet walks when in residence at Saint-Cloud where, according to the doctors, the air was better for me than in Paris. I did a lot of reading and studying as if in preparation for a vital part in state affairs which seemed unlikely ever to be mine. And presently I had the mixed blessing of Mama's presence. She arrived importantly from Madrid and gave me more comfort than one might have expected. Her ceaseless chatter was not unwelcome distraction, for I was dreading the ordeal which lay before me, not the pain so much as the entire lack of privacy. To be compelled to give birth in public—that, I knew, would be the real ordeal, the more so since the most prominent of the official witnesses, the one most vitally and personally concerned, would be the hated Plonplon. I pleaded with Napoleon to spare me at least that ghastly presence, but to no avail.

"Uncle Jerome is ill and not likely to live much longer. His son is in effect my real heir and will remain so until the moment of my son's birth. He above all people must bear witness to the fact that no trickery is practiced, no changeling smuggled into your bed if the child is stillborn or—well—"

"Or a girl."

"God will give me a son."

"There are other witnesses more reliable than Plonplon."

"Really, *chérie,* must you insist on using that offensive nickname?"

"You use it on occasion yourself."

Napoleon smiled and shrugged. "So does everybody else, even his father and sister."

"A most important witness, that coward Plonplon!"

"Refuse him admittance and any suggestion of trickery he might feel inclined to circulate would never be fully discredited."

At the beginning of March, Conneau and Dubois were asked to estimate as closely as possible the date of my confinement and after a weighty consultation they named the twelfth of the month.

"The twentieth would be more to my liking," said Napoleon.

That date was the anniversary of the birth of the first Napoleon's only legitimate son, the King of Rome. Clearly, then, the third Napoleon was hoping for the coincidence of an important link with the Imperial past.

"If only we could be sure of it," he said dreamily.

"Are you asking me to perform a miracle and hold back the birth?" I asked tartly.

"No, *chérie,* I leave that to the doctors."

There was another weighty consultation after which, thinking to delay the birth, those medical specialists gave me morphine. Day by day they increased the doses until, nauseated, I became so ill they desisted in the fear of bringing on the pains prematurely. The pains actually started on the evening of the fourteenth, but it was not until three o'clock on the morning of the sixteenth, Palm Sunday, that my son was born. I suffered horribly.

Meanwhile people streamed up and down the Rue de Rivoli and congregated in the palace gardens while Napoleon, distracted and agonized, paced my apartments untiringly. I was very brave, he kept telling me, whereas he himself, unable to bear suffering in others, was the greatest coward on earth. Was I really "very brave"?

All I can remember, apart from the pain, is the horror I felt at the sight of Plonplon's glassy stare. For he had taken to wearing a monocle as if in need of extra sight to reveal the appalling truth of his disinheritance. That monocle seemed to hover over me that whole time, night, day and night again, but it was only toward the end that it made its full appearance. Mama took care of that by keeping him behind a screen most of the time, bless her! I fainted when I could bear no more—neither the pain nor the Plonplon monocle, and on recovering heard the distant boom of cannon. I counted forty shots before fully realizing the truth. Twenty-one for a girl, a hundred-and-one for a boy. A *boy,* I thought stupidly. A Prince Imperial! A future Emperor for the Bonaparte dynasty!

Napoleon was so overjoyed he embraced everybody in sight, everybody but Plonplon who ran from him cursing and for a time refused to sign his name as a witness of the *acte de naissance*. Finally Mathilde told him sharply not to be a fool and, splashing ink everywhere as if to obliterate his signature, he signed. Thereupon Napoleon embraced everybody again, even his mother-in-law, though he had the presence of mind to refuse her request that she should be allowed to remain indefinitely in Paris. An occasional visit but no lengthy stay, my dear *belle-mère.* Then he issued rapid, excited orders to his secretary: a million francs to be distributed among the poor; he to be godfather, I godmother, to every *legitimate* child born in France that day; amnesty for the political proscripts providing—oh, that lovely presence of mind!—providing they declared themselves loyal to the Imperial government.

"My warmest congratulations, Madame," Plonplon said, bending over me menacingly. "We pray, my sister and I, that the Prince Imperial will live to mount the throne. Not that we expect our prayers to be an-

166

swered. History is weighted against it. Not since the accession of Louis XIV has a ruler of France been succeeded at his death by his son."

Chapter Thirteen

HOW I RESENTED the illness which followed the birth of my son! It was two months before I was well enough to leave my bedroom at the Tuileries, two months during which I saw little of my baby, precious months to any mother. An occasional glimpse, a few brief moments in my arms as I grew stronger, then away he was whisked to be fed by the wet-nurse, a healthy peasant from Burgundy.

Napoleon-Eugene-Louis-Jean-Joseph—those were the names given him at the private baptism on the day of his birth. His father brought him to me afterward—a very important baby swathed in a cloak of blue velvet around which was the Grand Cordon of the Legion of Honor. His Holiness the Pope, Napoleon told me, was his godfather; General Fleury murmured gravely that the Prince Imperial had remained calm throughout the ceremony.

"Madame, His Imperial Highness clearly understood, without any surprise at all and with full Imperial dignity, all the honors that were being paid him."

A baby only a few hours old? How ridiculous!

At the end of the two months, I went to Saint-Cloud and there I remained another month, slowly recovering my strength. It was a joy to hold my baby in my arms, but I was terrified of dropping him. Was he really mine? He, the Child of France, belonged to France. I had borne an heir to the Empire, not to my husband.

While I was at Saint-Cloud the Archduke Maximilian, brother of the Emperor Franz Joseph of Austria, came to France on a state visit. Maximilian was making what might be called a goodwill tour, his purpose being to bring France and Austria closer together now that the Crimean War was at an end.

I dreaded even a brief informal intrusion upon my privacy at the château, but when Maximilian was presented by Napoleon, an amazing and gratifying thing happened. The young man made me laugh. The laughter made me feel a great deal better and before the end of his visit I was able to attend a review given in his honor. Immediately after the presentation, Maximilian addressed me in very good Spanish, a courtesy I much appreciated, and for a few moments we conversed in Spanish with Napoleon standing somewhat awkwardly at my side.

"I believe you were met at the Gare de l'Est by Prince Napoleon," I said.

"He who is called Plonplon, Madame?"

"None other. You found him agreeable, I trust?"

"On the contrary, his manner was cold and stiff."

"Plonplon is almost always rude. I beg you to forget the bad impression he made upon you."

Maximilian was twenty-four at that time, an elderly looking young man, really quite owlish, if one can conjure up a picture of an owl with twinkling eyes.

"Not really a bad impression," he said meditatively. "That booming voice of his, a voice that has passed its best. The booming in addition to the heaviness of the man. Forgive me, Your Majesty, but—"

"Plonplon is no friend of mine," I murmured.

Maximilian bowed. "I shall always think of Prince Plonplon as a singer, a bass singer, let us say, a wornout fugitive basso from a small, little-known Italian opera house."

It was then, of course, that I laughed, and from then on Maximilian's visit, as far as *I* was concerned, was an assured success. Napoleon, for that matter, was quickly won over himself during a sightseeing tour of Paris. The archduke, it seemed, was something of an architect, an amateur but expert designer of public buildings and churches. The changes which had taken place in Paris during the last four years amazed him. He admired everything. A magician, he said, had been at work.

Napoleon when not in residence at Saint-Cloud came daily to see his son. He spent hours at the Imperial cradle, at times in dreamy silence, at others uttering little spates of crazy baby talk. He was the most indulgent of fathers and would oppose me, I suspected, if for the child's sake I attempted any form of discipline. As far as I was concerned, Napoleon was gentle and kind and grateful. He flattered me, too, saying that I had emerged from my ordeal looking more beautiful than ever, with a figure that had suffered not at all and a waist perhaps even slightly slimmer.

"Are you making love to me?" I asked somewhat tremulously.

"You'd like me to do that, *chérie?*"

A strange thing had happened. There was a new softness within me, a longing such as I had never known since those far-off days of my desperate, unrequited love for Alba. Napoleon's unfaithfulness was forgotten, past and present. His little "attachments"—there were several now, I knew—seemed not to matter.

"You gave me your word," I said coquettishly.

"Well—I'd changed my mind. I wasn't going to keep it."

"I don't think I would have forced you to keep it, Napoleon."

He flung himself into a chair and lit a cigarette. "You must buy yourself some clothes. Your new beauty cries out for adornment."

The thought of new clothes always excited me, often more than the actual acquisition, just as the smell of bacon in the kitchen is more appetizing than the taste of it.

"I have many more than I need," I said perversely. "I feel like a child who has eaten too much jam."

"Very well, then," he said roughly. "Go about in rags—smear dirt on your face—turn yourself into an ugly old crone! That, perhaps, will serve the purpose of dampening my ardor."

I shuddered in mock horror. "Rather than make such a fright of myself, I'd gladly drive you crazy with hopeless desire."

"Hopeless, yes!"

"Napoleon—"

He sprang up violently. "For the love of God, Eugenie, have a talk with Dubois. I'll send him to you at once."

And so, unhappily and unwillingly, Dubois told me the truth. He and Conneau, after several consultations with other doctors, had reached the conclusion that a second pregnancy would kill me. I was still in need of painful treatment before I would be perfectly well again, but even treatment, however long continued, would never remove the danger.

"Perfectly well again!" I jeered.

"We must count our blessings, Madame. We must thank God you gave us a boy."

"And at the same time a whole string of new mistresses for the Emperor."

"There would be mistresses in any case, Madame," Dubois said gravely.

That, of course, was true enough. But what an ironical quirk of fate that I should desire Napoleon now when it had become impossible. And because of his kindness in thinking only of my safety, I wanted him even more. Small wonder that with desire growing sour within me I was often a veritable shrew and made the poor Emperor many violent scenes about things of no consequence whatever.

I returned to Paris for the second baptismal ceremony, that enormous public display at Notre Dame. The city was *en fête* once more, everybody wanted to catch a glimpse of the little Prince Imperial, the new actor in the Bonaparte drama.

Later in the day, the Municipality of Paris gave us a banquet at the Hôtel de Ville. Eighteen thousand candles lit the tables for the four hundred guests. The flowers alone cost fifty thousand francs; the whole banquet, a quarter of a million. While listening to the enthusiastic speeches I kept thinking of all that wasted money. We could have founded three orphanages had the banquet not been thought necessary. I resolved then that in the future the poor and the destitute should not be neglected.

By this I don't mean that I became a recluse preoccupied solely with good works, one of those frightening, plainly garbed, grimly serious, humorless, quite relentless social workers. There was still gaiety in my life, and, besides, was I not the leader of fashion? The crinoline, which I had intended dispensing with when I needed it no longer, was now all the rage. And with the addition of several petticoats as well as many lengths of whalebone, it was growing monstrous. The dresses themselves had become much more elaborate with the cunning inclusion of ruches and flounces. Most of mine called for as many as thirty yards of material. Oh, that dreadful weight borne in the name of high fashion!

Most certainly I enjoyed my life during the next two years: the state balls and receptions, the state dinners, the more intimate private dinners with close friends, the hunting parties, the Imperial progresses throughout the country, the visits of Biarritz. All that and a great deal more.

And what of Loulou as we called our Little Prince Imperial? Napoleon boasted that he could ride before he could walk, but that was just another fond exaggeration. When he was no more than six months old, he was strapped on the back of a pony and paraded up and down the gardens of the Tuileries. How the crowd loved it and cheered. The little Prince, the little *man!* The Master of the Horse strode at his side, bellowing instructions like a company sergeant-major, while Miss Shaw, his English nurse, trotted behind anxiously. Loulou was a soldier from birth, with a commission in the First Imperial Guard Regiment, and before he was a year old, Napoleon took him to his first military review. Poor little mite, I can see him now sitting in front of his father on the Imperial charger. He wears full military uniform, the top-heavy bearskin almost as large as himself.

"Peace is my aim," said Napoleon, "but tradition demands a military Empire. Therefore my son must understand from the first that he, a soldier and the future Emperor, is in the care of the Army."

During those two years, I managed for a time to ignore my husband's love affairs which he no longer made any pretense of hiding. It was tacitly understood that no official mistress would ever be established, as had been the custom in the days of Louis XV. He had convinced himself, I think, that to take yet another mistress was no longer an act of unfaithfulness. After all, how could one really be unfaithful to a wife who was, as they say, a wife in name only?

Full and, on the whole, happy as my life was during those two years of peace abroad and at home, I was conscious at times of an emptiness within myself, a little isolated vacuum of nothingness. I fell to wondering if an active interest in state affairs would fill that emptiness. Would an opportunity ever arise? I doubted it since that was the one thing Napoleon denied me, but I found myself waiting hopefully, even patiently. I was waiting —how absurd it sounds!—for an event of as little seeming importance as a state visit to the opera.

It so happened that the baritone Massol, then on the point of retiring, was being given one of those quite often boring benefit performances. The program was depressing, including as it did the execution scene from an opera based on the tragic life of Mary, Queen of Scots. Despite the coldness of that January night, the vicinity of the Opera House, the Rue Lepelletier especially, was crowded with people when our carriage approached. Massol was a popular singer and the Emperor and Empress, assuring by their presence the success of his benefit, were acting with the utmost graciousness, even if one suspected that once again they were seizing an opportunity to play to the gallery.

"We are late," Napoleon said. "The performance will have begun by now."

"So much the better if the execution scene—"

The rest of my sentence was drowned by a sudden, violent explosion. It was followed almost immediately by a second and a third. The carriage rocked perilously but remained upright. All the gaslights in the street and those which had illuminated the front of the Opera House went out simultaneously.

"Eugenie?" Napoleon asked urgently in the darkness.

"I—I appear to be uninjured," I replied shakily.

"Splendid! Try to keep calm."

We sat in silence listening to the tinkling of the glass as it fell from the shattered windows, the pitiful neighing of the horses and the cries of the injured in the street. Torches were brought at last and Napoleon hurried up and down inspecting the damage and talking to the victims. Rouguet, the aide riding with us in the carriage, assured me that he was quite unharmed although blood was streaming from his face. Napoleon returned after a few moments, followed by a group of cheering people.

"As you see, the Empress is perfectly safe," he said, and to me in a whisper, "Speak to them, *chérie*."

"I beg you not to trouble about us," I said with that false calmness a severe shock sometimes gives one. "Please give your attention to the wounded."

"Bravo," Napoleon said approvingly.

The benefit performance was continuing as if nothing had happened. Adelaide Ristori's powerful voice floated out as the manager of the Opera House came to escort us into the auditorium. The audience, though intimidated by her shrieking, was seething with alarm as a garbled version of what had happened in the street was passed from row to row. A great shout rose from the front of the house as Napoleon and I entered the box and for the moment Ristori was silenced. Rouguet's blood had spotted the skirt of my white cashmere dress, and Napoleon's hat, which he waved to the audience, had been pierced in many places by bomb fragments.

At the end of the performance we drove back to the Tuileries where an impromptu reception had gathered to congratulate us on our escape. We learned then that our coachman and footmen had been badly injured, that a hundred and fifty people had been wounded and twelve killed.

Napoleon had escaped; I had escaped; we would always escape, or so Napoleon believed, but what of our son, a helpless baby? As soon as it was possible, I hurried to the nursery—Napoleon close on my heels—and there, as we stood at the cot, the horror of it all got the better of me and I wept bitterly.

"My faith is as unshaken as ever," Napoleon said softly. "While I live the Empire lives with me." He touched the sleeping Loulou gently. "Had I fallen tonight the Empire would have been consolidated by my death and would have lived on in my son."

"Aren't you afraid of further attempts?"

He looked at me with that blank stare of his, the stare which hid so many things. "Let us say that I have taken heed. Adequate provision shall be made for the future."

The Orsini Plot, as we called it, was the work of five men, four of whom were arrested in Paris. Orsini was the ringleader; his accomplices were Gomez, Rudio,

Pieri and Bernard. The four men who had been appre-
hended had come from England where the plot was
hatched. Their bombs had actually been made in England by an engineer named Taylor. Bernard, the fifth
man, was a French doctor who had remained in England. All five were political refugees.

To my dismay, our relations with England were immediately strained. The French newspapers raged un-
ceasingly. Even the official *Moniteur* quoted certain
army leaders who demanded "satisfaction" of the country which had given shelter to the "monsters" who had
struck at the life of their beloved Emperor. An official
protest was sent to Victoria's government, but Napoleon himself apologized for the *Moniteur's* story and
hoped privately that the storm he was unable to quell
would die down of its own accord.

And then, taking me completely by surprise, in an
Imperial message to the Senate, Napoleon urged a
change in the Constitution, and the Senate, with only a
few Liberals objecting, accepted the suggestion. In the
event of the Emperor's death, I, the Empress, was to
become Regent during my son's minority.

"Are you satisfied?" Napoleon asked me.

"You were always so set against my meddling in state
affairs."

"As Regent you would be ruling, not meddling."

"I think I understand. I may never be Regent. I must
still not meddle."

"You may become Regent sooner than you think."

"Napoleon!"

"Not through my death." However, he refused to en-
large on this puzzling statement and went on gaily,
"You have the liberty to discuss affairs of state with me
and my ministers. Let us begin with Plonplon's marriage to Victor Emmanuel's daughter Clothilde. Do you
favor the match?"

"How old is the Princess?"

"Barely sixteen. She would rather become a nun than marry any man."

"Plonplon is a monster. I certainly do *not* approve."

"So speaks the tender-hearted woman, not the Regent-elect. Victor Emmanuel and I have reached an agreement. The girl is resigned to her fate. Victor Emmanuel has convinced her that she will be performing a very special act of patriotism."

"May I know why this alliance is so necessary to you?"

"As Regent-elect, *you* tell *me*."

"Victor Emmanuel aims at the unification of the Italian states. He can see no possibility of that while Austria holds Lombardy and Venetia and really dominates the Italian Peninsula. I think he would go to war with Austria, except that his Sardinian army isn't strong enough. He supported you in the Crimea hoping, perhaps, to win an alliance against Austria later. You once spoke of bait for the trap?"

"Ah yes, la Belle Castiglione. But proceed, *chérie!*"

"You said you would enter the trap only if it suited you. Now we have this marriage. Do *you* want war with Austria?"

"Austria is a threat to the peace of Europe. Only a united, independent Italy, an Italy strongly allied to France, can remove that threat."

"Another war is unthinkable, Napoleon."

"If Austria behaves herself, war may be averted."

"Even so, a united Italy would be a threat to the Pope and the Papal states."

"Now you speak as an ardent Catholic and think only of the Holy Father."

"I thought you were an ardent Catholic yourself."

"We are not concerned here with religion."

"Your greatest strength as Emperor of France comes from the support of the French Catholics."

Napoleon shook his head. "My greatest strength, my *only* strength, lies within myself. We must think of the

177

dynasty. So must the French Catholics. They must be made to see—*you* must be made to see—that this is not a religious issue."

"Do you expect Austria to behave herself?"

"Frankly, no."

"Then a war is inevitable?"

"If Austria provides a reasonable excuse, yes."

A reasonable excuse, I thought. Reasonable excuses, entirely unreasonable in their "reasonableness," had been the cause of many a war.

"Orsini is an Italian patriot," Napoleon went on. "He wants a united Italy but not through what he calls French interference. Hence his attempt to kill me. Orsini is no ordinary anarchist. There may be others waiting to follow him, hoping to succeed where he failed. For that reason alone, I must waste no time in achieving my ambition for Italy."

Meanwhile, relations with England had become even more strained. There was talk of war in both countries and as far as the newspapers on both sides of the Channel were concerned, war had been declared already.

Napoleon sent a new ambassador to London. The diplomats conferred, the newspapers advised and scolded, and armchair generals in both countries cried out for vengeance. The situation deteriorated still furthur when the fifth conspirator, the French doctor who had remained in England, was brought to trial there and acquitted. Victoria and her ministers said it was an unjust verdict, diplomatic negotiations continued and finally, to my vast relief, a settlement was reached. The water was to be allowed to slip quietly under the birdge. The pen of the diplomat, if not that of the journalist, was mightier than the sword.

"Ill feeling remains," Napoleon said bitterly. "Our happy understanding with England is now reduced to a few polite and meaningless phrases."

"If Queen Victoria were to visit us again . . ." I suggested.

"It would be embarrassing meeting her, but yet . . ."

Lord Cowley was consulted and we learned that Victoria and Albert were soon to visit their daughter at Coblenz. Young Vicky was now married to Prince Frederick William of Prussia. That provided an acceptable excuse. If the Emperor cared to issue an invitation, they would call—as it were—in passing. No, they would not visit Paris, but the Emperor and Empress could, if it were convenient, meet them at Cherbourg. And so it was arranged, but Napoleon went first to Plombières.

"Plombières," ran the official announcement, "is the Emperor's favorite spa. His majesty is in poor health and will take the waters there."

Anyone could see that Napoleon was in poor health, but he need not have gone so far afield as Plombières. It so happened that Victor Emmanuel's Prime Minister was on the point of making a holiday visit to Germany and would pass through the spa en route. He and Napoleon met there secretly and secretly they committed France and Sardinia to war with Austria, should that country provide a reasonable excuse. It was a well-kept secret. Not even I discovered the truth of the Plombières meeting until Austria issued an ultimatum.

On reaching Cherbourg, Napoleon and I went aboard the Imperial yacht *Bretagne* in which we were later to sail for Brest en route for a state tour of Brittany. I have always liked the motion of a deck beneath my feet and enjoyed very much that little period of residence afloat in Cherbourg harbor. Shortly after our arrival, the *Victoria and Albert* appeared with an escort of six British warships. The *Bretagne* had an escort of nine French warships and at Cherbourg, waiting to be reviewed, an impressive military force was encamped. This deliberate show of arms made me feel uneasy. Napoleon was embarrassed, yes, but at the same time belligerent.

During the cool of that August evening, we went

179

aboard the *Victoria and Albert* unaccompanied by any members of the Imperial court. Prince Albert met us at the foot of the ladder. Queen Victoria, unattended as we were, was waiting on the deck above. I studied her curiously as Albert handed me up the ladder. She certainly had no intention of putting me to shame in the fashion race. She wore a crinoline, yes, but it was moderately proportioned and reminded me instantly of a wine tub.

Albert himself led me to the staircase, glanced at my enormous crinoline quizzically and handed me up safely.

"Splendid!" Victoria said, in relief.

"We had the gang-ladder and the staircase widened," Albert laughed.

Victoria now gave Napoleon her hand to kiss. Albert kissed mine. Victoria then saluted Napoleon briefly on each cheek. I saluted Albert in the same way. Napoleon and Albert shook hands. Victoria and I embraced. There was a momentary silence. We were embarrassed, all of us. Albert laughed nervously and bowed me to a chair.

"Your majesty is able to sit in that amazing contraption?"

I demonstrated, quite regally, that I was indeed able to sit. Victoria had already seated herself and was absently turning the pages of a book. She looked up guiltily.

"How rude of me! A most interesting book. *Jane Eyre*. Have you read it?"

"No," said I.

"I myself read only the English newspapers," Napoleon said gruffly.

"One should take little notice of what *they* say," Albert said quietly.

"French newspapers can be just as misleading," I interposed.

"Great harm can be done by the newspapers," Victoria added, with a quick little cough.

"In a country where the press is entirely free," said Napoleon.

"In such a country the government cannot hold itself responsible," Albert pointed out.

"I wonder if the weather is as hot in London as it is in Paris," I said, trying to change the subject.

"Perhaps even hotter," Victoria murmured.

"Censorship is not always sufficient," Napoleon persisted roughly. "In my country many things appear in print without my knowledge. Provocative statements are sometimes made contrary to my approval."

Victoria's eyes softened. He was apologizing for the French newspapers without exactly committing himself to an apology.

"The weather is so hot in London," she sighed, "that the ink has been known to reach boiling point in the inkpots—even those in use at the office of *The Times*."

Thus she, too, was apologizing for all that had been published by the London newspapers. For *The Times* had been particularly offensive to Napoleon.

"The heat in London this summer is so dreadful that we have all suffered from terrible headaches," Albert went on. "The state of the Thames is appalling, the smell frightful."

"We have never cared very much for London in the summer," Victoria said. "Even in winter I sometimes grow fretful."

There was another dragging silence.

"You must miss Vicky very much," I said.

"We miss her terribly." Victoria was fingering the book again. "*Jane Eyre*. A most interesting book, as I said. Shall we read a little of it together while the men inspect the yacht?"

Albert and Napoleon withdrew obediently. Victoria at once cast the book aside and smiled mischievously.

"What an ordeal! Were you as nervous as I was?"

"My knees were shaking violently."

"We are still good friends, you and I?"

"Can you doubt it, Madame?"

Victoria made me sit at her side, patted my hand and told me with tears in her eyes that she loved me dearly and would always feel concern on my behalf. Her only wish, politics aside, was that we should live to enjoy many little talks together whenever it was possible to escape from our separate duties.

"You appear to be able to sit with greater ease in your crinoline than I in mine," she said.

"A clumsy sort of ease," I laughed, and told her about a recent invention, the slender collapsible steel frame which in Paris had done away with heavy petticoats and any sort of padding. "I'm wearing only one light underskirt, Madame. Such a heavenly relief."

"I wondered why you weren't sweating," Victoria said brightly. "And now—babies! You are not yet expecting another?"

"No," I said, and told her the reason.

"How very sad. Vicky is expecting a baby. How strange to think that I shall soon be a grandmother. Vicky is not very strong. I shall advise her to have chloroform. I had it myself at my last two confinements. I hesitated the first time because of religious prejudice, but as I listened to the arguments I grew very, *very* angry. It was a sacrilege to rob childbirth of pain, they told me, adding that chloroform was a decoy of Satan. God meant women to suffer. It was a divine means of causing them to cry out to Him for help. Can you believe it? Is God as cruel a Father as that? But how I run on! Naturally you are wondering why I dismissed our husbands and what I want to say to you privately."

"The thought was in my mind," I smiled.

"We are very worried about the Emperor's health. We had heard that he was looking ill. I sense an irritation in his manner that was never there before. Ill health is often the cause of that, and other things, too. Apathy, for example, even infirmity of purpose. One's judgment can also be impaired and in a monarch that is very dangerous. I am not suggesting that the peace of Europe is at stake because of the Emperor's ill health, but it *could* be."

Fortunately Victoria spoke of "ill health," not "further excesses."

"Your responsibility is very great," she went on. "You are clever and kind. You have a great love of humanity, a great hatred of war. The lessons of the past are well known to you. I do urge you, Madame, to apply them in any attempt you may make to shape the Emperor's policy. Forgive me if I alarm you about his health, but I should like you to look to the future bravely, envisaging all manner of possibilities."

"Are you concerned about the Emperor's Italian policy?" I asked frankly.

"I know very little about it. Nor would I permit you to confide in me. My chief concern is the unstable conditions left by the Crimean War, conditions which seem to encourage a warlike attitude on the part of Sardinia. All wars are mistakes, and the Crimean War was no exception. If the outcome is another conflict, the peace of Europe may be shattered for many years to come. Wars decide nothing. They breed only other wars."

The *Victoria and Albert* and the *Bretagne* remained together in Cherbourg harbor for three days. There was a luncheon for our guests ashore at the Prefecture and a state dinner aboard the *Bretagne*. Napoleon could not seem to rid himself of his embarrassment and was often silent, his face a mask. When he proposed our visitors' health at the dinner, I sensed an emptiness beneath his seemingly cordial words, a meaningless pomposity, as if he were dictating a leading article for one of the newspapers: "The fact that the rulers of England and France are dining together now is proof enough that hostile passions, encouraged by certain unfortunate incidents, can change neither the friendship of the two crowns nor the desire of our peoples to remain at peace."

He was roundly applauded. Prince Albert made a gracious speech in reply, but even his words rang meaninglessly in my ears. Napoleon invited the royal couple to remain at Cherbourg for a military review but they declined and sailed the next morning.

"The Prince distrusts me," Napoleon said as we waved from the poop of the *Bretagne*. "To him my display of military and naval strength means only one thing—a challenge, if not an actual threat. How wrong he is! I differ from my uncle in at least one respect. I know better than to make war on England. My eyes are turned in another direction as Albert will presently discover."

Less than a year after the Cherbourg meeting, Austria issued her ultimatum to Sardinia, calling on Victor Emmanuel to disarm. He refused to comply with the demand and an Austrian army marched into northern Italy. There, then, was Napoleon's "reasonable" excuse. He promptly declared war on Austria and announced that he would lead the French army himself. France accepted it as a democratic war, and so did England, though reluctantly.

And what of me? I became Regent overnight, not through Napoleon's death but because of a war I was powerless to avert. The whole world knew that. My worst enemies knew it. I have been held responsible for many things, but nobody—not even Plonplon— blamed me for the Franco-Austrian War. He wouldn't! It was a short war and ended in victory for France. To blame would have been to praise.

My "rule" was brief and ineffectual. I rolled bandages, made speeches and presided over the Council of State. One speech sticks in my mind, and how proud of it I was at the time: "No matter how difficult my task

184

may be, I feel confident in my loyal French heart that I shall be able to carry it through. I am encouraged, gentlemen, by your faithful co-operation and by the support of the Nation which, during the absence of its self-elected ruler, is unlikely to offend against a woman and a child."

That little effort, I remember, was described as a speech of "regal dignity." But surely—heaven help me—I was indulging in a bit of editorial writing myself.

Oh yes, a brief and ineffectual "rule," for Napoleon still ruled firmly from a distance. Nevertheless, that first Regency of mine had one important outcome. Napoleon permitted me thereafter to sit at his side at certain council meetings. I was being taken seriously at last in the world of politics as well as the world of fashion. Or so I told myself . . .

Chapter Fourteen

I WAS DREAMING last night about dear Pauline
Metternich. Pauline was the wife of the new Austrian
Ambassador, Prince Richard Metternich, who took up
his duties in Paris soon after the end of the Franco-Austrian War. I don't think Napoleon ever fully approved
of Pauline Metternich—she had a neat way of manag-
ing her husband, for one thing—but I liked her instantly
and soon she was one of my closest friends. Her first
words, when the formality of the official reception was
over and done with, were outrageously provocative.

"France has won one war, but I, on behalf of the
women of Austria, propose to win another of greater
importance."

"And what is that, Princess?"

"Madame, it is my firm intention to challenge your
leadership in the world of fashion. Can you blame me?
In beauty alone I could never compete. Just look at my
face! One would think an ape had fathered me."

"Oh, come now, Princess!"

"This is not a peace conference. One need not be polite. But not the *mind* of a monkey. I never imitate."

"You are certainly *à la mode* at this moment, Princess. That in itself gives the lie to your claim. *I* made
the crinoline fashionable; *you,* like all the rest, have
copied it."

Pauline chuckled. "I shall dispense with the crinoline
and others will follow my lead."

She was thirty at that time, four years younger than

myself. The face of a monkey? In part that was true enough, yet there was beauty in her animated countenance, the beauty of a madcap joy of life. Nor could I find any fault with her figure or at all events those portions not hidden by the crinoline. She had a slim waist and her shoulders were superb. Her hair, which she wore loose instead of dragged back cruelly in the prevailing Chinese fashion, was a mass of golden lights.

"What a frighteningly dull court," she announced, when she came to take tea with me that first afternoon. "Are they dumb or congenital idiots, Your Majesty's ladies-in-waiting? I tried to talk to them about everything under the sun, but all they could say, one after the other like a cageful of parrots, was 'We have not Her Majesty's ear.'"

"Obviously you were questioning them about me. In actual fact they have my ear in all things but politics."

"Politics bore me, Madame. Is the size of the Imperial slipper, for instance, a dark political secret? And the *dress* of your ladies! To say nothing of the way they drag back their hair! Not one of them, I swear, is able to close her eyes. How ridiculous! How depressing! Is it true that even at Biarritz you still insist on formal clothes? I see by your face that it is. How many falls do your ladies take when tripping across the sand in a crinoline? I suggest short skirts for such outings."

"Would you advise your own Empress to wear short skirts?"

"We-ell . . ."

"I doubt it very much!"

"True," said Pauline, smiling mischievously. "But then *she* was born a Princess."

Amazingly enough I was in no way affronted, though I tried to be. Indeed, I laughed with real abandon and my Imperial dignity—how stifling it had become of late!—fell from me. Pauline above all others was able to make me laugh at myself. In time, I came to call her my Ambassadress of Fun.

During tea, which we enjoyed all the more by throwing off our slippers, she told me that she had always been in revolt against the strict, stiff etiquette of the Austrian court. Her pranks there had shocked everybody; the older members referred to her as "The Terror," but she was tolerated because the Emperor himself tolerated her. Pauline, ran the Imperial decree, could not be blamed for having inherited so many eccentricities from a most eccentric father.

"Father was Count Sandor, a Hungarian nobleman and one of the Emperor's close friends. He was a reckless horseman and at one time or other broke every bone in his body. In the end he broke his neck. He could never resist a bet, you see, and when somebody dared him to drive his coach-and-four into the Danube from the top of a high cliff, he did precisely that. And now, Your Majesty, let us discuss the first engagement of our private fashion war."

"People will laugh at you if you appear at court without a crinoline."

"On the contrary—they'll copy me."

"Not while *I* wear a crinoline, Princess."

"We shall see, Empress."

But to my surprise, Pauline clung to the crinoline during the following months. Clung indeed! Certainly it didn't cling to her. That would have been impossible, so large and well nigh uncontrollable had it become by the example I set myself. Pauline went even further than I, until it seemed that every doorway at the Austrian Embassy, if not at the Tuileries, would have to be widened. Her tactics were clear enough: she aimed at making the crinoline preposterous. Finally, when she appeared at one of my "Mondays," the monstrous crinoline she wore prevented her complete entry. There she hung, the upper part of her body in the room, the rest of her held back in the vestibule and not very modestly, I must say.

"Your Majesty's Mondays are much too inconvenient," she complained. "All I can do is set aside a special day of the week for myself."

My Mondays were an established institution. Even Napoleon approved of them and graced them unfailingly with his Imperial presence. My match-making days, he used to call them, for I brought many young people together at my informal Monday parties and often enough the result was a satisfactory if not always an entirely happy marriage. Receiving my guests in a special boudoir, two or three at a time, I joined them later for an informal ball either in the *Salon du premier Consul* or the Salle des Maréchaux.

Pauline duly established her Thursdays and I went gladly to the first one, though rather in the guise of an enemy spy preparing for battle. Pauline had gathered together the most ill-assorted crowd of people: bohemians rubbed shoulders with legitimate artists and writers; aristocrats with stern republicans; opera singers with cancan dancers. But her crazy, happy knack of making everybody feel at home bound us all closely together in an evening of wild enjoyment.

My sister Paca was with me that night. Dear Paca, she tried hard to be shocked and wondered what I saw in Pauline Metternich, but soon her eyes, too, were sparkling and she was enjoying herself as much as I was. It had been a great joy to me to see so much more of Paca; she and her family were now spending much time in France. I had in fact built a new house for her, the Hôtel d'Albe, in the Avenue des Champs Élysées. Mama was staying there at this time and both of us worried about Paca's health. Paca herself made light of it. A mere pain in the back was nothing to be concerned about, she said.

We left Pauline's soon after midnight and wondered a trifle anxiously what Napoleon would say when a description of the party reached his ears. Pauline had actually been smoking a cigar when we withdrew and singing a very risqué song with a popular singer from one of the music halls.

The fashion war was interrupted before any serious fighting could take place by a state visit to the territories which had come to France as a result of the Franco-Austrian War. We gained Savoy and Nice—or rather we regained them, for they had been part of France until the fall of the first Napoleon—and Victor Emmanuel annexed Modena, Parma and Romagna. Nevertheless, Victor Emmanuel was far from satisfied and still angry with Napoleon for making peace before the whole of Italy could be unified. I myself was horrified at this attack on Papal territory, while the French Catholics were beginning to regard my husband with loathing. His Holiness excommunicated Victor Emmanuel and came close to excommunicating Napoleon also. I argued violently at council meetings, pleaded with Napoleon in private, and wept bitterly. But the most I was able to achieve was the promise that the French garrison at Rome should remain stationed there to protect the Pope from any attack planned by his enemies.

After visiting Savoy and Nice, Napoleon and I embarked on the longest journey of our reign. We sailed from Marseilles and landed at Algiers, to be received there with the utmost pomp and ceremony by French officials and Arab chiefs alike. Meanwhile, the position in Italy was growing worse. Garibaldi, a revolutionary agitator, had already taken the whole of Sicily and was marching on Naples, while Sardinian and Papal troops were fighting in Umbria. Nobody knew Napoleon's plans. He merely said that it was a good time to be away from Paris. Several of his ministers wanted war with our former ally, Victor Emmanuel; Napoleon did not. A united Italy, yes, but let Victor Emmanuel and Garibaldi do the fighting.

A special messenger was waiting when we reached Algiers. Napoleon received him alone, and after they had been closeted for only a few moments he emerged in gravefaced silence.

"Is it bad news from Italy?" I asked.

"We have certain duties to perform," he evaded. "Let us perform them."

It was a very full day, a happy, exciting day. I rode a camel—imagine sitting on a camel in a crinoline!—I received the obeisances of the Arab chiefs with a thrill such as I had never felt before, I ate strange native food with relish, and that night at a ball given by the Governor-General of Algeria, I danced until I was exhausted.

"I felt like a princess of the desert, not an Empress," I told Napoleon afterwards.

"You charmed everybody," he said gruffly. "The success of this visit is entirely due to you."

"The Arabs admired your horsemanship."

"As I intended."

"You sound anything but pleased, Napoleon."

He took my hand roughly in his. "*Chérie,* that messenger this morning—He brought a telegram—"

"The Pope has been attacked?"

"The telegram came from your mother. It said that your sister is seriously ill."

Even then I had no suspicion of the real truth. But Napoleon's despicable action in not informing me at once made me fly into a rage. I told him wildly that he cared nothing for my personal feelings. Had he told me that morning, I would have been too distracted to charm anybody, as he knew only too well.

"Duty, duty, duty!" I sobbed.

"*Chérie,* I wanted you to enjoy yourself with a free mind."

"A lie and you know it!"

"As you wish."

"I must leave for Paris at once. *At once,* Napoleon!"

His face became inscrutable, his voice impersonal. "Fetes have been organized, receptions, tours of inspection. As Emperor and Empress, we are in no position to please ourselves."

I remember very little of the rest of our stay. As a professional Empress, I acquitted myself admirably—or so I was told. But I do remember vividly how Napoleon sent Pepa to me the moment we sailed and came himself, nervously and reluctantly, while the weeping woman was still at my side. He begged me to be brave, saying that it was the will of God.

"Do you think me entirely heartless?" Napoleon said. "I wanted to prepare you gradually. I had hoped you would guess the worst."

"I don't believe you. Seriously ill indeed! When Paca was lying *dead* in Paris!"

"Forgive me, Eugenie."

"All you cared about was making sure I'd complete the rest of my duties."

"Paca was dead. Telling you earlier would have made no difference. But for the invention of the telegraph, we would still be in ignorance."

"And that makes everything right! Logic, male logic!"

Bad weather delayed our voyage. As a result, I was deprived of the privilege of seeing my sister's face in death, of following her coffin to the grave. Yes, in securing a crown for myself I had trampled on my own heart. Even the terrible news that the Papal forces had been shockingly defeated left me unmoved. His Holiness was safe, I was told; the French garrison would see to it that no harm touched him. Napoleon was looking after him, but he showed no dismay over the fact that he had been deprived of the greater part of his territories.

"The best remedy for grief is hard work," Napoleon pronounced. "We miss you at the council meetings—your fiery opposition, your shattering comments. I beg you, *chérie*—"

"I'll never attend another meeting!"

"Plonplon will be delighted."

Even that statement left me unmoved.

"I think I know how you feel," Napoleon went on quickly. "You want to get away from everything. Well now, that might be a remedy. Would it please you to go to England for a time? Or rather Scotland, which would mean that you must pass through England. You would travel incognito, of course, taking only two or three people with you. And while in London you would avoid a meeting with our ambassador."

"You seem intent on making plans for me."

"No one would question your desire to travel abroad as a means of recovering from your grief. Scotland, however, would be a mere pretext. England and a private visit to Queen Victoria would be your objective."

"But why, Napoleon?"

"I want to discover the Queen's private thoughts about the moves I've made of late."

"You are trying to make good use of Paca's death!"

"My rule is to seize any opportunity that presents itself. Victoria is still your friend, whatever she may think of me. She is also a soft-hearted woman. She will weep for you and with you."

"How harsh you sound!"

"A flood of tears would do neither of us any good at this moment, but a whole torrent of them may help— with Victoria."

I left Paris one dull November day accompanied by two ladies-in-waiting, an equerry and one of Napoleon's aides. Reservations had been made at Claridge's Hotel in London for the Comtesse de Pierrefonds and her party. Napoleon saw me off at the Gare du Nord. Pepa was there also with a message from Pauline Metternich: during my absence there would be no attack on the crinoline. I remember that I laughed with almost real feeling. Thank God for Pauline and her sense of humor!

I spent two days in London before going to Scotland. My heavy mourning prevented any recognition when I went shopping—oh no, not for *clothes,* but for English toys for Loulou and presents for dear Paca's children. In Scotland, however, I was recognized, and much was made of the fact that not since Mary Queen of Scots, then the widow of a young French King, had a royal lady of France set foot in Scotland. I visited Holyrood to inspect Mary's relics and I wondered somberly if relics of mine would ever be preserved in Paris.

Leaving Scotland and its mists and fogs, I found more mists and fogs in London. A French diarist said that the weather in both places was in harmony with the melancholy of my mind. Far be it from me to quibble with his dreary romanticism. My heart, coming suddenly to life again, was in Paris with my little son, and—oddly—with Pauline Metternich. Thank God for Pauline! The Battle of the Crinoline, frivolous as it may seem, was an important factor in bringing me back to normality.

At Claridge's I learned that Queen Victoria was anxious for the Comtesse de Pierrefonds to visit her at Windsor. Accordingly, I slipped away from London unattended—and found myself bewildered when I had to buy my ticket at the railway station. Not once since becoming Empress had I attended to such mundane matters myself. Fortunately I had enough money in my purse, and during the short train journey I began to enjoy my new, if temporary, independence. An equerry met me at Windsor station and Prince Albert himself at the Castle gates.

"The Comtesse de Pierrefonds, I presume?"

"None other, Your Highness."

Albert led me at once to the private drawing room where Victoria was waiting. They were overjoyed to see me, they said, even though I came in sadness. I was with friends again, that I knew without question. Old friends, dear friends. Victoria and I wept a little, but there was no flood of tears. The thought that Napoleon had sent me for a specific purpose, that I had come under false colors, covered me with shame, and I resolved that politics would not be discussed unless Victoria herself introduced the subject.

"Did you observe," she said darkly, "that we now have special smoking compartments in our trains?"

I nodded gravely. "In fact, Madame, I occupied one by mistake."

"How dreadful for you!"

During lunch she asked about my son. "He will be four next March, won't he? How time does fly! I'm told he is a very spirited little prince."

"He's often naughty," I laughed.

"And you, of course, have the task of correcting him."

"Naturally! Loulou can do no wrong, not in his father's eyes."

The boy was actually no naughtier than most healthy boys of his age. His only real fault was the stubbornness he had inherited from Napoleon, but this his father regarded as a sign of inner strength. Almost always when I corrected the child, Napoleon gave him presents, embraced him, pampered him. The Emperor, people said, was a loving father; the Empress, a stern, unfeeling mother.

Victoria laughed gently. "It is often a mother's difficult duty, correcting the children. My husband was always just as weak as yours in that direction. Is Miss Shaw entirely satisfactory?"

Miss Shaw, our English nanny, had been appointed on Victoria's recommendation. She spoiled Loulou almost as much as his father did, but I liked and trusted her. Perhaps the most remarkable thing about the red-cheeked, motherly Miss Shaw was her implicit faith in the healing qualities of bacon. Whenever Loulou suffered some childish ailment, she'd say, "One rasher of fried bacon will cure him instantly." I told Victoria this and she laughed heartily.

"And just think," she said pensively, "in the not too distant future, you will be faced with the problem of finding a suitable wife for the Prince Imperial. Oh, the difficulty of these royal alliances. You must choose well for your country's sake, but if at the same time you choose well for your son's, I shall be very happy for you all."

Politics? There was an opening here but Victoria refrained, as I did, from taking it. Instead she spoke lovingly of her first grandchild, Vicky's son William. He was thriving, in spite of a stunted left arm. Such a sad affliction! Such a terrible cross to bear!

The difficulty of royal alliances indeed! The danger of the choice, however well one might think one has chosen! Happily Victoria was unable to look into the future. That particular grandson became William II, the German Emperor, the ambitious Kaiser, the savage warmonger whose cross the whole world bore from the outbreak of war in 1914 until his defeat in 1918.

"I am marrying off another daughter," Victoria ran on. "Soon I shall be a practiced matchmaker."

"And your eldest son, the Prince of Wales?" I asked.

"Ah yes, dear Bertie! He is now twenty. The choice of a daughter-in-law is more difficult for a mother than the choice of a son-in-law, but I am much taken with all I hear of Princess Alexandra of Denmark."

I turned to Prince Albert. "And you, Sir?"

Albert laughed mischievously. "Have I any say in the matter? I am the husband of the house, yes, but not the master."

Victoria laughed fondly. "Albert loves to tease me. Everybody knows that I rely on him in all things and trust his judgment fully. We women are not made for governing."

I sensed the perfect accord between them just as I sensed, the moment Albert spoke again, that Victoria's political point of view was to be outlined by the husband, whether or not he were the master.

"How would our alliance with Denmark be regarded in France?" he asked. "Speak," he added with a laugh, "as the Comtesse de Pierrefonds, an interested observer."

"The Emperor and his ministers would surely welcome England's alliance with a friendly power to the north of Prussia."

"And Prussia herself?"

I hesitated. Prussia, of which Vicky's father-in-law was then Prince Regent, had shown concern at Napoleon's annexation of Nice and Savoy. Prussia, therefore, would rather see the Prince of Wales married to a German princess, or so I thought.

"The Comtesse de Pierrefonds," I said diplomatically, "has little understanding of Prussian sentiment in that direction."

"There is a general feeling in Europe," he went on, "that Frenchmen are being taught to regard German territory as their own property. Does Madame la Comtesse feel there is any truth in it?"

"How can she, knowing as she does that the Emperor made peace with Austria rather than run the risk of war with Prussia?"

"Prussia is not the whole of Germany, Madame."

"War could bind all the German states together," I said, unknowingly uttering a prophecy.

"My dear, you are beginning to bore the Comtesse," Victoria broke in. "Have you had time to do any shopping in London, my dear?"

Thus obliquely she told Albert that he had made his point, but I managed to get in the last word, politically.

"A *little* shopping," I laughed, "but I might as well have remained in Paris to do it, the London shops are so filled with French goods. But," I corrected, "the French shops are also filled with English goods. Englishmen may shop in peace in Paris, if they wish, and

Frenchmen in London. The Comtesse de Pierrefonds, as an interested observer, believes that nothing will ever prevent it."

"Nothing, please God," Victoria said.

When we parted she spoke of my dear visit and the pleasure it had given her. She sent affectionate remembrances to Napoleon, but from her voice I knew that she no longer trusted him nor felt for him any real affection.

"We look hopefully to the future," she said finally, "*Your* future and France's."

Her meaning was clear enough: I must endeavor to shape Napoleon's policy.

"At the Gare du Nord," I said, "the Comtesse de Pierrefonds will cease to exist and the Empress will hurry to the council chamber."

Leaving England in excellent physical and mental health, I felt amazingly alert. My future and France's future were one and the same thing, and that "thing" represented the future of my son. When he became Napoleon IV, he would, through his mother's efforts, inherit an Empire at peace with the whole world. Confident of success, I was ready for two battles, the Battle of the Council Board and the Battle of the Crinoline.

Undoubtedly the latter sounds frivolous from the male point of view. But what fools men are when it comes to understanding women. An apparent preoccupation with fashion is often a means of steady concentration on higher things, as well as the mortification of other women and the conquest of the mere male. *Conquest* did I say! What did I find at the Tuileries after a month's absence? I found the door of the council chamber firmly closed against me!

Chapter Fifteen

THE SIGHT OF the Tuileries, which I liked least of all the Imperial palaces, depressed me a little. It seemed as if, in spite of all my hopes for the future, I was returning to a prison. I felt happier, however, on reaching my own apartments. My favorite chair was in its right place before a brightly burning fire and there were flowers everywhere.

"From the Emperor," Pepa said scornfully.

"A very charming gesture."

"Ha!" she barked. "Your Majesty proposes to attend the dinner party tonight?"

"Certainly."

"How headstrong we are! I shall inform the Emperor that the Empress is much too tired."

"Nonsense! A little gaiety will be good for me."

"Gaiety? Ha! Well, we shall see."

The meaning of her "Ha!" became all too clear when I joined the assembled guests in the *Salon d'Apollon*. La Belle Castiglione! There she stood with Plonplon and his young wife Clothilde, a smug expression on her face as she glanced at Napoleon who was chatting with Richard Metternich. Castiglione, an honored guest at an intimate dinner party!

Castiglione looked even lovelier than when I had first seen her four years ago, and much more self-assured—if that were possible. I took quick note of her nymph-like figure, her flashing green eyes, her smooth pink-tinged arms and neck and boiled with fury. I had tolerated the *affaire,* yes, but never before had I been called upon to tolerate her presence at a private dinner party. Napoleon had pursued her with secrecy and after peace was made with Austria had shown no concern when she had departed for Turin, apparently to rejoin her complaisant husband.

"Flowers!" I hissed, when Napoleon joined me.

"I hope you liked them, *chérie.*"

"Obviously you sent them to the wrong place!"

Instantly his face became a mask. "You have yet to greet the Comtesse de Castiglione."

"How very impolite of me!"

"The Comtesse has come to Paris on a very special mission—"

"Ha!" said I, my voice sounding exactly like Pepa's.

"—and must be shown every courtesy," he concluded. His imperturbability was absolutely infuriating.

"Why not speak the truth?" I said. "Unpalatable, yes, but more acceptable."

"Shall we go in to dinner?" he asked.

Plonplon blundered up and took my arm; Napoleon took Clothilde's, and that was that.

"How pleasing to see that you have come out of mourning at last, Madame," Plonplon murmured.

I had done so unwillingly, but how glad I was that Pepa, knowing what faced me, had persuaded me to wear a simple white velvet dinner dress. The Empress in deep mourning, shrouded, isolated—*that* would have been a mighty triumph for Castiglione. The simplicity of my attire that night, I'm happy to say, made her look cheaply overdressed for all her aristocratic breeding.

"One had wondered," she said, in no way dismayed by my refusal to greet her, "why Your Majesty should choose to go to Scotland in winter, but one realizes now that you had a good reason for facing that dreadful climate."

"Indeed?"

"Your Majesty knew that the cold weather would restore your health and increase your beauty."

"That is what we all think," said Napoleon.

Pauline Metternich laughed serenely. "I myself would gain only chapped fingers and a red nose. And so, I feel sure, would Madame de Castiglione."

"The Sardinian climate would be kinder to both of you," said Plonplon, thus introducing the subject of Victor Emmanuel and Italy and bringing a slight frown to Napoleon's face. "And as for its influence upon men, all I can suggest is that it breeds a race of fearsome warriors. How long will it be, I wonder, before Victor Emmanuel becomes king of the whole of Italy?"

"What do you say, Comtesse?" I asked.

The wretched Castiglione shrugged her lovely shoulders languorously. "As everybody knows, I once had a place in the King of Sardinia's bed but never one at his council table. Politics are beyond my understanding and bore me."

"The bed and the council table are often one and the same thing, or so history teaches," said Pauline Metternich.

The dinner, an unpleasant one for me—if not for Napoleon—came to an end at last and Plonplon was asked to propose my health. He did so with a heartiness that surprised me, until I saw that his eyes were on Castiglione. And in order to make his meaning clear, he referred to me once as Madame la Comtesse.

"But forgive me," he laughed, as Napoleon coughed pointedly, "the incognito has been dropped. Naturally I speak of Her Majesty the Empress, not Madame la Comtesse de Pierrefonds."

Nobody was deceived. Plonplon had toasted Castiglione.

"The poor Emperor is in for a bad quarter of an hour," he drawled as he led me back to the drawing room. "No one will blame him if he takes refuge at the Rue Matignon this night." He waited for me to ask the obvious question, showed no disappointment when I refrained and added sagely, "Be wise, Cousin. Smile and accept the inevitable. Only a fool comes between a dog and his bone."

Normally we spent two hours in the drawing room with our guests, but on this occasion Napoleon, the considerate husband, explained that I was very tired after my long journey and dismissed them early. Then he bade me goodnight in the presence of my ladies, murmured the word, work, and went straight to his study. Thus deprived of the chance to make a scene, I raged at Pepa until the poor creature burst into tears.

"I tried to keep you from the dinner party," she sobbed.

"Precisely!" I said unreasonably. "And if you had succeeded, fool that you are, it would now be said that I, the Empress, was afraid to face the Emperor's mistress."

"I can never do the right thing," Pepa moaned. "Even if I had written to you in England and told you the truth, that, too, would have been wrong."

"Nonsense! It was your duty to forewarn me."

And then the whole story came out. Castiglione had come back to Paris two months before my departure for England. Napoleon had taken a house for her in the Rue Matignon and there, strangely enough, she had remained in hiding as it were. After my departure, she had emerged and came many times to the Tuileries, both publicly and privately.

"She will never come again," I said furiously.

The morning after my return from England the routine of my normal day at the Tuileries was resumed almost as if there had been no interruption. And I knew that Napoleon, maintaining his own routine, would have no speech with me until, by long established habit, we took lunch together. Immediately after breakfast, a very light meal I scarcely touched, I went through an accumulation of accounts with Pepa, my self-styled treasurer.

"Are you still exacting special discounts of which I am supposed to be ignorant?" I asked grumpily.

"There is much competition for Your Majesty's patronage," she said, cringing but unafraid. "Pepa on occasion accepts the presents which are thrust upon her."

My next task was to read the many petitions which had been gathering dust during my absence. Damas-Hinard, my secretary, had marked those he considered worthy of immediate charity, those which were doubtful and those which were patently the work of professional cadgers. There was still time before lunch to visit the widows of three soldiers who had died in the Crimea; and this I did, going forth as usual in a hired carriage, Pepa at my side jealously holding the purse. There was even time to call at one of the hospitals in which I took a personal interest.

Frustratingly enough, Napoleon and I were not alone at the luncheon table. My request, conveyed to him through Pepa and his secretary, that we should have complete privacy had been deliberately ignored. However, if habit still prevailed, my opportunity would come later when Napoleon rose from the table and accompanied me to my workroom, as I called my study-cum-boudoir, to smoke a cigarette before going about his own business.

"And now . . ." he said, pushing back his chair.

That was the usual signal.

We retired to my workroom. Napoleon made himself comfortable in a chair, lit a cigarette and looked at me with a benign expression on his face: His Imperial Majesty, Napoleon III. In a word, the King who could do no wrong.

"Tell me about your conversation with Victoria, *chérie*."

I gave him a brief account, the words all but choking me.

"Precisely what I expected," he commented. "I know even a little more than you were able to discover. Victo-

203

ria has warned one of her German relatives that the German states must look to their defenses."

"You sent me merely to get me out of the way. You were panting to bring Castiglione to court."

"She is here on a very special mission, as I told you. Because of her mission it is necessary that both you and I should receive her graciously." That benign expression still!

"She has denied any interest in politics. A very special mission indeed! Very well, Napoleon! Bring her to the next council meeting. Let her mission be fully discussed."

"She is here in an unofficial capacity. Official discussions are taking place with Victor Emmanuel's new Ambassador, Nigra."

"Pauline Metternich was right," I said scathingly. "The bed and the council table are often one and the same place."

Napoleon lit another cigarette. His hands shook slightly, but his voice was calm enough. "Secrets have never been wormed out of me in any bed or at any council table." He laughed shortly. "An occasional deliberate slip of the tongue, never more than that."

"May I know the nature of her mission?"

"Victor Emmanuel's eyes are fixed on Rome. He claims that without Rome, he will never have a fully united Italy."

"Do you agree?"

"I can see his point of view, but that, politically, doesn't mean that I agree to his occupying Rome. Our garrison is still there, guarding the Pope. Please remember that, Eugenie."

I looked at him doubtfully. "May we have a full discussion at the next council meeting?"

Napoleon rose abruptly. "Henceforth the council chamber is closed to you."

And with that he left me to my raging, troubled thoughts. Castiglione had forced him to accept her at court and I was compelled to do so also. I wondered if she had also forced him to keep me from the council chamber but—on reflection—doubted it. Knowing I disapproved of his anti-clerical policy, Napoleon himself would want to keep me out.

These thoughts remained at the back of my mind as the routine of the day continued. Damas-Hinard appeared a few moments after Napoleon left my workroom. He was an efficient secretary—old, thin, white-haired and so prone to bowing obsequiously that he rarely stood with a straight back. Some new petitions were set aside for my attention the next morning and then, until two o'clock, I dictated letters and wrote a private one to my mother in Spain.

Two of my ladies appeared on the stroke of two. The carriage and military escort were waiting and as usual, when the weather was fine, I went for a drive in the Bois de Boulogne. Long ago Napoleon had set the exact time for this drive. The Bois was a fashionable sauntering place in the middle of the afternoon, and there, at that time, the Empress exhibited herself in public, bowed to right and to left, smiled, waved, stopped to chat with friends and strangers alike, gave not a thought to any would-be assassin who might have been lurking there, then—drove back to the Tuileries. Her Imperial Majesty the Empress, gay as ever, beautiful, smiling, charitable, fearless. I, Eugenia! I beg your pardon, Frenchmen—I, *Eugénie*.

That day I returned earlier than usual from my drive. There was still time before dressing for dinner to read a small pile of Napoleon's letters and other documents Damas-Hinard had placed on my desk. This, after what Napoleon had said, surprised me. Amazing that I, the mouse that gathered up the Emperor's crumbs, should still be permitted to read his confidential papers. A quick glance, however, was enough to show me that nothing of political significance had been included, except a memorandum several pages in length on the relaxation of the newspaper censorship. But between the pages, left there obviously in error, was a very private letter. The writer addressed Napoleon as "Dearest Louis-Napoleon," reproached him for his recent neglect and signed herself "Anne-Marie."

"Ah, you found it," said Pepa, who had come to discuss my choice of gown for dinner. "La Castiglione is not the *only* one, you see. Paramount among the *putas*, but not always available. A formidable man, the Emperor. This Anne-Marie must have displeased him in some way. I could draw up a list of a dozen others and none of them as yet neglected."

"Do so then!"

"Presently, but at the moment clothes are more important."

They were, indeed they were, and I insisted upon a full inspection of the wardrobe I had left behind a month ago. This entailed a visit to the floor above where my clothes were stored. I seem to remember now that, at the time my dressing-lift—a convenience much appreciated by my ladies—had been installed Loulou had taken great delight in riding up and down in it. Sometimes he concealed himself beneath the mannequin on which the dress of my choice had been fitted. After the first time, when the young wretch really did frighten us, we always screamed in pretended alarm as he leaped out with a warlike whoop.

"Your Majesty's wardrobe is somewhat depleted," Pepa announced before I could comment on that fact myself. "Unhappily Your Majesty was away for the semi-annual reformation."

Reformation! I could but laugh. Pepa made it sound like an important period in history, strongly religious in flavor. What actually happened was that twice a year I weeded out the clothes I no longer wanted and gave them away, usually to Pepa and the under-maids. They, in their turn, sold them, not in France—Napoleon wouldn't permit that—but abroad.

"You actually took it upon yourself—" I began.

"Pepa could do no less. The rhythm of the Imperial year would have been destroyed had she hesitated."

"How many dresses did you keep for yourself?"

"It was wrong of Pepa, but she thought only of the future security of herself and her husband."

"You sold the blue muslin, the one with the yellow bows?" I asked angrily. "You knew I was fond of it."

"It had grown shabby."

"How much did you get for it?"

"Seventeen hundred francs."

"It cost only fifteen hundred. Never before has a dress of mine been sold for more than the original cost."

Pepa's eyes snapped greedily. "One must be thankful for the craziness of the Americans. Their country has become the most profitable market. They would even buy the Tuileries if it were possible to transport it across the Atlantic."

"Watch your step, Pepa," I warned. "I may yet be tempted to sell you to the Americans."

I chose a dress at random; my ladies fitted it onto the mannequin, an iron frame cast in my own shape, and then, in headless effigy, the Empress of France went down in the lift to the dressing room below. It came as a shock to me, once I was dressed and ready to go to dinner, to discover that the crinoline was beginning to bore me. What of my war with Pauline Metternich? I shrugged impatiently. I was the sworn protector of my own creation and that, heaven help me, was that.

In a rebellious mood I sought revolt elsewhere. I was free that night of any state duties and on such rare nights dinner was supposed to be an informal meal. Informal! What utter nonsense! At least ten people would dine with me—ladies-in-waiting, officials of my household, occasionally Napoleon himself. But whether or not he was present, etiquette as crushing as that of a state dinner would prevail. I sent for my chamberlain.

"Are we expecting the Emperor tonight?"

"No, Madame."

That was annoying. His absence would take the sting out of my revolt.

"Send everybody away. Let them dine where they will. Tell Bignet to serve my dinner, one course only, in the Blue Drawing Room. And—yes—on the tea table close to the fire."

"As Your Majesty wishes." The poor fellow was absolutely appalled.

"Wait, Monsieur! The Prince Imperial shall join me. Inform Miss Shaw at once."

That was worse, much worse. Loulou was not yet old enough to dine with adults. In any case, he was in bed, probably fighting off sleep. I was in revolt, you see, against myself, my strict ideas of parental discipline. And I was lonely too, isolated by those dark troubled thoughts which lurked in the back of my mind.

Miss Shaw, flustered and disapproving, brought the little Prince to me in his dressing gown and slippers. He climbed on my knee, a very sleepy little boy not really fighting off sleep.

"This is a dream, Mama."

"A nice one, darling?"

He yawned and pointed at Miss Shaw. "That's a witch. Nice one, though. Nice dream too."

Loulou was fast asleep by the time Bignet brought in the tea table. I ignored the food and sat there by the fire, holding my son close and telling myself that for these few moments I was an ordinary mother behaving in an ordinary fashion. I grew slowly calmer, then drowsy, and finally I fell asleep myself. A terrified Miss Shaw woke me at half-past ten. The Emperor had returned to the Tuileries!

"With Your Majesty's permission . . ." she gasped and, gathering Loulou up in her arms, she hurried away with him.

A few moments later Napoleon strode into the room.

208

"How displeased you look," I said happily.

"I hurried to the nursery, as usual, and found the bed empty," he gasped. "Imagine my thoughts! I alerted the guards, I— And then Miss Shaw came with Loulou in her arms and explained everything."

"I'm sorry, Napoleon."

"How unlike you to spoil the boy."

"I was spoiling myself. Did you have a pleasant dinner? Does your beautiful Castiglione possess a good chef?"

"I did not dine with the Comtesse."

I picked up the list of names which Pepa had placed on my desk.

"With Anne-Marie? Or Brigitte? Or Suzanne? Or . . . ?" Aloud I read down the whole list.

"I dined with Plonplon," he said. "What a waste of time—going to the trouble of compiling that list. The girls mean nothing to me, nothing whatever."

"They mean one thing surely!"

"Be patient, Eugenie, be patient." He seemed to be pleading with himself rather than with me. "I can't help myself. I feel that time is running out. I must fill every moment."

"Sit down. Smoke a cigarette. I want to talk to you."

Napoleon sank wearily into a chair and I offered him the box of cigarettes which was always in readiness on my desk.

"Please be brief," he said, thrusting aside the box.

"A council meeting has been called for tomorrow. I intend to be present. That is all I have to say."

"Are you threatening me with that list of names?" he asked stupidly, for I was flourishing it in his face. "Exposure unless I comply?"

"Exposure?" I dwelt on the word.

"A futile gesture, *chérie*. What is there to expose? Everybody knows already."

Exposure, I thought, but of a very different order. Exposure to the sort of ridicule which the Emperor of

France would never stomach. The threat of it, at all events.

"I shall be present at the council meeting. Goodnight, Napoleon."

It was really quite simple. Plonplon was a few minutes late for the meeting. The others had already followed Napoleon into the council chamber when the gross creature appeared, hurrying and panting a little under his great weight. I slipped behind him as he opened the door. Then I realized that my crinoline—those damned crinolines!—might betray me. It brushed against the door jamb with a distinct rattle. Plonplon turned—*I* turned with him—another, louder rattle. But I was now in the room and a moment later, while Plonplon was still gazing curiously up and down the corridor, I slipped quickly into his seat at the table. There were no other vacant seats. Dear Plonplon was obliged to stand, to pace up and down behind me, to gasp and snarl and make unpleasant remarks under his breath. I stole a sly glance at Napoleon. His face—how irritating!—remained inscrutable. Well, no matter! *That* would soon be changed. As deliberately as a judge I took from the neck of my dress a folded sheet of paper, unfolded it and placed it solemnly on the top of a pile of documents in front of the mighty Emperor.

"A memorandum, Sire. I earnestly beg Your Majesty to bring my suggestions to the attention of Your Majesty's most honored and honorable Privy Council."

As if mesmerized by my hypnotic stare, Napoleon began to read aloud: Under the present grave circumstances, and after carefully considering every possible exigency, I, the Empress . . .

Then he stopped, mesmerized no longer, and read on in silence, without the slightest flicker of emotion on his face. What he read was this: I, the Empress, have decided to withdraw from His Imperial Majesty's court.

Divorce, for obvious reasons, is in my mind, but neither I nor my religion countenance divorce. Therefore, while seeking shelter in England, a country ever hospitable to refugees, I shall instruct my legal advisers to negotiate the terms of a judicial separation.

"We are all attention, Sire," Plonplon barked.

"Quite," said Napoleon. "Her Majesty the Empress makes a suggestion which I, the Emperor, endorse most —hum—heartily."

I held my breath. Had I failed? Was it possible that—

"Her Majesty," the cunning fellow went on smoothly, "is of the opinion that autocracy is a grave mistake and that the very real damage done by our alienation of the clerical party should be offset by a steady wooing of the liberals. This suggestion arises out of Her Majesty's careful appraisal of our relaxation of the censorship, it in itself being a liberal gesture."

"Amazing!" Plonplon gasped.

Dazed as I was, I glanced at Thouvenal, the present Minister of Foreign Affairs and the most active enemy of the Pope in France. His eyes narrowed.

"Intolerable!" he rasped.

Napoleon rose. "Gentlemen, this is the shortest council meeting since my reign began. I beg you to retire and give Her Majesty's suggestion every consideration."

The ministers filed out. Plonplon followed them unwillingly. The Emperor and the Empress were left facing each other across the table.

"I would never have made such a suggestion, never!" I stormed.

"True. You lean to autocracy and the Church and in consequence hate liberalism. You hate it, I suggest, because Plonplon has set himself up as a liberal. He would set himself up as anything in his craving for popularity. Autocracy, I agree, is necessary in time of war. We now have peace. A liberal policy, carefully nurtured, will pre-

211

serve the peace. Be wise. Set aside your hatred of Plonplon. It comes between you and sound judgment."

"My judgment is sound enough in respect to the Church, as well as to your anti-clerical policy which is Plonplon's also. Dismiss him, as you've dismissed me. Do that and I'll abide by your ruling."

"Otherwise you really will seek a legal separation?"

"Yes!"

"I don't believe you, *chérie*. You would never separate yourself from your son. I even doubt if you would ever separate yourself from me. Your loyalty which you may well regard as a curse would prevent it."

"A curse, yes!" I all but wept.

Napoleon tore my memorandum into tiny pieces and stuffed them in his pocket. I rose and went miserably to the door.

"Wait!" Napoleon commanded. "The meeting is not yet closed. Two important members of the council are still present. If you have any other suggestions to make, let us discuss them now before bringing them up at the next full session."

"I'm not dismissed after all?" I said in wonder.

"No," Napoleon laughed, "you are much too resourceful to be set aside."

"And . . . Plonplon?"

"He remains, naturally, but please don't stir up any trouble about my loyalty to the Bonaparte clan."

"Castiglione will not be pleased."

"My *wife* is pleased."

"You will insist on my receiving her at court?"

"It is either that or your own absence from the council chamber."

"You give me no choice," I said chokingly.

"Splendid!"

"I shall oppose your anti-clerical policy again and again."

"That is understood. May I know your next step?"

"I want Thouvenal dismissed from office."

"It would make a good impression on French Catholics. Very well! Dismissed he is. Drouhn de Lhuys shall be brought back, You approve of that?"

"You could do much worse."

"You think, perhaps, that this is a gesture only—that my policy is unchanged? Well, who knows? I honor and respect the Pope as a spiritual ruler. I can do no less. In my own way I am as good a Catholic as you. But His Holiness as a temporal ruler? That is another matter. Nevertheless, I give you my word that no harm will come to him. I promise to leave our garrison at Rome as long as danger exists."

And with that I had to be satisfied. But a dismaying uneasiness touched me and, in spite of the promise, in spite of my reinstatement, I began to feel that I could no longer trust Napoleon. Oh, not because he held to one policy and I to another, but because I feared he was following a course as devious and secretive as that which had led to the Franco-Austrian War. Napoleon sometimes said that it was unwise to let one's left hand know what one's right hand was doing, but there were times, I often suspected, when his left hand was unaware of what it was doing.

Chapter Sixteen

AND NOW I have the all-important Battle of the Crinoline to look back on—pleasurably after all these years, if not completely so at the time.

"It appears that I have an ally though not one of my own choosing," I remember Pauline Metternich saying. "The Comtesse de Castiglione has been to Monsieur Worth, himself an enemy of the crinoline."

"Monsieur Worth? Who, pray, is he?"

"In actual fact, Mr. Worth. The fellow is an Englishman."

"You mean he's a dressmaker?"

"Yes."

"A *male* dictator of fashion? Ludicrous! Nobody will take him seriously."

Pauline chuckled richly. "He and I together will get you out of crinolines. After which, everybody will take him seriously."

There was a fancy dress ball at the Tuileries later that week, and rumor had it that Castiglione would appear in a costume designed especially for her by Mr. Worth, though she was heard to remark that no dressmaker, male or female, was capable of doing her superb figure complete justice.

"In that case," Pauline laughed, "we must challenge her to appear in the guise of Ingres' painting, 'La Source.' In a word—entirely nude."

Thereafter a number of anonymous letters reached the vain young woman. Pauline wrote six, carefully disguising her handwriting. I myself, following her lead, wrote three. It seemed a grand idea—all to the good if she accepted the challenge. Napoleon, accustomed as he was to such a display in private, would be vastly shocked over such an exhibition in public.

Castiglione arrived late at the ball but she had sent servants ahead of her to place in position a grotto of imitation rocks. Then she made a spectacular entry, wearing a shapeless sack which covered her from neck to feet. When all had recognized her, she drew a hood over her head, seated herself at the entrance of her cave and invited Napoleon to join her in deep meditation.

"Gladly, Madame Hermit!"

Castiglione crawled into the cave and Napoleon, wearing a Tudor costume, crawled after her on all fours, a by no means dignified sight. A delighted crowd of revelers gathered about the cave, Plonplon among them. A moment later there was a muffled giggle from within.

"Ah!" said Plonplon, thrusting his head and shoulders through the entrance.

"Ah!" cried the revelers as Plonplon drew back with a laugh, Castiglione's sack in one hand.

" 'La Source' in all her glory," he announced.

He then uttered a sharp command and Castiglione's servants slowly pushed the cave which was set on a platform equipped with wheels, from the Salle des Maréchaux. It was an hour before Napoleon reappeared, a nonchalant Napoleon smoking a cigarette. Castiglione followed a few moments later, wearing a Roman tunic such as Josephine had worn in the wild, abandoned days of the Directory. She would have looked *more* respectable as "La Source."

"This is the end," I told Pauline frantically. "I shall never receive her again. If the Emperor still insists on bringing her to court, I shall turn my back on her."

"And at the same time your back on the council chamber," Pauline warned soberly. "She must be disposed of, yes, but not at so disastrous a cost," she lowered her voice. "People are beginning to stare. I urge you to dance, to smile, to behave as if nothing has happened to disturb you."

Accordingly, I danced with Pauline's husband, then with Nigra—the Chevalier Nigra, Victor Emmanuel's Ambassador—whose presence I detested almost as much as Castiglione's. And, of course, I smiled! It was easy. Had I not learned to smile with a frightening brightness that deceived everybody but myself? Meanwhile, I was considering Pauline's warning. She was as much against a united Italy as I was but for a different reason. Victor Emmanuel had gained too much already for Austria's comfort. Pauline, expressing her country's views, regarded a too powerful Italy as a threat of future war. Naturally she wanted Castiglione's influence removed, but not at the cost of my own removal from the Privy Council.

"Is this a sign that Your Majesty has forgiven me?" Nigra asked.

At our last meeting, he had spoken of the good Victor Emmanuel was doing in Italy and, losing my head, I'd called him a brigand, a thief and an atheist.

"When a man waltzes as divinely as you do, Monsieur, all else is forgiven."

Reckless now, I danced with him four times and when Napoleon approached me just before the end of the ball, I told him that I had promised Nigra the last waltz.

Pauline, standing close by, chuckled softly as the Emperor turned coldly away.

"The Chevalier Nigra is a handsome man, cultured, too," she said reflectively. "He even writes poetry and is much sought after in society. He has none of the crudeness of Victor Emmanuel or Cavour. If I were heart-free myself . . ." She broke off with a shrug. "The Emperor is well aware that Nigra has a fascination for women."

216

"Pauline, you're not suggesting—!"

She nodded and laughed, her monkey face alight with mischief. "Arouse a fierce jealousy in the Emperor's breast and that may well be the end of Castiglione."

I next met Nigra when he gave a ball in celebration of the proclamation of the Kingdom of Italy; Victor Emmanuel had at last become King. I myself would rather have worn sackcloth and ashes over this event than an elaboarate ball gown. There was a small crumb of comfort in the fact that the Pope was still safe, still guarded by the French garrison. Only Venetia and Rome and a few scraps of papal territory now remained beyond Victor Emmanuel's grasp.

"Knowing Your Majesty's views," said Nigra as we waltzed together, "I was expecting a convenient migraine to keep you from my ball."

"The Emperor has acknowledged the new kingdom and its first King. The Empress can do no less. One must not want what one knows one cannot have."

Nigra's eyes twinkled. "A political rule, but never, to my mind, a rule in the pursuit of love."

"You have a very low opinion of women, Chevalier."

"On the contrary, a very *high* opinion. I write poetry about them. I sing their praises constantly. My muse is never idle."

It was a gay flirtation. We continued it during many dances that night. Napoleon missed nothing but his face, confound him, remained as inscrutable as ever.

Two days later I invited Nigra to tea in the Salon d'Appollon and I made a point of asking him to bring some of his verses. What an uncomfortable little tea party that was! Napoleon, even at his most inscrutable, had a way of making everybody else feel uneasy when, beneath his mask, he himself was uneasy or unhappy or angry. He smoked and smoked until the atmosphere grew vile. I used my fan continually, pointedly, but that encouraged him all the more.

"Did you bring your verses?" I asked Nigra, during a ghastly lull in the ghastly, disjointed conversation.

Nigra bowed, "Yes, Your Majesty."

"Please read them to us, my dear Nigra."

"Your Majesty is much too kind." He took a few crumpled sheets of manuscript from his pocket and glanced at Napoleon. "With Your Majesty's permission?"

Napoleon took out his watch. "Have you brought a short poem?"

Nigra leafed through the sheets. "A sonnet, Your Majesty."

"And the subject?"

"Love. Lines to a beautiful lady who must of necessity remain nameless."

"Her nationality?"

"Nameless, also, Your Majesty. Love transcends all nationalities."

"Proceed."

The Chevalier Nigra had a good voice and made excellent use of it. He might have been a virtuoso of the violin employing his bow on the D and G strings only. You could feel his voice within your breast. I found myself listening with my lips slightly apart and, since Napoleon's expressionless eyes were upon me, they remained apart. And the sonnet? It was prettily and sentimentally worded but of no real poetic value.

Napoleon rose. "Why not set your lines to music?"

And with that he marched from the room, a short, stout figure puffing smoke like an incense burner.

"Stay a little longer," I commanded Nigra while Napoleon was still within earshot. "I want to hear the rest of your poems. Are they all about love?"

The next afternoon I drove in the Bois as usual. It so happened that Nigra was riding there. He dismounted and came to chat with me. Presently, after a glance at my mounted military escort, he suggested a stroll. I declined.

218

"Tomorrow, perhaps?"

"Perhaps."

The weather was inclement the following afternoon. Nevertheless I went to the Bois. Very few people were abroad. Nobody expected to see the Empress in the Bois on a wet afternoon. Only one person, coming upon us as if by chance, saw me walking in a fine drizzle with the Chevalier Nigra. He was a policeman in a frock coat, one of a select company whose duty it was to guard both Napoleon and myself. Splendid! I was being watched as well as guarded.

The court went to Compiègne for a few days. Napoleon spent most of his time working with his secretary and conferring with various ministers. I spent most of mine riding with Nigra, conscious always of watching eyes. We returned to the Tuileries for a series of receptions and state dinners. When Napoleon appeared to forget to invite Nigra, I invited him myself.

If Napoleon fumed inwardly, he showed little sign of it. Accordingly, I made one last desperate bid to bring his jealousy to the boiling point. How clever I thought myself when I visited a hospital one afternoon with two ladies in attendance.

"Wait in the carriage. I won't be long."

I entered the hospital but left it immediately by a side entrance. I wore a veil, and thus veiled I hailed a passing public carriage. Nobody recognized me as I drove in the Bois for almost three hours, not even Nigra, though he passed me twice.

Napoleon appeared suddenly as I was dressing for dinner. "Well?" he demanded, having dismissed my ladies.

"Well?" I countered.

He took a sheet of paper from his pocket. "I have here a record of your meetings with Nigra—the places, the dates, the times. Only your movements this afternoon from the time you abandoned your ladies at the hospital to the time you returned to the Tuileries remain unaccounted for."

"Obviously your spies are stupid."

"Where did you go?"

"It was very pleasant in the Bois."

"You were not seen there."

"How peculiar."

"Tell me the name of your companion."

"My companion in sin, you mean?"

I thought he was going to strike me. The inscrutable Napoleon had given place to an elderly gentleman— how he would have hated such a description of himself at the age of fifty-three!—quivering with anger and, I felt confident, an all-consuming jealousy.

"Nigra's movements have been accounted for, too," he went on, struggling to control himself. "He was in the Bois, yes, but alone the whole time. Earlier he was at Mathilde's, later at Plonplon's."

"Ah!" said I, cudgeling my brains for inspiration.

"If your expedition was an innocent one, give me proof of it!"

"Not entirely innocent, Sire." I'd found my inspiration and pressed on with it before Napoleon could speak again. "As you often say, it's wise not to let your left hand know what your right is doing."

"So?"

"Nigra is my left hand."

He laughed shakily. "I think I understand. You've been using him to mask a real intrigue."

"You should be grateful, not angry. Have I not done everything in my power to avoid a scandal? Press me too hard and I'll conduct the *affaire* as you conduct yours—openly! Please understand that I am very deeply in love."

"An all-consuming passion?" Napoleon growled.

I bowed my head. "It has never happened before."

He paced the room for a few moments, deep in thought. Finally he came to rest in front of the mannequin, the headless iron frame which still wore my dinner gown.

"I understand how desperately serious it is," he muttered, addressing the mannequin. "A woman of your age—the intensity of feeling which sometimes heralds the menopause—"

"I'm only thirty-five!" I flared up instantly.

"True," he told the mannequin, "but your warm Spanish blood, the early maturity of the south . . . A quick ripening," he added, *he* the undoubted authority, "and as a result—" He turned to face me. "How foolish of me to be blinded by jealousy. I have nothing to fear. What of Conneau's warning—the warning supported by all the other doctors? You would never take the risk."

I burst instantly into tears. Tears of frustration, for it seemed that I'd failed after all. And because I had, the tears came easily.

"I can't hold back," I sobbed. "The risk of death means nothing; realization everything."

Napoleon swung round on the mannequin and sent "her" crashing to the floor.

"I eluded your spies today, Napoleon. I shall do so again and again."

He picked up the mannequin, shook the figure and flung it away. Then, in apparent control of himself, he turned to me with an expression of deadly calm on his face.

"Will you bargain with me, *chérie?*"

"Sire—"

"No, wait! I'm asking you to make a great sacrifice. I in my turn will make a great one too. It will cost me dear but the Comtesse de Castiglione shall never be invited to court again. I may even in time find the strength to forget her."

"Give me time to think," I begged, realizing that too quick an agreement might make him suspect my trickery. "To—to steel myself," I added.

Napoleon bowed. "Gladly."

Dinner that night was followed by a small private ball. Castiglione, as it happened, had not been invited. Nevertheless, she appeared at ten o'clock, self-assured as ever, and curtsied before me with her usual insolence. I turned away my head. Napoleon was watching with interest, Pauline Metternich at his side. Castiglione curtsied again, and again I ignored her. Napoleon strolled up with Pauline but said not a word.

"Is an invitation always necessary?" Castiglione asked petulantly.

I summoned a lackey. "Madame la Comtesse de Castiglione is leaving. Escort her to her carriage."

She turned furiously to Napoleon. "Sire!"

Napoleon stifled a yawn and slipped his arm through Pauline's. "As I was saying, Princess . . ."

Castiglione went. She was never seen at court again. At Mathilde's, yes; at Plonplon's, yes; in fact she became Plonplon's mistress and brought him close to beggary before she found another lover. Her beauty began to fade while she was still young, poor thing. She withdrew from society, became a hermit and died in a house in which not a single mirror had been permitted for years.

While smoking his usual after-luncheon cigarette in my study the next day, Napoleon said quietly, "The coachman of a public carriage was questioned last night. I am satisfied that you were the veiled woman who spent three hours driving in the Bois."

"Was he questioned before Castiglione appeared at the ball?"

"Yes."

"Yet you allowed me to send her away!" I exclaimed in wonder.

"I was on the point of sending her away myself, but out of kindness I left it to you."

"You'd grown suddenly tired of her?"

Napoleon ignored this. *"Mon dieu,* how skillfully you fooled me! Jealousy deprived me of my senses. I ought to have realized that your loyalty would always prevent you from taking a lover."

"Irritatingly enough, I think it would."

Napoleon drew deeply on his cigarette. "Castiglione is of no further use to me. A happy coincidence that I should have discovered the fact before I bargained with you."

"Surely the bargaining was a pretense on your part also?"

"No. I still believed in your love affair at that time. Castiglione is of no further use to me because her uncle, Count Cavour, has died suddenly. The news has not yet been announced in Paris. She represented Cavour, not Victor Emmanuel, as I allowed you to believe."

"Is there any real difference politically?"

"Cavour was the king-maker, and as such, more important to me than the king he made. I trusted him more than I could ever trust Victor Emmanuel. Castiglione had great influence with her uncle. She is deeply religious, though you may not believe it, and is alarmed at Victor Emmanuel's policy. Through her I counted on Cavour to restrain him."

It was heartening to know that Napoleon was still determined to protect the Pope in spite of what he'd said about temporal power. I spoke of this and thanked him humbly.

"I'm more concerned about restraint in another direction, *chérie*. What if Victor Emmanuel's ambition drives him too far? We must warn him about that by strengthening our forces on the Italian border. In addition, we must become better friends with Austria."

"How ironical that you should once have gone to war with Austria for Victor Emmanuel's sake and now need Austria as a means of limiting his power."

"Italy is still an ally. I need *both* Austria and Italy. A balance of power, that is my aim, a balance of power and no fear of war. Did I cause much damage to your mannequin last night?"

"You bent it a little."

"And I ruined one of your pretty dresses. Buy a dozen new ones and have the account sent to me."

"So very generous of you!"

Napoleon rose. The ritual of the after-luncheon cigarette was at an end.

"A *dozen* new dresses?" Pauline Metternich exclaimed, while driving with me in the Bois that afternoon. "How splendid! You must pay Mr. Worth a visit."

"Never!"

"At all events, it will do no harm to inspect the new dresses I bought from him last week—bought but have not yet worn."

"Ah, the battle is on!"

"And my weapons in readiness, Madame!"

Naturally I was dying of curiosity and wasted no time in entering the enemy camp. That is to say, Pauline's boudoir at the Austrian Embassy. The weapons, displayed on four mannequins, formed an advance guard sternly determined on the destruction of the poor crinoline. I inspected them from left to right. Number one wore a small crinoline such as I had worn before Loulou's birth; number two, an even smaller one; number three, a modified version suggestive merely of things long passed; and number four! I averted my eyes quickly.

"Monstrous!"

"Why not try it on?" Pauline purred.

I looked again at the monstrosity. Blue silk. My favorite color. The *exact* shade. The skirt flowed from the waist and fell in lovely folds to the floor. A rippling waterfall, the motion caught and held as if by an artist's brush. I could well imagine how it would feel to move in such a lovely gown.

"Monstrous!" I repeated.

"Why should a woman hide her slimness beneath a crinoline?" Pauline argued. "Who wants to give an ev-

224

erlasting impression of hidden but apparently permanent pregnancy?"

She sent for her women. They arrayed her in the new gown. I grew sick with envy.

"Mr. Worth," she said, "is of the opinion that Your Majesty clings to the crinoline because it emphasizes the loveliness of the Imperial bosom. Did it ever do that for mine? Whereas *now* . . . !"

We stood side by side in front of the long mirror. Pauline's bosom was by no means as lovely as mine, yet in the Worth creation it looked lovelier.

"Disgusting! I shall send for Mr. Worth and—*yes,* I shall threaten him with exile unless he desists."

When Charles Frederick Worth first appeared at the Tuileries, he was thirty-five, tall, quite good-looking, not yet heavy-jowled and thick-necked as success was later to make him. His mustache was untrimmed and his beardless chin rather chubby and very determined. He was fond of describing himself as a poet, a *couturier* who composed rather than designed his creations. He wore a loose black velvet jacket, a carelessly tied cravat and dark grey trousers. No other man would have dared to present himself at court in anything but a formal tailcoat. The disrespect of it! Small wonder I regarded him from the first with a lively interest.

At that first visit to the Tuileries, Mr. Worth was accompanied by six *vendeuses*. Five of them carried rolls of materials—satins, silks, laces; and the sixth, a large flat box tied with ribbon. Before I could protest, the materials were unrolled and my drawing room became a second, if temporary, Worth atelier.

"An entrancing sight, Mr. Worth," I said tartly, "but what of the new fashion you and Princess Metternich would force upon me?"

Mr. Worth bowed and with one sweeping gesture drew my attention to his six assistants whose dresses I had refused to notice. The girls had been chosen cunningly for their height, slimness, their small waists and their beautiful bosoms. Six Paulines prancing in new Worth creations and looking almost as elegant as Pauline in hers.

"It was I, Madame, who discovered the real art of cutting out," said Mr. Worth. "Snip-snip go the scissors with the run of the cloth, not *against* it. Observe, please, the way in which my young ladies' gowns fit the body so that one realizes it really is a body. Material and body flow together. With the crinoline my art is of little avail. The unseen body below the waist may move, I grant you, but the crinoline, disguising all beneath it, billows out in all directions like a bell tent."

I looked at him haughtily. So the Empress of France resembled a bell tent!

"I have merely scratched the surface, Madame," Mr. Worth went on, his voice as resonant as Nigra's reading poetry. "What can I do of any real significance for these clumsy girls? Complete success eludes me. How can it be otherwise when I have not yet been permitted to compose a gown for the most elegant lady in the world?"

"A pretty speech for an Englishman."

"One learns quickly in Paris, Your Majesty. But then, Paris was always my spiritual home."

"You regard your profession as a thing of the spirit?"

"Assuredly, Madame. Your seamstresses, for that is all your female dressmakers are, attack their task in an earthy manner. They make the mistake of dressing their clients for the edification—forgive me, Your Majesty—for the *earthy* edification of men. How sadly they miss the true intent of female fashion! Women may not admit it, but they dress for other women, for the mortification of their female rivals. Each would outshine the other. The male is of no importance. He is tempted—he will always be tempted—whatever a woman wears. The crinoline, the ugly crinoline, is proof enough of that."

I swallowed the insult to my own creation, for I was thinking how right he was. Dressed by Worth, Pauline Metternich would outshine me at my own court if I insisted on clinging to the crinoline.

"You believe that only a male dressmaker can show a woman how to outshine another woman?"

"Providing his name is Worth, Your Majesty."

"A very spiritual calling," I said dryly.

Mr. Worth bowed. "What could be more spiritual, more heavenly, than a heavenly Worth creation?"

"The crinoline was heavenly in your own eyes when you favored it."

"Truly, Madame." He smiled reminiscently. "Especially one formidable creation containing a hundred yards of silk."

"I venture to predict that you will reach the pinnacle of success if you design for me another containing two hundred yards."

"Could Your Majesty sustain the weight?"

"You refuse the commission, Mr. Worth?"

"Mindful of Your Majesty's health, yes."

"Nevertheless, crinolines will still be worn at Court. *That* is an Imperial decree."

Mr. Worth bowed again and withdrew. His six assistants rolled up the lovely materials and followed him, sorrowfully but elegantly. I then discovered that the large flat box had been left behind, unopened. Can any woman turn her back on a box of that size and shape? The pretty ribbon simply must be untied, the lid opened, the tissue paper cast aside. I was cunning, though. Dismissing my ladies, I snatched up the box, sneaked into my boudoir like a felon and locked the door.

Worth had excelled himself. Clever as he was, he never created anything more elegant and original than that first Imperial, crinoline-less gown. The material was a gorgeous silk brocade, handwoven at Lyons, while the design was a breath-taking representation of

Chinese flowers. The fit was perfect; Pauline, providing my measurements, had seen to that. My fingers were all thumbs as I changed into it. The lightness was intoxicating. I could even think more clearly. Not a single minister, not even Napoleon himself, would get the better of me at the council board—crinoline-less.

Handwoven at Lyons, I thought. Lyons, where the masters of the craft were facing ruin because of the competition of steam-driven looms. What a magnificent service I, the Empress, would render the poor Lyonnais if I wore this gown and caused others to copy it. "Think also of the political significance," the Devil whispered in my ear. No, not the Devil—the Serpent proffering a new sort of apple.

Nevertheless, I appeared at dinner that night wearing the most enormous crinoline in my possession. Had I not issued an Imperial decree? Even Pauline must obey or stay away from court. I must have obedience from Pauline; *then* would come my own gracious capitulation. But Pauline stayed away from court, and at her own dinner parties, which I refused to attend, wore a succession of Worth creations.

Impasse!

"Franco-Austrian relations are being severely strained," Napoleon laughed.

However, my resistance collapsed when I heard that Castiglione was returning from her uncle's funeral. Nothing could prevent her now from appearing in society without a crinoline. Once that happened, I'd be condemned to wear the hated contraption for the rest of my life or have it said that I was following a fashion approved by the Emperor's ex-mistress. Acting without hesitation, I went to dinner in my first Worth creation and I issued a new decree.

"Crinolines," I told my secretary, "are not to be worn again at court."

Then I ordered six new dresses, all of silk brocade. That was sufficient to put the Lyonnais on their feet again. During the next ten years the production of handwoven brocade was doubled. I adored those gowns but pretended that I wore them only in the course of Imperial duty and called them my *robes politiques*. In addition, Worth "composed" for me a new town dress which he called an ensemble. In a word, there was a jacket to be worn over the dress, and both were of grey taffeta bedecked with little black velvet bows. The first ensemble, but goodness—*not* the last!

Worth was inundated with orders. His workrooms were extended and additional seamstresses employed overnight. Since he now enjoyed Imperial patronage, people jeered no longer at a male dictator of fashion. Worth made a fortune, the eight hundred thousand francs he spent on a new villa at Suresnes being a mere bagatelle.

"Are you satisfied?" I asked Pauline when she saw me for the first time without a crinoline. "Is victory sweet enough?"

She nodded and grinned. "But the victory is really Mr. Worth's. *He* killed the crinoline. Long live the Empress!"

Chapter Seventeen

THE DAILY ROUTINE of life at the Tuileries was not, thank heaven, imposed upon me every day of every year. The wider yearly routine of my life included visits to Saint-Cloud, Compiègne, Fontainebleau and Biarritz. Just as we spent the winter season with its round of social activities at the Tuileries, so we spent a part of the autumn at Biarritz, only a hop, skip and a jump from the Spanish border. I loved the villa there, the Villa Eugenie. It belonged to me alone; in later years I was obliged to sell it and see it turned for a time into a casino. But in my own day, Biarritz was unspoiled and secluded; nobody dreamed then that it would ever become a popular seaside resort.

The Biarritz of September 1861 stands out more clearly in my mind than any other. A political scheme, said to be of my own devising, was hatched at that time —it led to a disastrous war, heaven forgive us—and Loulou learned to swim. The poor boy was much afraid of the water and refused, as he'd done the year before, to venture deeper than his knees. Even the smallest wave breaking in his direction sent him scampering to the safety of the sand.

"It isn't really fear," he said, when I chided him one day during the second week of the holiday. "It would be different if I could swim."

"Monsieur Mérimée is waiting to teach you."

"He's clumsy, Mama. Do you want him to drown me?"

"Come, Monseigneur," Mérimée coaxed and strode into the water.

Loulou set his chin stubbornly. "The water is much too deep."

"Give him time," Napoleon said. "Let him gain a little confidence. It would be foolish to force him."

"Jacques swims very well," I said, pointing innocently to a group of Loulou's young friends. "How old is he?"

"Six."

"Darling! Six?"

"Five, then."

"And you are six months older."

Napoleon jumped up with an abruptness that spoke volumes. His son, the Prince Imperial, put to shame by the son of the local postmaster?

"Take my hand, Loulou. We'll try the water together."

Loulou hung back. "Jacques isn't brave. He runs when I fire my cannon."

"And *you* run when a wave breaks on the beach," I said.

"You don't understand, Mama. I'm in command of the cannon but I can't command the sea."

"A sensible explanation," Napoleon commented. "My son is wise beyond his years." And with that the proud father went bathing alone, leaving me to snatch Loulou up in my arms in sudden fury.

Afterward everybody swore I threw the boy head first into the water, but all I did was drop him because he struggled beyond my control. In fact, I disappeared under the surface myself and, coming up in water no deeper than my knees, saw Napoleon swimming in my direction, bobbing up and down in frantic haste, drooping mustache visible one moment, under the water, the next. I spluttered with laughter at the sight. Surely this was not the Emperor of France, rather a very angry seal.

Meanwhile Miss Shaw had waded fully dressed into the surf.

"Nous avons drowned our *petit* prince!" she shrieked, getting her English and French confused as she usually did when agitated. "Your Majesty should *prenez garde.* You have only one *enfant."*

But all was well. Loulou, "rescued" by Mérimée, had torn himself free on reaching the beach and was running along the sand as if pursued by the devil himself. A moment later he collided with an immaculately dressed gentleman and clung wetly to his beautiful trousers.

A delightful little scene followed. The immaculate gentleman, who proved to be none other than Don Jose Hidalgo, was joined to my surprise by Mama—Mama in an over-large crinoline! I hurried from the water. So did the angry seal. The four of us—the dripping, sobbing Loulou between us and myself and the angry seal dripping too—met on a patch of dry, warm sand. Mama curtsied; Don Jose bowed. Napoleon kissed Mama's hand; Don Jose kissed mine.

"Your Majesty . . ." He turned to Napoleon. "Sire . . ."

"You are very welcome, Don Jose." Napoleon, darting angry little glances at me, was trying to be jovial. "Dona Manuela, how *nice* to see you again." And then, explosively: "She threw Monseigneur into the water!"

Mama agreed at once. "I saw her."

"Crinolines are no longer worn, Mama," said I.

She eyed my attire disapprovingly. "So I perceive."

"Jacques learned to swim naked," Loulou ventured. "He always swims naked, except when the court is at Biarritz."

"As would I, Monseigneur," Don Jose murmured. "How else can one really enjoy the water? If you learn that way, you will soon be swimming like a fish."

"I—I shall think about it," said Loulou, slipping his hand into Don Jose's.

Napoleon and I retired to our respective bathing machines and presently, having changed—what a relief to get rid of my sodden corset!—we trouped up to the villa with our unexpected guests. Lagging behind, for the climb was a steep one, Mama whispered that Don Jose had been kind enough to escort her to Biarritz and if the Emperor had no objection would remain until she was ready to return to Madrid.

"I want you to have a long private talk with the dear Jose," Mama said gaily.

"Are you in debt again, in spite of his gallant efforts?"

"Indeed I am not!" she said virtuously.

Ah, I thought, Mexico once more!

"May I have a party for my friends?" Loulou asked his father.

"You had one yesterday," I interposed. "Lessons were neglected. Monsieur Monnier will be very upset if you neglect them again this afternoon."

"This is a holiday, Mama!"

"With one hour set aside for lessons. *One* hour only, remember."

"*Three* hours tomorrow, Mama, to make up," Loulou coaxed.

"Let him have his way," said Napoleon. "A small compensation for having been flung into the sea."

Loulou gave a whoop of joy and ran ahead of us up the path, and by the time we reached the villa, the children's party had sprung into being with a dozen wild animals, ages ranging from five to eight, creating havoc in the main *salon*.

"Only one thing will make it possible for us to hear ourselves talk," said Napoleon.

"Food," Mama agreed.

The order was scarcely given when Louis-Napoleon, Dr. Conneau's young son, gave a yelp of pain as his head struck the edge of a table. There was instant silence. Everybody had seen Loulou trip him. Loulou hung his head in shame while the others stood about shuffling their feet.

"You saw what happened?" I asked Napoleon.

"It was an accident."

"Napoleon—"

"I saw," he said gruffly.

"Loulou must be punished."

"You're better at that than I am."

"*Please,* Napoleon!"

"Do you want the child to hate me?"

That was always Napoleon's plea. Small wonder people said I was too severe a parent.

Mérimée had now helped young Conneau to his feet. No serious injury had been sustained, though a small lump was already appearing on the side of his head. He and Loulou were very close friends. Much the same age, they did almost everything together, even their lessons in the schoolroom at the Tuileries.

"Aren't you ashamed of yourself?" I asked Loulou.

"It was war, Mama. I—I didn't stop to think."

"That is the trouble with war," said Mérimée.

"War?" I asked.

It turned out that the game was a counterpart of the American Civil War which had broken out a few months earlier. Loulou was a Federal leader; Louis-Napoleon Conneau, by no choice of his own, a Confederate. He possessed a slave, did the little Conneau, none other than Jacques whose face was smeared with soot. Confederate Conneau's purpose was to hold the slave; Federal Loulou's was to free the wretch.

"A noble aim," said Napoleon. "We none of us believe in slavery. However, our government has recognized the Confederate States as belligerents. So has Queen Victoria's."

"This is a history lesson, Papa," Loulou giggled.

"And that shall be your punishment," said I. "Go to Monsieur Monnier at once."

At that moment trays of delectable confections were brought in and placed on the sideboard. Loulou turned up his eyes and groaned in dismay. So did I, silently.

What a heartless wretch the Empress-Mother was compelled to make of herself.

"Let us have a history lesson here while the children eat," Don Jose suggested, offering a compromise which I gratefully accepted. "I myself will give it."

"We'd rather have a story, Don Jose," young Conneau begged, for Hidalgo was very good at story telling.

"That is my intention. History makes a lovely story when told properly."

"No dates?" Loulou asked urgently.

"Not a single date," Don Jose promised. He dropped his voice to an intriguing whisper. "I shall tell you the story of Santa Anna's leg."

The children gathered round him eagerly while servants supplied them with over-loaded plates of cakes and sweets and glasses of bubbling soda-water flavored with orange syrup, a concoction of Napoleon's known as the "Emperor's Champagne."

"Antonio Lopez de Santa Anna," Don Jose began, "lost a leg in battle in the year— But no, dates are forbidden!"

"Forbidden, Monsieur," Loulou cried gleefully.

"Soldiers often lose legs in battle," said young Conneau.

"Ah, but this was a very special leg. A *president's* leg. Santa Anna was President of Mexico at that time."

"Was the leg shot off?" Loulou wanted to know.

"No, Monseigneur, but the doctors were obliged to amputate it, after which, since it was such an important leg, it was taken to the capital for burial. Oh, it was a very grand funeral and later a monument was erected above the leg's grave. The unveiling ceremony was even grander than the funeral, and everybody wept at the sight of the gallant Santa Anna stumping about on his new wooden leg."

"Is that all?" Loulou asked.

"Dear me, no! Santa Anna was overthrown by his enemies, the monument was destroyed and the leg—

they dug it up, you see—was carried through the streets with people shouting 'Down with Santa Anna's leg!' Then they built a bonfire and threw the leg into the flames. As for Santa Anna, he bobbed up again, wooden leg and all, vanquished his enemies and, since the real leg was no more, everybody cried, 'Long live Santa Anna's wooden leg!' "

The children clapped and demanded another story.

"Gladly!" said Don Jose, giving me a really sly glance. "Can anyone tell me where Texas is?"

"In America," said Loulou, his mouth full of cake. "It's one of Louis Conneau's Confederate States."

"Correct, Monseigneur, but before that it was a republic, and before *that* a province of Mexico. It all came about because some Americans from the southern states of the Union went and settled in that part of Mexico. Land was very cheap there, you see. They took their slaves with them, not wanting to work too hard themselves. Now the Mexicans didn't like slavery and told the Americans to free their slaves. The Americans refused and revolted against Mexico. It was a successful revolt and Texas was turned into a separate republic. Later on, it became a new state in the American Union."

"Do the children know that Mexico was once a Spanish colony?" Mama asked.

"I was about to tell them," Don Jose said quickly. "Mexico is now an independent nation, children. And that, Monseigneur, really came about because of your noble ancestor, the First Emperor of France."

"The Monroe Doctrine was surely the cause," Mérimée protested.

"The Doctrine protects Mexican independence, yes, but Emperor Napoleon I's domination of Spain, followed by his fall and exile, encouraged the Mexicans to revolt against Spain."

The children's attention was straying and Napoleon, who had sat listening in silence, rose and suggested a new game out-of-doors. They ran ahead, screaming wildly. Napoleon paused and turned politely to Don Jose.

"You omitted to tell the children that Santa Anna lost his leg while fighting against a French force sent to Mexico by Louis-Philippe. You omitted to tell them also that the loss of Santa Anna's leg, or at all events the campaign in which it was lost, contributed considerably to the loss of Louis-Philippe's throne."

"A fortunate circumstance for Your Majesty," Don Jose murmured.

"To that I agree, Don Jose, but no more legs shall be lost in Mexico because of France."

So much for Don Jose Hidalgo's latest scheme, I thought, as Napoleon went out to join the children, leaving Mérimée and Don Jose to argue with one another. I smiled tolerantly as I listened. When Don Jose expressed a point of view held by Mérimée, dear Mérimée contradicted him flatly. And it was the same with Don Jose when Mérimée expressed one of his points of view. Each was jealous of the other's friendship with Mama, and how dear Mama reveled in it all!

"So Mexican independence is not to your liking!" Mérimée cried triumphantly.

"I said nothing of the kind!" Don Jose protested.

"You inferred it, my friend!"

"I neither said it nor inferred it. I am concerned solely with the troubles of the Spanish Mexicans. Separation from Spain brought chaos and revolution, and chaos still reigns in spite of independence. And what of religion? The Church no longer exists in Mexico. President Juárez' government is violently anti-clerical. The churches have been closed, church property confiscated. There is no one to protect religion in Mexico today as there is, thank heaven, in Rome."

"You heard what the Emperor said," Mérimée said. "You must look elsewhere for help, my friend." With that he rose and stamped out to the garden.

"Dona Manuela, if you would be so kind?" Don Jose said.

"Ah, you want to get rid of me, you wretch!"

Don Jose bowed. "You were never very good at keeping secrets."

"I also heard what the Emperor said," I reminded him, when Mama had departed in mock indignation.

Don Jose shrugged easily. "You have a voice in state affairs, Madame, a powerful voice. This is no wild scheme of my own. I represent the Mexican Absolutists. They seek the overthrow of that arch fiend, Juárez, and the setting up of a Mexican monarchy. The mere presence of French troops would restore order and re-establish the Church. It is my hope, my prayer, that Your Majesty will listen with sympathy and will induce in the Emperor a like sympathy."

Don Jose went on to explain his position at length, talking softly and persuasively. When finally his voice died away, it seemed to me that God had called upon me to fulfill a holy mission. Even so, I drew back. What if the holy mission led to war? Napoleon had spoken of the Crimean conflict as a holy war, but was war ever holy?

"The most I can promise you, Don Jose, is a private interview with the Emperor."

Don Jose kissed my hand. "For that I am deeply grateful."

Napoleon received Don Jose after dinner that night, I being the only other person present in the study. Napoleon yawned, stretched and remarked that the sea air always made him sleepy.

"A bedtime story is all I need to set me slumbering in my chair," he laughed.

Nevertheless, he listened attentively and courteously, assumed his habitual mask-like expression and smoked endless cigarettes, while Don Jose expounded passionately on the iniquities of Benito Juárez who had been in full power little more than six months. Juárez was a

Mexican Indian, the possessor of a native cunning as well as a native cleverness. Educated by a wealthy trader, he practiced law before entering politics. He had long ago sworn to destroy the Christian religion in Mexico and now, within six months, he had succeeded.

"The whole of the Catholic world will honor you, Sire, if you restore the Church in Mexico," Don Jose said dreamily.

"You suggest that I should ignore the Monroe Doctrine? Are you fully conversant with it, Don Jose? President Monroe's declaration of 1823 states clearly that the United States would consider any attempt on the part of a European power to extend its system to any portion of the American continent as dangerous to the Union's own peace and safety. You are as well aware as I that the United states would never tolerate an attempt on my part to interfere with or control the destiny of Mexico."

Don Jose smiled blandly. "The situation has changed radically during the past few months. The Americans are busy with their own destiny, bloodily busy. If they were at peace within their own borders I would not have dreamed of approaching you. They are powerless at present to do little more than protest, as I think Your Majesty realizes."

Napoleon rose and brushed some cigarette ash from his sleeve. It was a definite gesture of dismissal. Don Jose ignored it.

"Sire, I have another card up my sleeve. I have received dismaying news from Mexico, news which by now must have reached the French Foreign Office in Paris. The Republic of Mexico has suspended payment on all foreign loans. Juárez refuses absolutely to honor the debts incurred by the former president. Three countries stand to lose a great deal of money—France, England and Spain."

"Now you talk like a businessman, not a religious fanatic," said Napoleon. "Unfortunately I am in no mood tonight for either business or religion."

Don Jose bowed and withdrew.

"I wonder how much money our worthy friend stands to lose in Mexico?" Napoleon asked me dryly. "'The whole of the Catholic world will honor you, Sire.' Be that as it may, I can see the flash of gold rather than the elevation of the Host, hear the clink of coin on coin rather than the tinkle of the Mass bell." Napoleon smiled dreamily. "Intervention in Mexico would be a recompense for the temporal restrictions forced upon the Pope, restrictions for which *I* am blamed, protect him though I do. A recompense? The full support of French Catholics regained, perhaps? Well, who knows?"

The next morning a batch of telegrams was sent from Biarritz to Paris. One went to Morny, another to Walewski, the rest to friends with no active interest in politics. We were on holiday, said Napoleon, but even so one was compelled to mix business with pleasure. The telegrams were all worded the same: "Your presence is commanded, be sure to come sans culottes." That was copying, Mérimée, my Minister of Pleasure at Biarritz, for he, with my delighted permission, often worded invitations with the phrase: "Venez sans culottes."

"Are the gentlemen really to come without their trousers?" Loulou asked in wide-eyed wonder.

"It's only a figure of speech," I explained. "Papa means them to come informally, not to worry about etiquette. But when you put *sans* and *culottes* together, there's a different meaning. *Sans-culottes* was the name given to the democratic party by the court party at the beginning of the Revolution years and years ago. In the eyes of the aristocrats the *sans-culottes* were very unpleasant people. Republicans are sometimes called *sans-culottes,* even today."

Loulou laughed mischievously. "This is almost a history lesson, Mama."

240

"So it is, and speaking of lessons, here comes Monsieur Monnier."

"Oh *no*, Mama!"

"Three hours today, darling. You decreed it yourself."

Monnier, the recently appointed tutor, greeted me with a deferential little bow and took Loulou by the hand. "Come, Monseigneur."

Loulou hung back. "Not three whole hours, Mama. Yesterday Don Jose—"

"That was less than half an hour."

He smiled beatifically. "Would a swimming lesson be counted, Mama?"

"If this is a trick, Loulou—"

"Jacques' uncle is waiting to teach me. He taught Jacques. If I can go into the water naked, I won't—I mean, I'll learn quicker just as Don Jose did."

It was no trick. Loulou was able to swim quite well before we returned to Paris. He had no other lessons, naturally, but I was well content. Our little Prince was no longer afraid of the water.

A larger party than Napoleon had actually invited reached Biarritz; it included Plonplon and his wife and Prince and Princess Metternich. To be sure, the former were "family" and needed no invitation while the latter were *personae gratae* at all times. Pauline and I bathed during the afternoon. The detestable Plonplon followed us down to the beach but not having much liking for the water remained, a most ungainly sight, on the edge warning us against swimming out too far.

"I think we really are a little too daring," I remarked.

"We simply had to shake him off," said Pauline. "He's dying of curiosity. That's why he came to Biarritz. His spies must have told him that Richard and I were visited by a Mexican emissary."

"A Mexican emissary, Pauline?"

It appeared that the leader of the Mexican Absolutists was the Mexican exile, Gutiérrez de Estrada, and that his two most trusted supporters were Don Jose Hidalgo and Don Juan Almonte. The latter had approached Richard Metternich, while Don Jose because of his friendship with me had concentrated on Napoleon.

"So Austria is likely to lose money in Mexico, too," I said.

"I know nothing of that. Almonte wanted to know if the Emperor of Austria's brother, the Archduke Maximilian, would care to accept the Mexican throne."

"Don Jose made no mention of that."

"It was necessary first to consult Austria."

"And Austria . . .?"

"The Emperor Franz Joseph is interested on his brother's behalf. Richard sent him a telegram and received an immediate reply. What do you think of the idea yourself, Eugenie?"

It was over five years since Maximilian's memorable visit to Saint-Cloud and he was now married to one of Queen Victoria's cousins. It was easy to understand why the Mexicans were interested in him. He was a descendant of Charles V of Spain under whose rule the Aztec Empire had fallen three hundred years ago.

"The Archduke Maximilian is a suitable choice," I said.

"I hope the Emperor will think so too," Pauline said significantly.

Then we both laughed at the thought of two women floating languidly in the sea while planning, anything but languidly, the destiny of Mexico. But I myself grew serious again as we swam back to the beach. A Catholic Empire in Mexico in place of the anti-clerical Republic of Benito Juárez . . . Stability and religion in place of near anarchy . . . My interest deepened, but the decision was Napoleon's, not mine.

After dinner that night, while Loulou was organizing a magic-lantern show for his young friends, Napoleon summoned Morny, Walewski, Plonplon and myself to his study and repeated all that Don Jose had said. Morny, Napoleon's illegitimate half-brother, expressed immediate approval. He was concerned solely with the financial aspect of the case. The Mexican government must be made to honor its debts, otherwise the French economy would suffer badly. Certain French bankers had spoken to him and were very disturbed about the situation.

"More disturbed than if we permitted you, through this, to destroy the Empire?" Plonplon asked scathingly.

Morny ignored the question, feeling, no doubt, that Plonplon's opposition was prompted entirely by jealousy. Plonplon, as everybody knew, resented the fact that Napoleon had made Morny Chief Minister and Titular Head of the Government.

"I think I can count on Walewski's support," Morny said at last.

"You can," Walewski agreed, "but my interest is religious, not financial."

Count Walewski was the son of Napoleon's uncle and the Polish countess Marie Walewska. He was a year older than Morny, tall, very pleasing of manner and handsome. Many ill things were said of him but I knew him to be an honest man. Here then was another ally for me in the Mexican venture. The thought startled me. Obviously I was more committed than I'd cared to admit.

"Surely we can find a peaceful means of inducing Mexico to pay her debts," Plonplon said.

"Let us hope so," said Napoleon, "but what of the suggested Mexican Empire?"

"I'll have no part in that."

"What a pity," I couldn't resist saying. "I was hoping that His Imperial Highness, the Prince Napoleon, would gladly accept the Mexican throne."

"Plonplon an Emperor after all!" Morny laughed.

"The Mexicans would never accept a free thinker," said Walewski. "I myself would suggest Prince de Joinville."

"A happy thought," Napoleon agreed. "Prince de Joinville, a son of Louis-Philippe. It would please the Orleanists, ever a political thorn in my flesh. It would please the Queen of Spain, too, since her younger sister is married to de Joinville's brother. And as for my wife, Spanish by birth—"

"Your wife," I interposed, "was about to suggest the Archduke Maximilian."

"Whose voice is this we hear?" Plonplon asked, as if mightily puzzled. "That of Pauline Metternich?"

"Let the Empress explain her reasons," Napoleon commanded.

There were several; I had assembled them carefully.

"Apart from the obvious Mexican interest in the Archduke, is he not a Hapsburg? That would please Spain, too, notwithstanding his closeness to the Austrian throne. His wife Charlotte is the only daughter of Queen Victoria's Uncle Leopold, and that would please Her Majesty, if not Her Majesty's government. Charlotte's mother was a daughter of Louis-Philippe. Therefore the Orleanists would be just as pleased as if we chose Prince de Joinville. Finally, your own position, as you have already admitted, would be strengthened *in France* by the support and approval of the French Catholics."

"You begin to convince me," said Napoleon, "that the Archduke Maximilian is a better candidate than Prince de Joinville."

"A strong Catholic Empire in Mexico would be a check to the territorial ambitions of the United States," Walewski said. "Ironically enough, the taking of Texas, a state committed to slavery, led to the present Civil War. Now is the time to act. Quick action will place the

244

Archduke Maximilian on the Mexican throne long before the Americans give up slaughtering each other."

Napoleon rose up from his desk. "I have been presented with some interesting arguments." He stretched lazily. "Shall we join Loulou's magic-lantern show?"

At that moment his secretary entered, whispered in his ear briefly and withdrew.

"Well, well," said Napoleon, "Hidalgo is in receipt of some interesting information from Madrid. Spain is on the point of intervening in Mexico."

"Splendid!" Plonplon cried. "Leave it to Spain to pull the chestnuts out of the fire."

"And at the same time give her the chance of making Mexico a part of Spain once more?" Morny asked quickly. "Pressure must be brought to bear on Spain."

"By France?"

"By France and England. If we can win the support of England, Spain will refrain from acting alone. Three countries are concerned financially—France, England and Spain. A joint expedition, that is what I envisage."

"Three big boys flourishing three big sticks," Napoleon mused. "The Juárez government intimidated; not a blow struck. Yes, an interesting suggestion."

"An international expedition," Morny said pointedly. "An international law invoked. The collection of debts is surely legal."

"As I was about to say myself," Napoleon said imperturbably. "Go back to Paris tomorrow, my dear fellow. Open up negotiations with the British and Spanish ambassadors."

"Gladly, Sire," said Morny, smiling triumphantly at Plonplon.

Scarcely eight weeks after the discussions at Biarritz, an agreement was signed in London by England, France and Spain. All three countries were to engage in a joint occupation of the Mexican port of Vera Cruz.

Spain sent six thousand troops, France two thousand and England only a few hundred. A small army of occupation, but certainly not an army prepared to make war. At the last moment the United States—the dis-United States, as Morny put it—was invited to join the expedition, but this, as Morny had calculated, that country was neither prepared nor willing to do. The allied debt-collecting expedition was legal, the United States agreed, but warned against either a permanent occupation of Vera Cruz or interference in Mexican domestic affairs.

Meanwhile, the Archduke Maximilian expressed a lively interest in the offer of the Mexican throne but refused to give an immediate decision. He hesitated, Napoleon said, because of the unexpected disapproval expressed by the British government if not by Queen Victoria herself. She, poor woman, was too distressed by a private sorrow to give much attention to state affairs, for Prince Albert had died of typhoid fever before the joint expedition reached Vera Cruz. "The things of this life are of no interest to me now," she wrote in reply to my ill-phrased, awkward letter of sympathy.

I waited for news from Vera Cruz with an anxiety I told myself was unreasonable. The trans-Atlantic cable was not yet in operation and letters took six weeks or more to reach France from Mexico. In his first letter, our ambassador wrote of differences of opinion between the allied debt collectors. These, he felt sure, could be smoothed out, since the occupation had met with no active opposition. At last, after four months of futile negotiating, the English and Spanish forces were withdrawn.

And then came news of disaster. The French forces were defeated in an engagement with the Mexican army. What a sorry blow that was to French pride! The French army, supposedly invincible, defeated by an ill-armed band of Indians? *Defeated?* Napoleon, thinking only of French prestige, refused to admit defeat. Withdrawal? Preposterous!

"Reinforcements are being sent to Mexico," he told me. "You now have your mission, your holy mission."

Chapter Eighteen

TWENTY-TWO MONTHS after the defeat of that small French force in Mexico, the Archduke Maximilian brought his wife Charlotte to Paris. I never think of their arrival at the Tuileries without thinking also of spaghetti and of the new toy acquired by Loulou at that time, a living, breathing lovely toy, the little striped donkey given to him by Victor Emmanuel.

I must try and list in correct order the events of those twenty-two months. To begin with, reinforcements were sent to Mexico until, gradually, a French army of forty thousand were assembled there, supported by thirteen thousand Mexican volunteers. France was merely assisting the Mexican Absolutists with money, arms and men, Napoleon insisted. It was their war, not ours.

Meanwhile Maximilian himself was wavering. He had a clever brain, a too clever brain. He could see both sides of a question as well as several additional sides of his own making. "Write to his wife," Napoleon instructed me; Charlotte was known to be ambitious and eager for a crown. I wrote readily enough, stressing the importance of the religious issue. But still Maximilian wavered. He was waiting, Charlotte wrote, for a sign.

A sign of sorts was soon revealed. The French commander occupied the capital of Mexico and Juárez was driven north with a small army that was rapidly disintegrating. A new government was set up in Mexico City and an hereditary monarchy proclaimed. But the throne remained unoccupied, Maximilian refusing to move until the Mexican people ratified the decree of the new government.

Now Napoleon began to lose patience and once again I wrote to Charlotte, telling her that unless her husband made up his mind at once, another prince would be sent to Mexico. That appeared to be sufficient—or almost. Maximilian said he would accept the Mexican throne providing the French guarantees were in accordance with his own desires. And to discuss those guarantees he and Charlotte came to Paris.

Napoleon and I received the future Emperor and Empress of Mexico in private that first day at the Tuileries. Warned of their arrival, we were waiting in the Salle des Maréchaux when a great clatter and much excited shouting reached our ears.

"In the name of heaven!" Napoleon exclaimed.

We hurried to the top of the grand stairway. Loulou was already half-way up—on his donkey! Miss Shaw was wringing her hands and shrieking while Monnier stood placidly by and the servants rushed up and down in despair. Only the *cent-gardes* remained immovable as Loulou continued his adventurous progress. Behind him, behaving as if a donkey on the grand stairway was an everyday event, came the archducal party. Trying to keep a straight face, I appealed quickly to the overindulgent tutor.

"Monnier, are you out of your mind?"

Monnier bowed, seized the bridle and attempted to lead the donkey back down the stairway. It slipped in its stubbornness, turned and bounded up again, encouraged, of course, by Loulou. Monnier was quickly shaken off and so was Napoleon when he tried to intervene. Loulou and the donkey then disappeared from sight with Maximilian, a look of concern on his face, in hot pursuit. Prince Metternich solemnly presented Charlotte and a few moments later, in the Salle des Maréchaux, Maximilian dismounted from the donkey to kiss my hand.

"I made him have a ride," said a delighted Loulou. "Now watch, please!"

Thereupon, to my horror, he dragged long strings of boiled spaghetti from the pocket of his black velvet jacket and began to feed them to the donkey. An amusing sight certainly, this of the spaghetti disappearing into the donkey's mouth. It was guided so skillfully by Loulou that not a single length was broken.

"Are we having spaghetti for lunch?" Napoleon asked mildly.

"No," said Loulou, "there isn't enough left."

During lunch, Pauline Metternich talked about Mexico and Charlotte encouraged her avidly. Maximilian nodded and smiled in the most amiable manner in the world and talked about Miramar—Miramar and nothing else.

"Max is crazy about the place," Charlotte said crossly.

Miramar was their country estate, a newly built castle on the Adriatic near Trieste. Maximilian had designed it himself and was still adding extra rooms. It seemed that it would never be completed to his satisfaction and as for the grounds, there were acres yet to be laid out.

"A very absorbing interest," Napoleon commented heavily.

"Maddeningly so," said Charlotte. "I shall be glad to leave for Mexico."

"Where a palace awaits you," said Pauline, "as well as the Chapultepec Castle on the outskirts of Mexico City. Both, I believe, need restoring and would be projects worthy of the Archduke's special attention."

Maximilian seemed not to hear. "I wish you could see my Moorish pavilion at Miramar. My study, too." His eyes grew dreamy. "Do you think I'm making a mistake in planning an Oriental garden at Miramar? I'm somewhat anxious about the tropical plants. They aren't flourishing as well as I'd hoped."

"Mexico is the place for tropical plants," I said gaily.

250

"It is all a question of getting them acclimatized," he decided, smiling as if he had scored a major triumph.

Luncheon over, Napoleon led the way to my study and smoked four cigarettes before losing patience. Mexico? One would have thought the Archduke had never heard of the place. When I suggested that it would be exciting to sail across the Atlantic in his frigate, he talked about the Mediterranean and the voyages he and Charlotte had made to Greece and Egypt and Spain.

He turned to Napoleon. "One dream of mine is to sail through your new canal. When will the work be completed at Suez?"

"It isn't *my* canal," Napoleon said brusquely. "My interest in it is, of course, intense. So is my interest in Mexico. Would Your Highness care to take a drive this afternoon? More improvements have been made since your last visit. You may find inspiration for the improvements you will undoubtedly want to make in Mexico City."

While Maximilian went sightseeing with Napoleon and the Metternichs, Charlotte remained with me at the Tuileries. She wanted to see everything and sought my advice on the setting up of a court in Mexico. How bored she was with Miramar! Max was a dear, of course, very handsome and morally irreproachable, but his lack of ambition was lamentable. I observed the determined glint in her brown eyes. She, I thought, would be the real ruler of Mexico if only we could get Maximilian across the Atlantic. She was twenty-four at that time, tall, slim, quite regal in appearance, but not really beautiful.

"I would go with Max to the end of the earth," she asserted.

"Our sole concern is that *he* should go with *you*."

"Cousin Victoria made the same remark to Papa."

"It's pleasing to know that Queen Victoria now approves of the undertaking."

"Papa is responsible for that. Even the British government is beginning to approve. Cousin Victoria reigns over a nation of shopkeepers. The promise of profitable trade with Mexico is attractive. The Mexican funds are rising steadily on the London Stock Exchange. What of the Paris Bourse, Madame?"

"A rise there also, but I myself am more concerned with the religious aspect of the undertaking."

Charlotte gave me a well-bred stare. "I am just as devout as you. One must accumulate treasure in heaven also. The spiritual Stock Exchange, as it were."

The next day there was a state dinner followed by a state ball. I was particularly delighted with my new Worth creation, the more so since the material—white tulle threaded with silver—had not been seen at court before. The decorations were unique, too—tiny bunches of pink cowslips peeping out of tufts of grass. Charlotte looked at me disdainfully. Somewhat dismayed, I began to suspect that she regarded me as an upstart, one to be used because of my position. For that reason alone, I decided, she must be hurried away to Mexico without further waste of time.

"The Emperor's patience is exhausted," I told her privately. "In fact, my dear, he is on the point of discussing Mexico with Prince de Joinville."

That was more than sufficient. Pauline reported that Charlotte had been heard screaming at the Archduke during the night, and Maximilian announced the next morning that he was now prepared to discuss the real purpose of his visit. He realized, he said, that the Mexicans, wanting an Emperor so badly, could not be kept waiting indefinitely. "I cannot with honor continue to dally," he declared.

An agreement was discussed, drafted and redrafted. Mexico was called upon to pay the full cost of the expedition and the continued cost of maintaining French troops in Mexico until it was possible to withdraw them. Meanwhile, the French commander, not Maximilian, would have control of the army. In addition—the crux

of the whole matter as far as Morny was concerned—
the remainder of the debts not yet collected was to be
paid in full. Maximilian argued spiritedly and initialed
the agreement only when a secret clause was added:
French troops must not be withdrawn too hurriedly,
and French assistance must always be available whatever happened in Europe.

"The eleventh hour is passed," said Napoleon, when
Maximilian and Charlotte had departed. "We now have
nothing to fear."

"They have yet to sail for Mexico."

"I was thinking of my own particular eleventh hour,
chérie. My dynasty is firmly established after eleven
years of consolidation. I have brought it safely to the
point where we can look forward to a long era of peace
and prosperity." He was closing his eyes—indeed we all
were at that time—to Prussian ambition. He sighed
wearily but with full satisfaction. "I now have a splendid legacy to leave to my son—" he smiled apologet-
ically, "—to *our* son. Forgive me for regarding him as
mine alone."

"Let us regard him as yours alone today," I laughed.
"The young imp rode his donkey up the grand stairway
again not an hour ago and this morning fed spaghetti to
the ostriches at the Jardin des Plantes. A little sternness
on the part of his father is all I ask."

"Do you want him to hate me?" Napoleon said, kissing my cheek affectionately. "Today he possesses only a
mother. Correct him, yourself, *chérie*."

And suddenly I was thirty-nine.

I say "suddenly" because of those words of Mama's:
"Thirty-nine comes upon a woman so suddenly." After
all, in many cases forty never comes at all. My thirty-
ninth birthday was a memorable one because it was
celebrated during my second Regency. The Franco-
Austrian war brought about my first Regency, and one

of Napoleon's love affairs my second. But for that fact I'd scorn to waste ink on *l'affaire Béllanger,* even though, in retrospect, I am able to laugh a little at the anger and indignation which shook me so violently at the time.

I discovered the Béllanger affair because of Loulou's donkey. Dear boy, I had deprived him of his pet for a few days because of some naughtiness which I cannot now remember. It was impossible, of course, to hide the donkey from him in the Imperial stables, so I had placed it in the care of a horse dealer from whom I sometimes bought horses. In due course, the dealer returned the donkey and presented his account to me personally, for I'd asked him to wait on me and discuss a further purchase.

"Pay him immediately," I said, passing the account to Pepa.

Pepa, thus deprived of making a profit for herself, scowled heavily but a moment later, as she stared at the account, she was convulsed with ribald laughter.

"A strange way of presenting an account," she chuckled and read aloud what was in reality a letter:

"Dear little father,

I have taken the liberty of buying two horses which will do honor to your excellent taste and your generous purse. Is the sum of 25,000 francs too great for the pleasure the gift will give me? You know it is not. Therefore, pay the money to the bearer of this note and your dearest Marguerite will return it with 25,000 kisses."

"An exhausting task," I commented tartly.

The poor dealer was immediately covered in confusion. He had made a mistake—a *dreadful* mistake! Hurriedly he snatched from his pocket the account for the donkey's board and lodgings.

"May I know the name of the 'dear little father'?" I asked.

"That I cannot say, Your Majesty," he stammered.

"Well, never mind."

I sent him away but kept the letter, and though I was determined not to make a scene, I gave it to Napoleon when he was smoking his after-luncheon cigarette in my study that afternoon. He read it, folded it and put it in his pocket.

"Are you driving in the Bois this afternoon, *chérie?*"

"If you insist, 'little father.' "

"Routine often becomes a bore," he said generously. "You may please yourself."

I smiled sweetly. "A Russian mistress is perhaps a novelty."

"Marguerite is French. As a matter of fact, she usually calls me Seigneur. Morny, by the way, is ill. It would be a kindness if you—"

"Aren't you curious to know how that letter came into my possession?" I broke in, exasperated beyond endurance.

"Obviously a mistake was made."

"How old is she?"

"Eighteen."

"And you are fifty-seven."

"True."

"Have you bought her a house?"

"Yes."

"Where?"

Napoleon rose. *"Chérie,* will you never accept the fact that these affairs are of no importance whatever? I need the release they give me. I—"

"Very well," I sighed. "I won't make a scene, providing the girl is never brought to court."

Napoleon looked shocked. "Marguerite is a peasant."

"So were the Bonapartes not so very long ago."

"No," said Napoleon, as if talking to an unreasonable child, "they were gentry even in Italy before migrating to Corsica. My grandfather was an advocate. Still, if one goes back far enough, all families—"

"True. Back and back to Adam and Eve. Gardeners if not actually peasants."

The matter would have been forgotten as far as I was concerned, nor would I have learned this "peasant's" name, had it not been for Plonplon. He appeared at a fancy dress ball attired as a Nubian slave and squatted outside a striped tent in the Salle des Maréchaux. There Napoleon and I came upon him when we made our own appearance. The tent, he said, contained a fortune teller. Her charge was the modest sum of fifty francs.

"Are you raising money for charity?" I asked politely.

"A very special charity," he replied. "We need twenty-five thousand francs for a poor horse dealer. Alternatively, twenty-five thousand kisses for a poor Emperor."

Napoleon's face stiffened. "Take M'm'selle Béllanger home at once, Plonplon."

"The privilege is surely yours, Sire."

"Do as I say!" Napoleon said angrily.

Plonplon shrugged and dragged the fortune teller from the tent. A peasant, Napoleon had said, but a very pretty one. Her hair was fair, her large eyes blue and her cheeks alive with health and youthful vigor. There was a mischievous smile about her full red lips. She looked even younger than eighteen. Small wonder the aging, jaded Emperor had fallen under her spell despite the fact that he looked—and indeed was—old enough to be her grandfather.

"I give you my word," Napoleon said, watching wistfully as Plonplon led her away, "I would never have brought her to court myself."

"Can you trust Plonplon with her?"

"I can at least trust her with *him*."

Be that as it may, Napoleon disappeared from the ball less than an hour later.

The new Emperor and Empress of Mexico had, by this time, sailed for Mexico. Ten months after their arrival Morny died. Napoleon felt his loss severely and, with his own health deteriorating, again grew despondent. Morny was irreplaceable, he said. But for Morny, the Empire might never have been created. Could he maintain it without Morny? His words shocked me. This was no longer the man who had boasted that he had created a splendid legacy for his son.

During the next few weeks, his health grew steadily worse. He tackled state affairs half-heartedly and seemed unable to make even the smallest of decisions. Finally he was taken seriously ill while the court was in residence at Saint-Cloud. Dr. Conneau roused me in the middle of the night, but when I started to go at once to Napoleon's bedroom, Conneau coughed discreetly and suggested that a negligee was insufficient covering for even a short journey into the night.

"What do you mean by that, Monsieur?"

"His Majesty was taken ill at the house of a friend. It would be unwise to move him."

"The house of a friend?"

"I beg Your Majesty to hurry. The Emperor's condition is very serious. Otherwise I would have hesitated to impose this indignity upon you."

"So! The house of M'm'selle Béllanger!"

"Yes," Conneau admitted with a hollow laugh.

I dressed hurriedly but on rejoining Conneau in the anteroom learned that a message had just been received. The Emperor had rallied. All danger was past. He was being brought back to Saint-Cloud. Conneau regretted having alarmed me.

You can imagine the difficulty I had in controlling the fury which consumed me as I sat by Napoleon's bed during the early hours of the morning. His face was flushed, his cheeks puffy. He asked for cigarette after cigarette. The doctors had at first diagnosed a seizure but were satisfied now that he was suffering merely from nervous exhaustion.

I remained with him until dawn, leaving him only when he had made two promises, both of which he uttered with pitiful eagerness: Marguerite Béllanger would be sent away; he himself would go to Algeria, a colony always dear to his heart, to recuperate.

And so, because of *l'affaire Béllanger,* I entered upon my second Regency, but with Plonplon, the detestable Plonplon, on hand to "assist" me as Vice-President of the Council. In other words, to oppose me at every turn.

My first council meeting was a stormy one. Plonplon called for a discussion of progress in Mexico, but I saw no trouble in that. Things were going smoothly enough. Maximilian had recently returned from a long tour of the inland during which time Charlotte had acted as Regent. They were apparently quite happy. They felt that the Mexican people as a whole were with them. Maximilian had discovered that the government officials were corrupt—what a surprise!—but was determined to change all that. Charlotte complained only of the insects and asked for a steady supply of insect powder.

"It would seem," I summed up, trying to make everybody laugh, "that we must make the Empress of Mexico a present of a ton or so of insect powder."

Plonplon thumped the table impatiently. "Insect powder! A fine protection against an American invasion of Mexico!" He jumped to his feet and stamped about the room. "The Civil War is drawing to a close. The moment peace is made, American arms will pour into Mexico. Juárez is still at large. American arms first, then American troops. The time has come for the withdrawal of French troops. I demand it! I absolutely demand it!"

"President Lincoln's foreign minister has protested again and again at the presence of a French army in Mexico," I admitted, "but always in the most respectful of language. Morny was growing to regard the protests as a mere matter of form. Morny felt that President Lincoln in time could be induced to acknowledge Maximilian as Emperor of Mexico. Morny—"

"Morny may be dead, but apparently he pulls the strings from the grave," Plonplon interrupted. "Or do we have here an ambitious woman determined to take his place?"

"Determined, yes!" I cried. "Determined to carry on the good work he was doing for France."

"The *good* work!" Plonplon sneered. "May I ask, Madame, if you, too, made a large profit from the Mexican venture?"

And then the appalling story was revealed. Plonplon quoted facts and figures and supplied all the documentary evidence that was needed. Morny had supported the Mexican venture and worked for its success for one reason only—personal financial gain. The banker Jecker, a Swiss by birth but French by naturalization, had seventy-five million francs at stake in Mexico. He had approached Morny. A secret agreement had been reached. Morny, assured of a commission of thirty per cent, had then set to work.

"Was the Emperor aware of this?" I asked fearfully.

"No," Plonplon was honest enough to admit. "Have no fear. Secrecy will be preserved as long as possible. Publicity would injure French prestige, wouldn't it! Or rather, the prestige of the Emperor's government."

"Of which you are a member," I pointed out.

"While it remains in existence, yes."

"If the government fell, you would fall with it."

"Possibly, but . . . who knows? Did I create the present Empire?"

And with that, Plonplon stamped from the room, leaving me to wonder whether he would keep silent or shout the damaging story from the housetops. What, I asked myself, would he gain by revealing the facts? Personal prestige, perhaps?

Then an idea for getting him away from Paris for a

time occurred to me. Personal prestige in another direction! Napoleon intended returning to France by way of Corsica, there to unveil a monument, a group of statues representing Napoleon the Great and his four brothers. The monument was regarded with a good deal of veneration since the last brother, ex-King Jerome, was now dead. Plonplon, envious always of his cousin, would welcome the task himself. Later that day I sent a telegram in code to Napoleon, telling him the whole shocking story of Morny's dishonesty. Two days later Plonplon received a telegram from Napoleon and left importantly for Ajaccio.

Thereafter the council meetings were peaceful. I listened attentively, earnestly and calmly to everybody and when convinced that I was in the wrong, I bowed gracefully to the opinions of others. In the same way I discussed various foreign affairs with various foreign ambassadors. Lord Cowley was particularly impressed when he and I discussed Prussia and Austria and the short war they had made jointly on Denmark, a war in which the two countries had taken three Baltic States from Denmark. However, it seemed to us that Prussia and Austria would come to blows themselves in time, so we agreed that both England and France, come what may, must preserve a strict neutrality.

"The Emperor will have nothing to do when he returns, now that you are handling state affairs so ably," Cowley said with a smile.

But at Ajaccio Plonplon indulged in an amazing *faux pas*. While not committed to republicanism to the degree of supporting the thirty-five republican members of the Chamber of Deputies, he had his own ideas of Bonaparte republicanism and was dreaming of setting up a role of his own if Napoleon's Empire fell. Blown up like the frog who would a-wooing go and, at the same time, gesticulating like a worn-out basso returning inadvisedly to the stage, he croaked and boomed his way through a speech in which he criticized and condemned every political party in France except his own, the one-man Plonplon party. In short, he attacked the government which was the same thing as attacking his cousin the Emperor. In addition, he ranted about the temporal power of the Pope and referred to his Holiness as "a medieval fortress." Clearly he was telling the whole world that he, the hereditary Prince of France, was the only man who knew how to save the Empire from ruin.

When the full report of this speech reached Napoleon, he stirred himself to reply to it in a letter addressed personally to Plonplon, a letter which he sent to me with the covering note: "If the Empress-Regent thinks fit, let it be published in the *Moniteur*." I read it avidly and chuckled at the broad hint the note contained—Plonplon must either resign or suffer dismissal. I published the letter and Plonplon resigned.

Funny, isn't it! Plonplon had been the one who brought Marguerite Béllanger to Napoleon's notice, thus causing Napoleon's physical collapse, my second Regency and his own political downfall. I was about to add "and Béllanger's dismissal," but that promise Napoleon failed to keep. The pretty little peasant joined the Imperial yacht at Marseilles, traveled with him to Algeria, returned with him to Paris and remained his mistress till the fall of the Empire. Small wonder Napoleon's health showed little improvement after the Algerian holiday. However, I held my peace, for on his return he insisted upon my attending every council meeting.

"You must gain a full grasp of all phases of government," he said. "Morny's deceit has shaken me badly. I am left now to suspect all my ministers. I can rely on you, only on you. And you, *chérie,* must be ready to assume full power at any moment."

I come now to the Biarritz plot of the autumn which followed my thirty-ninth birthday.

Just as I never think of Maximilian and Charlotte's arrival at the Tuileries without thinking of spaghetti and Loulou's donkey, so do I think always of Loulou's dog in relation to Bismarck when that gentleman visited us at Biarritz. It was a friendly creature, that dog—huge, clumsy and determined, with a liking for dislodging people from his favorite chairs. How clearly that particular scene at the Villa Eugenie remains in my memory! There stands Bismarck, bowing stiffly from the waist, an enormous man in a white uniform, one hand resting on his sword, the other grasping his ridiculous German helmet. And there stands the dog, slowly wagging his tail and eyeing the chair in which Bismarck is about to sit. Bismarck lowers himself, the dog leaps joyfully forward and—*voilà!* I savor it still—the sight of Bismarck lying on the carpet and the dog snugly ensconced in the chair. If only Bismarck had broken his neck!

Otto Eduard Leopold von Bismarck had been the head of the Prussian government for the last three years. He was fifty, ambitious and determined to bring all the German states together under one crowned head, that of the King of Prussia. He was inspired, he said, by Napoleon's all-Italy policy. Why not, then, an all-Germany policy? Austria stood in his way and must be made to see reason. But Austria, though a co-member of the German "bund," was proving stubborn. A strong, united Germany and a strongly established French Empire—what could be better than that for the preservation of the right balance of power in Europe? All Bismarck asked was French neutrality patterned on English neutrality if Austria forced war upon Prussia. Concessions? Luxembourg for France; possibly Belgium also.

Neutrality meant peace, and how Napoleon and I wanted peace. An agreement was reached, but no treaty was signed, no pen put to paper. It was a gentleman's agreement, and Bismarck went off well satisfied, still wearing his sword and helmet, and one or two bruises caused by Loulou's dog. He soon reached another agreement with Italy, an openly declared defensive-offensive pact.

Then Austria grew alarmed and demanded the demobilization of the Prussian army. Prussia replied by marching into Saxony and Hanover. Austria declared war and Napoleon announced French neutrality. It was a short war. Napoleon, the Peacemaker, mediated on behalf of Austria. Prussia gained additional territory, Austria surrendered Venetia to Italy and France gained nothing at all.

"Did we do the wrong thing?" Napoleon asked.

"We wanted peace. We still have peace."

"And preserve it we must, whatever happens in Mexico."

The position had changed rapidly in America. There was no need now for Plonplon to demand the withdrawal of French troops from Mexico. The American Civil War was at an end. It had actually ended while Plonplon was making that demand of his and the United States, the Union preserved and strengthened, had now asked pointedly for withdrawal. Napoleon and I had agreed. We could do no less, and Maximilian, fearing the result if he were left to stand alone, sent Charlotte to France to plead with us.

Charlotte, now the Empress Carlota, reached Paris when the court was in residence at Saint-Cloud. Napoleon said he was too ill to see her and gave me the unhappy task of greeting her at the Grand Hôtel. Illness was no mere excuse. The doctors had sent him to Vichy to take the waters, but his condition was no better when he returned. There was a sharp fall on the Bourse and reports in the London newspapers of his impending death. As for Marguerite Béllanger, she returned from Vichy in bounding health.

Charlotte met me on the stairway of the hotel, and

there, watched by many curious eyes, we embraced and smiled and asked polite questions about the state of our husbands' healths. Then we retired to the privacy of Charlotte's suite and she flew into a violent temper.

She was so beside herself she scarcely knew what she was saying. Her eyes had a wild, almost demented look. Our ambassador in Mexico had warned us to be prepared for a change in her. When balked, she was likely, he said, to fly into an unreasoning rage as the Mexican ministers had soon discovered.

"When may I see the Emperor?" she demanded.

"The Emperor, as you know——"

"Does he want me to come to Saint-Cloud uninvited? Am I being compelled to force my way into his august presence?"

"Very well," I said reluctantly. "His Majesty will receive you tomorrow afternoon."

Returning to Saint-Cloud, I found Napoleon alone in his study. He was staring blankly at the wall, not even smoking. In my absence, he muttered, he had received the Prussian ambassador. Bismarck's attitude was stiffening against France; he considered the continued presence of French troops in Rome a provocation to Victor Emmanuel.

"It would seem that I must honor my promise and withdraw them," he added dully.

"You actually *promised?*" I gasped. "But when?"

"Two years ago. It was a secret agreement. Please don't be angry, *chérie*. Surely you realize that war with Prussia is as unthinkable as war with the United States."

"Oh yes, I realize it," I said bitterly.

"I'll delay the withdrawal as long as possible. Must I really face Charlotte tomorrow?"

"If you can face Marguerite Béllanger . . . !"

Charlotte came to Saint-Cloud with two ladies-in-waiting. She looked amazingly calm and laughed gaily as she drew my attention to the new hat she had bought that morning. That, however, failed to reassure me. In a desperate situation a woman often thinks about hats.

As soon as we reached the privacy of Napoleon's study, she ignored me completely and addressed herself solely to my husband.

"The Mexican cause is yours, Sire," she said quietly. "Otherwise I would not ask you to save it."

Napoleon cast an appealing glance in my direction. "My cause is peace."

"Then I beg you to preserve it by leaving your army in Mexico. Juárez is rising again. Do you want him to murder us all?"

"We talk at cross purposes, Madame. The United States—Believe me, the Empress and I have every sympathy with you, but we are helpless, quite helpless."

"Why not appeal to Austria?" I suggested.

Charlotte looked at me in disgust. "Prussia has warned Austria not to interfere. Has she warned France also? Is that why you stand aloof?"

Napoleon shook his head. "It would please Bismarck to see France weakened by war with the United States."

"Poor little France, trembling between Prussia and the United States," Charlotte laughed scornfully. "What has happened to your whip, little circus master?"

And then the storm broke. She sprang to her feet, tore off her new hat and flung it to the floor. The hat, for the moment, had become France. She trampled on it, laughing hysterically.

"A circus master!" she cried, pointing a finger at Napoleon. "Max always called you that privately. We laughed. How we laughed! Yet we trusted you; we believed in you. What fools we were, myself especially! I ought to have known better, I, the granddaughter of a *real* French King." She pointed her finger at my husband again. "Louis-Napoleon Bonaparte, the dangerous adventurer. And your court, your new city of Paris! The work of a parvenu, *all* of it. How many people are still deceived by the spurious magnificence? Oh, it won't last; it can't last! Max predicted that after his first visit to Paris. Your little house of cards, your comic-opera throne—you'll bring them all toppling down yourself." She swung round on me. "Or the Spanish woman will."

With that, she fell into a chair exhausted and wept bitterly. Napoleon bent over her solicitously. There were tears in his eyes; he was trembling violently. "The decision isn't mine alone. My ministers, everybody—"

"Naturally your ministers don't care what happens to Max and me," she sobbed. "Haven't they grown fat out of your Mexican venture?"

So she knew about Morny as did everyone now. Our efforts to conceal his perfidy had succeeded only in tarnishing us with his own guilt. But I saw the futility of pleading our innocence, of pointing out that more French money had been squandered in Mexico than would ever be recovered, that four thousand French soldiers had died there. Steadying myself, I poured a glass of orange syrup from the decanter on Napoleon's desk and offered it to her.

"Drink this. It will make you feel better."

Charlotte dashed it from my hand. "Now you are trying to poison me!"

There was nothing more to be done but summon her ladies. They soothed her and presently led her from the room, one carrying the battered hat. Not surprisingly she bought another before leaving Paris. She could well afford the extravagance, she told everybody gaily, for a kind old gentleman had left her a fortune large enough to buy up all the hats in the world.

From Paris she traveled by easy stages to Miramar and there dressed herself in deep mourning. Her one fear was that the imaginary French spies she saw lurking in every corner would succeed in poisoning her. Insanity became undeniable when at last she went to Rome. There she broke in upon the Pope at breakfast, plunged her forefinger into his cup of chocolate to test it and then, satisfied, drank deeply and greedily. She is still alive today as I pen these words—an old lady of almost eighty, but she has never recovered her senses.

And Maximilian? After the withdrawal of the French troops, he found his dwindling Mexican army attacked on all sides by Juárez' ever-growing forces, but he refused to escape while escape was still possible. Finally he was betrayed by one of his own officers, taken prisoner and condemned to death. News of his execution was to cast deep gloom over the most brilliant spectacle of the Second Empire, as I shall relate later. His enemies regarded him as a traitor, so they shot him with his back to a wall. He died bravely, fortified by the belief that he was about to join Charlotte. A false report had reached him that death had already released her from her incurable madness.

"It is easier to die than I thought," he said. "Death is my good angel."

Chapter Nineteen

TEMPER, I FIRMLY believe, is my own particular recipe for longevity. Be that as it may, I indulged in a first-class display of that temper when finally Napoleon told me he was about to order the withdrawal of the French garrison at Rome. A sobering reflection, even now after more than fifty years.

"You promise me one thing and Victor Emmanuel another," I raged. "The left hand, the right hand! How fortunate you don't possess as many hands as that Hindu goddess, Kali!"

"I'm keeping my word with you and the same time my word with Victor Emmanuel."

"A magician, not a circus master!"

"*Chérie,* Victor Emmanuel has given *his* word, too. The Pope is in no danger. Victor Emmanuel will neither attack Rome nor permit anybody else to do so."

"A signed agreement?"

"No."

"Not that it matters. Signed agreements are easily torn to shreds. Do you mean to tell me that Prussia will attack France if you leave the garrison in Rome?"

"How can I possibly say?"

"Just a small risk?"

"For all I know, a large one."

"*Bradago!*" I flung at him, simply because he was wearing a white waistcoat.

"Ah, a bull-fighting term! Uncomplimentary, too, by

the sound of your voice. May I know the meaning of the word?"

"A bull with a white liver," I said, untruthfully.

Paling under the insult, Napoleon said, "I gave you my word to leave the garrison in Rome while any danger existed. There's no danger now." He turned away. *"Bradago . . ."*

"I'm sorry," I said, suddenly contrite. "A *bradago* is a bull with a white belly. Some of the bravest bulls have white bellies."

"Bradago . . ."

"It isn't cowardly to be afraid of war. I fear and hate it myself."

"There's no room in our profession for tender-heartedness," Napoleon said sadly. "What did we gain by neutrality? Or more to the point, what did we lose? France and Austria together could have defeated Prussia, put an end to Bismarck's ambition. I let the right moment pass."

"Forsake the Pope and your son will never mount the throne. Call it superstition on my part if you like—or presentiment—or sheer instinct. But I feel it, Napoleon, I know it." And I did. It was no trick. I was trembling violently.

"I am not forsaking the Pope," Napoleon insisted, shaken as he was by my words.

Not long after that, Napoleon became seriously ill and suffered so severe a bout of pain, Conneau told me, that drugs were being administered. As to the disease itself, Conneau was vague and noncommittal as doctors often are. We would have to wait and see. Much, he suggested, would depend on whether or not the Emperor could be persuaded to lead a quieter and—hum—more continent life.

"Please, not a lecture," Napoleon begged, when he was able to talk to me. "I am what I am. Nothing can change me." Then, displaying a feverish vigor, he spoke of the need to bring together those two opposing forces, the Clerical Party and the Liberals. I looked at him helplessly. The withdrawal from Rome was a Liberal triumph. The Clerical Party had been routed; that was their boast.

"What we must have now," he went on, his mind on another track, "is a grand spectacle in Paris. Another exhibition, one greater than that of 1855. French industrial achievement displayed to the whole world. The emphasis upon the pursuits of peace. Everywhere one hears talk of war. Let *us* talk peace, think peace, make others envious and ready to challenge us peacefully."

It was a glittering spectacle, our *Exposition Universelle des Beaux-Arts et de l'Industrie,* but the emphasis on peace alone? There were military displays. Why not? France was jealous of her peaceful way of life and fully prepared to guard it. France had even conjured up a new gun, the bolt-action, breech-loading *chassepot,* so called because of the inventor, Monsieur Antoine Chassepot. Why had Austria been defeated by Prussia? Simply because the Austrian muzzle-loader was inferior to the Prussian needle gun. Ah yes, but the needle gun was no better than the broadsword when compared with the *chassepot.* The new gun was exhibited proudly among the works of art and the numerous industrial inventions. So was yet another new Prussian weapon, the fifty-thousand-kilo gun from the Krupp workshops.

There was another important exhibit, one that walked, talked, smiled, listened, studied and made copious mental notes. In a word—Bismarck. He came to Paris with his master, King William of Prussia. Master indeed! Everybody knew the name of the real master of Prussia and the growing German Confederation, to say nothing of the new Krupp gun. That alone held Bismarck's interest at the exhibition. The artificial pearls were interesting, but who would dream of giving a lady cheap imitations? The best of French wines were worth a sip or two, but there were better wines in Germany. I'm forgetting, however, the locomobile which Bismarck studied thoughtfully. A significant new contraption, the horseless carriage. When fully developed, would it not come close to revolutionizing warfare?

Less important living exhibits graced our list of guests. It was quite a galaxy. The first Napoleon, silent on his column, must have turned green with envy, for never during his own reign did he succeed in gathering together so many crowned heads, princes and arch-dukes. The Tsar of Russia rubbed shoulders with the Sultan of Turkey and the King of Prussia—an ill-assort-ed trio, that! There were six other kings, three queens and among the thirty or more princes and grand dukes a little smiling, bowing princeling from Japan, at that time a far-off country of little importance.

Politics were not neglected. Napoleon was looking to Russia as the one possible counter to the growing power of Prussia. The Crimean War had been forgotten and forgiven so he hoped, and the Tsar, if only for his own sake, would surely be willing to consider an alliance.

"Your task, *chérie,* is to charm Alexander, *mine* to impress him with a display of French military strength."

I found Alexander very difficult to charm. Or more correctly, I found it impossible to discover whether or not my efforts were succeeding. He was an autocrat of autocrats, that Tsar of all the Russias, a very mighty but aloof "little father." His politeness was icily correct; his smile noncommittal; and even though he betrayed him-self in no way at that first reception, I was left with the uneasy feeling that in paying his respects he was su-premely conscious of my inferior origins.

The next day there was a grand review in the Bois de Boulogne, with the Tsar sitting his horse on one side of Napoleon, King William of Prussia on the other—the one to be impressed by the parade of sixty thousand troops; the other, one hoped, to be intimidated. After-ward Napoleon drove from the Bois with Alexander in his carriage, I following with King William in mine. Each carriage had a military escort and the route was lined with police. Even so, fanatics are ever desperate and as Napoleon's carriage reached the Grand Cascade, a single shot rang out.

"At whom was the assassin firing?" King William asked, as the police seized the man, "the Emperor of France or the Tsar of Russia?"

I stared apprehensively at Napoleon's carriage. Both men were standing and Napoleon, so much shorter than the Tsar, was reaching up to embrace his "brother."

"Now we have been under fire together!" Napoleon cried for the edification of the crowd.

"Touching," King William said plaintively. "No one appears to have been hurt. It must have been a wild shot."

I looked at him suspiciously. Was he wondering if this was a contrived affair? I listened to the cheering of the crowd. "Long live the Tsar!" rang out clearly above "Long live the Emperor!" A neatly placed claque? My suspicions, however, were unfounded. Alexander was the intended victim and the would-be assassin was a Pole sickened by the brutality inflicted upon his countrymen by the Tsar's Cossacks. Napoleon had merely taken swift advantage of an unexpected situation.

There was a ball that night at the Russian Embassy. Alexander opened it with me and as we danced, I tried to apologize for the incident. In spite of the strict watch kept on foreign refugees, I explained, the police were sometimes hoodwinked.

"I am safer in my own country," he said irritably.

"Indeed?" I retorted. "I was under the impression that your life had been attempted more often in Russia than the Emperor's in France. I felt sure you were well used to one of the common hazards of our profession."

Alexander's face softened. "Forgive me. You put me to shame. The Empress Eugenia is as famous for her bravery as she is for her charity. I honor her for it."

Napoleon was delighted. In the most unexpected manner imaginable, I had succeeded in charming the Tsar. He himself would waste no time in taking the political plunge. A private luncheon first, then an amiable, informal discussion while smoking a cigarette. The discussion took place in Napoleon's study rather than in mine, and I—well, Napoleon decided at the last moment to exclude me. I waited for an hour before impatience and indignation, to say nothing of outraged dignity, got the better of me.

"A surprising interruption," Alexander remarked coldly when I burst in upon them.

Napoleon tried to laugh it off. "The Empress is wearing a new gown and seeks your opinion."

"I observed it during lunch."

"And admired it, yes?" Napoleon asked anxiously.

"Petticoats, however pretty, are out of place in politics," said the unspeakable autocrat.

Thereupon he bowed distantly, failed to see the hand Napoleon offered him and withdrew. Later that day the Russian ambassador demanded the death of the unfortunate Polish national and seemed dissatisfied when told that judgment rested with the French courts. Alexander left for Russia the next day. The Pole was found guilty but his life was spared. Napoleon grumbled that my own conduct, in addition to the verdict, had deprived us of a Russian alliance. That was nonsense. Had Alexander wanted an alliance, nothing—not even a petticoat —would have been permitted to interfere.

The festivities, however, went forward smoothly enough without the presence of the mighty Tsar. There were more balls, more receptions and finally the grand climax of the prize-giving ceremony. This coincided with the shattering announcement of Maximilian's execution in Mexico. I was told afterward that I distributed the prizes with a calm smile on my face and that Napoleon delivered his prepared speech unfalteringly. If true, I remember nothing of those ghastly moments. Later, much later, I read Napoleon's speech, a few brief phrases of which still echo in my memory: "This exhibition marks a new era of harmony and progress . . . I am convinced that Providence blesses the efforts of all who desire to do well . . . I believe in the triumph of morality and justice . . . They alone consolidate all thrones, uplift all peoples, ennoble all humanity . . ."

The irony of it! Small wonder that I with my fixed calm smile and Napoleon with his unfaltering speech were condemned by many as heartless, calculating intriguers.

Not long after Maximilian's death, Napoleon suffered another severe attack of pain, and once again I sat by his bedside waiting for him to emerge from a drug-induced stupor. On opening his eyes he stared at me without recognition and muttered to himself about his recent failure to form an alliance with Austria. Presently he grasped feebly at my hand.

"Eugénie?"

"Has the pain gone, Napoleon?"

He struggled to a sitting position. "Did you seize the opportunity to send Marguerite away?"

"No."

"That was kind of you."

"Some other *puta* would have taken her place."

"Wise then, not kind." He laughed like a child well pleased with his shrewdness. "What of state affairs? Are you in full control?" He looked at me in amazement when I shook my head. "How silly! You aren't as wise as I thought. A really clever woman would have forced abdication upon me."

Abdication! Was he as serious as he sounded? I thought of the hints which Pauline Metternich had thrown out a few days earlier. There was a strong possibility of Austria being willing to negotiate a treaty if

Napoleon were out of the way—Napoleon, whose neutrality was of use to one nation only, Prussia.

"Abdication would require a special act," I said steadily. "Your own signature . . ."

"So it would," he agreed.

Abdication, I thought, while Loulou was still a child. My son the Emperor-Minor, myself the Empress-Regent with full power and the will to use that power wisely in a determined effort to preserve the dynasty.

Napoleon fingered the sheet. "Well, why not? Call a special council meeting for tomorrow morning. Bring the ministers to my bedside. Afterward I shall retire to Plombières or perhaps Vichy."

I could scarcely believe my ears. "Napoleon . . ."

"You wonder why I'm doing this? Gratitude, *chérie,* gratitude. A small reward because you refrained from sending Marguerite away."

"Are you absolutely serious?"

"I give you my word—my solemn word."

I grew vastly excited, but when calling the bedside council meeting, I said not a word about abdication, thus preventing the ministers from first discussing it among themselves.

We found Napoleon sitting up in bed with a mass of documents spread out before him. He was bright-eyed and brisk, greeted everybody affably, then growing grave addressed himself to the Minister of State.

"Has the story reached the Paris newspapers yet, Rouher?"

"No, Sire, but the London newspapers will be full of it and I expect their Paris correspondents to be informed by telegram at any moment."

The *London* newspapers? I found myself laughing in disbelief.

"Gentlemen," Napoleon went on tensely, "Garibaldi has invaded papal territory." He glanced quickly at me. "No, this is not a breach of faith on Victor Emmanuel's part. Garibaldi has acted once again on his own behalf. Victor Emmanuel has expressed strong disapproval and remains aloof. We must do the same."

I protested at once and so did Rouher. There were instant arguments for and against, and the meeting broke up without a decision being reached. To me only one line of action was possible, but Napoleon refused stubbornly to listen.

"France, I insist, must stand aloof."

"Is that why you changed your mind?"

"About abdication? I changed my mind before the news reached me."

"So much for your solemn word!"

"I was under the influence of drugs at the time."

That, of course, explained everything.

I argued with him for days and talked separately with each minister. At last I gained a majority and Napoleon agreed reluctantly to send an army corps from Toulon to Rome. A few red flags fluttered in the streets of Paris but the demonstrations organized by the communists were quickly broken up. Not even Napoleon was ready, then, to take the "reds" seriously. Only one army corps was needed in Rome. Garibaldi and his redshirts were soon scattered and in flight, and a French garrison was stationed once more in Rome. The Pope was safe. Napoleon III, Defender of the Faith!

"Is real faith ever in need of a defender?" Napoleon asked broodingly. "Faith is its own shield. Nothing can touch it. I defended the Church Temporal, the Church *Militant*, not the Faith."

"Why quibble?" I laughed. "The loyalty of every Catholic in France is now yours."

"At the expense of antagonizing Italy. I failed with Russia, again with Austria. A treaty with Victor Emmanuel is equally impossible now. France stands alone and alone must become self-sufficient. Harmony and progress at home—*that* I must have and through it build up the army, and the navy, and strengthen our defenses. No country will make war on us then. My only fear is the fear of revolution. Expressions of loyalty are pouring in from the Clerical Party but the Liberals are in an ugly mood.

"I spoke once of bringing the two parties together," he went on agitatedly. "The preservation of the dynasty is only possible that way. Out of the confusion which so often clouds my mind, one thing stands out clearly. Either I win over the Liberals or my son will never mount the throne. You stand against me, that I know. Therefore, I must build my Liberal Empire alone."

And he did, God bless him, short-lived as that brave new Empire was. Napoleon was right and I wrong. But for the greed and cunning of Bismarck, the Liberal Empire would still be flourishing today.

In 1868, to those of us who had witnessed the invention of the camera, having one's photograph taken was sitll an exciting adventure; to me it was always something of an ordeal. One assumed a fixed expression, held one's breath and waited in absolute agony while the photographer-magician, his head beneath the black cloth, moved this way and that until the tripod, giving him three extra legs, seemed to have become a living part of his body. Loulou, to whom the camera was as commonplace as the automobile is today to a boy of that age, was a dreadful little poseur when face to face with a photographer. The outrageous attitudes he struck, especially when wearing a military uniform!

"Do I look manly enough?" he demanded when he was being photographed on his twelfth birthday.

"As manly as your great ancestor at the Bridge of Lodi," Napoleon assured him fondly.

"I *do?* Then perhaps I ought to be photographed pointing a gun."

"Stand still, Loulou," I admonished. "Do you want to appear with two heads instead of one?"

"Loulou!" he expostulated. "I'm much too old for that baby name."

"As you wish, Monseigneur."

Since he now had his own special court—*la jeune cour,* we called it—the boy was inclined to take himself with tremendous seriousness. *La jeune cour,* replacing the easy-going Monnier, consisted of General Charles Frossard, the military governor, four aides-de-camp and Augustin Filon, the new tutor. Frossard, kindly but firm, was in complete charge. Not even Napoleon was permitted to interfere. Poor Napoleon! I well remember the dismayed expression on his face the first time he sent for Loulou during a lesson and was told that the Prince Imperial was not available. I was well satisfied with the new arrangement; my son was submitting to real and necessary discipline at last.

"I insist on being called Louis, really I do," he said.

"Old habits are hard to break," Napoleon laughed. "Think, for instance, of Bertie, the Prince of Wales. Some day he will be King Edward VII of England."

"Very well," Loulou conceded. "You and Mama may continue to call me Loulou, but only in private."

His twelfth birthday was an important one, celebrated by a public holiday throughout France, while at the Tuileries a reception was given in his honor.

Among the people received that day by Loulou was Émile Ollivier, a prominent Liberal, one of the five— *Le Cinq,* we called them—elected in opposition ten years ago. Violent in opposition then, a Republican rather than a Liberal, Ollivier had grown more moderate in his political outlook. Accordingly, Napoleon was striving to win his loyalty, but I myself still regarded him as a political enemy. When I looked at him, I saw only the menacing bulk of Plonplon, not the rather gentle social worker with whom I had at least one thing in common, an interest in prison reform.

"As you see, Ollivier," said Napoleon, bringing the

278

man to greet me, "the Empress and I take a back seat at the Tuileries today."

Ollivier smiled pleasantly. "People have been known to turn and listen attentively, thereupon making the back seat the front seat."

"Clearly you shun the round table with no man at the head, Monsieur," I said tartly.

Ollivier smiled charmingly. "Even at a round table Your Majesty's prominence would be undeniable."

"Flattery, Monsieur, from a man who never flatters?"

"We may stand in opposition, Madame, but I speak in all sincerity."

Napoleon laughed lightly and drew our attention to Loulou. "Every inch a Bonaparte, don't you agree, Ollivier?"

"You should remember, Sire," Ollivier said gently, "that I shed tears of anger when the bones of Napoleon Bonaparte were brought to Paris from St. Helena."

"I see no tears at the sight of your future Emperor."

"Possibly because he bears little resemblance to the Bonapartes."

"Even so, the hatred is passing?" Napoleon asked eagerly.

"It passed some time ago."

"We shall win you over yet," Napoleon laughed.

Ollivier glanced at me. *"We,* Your Majesty?"

"Say rather that you and I together shall win over the Empress."

I met Ollivier again at my own birthday party the following May. He sat at the Imperial dinner table along with Plonplon, Mathilde, a few of my intimate friends and Eugène Rouher, the Minister of State. Bringing Ollivier and Rouher together at a dinner party was another move of Napoleon's in the thankless task of trying to create friendship and understanding between the two opposing political forces. Rouher, an Absolutist, was as adamant as I myself and therefore a much needed ally.

That particular party provided another example of Plonplon's rudeness. Napoleon should have known better than to ask him to propose my health, but ask him he did.

"I drink to Her Majesty's forty-two years," said Plonplon, eyeing me balefully.

Ollivier rose instantly. "With the Emperor's permission, *I* drink to Her Majesty's *next* forty-two years."

Everybody drank—except Plonplon.

I must admit I felt somewhat drawn to Ollivier after that and no longer thought of the Plonplon shadow, for had Ollivier not dissociated himself from Plonplon, there at the dinner table? Nevertheless, though I talked with him from time to time and discussed the reforms he had in mind, I remained stubbornly against him. After all, had I not the still large government majority on my side, whatever the next general election might bring? It was *my* government now, I told myself; my husband the Emperor had gone over to the opposition.

Dear old Mérimée, always gloomy those days, predicted that Napoleon's hand would be forced—by which he meant *my* hand—after the general election. A new excitement was in the air, he said, and invited me to make a tour of the boulevards with him. We went in disguise—my own, I remember, included a pair of spectacles—and nobody recognized us. The bookshops held my attention first. Inflammatory anti-Empire books and pamphlets were boldly displayed and people were buying them eagerly. The first volume of Karl Marx' *Das Kapital* was also selling briskly.

Then we went from café to café and at one of them came upon Henri Rochefort holding court as he sipped an *apéritif*. His Republican pamphlet *La Lanterne*, itself an echo of the old revolutionary cry, "A la lanterne!" had been suppressed but not before thousands of copies had been sold. A warning of things to come, said Mérimée. But was revolution really in the air again? I studied the crowd of eager, hot-headed talkers who surrounded Rochefort, that tall, thin fanatic with an abnormally large forehead and a ridiculous goatee beard adorning his pointed chin. He and his friends wore *lanterne* buttons and were discussing Karl Marx, apparently, by the sound of their voices, for the purpose of provoking one hectic argument after another.

Revolution? No, I couldn't believe it. The state of France was much too stable for serious discontent. There was a large national debt, yes, but that was the Emperor's personal headache. The man in the street was happy enough. French industry was making rapid progress. There was plenty of work to be had and taxation, never crippling during Napoleon's reign, caused scarcely more than the normal token grumble.

"You're out of your mind," I told Mérimée.

"Wait for the general election," he said.

It took place the following April and, dear me, how fractious Napoleon grew while we waited for the final results to reach the Tuileries! He suffered a little bout of superstition, too, and all because of a new fashion introduced by Mr. Worth.

"I like your new dress but not its name," he said darkly.

"The polonaise? It's a pretty enough name."

"Worth developed it, I'm told, from the pannier of Louis XVI's reign. The pannier appeared at the end of his reign, the eve of disaster. Is Worth a prophet as well as a dressmaker? Are we being told through a resurrected fashion that my reign is coming to an end?"

"Would you like me to resurrect the crinoline just to be on the safe side?"

The final results were startling. Napoleon had introduced a few liberal reforms but, in spite of such vote-catching, the opposition emerged in greater strength with a gain of a million and a half votes.

"A warning I dare not ignore too long," said Napoleon.

Toward the end of that year, the Suez Canal which my cousin Ferdinand de Lesseps had begun ten years earlier was completed and the Viceroy of Egypt invited me to preside at the opening ceremony. That, the most glorious episode of my life, was my last personal triumph as Empress.

It all has a dreamlike quality now, right from the beginning to the end of that enchanting voyage in the Imperial yacht *l'Aigle*. Venice first, then Athens and Constantinople. The sheer magic of those names! I regretted not having insisted upon Loulou's accompanying me, but my two nieces, dear Paca's daughters, were there to share my joy. Loulou, in any case, would have been horrified at the sight of his mother lounging like an eastern queen in the crimson tent aboard the Sultan of Turkey's caïque or squatting in the richly decorated litter in which she was carried up from the Bosphorus to the palace.

And Cairo! My little son would have been jealous of the attentions paid me by the Viceroy, Ismail-Pacha, but I took it all for granted and reveled in it day and night. The Queen of the World—that's who Ismail-Pacha made me feel I was. The tropical air reminded me of southern Spain and oranges ripening in the sun. A flight of fancy mentioned in passing, and with a wave of the hand, there they were the next morning, row upon row of heavily laden orange trees transplanted to the palace garden during the night.

The dream continues. Port Said harbor crammed with ships from every part of the world, *l'Aigle* leading the procession into the new waterway, while the Queen of the World reclines on the deck surrounded by the Emperor of Austria, the Crown Prince of Prussia, the Emir of Persia and numerous princes and ambassadors. Ferdinand de Lesseps sits on her right. Let us not forget him—the real hero of that glorious day. A happy man, de Lesseps. Years of well-nigh insurmountable struggles, the impossible achieved at last. Presently he'll receive a silver cup in proof of it, the inscription reading: *L'Impératrice Eugénie à Ferdinand de Lesseps.*

The Emperor of Austria and the Crown Prince of Prussia were generous in their praise. It was particularly pleasing to me that Austria and Prussia should have been brought together on the deck of a French yacht. Only Bismarck's presence could have ruined that day for me. But Bismarck was ill, a nervous breakdown, the Crown Prince told me. The man had gone too far in many things, he said, and both he and his father King William had opposed him sternly. Hence, so very unexpectedly, so very gratifyingly—a nervous breakdown.

"The Emperor of France will be most interested," the Crown Prince murmured.

"If it should lead to a better understanding between Prussia and France, the whole world will be interested," I replied.

Franz Joseph of Austria was certainly interested. With Bismarck out of the way, a new era of peace lay before Europe or so he predicted. As far as he was concerned, the French failure in Mexico was best forgotten. Now was perhaps the time to discuss an alliance with France or even a triple alliance—France, Austria, Prussia . . .

Small wonder I returned to Paris glowing with a feeling of double achievement. I was even ready to listen more tolerantly to Ollivier's arguments; until I discovered that during my absence Napoleon himself had listened fully, had dismissed Rouher and had asked Ollivier to form a Liberal Ministry.

"The Liberal Empire is now in being," he told me.

"You sent me to Egypt to get me out of the way!"

"You went willingly, *chérie.* No pressure was exerted."

"Did you ask Ismail-Pacha to invite me?"

"Indeed I did, but not because I wanted to get rid of you. It was an opportunity, I admit, to conclude my task in peace, but your presence would not have deterred me. I sent you to Egypt for one reason only: I wanted you to have an important personal triumph there and through it consolidate your own position. Consolidate it further through friendship with Ollivier."

"Never!"

"You are still a member of the executive council. If I die while Loulou is still a minor, you will have all the power which I at this moment possess."

With that I grew calmer. Napoleon had created his revolution within the government. It was even possible that he had averted a rising, a real and bloody revolution. There was peace and prosperity at home and, with Europe growing calmer, every sign of lasting peace abroad.

"Shall we talk about Austria and Prussia?" I said.

"Gladly!"

"But remember this, my Napoleon, if I find Ollivier going too far I shall oppose him violently.

My husband was staring at my dress. "A pretty color. Is it a new shade of blue?"

"Yes. *Eau-de-nil.*"

"Ah, in honor of your trip down the Nile. No doubt every woman in Paris will be wearing it soon."

"But of course! I'm still the Empress of Fashion if nothing else."

Chapter Twenty

AT THE LIRIA PALACE there are still many re-
minders of the past—including a small framed photograph of Loulou taken just before his last birthday at the
Tuileries. His hair is in curly disarray in spite of his
many efforts to smooth it severely back, and he wears a
black velvet suit with a large white collar and a red tie
loosely knotted.

I well remember the last time he wore that velvet
suit. It was at a dinner party two months or so after his
fourteenth birthday. For the last six years he'd been allowed to dine with us in private, but now on occasion
his father was bringing him to important state functions
and allowing him to take part in the conversation. That
particular dinner was in celebration of the recent plebiscite at which the people had been asked to vote for or
against the new ministry and, at the same time (the
whole stated in one skillfully worded sentence), the
continuation of the dynasty.

The result was awaited tensely by all concerned and
under the strain, my temper suffered equally with Napoleon's health. The people of France had voted over-
whelmingly for the Empire almost twenty years ago.
Why ask them to vote again? Many an Imperialist, hating Liberal reforms, would be tempted to vote nay. And
how many Liberals, hating Imperialism, would fall into
the trap of voting *yea*?

There were near riots in Paris, barricades were erected and red flags carried through the streets, while little

groups of people sang the "Marseillaise," long ago forbidden. Nevertheless, when the votes were counted there were seven million yeas against a million and a half nays. It wasn't the overwhelming majority Napoleon had hoped for, but it was reason enough for merry-making.

And so the dinner party, with the guests gathered afterward in the Salon d'Apollon. Napoleon looked so ill that many people were shocked by his appearance, but he was more relaxed than usual and that put us all at our ease. Everybody congratulated him, but again nd again he shook his head.

"You must congratulate my son. The Empire is safe for Napoleon IV."

"Safe?" I remember Plonplon asking. "Are you as sure as you try to sound, Sire? There were nearly two million abstentions. Two million people unwilling to vote either yea or nay!" He turned to Lebœuf, the Minister of War. "And you, Monsieur, are you not alarmed at the spectacle of fifty thousand soldiers voting nay?"

"A disappointment," Napoleon admitted, "but no doubt they feared a reduction of the army and the loss of their jobs in these times of growing peace."

Loulou came up and slipped his hand into his father's. "Papa, may I be excused now?"

"What, bored already?"

"Papa, you promised. It won't take me long. I'll be back in ten minutes. Less, if I hurry."

Napoleon smiled and nodded. "I'd quite forgotten. Off you go."

"What do you think of the Spanish situation?" somebody asked.

"A domestic affair which the Spanish people must solve for themselves," Napoleon replied.

A Spanish revolution had removed Queen Isabella from the throne. She had offered to abdicate in favor of her son, the Prince of the Asturias, but the new government, contemptuous of the Spanish Bourbons, had rejected the offer. General Prim, now in control of Spain, was said to be negotiating with an Italian prince. Prim wanted a king on the throne of Spain, but one who would be little more than a puppet.

"Ah!" Napoleon cried.

Loulou had made a dramatic reappearance. Gone was the velvet suit. In its place he wore a new uniform, a *real* uniform, that of a sub-lieutenant of infantry. He was a real soldier at last, ready and eager to join his regiment.

"One need no longer play at being a soldier," he said proudly.

His words gave me such a queer, lost feeling. It was something quite apart from any military implication. I expect the same feeling would have struck me if the velvet suit had been replaced by grown-up evening clothes. Gone was the boy of only a few moments ago. An occasional glimpse during the shattering weeks that followed, yes, but I never really saw him again. Why, I thought, in sudden consternation, it will soon be necessary to find him a wife and then I'll lose him altogether.

The court was at Saint-Cloud when the Spanish situation, the "domestic affair which the Spanish people must solve for themselves," became very much the concern, the disastrous concern, of France. It was a quiet enough court, with entertainment reduced to a minimum. All Napoleon wanted to do was rest and regain his strength. A few quiet walks, no riding at all and many long hours alone in his study planning new reforms. Occasionally he roused himself and disappeared for a night. Marguerite Béllanger was still in favor. At the end of June he allowed Conneau to bring a number of eminent specialists to Saint-Cloud. They examined him on July first and retired to prepare their report. On the second, after a hurried talk with Gramont, the new

Foreign Minister, he called an immediate council meeting.

"General Prim," he announced wearily, "has invited Prince Leopold of Hohenzollern-Sigmaringen to accept the Spanish throne."

"A *German* prince," Gramont stressed unnecessarily. "An officer in the Prussian army!"

And then the whole story came out. Bismarck, completely recovered from his nervous breakdown, was in full power again. Even while ill or supposedly ill, he had intrigued secretly with General Prim, and there seemed every reason for believing that in approaching Leopold on behalf of the Spanish government, Prim had been prompted by Bismarck.

"Leopold is Bismarck's tool, that is undeniable," Napoleon said.

"Has Prince Leopold accepted the offer?" Ollivier asked.

"Apparently."

"Can we stand idly by while a German prince assumes the Spanish throne?" Gramont asked.

The answer, of course, was no.

The next morning when the newspapers published the startling story, the whole of Paris cried out against it and a few of the boulevard politicians shouted "*A Berlin!*" just as if war, unthinkable war, had been declared that moment. Messages began to pour in from the provinces. A German prince must be kept off the Spanish throne, whatever the cost. Another council meeting was called and it was decided that the strongest possible protest must be made to King William of Prussia. If he ignored it, said Gramont, war was inevitable. Leboeuf supported him instantly. I listened in dismay, my only consolation being Napoleon's refusal to be influenced.

"War is never inevitable," he insisted.

"King William will draw back when he realizes that the whole of France is roused against him," Ollivier said hopefully.

"We are dealing with Bismarck, not King William," Lebœuf said scathingly. "Bismarck throws down a challenge. I see only folly in permitting him to go on building up his forces. France was never stronger than at this moment. One quick, bold stroke and the French army will be marching through the streets of Berlin."

"Let us await the result of our protest," Napoleon begged, and closed the meeting.

That evening I asked him to let me see the report drawn up by the specialists. He laughed jauntily and said that the medical terms would only confuse and perhaps mislead me.

"As Conneau will tell you," he added, "the only treatment I need is a long rest. We shall go to Biarritz as soon as this Spanish affair has been settled."

Six days later we received a telegram from our ambassador in Germany. He had succeeded in having a long and satisfactory talk with the King of Prussia who was taking the waters at Ems. Bismarck had not been present. He was in Berlin. Our ambassador was confident of a happy outcome, a peaceful solution. Three days later a telegram from Madrid announced the withdrawal of Prince Leopold. Spain would look elsewhere for a king. France and Prussia were mobilizing their forces rapidly, but that meant nothing now.

"Peace!" Napoleon cried, the tears rolling down his cheeks.

There was instant consternation in Paris. Public opinion had been aroused to such an extent that the announcement caused frantic disappointment. Mighty France, invincible France, had been taunted and insulted. The withdrawal of Prince Leopold was not enough. The King of Prussia must apologize. Gramont was loud in this demand, so was Lebœuf and even Ollivier, caught up in the mass hysteria, supported them. Instructions were sent to our ambassador who must have been sorely embarrassed in his attempt to put the demand in diplomatic language. His reply stated tersely that King William was unwilling to do more than confirm Prince Leopold's withdrawal. Off went another telegram to Ems, sent independently by Gramont. The King of Prussia must give a personal guarantee against a revival of Leopold's candidature.

In reply, or so it seemed at the time, the German newspapers published a dispatch from King William at Ems to Bismarck in Berlin, and the French newspapers copied it immediately. King William, refusing to receive the French ambassador again, had told him that the matter was closed. To this was added a report from a French correspondent at Ems: King William, meeting the French ambassador by chance on the promenade, had turned his back upon him.

"France has received a slap in the face," Gramont said wildly.

The actual truth, as we later discovered, was that Bismarck had made public a dispatch which King William had commanded him to regard as a state secret. But Bismarck, furious at Prince Leopold's forced withdrawal, had disobeyed, thus waving the red flag in the face of the French bull, as he laughingly termed it. It was soon known, also, that King William had only turned his back on the French ambassador after another attempt, there on the promenade, to discuss the situation. That particular gentleman of the press would have been better employed reporting the angle at which King William wore his hat.

The French bull roared and pawed the ground. He roared in the council chamber at Saint-Cloud and along the boulevards of Paris, in the scented *salons* and the crowded cafes. There were three council meetings that day, one in the morning, another in the afternoon and the last at midnight. During the first and the second, Napoleon was badly outnumbered but stood firmly against war. Bismarck wanted war, yes, but because of certain alliances he did not dare declare it himself. Why, Napoleon asked, should France fall into the trap and

290

willingly permit herself to be stigmatized as the aggressor?

After the second meeting broke up, I went with Mérimée to Paris. Disguised once more, I looked this time like a well-to-do housewife making an ordinary shopping excursion, so Mérimée said. People were singing the "Marseillaise" and the cry *"A Berlin!"* was deafening. From time to time we talked with little groups of people or rather I left the talking to Mérimée, since I was afraid to betray myself by my Spanish accent. Political enemies of long standing had become firm friends overnight. Oh, they'd be at each other's throats again after the occupation of Berlin, but meanwhile, united in a national emergency, they formed an irresistible force, an invincible army in themselves. *A bas la Prusse!* At the same time, being French, they still had an eye to business. The bookshops were doing a thriving trade in dictionaries. More than one establishment carried over its door a placard that made everybody roar with laughter: FRENCH-GERMAN DICTIONARIES FOR THE CONVENIENCE OF FRENCHMEN IN BERLIN.

I returned sadly to Saint-Cloud. Paris was the council chamber now. There the decision had been made. The nation was already at war. The forbidden "Marseillaise" rang in my ears, and in my mind's eye I saw the mob of eighty years ago storming the Tuileries. The warning was dismayingly clear. If the Emperor Napoleon III held back, the Emperor Paris would turn on him savagely. It was either war or revolution and, like Napoleon, I had come to fear revolution more than war.

For the most part Napoleon sat in silence at that final, fateful, midnight council meeting, his face more mask-like than ever. Even when Lebœuf, Minister of War, flung his portfolio on the table, his expression remained unchanged.

"Either France declares war or I resign my office," Lebœuf challenged. "The honor of France is at stake. A short war, a glorious war. The army is stronger than ever before. We lack nothing, absolutely nothing. That I guarantee."

"France is certainly in better shape than Prussia," Gramont said. "Bismarck wants to intimidate us, but not at the cost of a ruinous war. His grip on the German states is not yet secure. The whole of southern Germany will revolt. Bismarck's stupid miscalculation is inspired by Providence."

"The honor of France is at stake," Lebœuf repeated. "Only war can preserve it."

I spoke up then myself, soberly and earnestly, not wildly and excitedly as Gramont reported later in his attempt to make me solely responsible. Honor, the insistence on honor, that had a strong appeal to me—a blinding appeal, as is often the case when the sword of honor cuts down all about it, even common-sense. The fear of revolution, that influenced me, too. But above all else the deciding factors were Marshal Lebœuf's guarantee and Gramont's opinion on the state of Germany.

"And so war is inevitable," I concluded.

The rest spoke up, all in favor of war. Lebœuf, seizing his portfolio, flung it down before him a second time.

Napoleon stirred himself and spoke at last. One word only.

"War!"

Lebœuf and Gramont embraced each other, then the latter rushed off to Paris to announce the council's decision to a Paris still thronged with people late as the hour was. The news spread rapidly. The Legislative Body had yet to debate the issue, but to the people that night it was a mere matter of form. Three thousand people danced round the Emperor Napoleon's column chanting *"A Berlin!"* and *"Vive l'Empereur!"* France declared war officially five days later, by which time the Chamber, with only ten members in opposition, had voted war credits recklessly.

The realization that France was at war came upon me fully and shatteringly when Sub-lieutenant Bonaparte, as Loulou insisted on calling himself, announced proudly that he was going with his father to the battlefield. I was much against it but agreed in the end, for I feared revolution if things went wrong and reasoned that my son would be safer with the army. In any case there would have been no holding Loulou back. He was the youngest soldier in the army. Think of it, the *youngest!* That meant more to him than being heir to the throne.

"The Prince Imperial isn't in the army to play at soldiers," said Napoleon, uttering the words which Loulou put into his mouth, "but to learn an Emperor's profession."

I packed my soldier son's little black trunk myself and I clipped a lock of hair from his head. "For Grandmama," I assured him, warned by the embarrassed look on his face. Grandmama, yes; old ladies could be excused for that sort of sentimentality.

"You must speak about honor and duty when you bid me good-by at the station," the lad said. "That will make a good impression on everybody."

Since the court was still at Saint-Cloud, Napoleon decided to leave for army headquarters at Metz by way of the little private railway station in the park. No time was wasted; the sooner he, the Commander-in-Chief, reached Metz, the sooner an offensive would be launched.

A change in the weather added to the gloom of the leave-taking. The brilliant, hot dry summer gave place that twenty-eighth day of August to an early autumn. The sky was heavily clouded and a gusty wind carried showers of fallen leaves before it as I drove Napoleon to the station in my open pony carriage. Members of the Imperial household stood on the platform, as conscious as I of the protracted deadlines of all leave-takings.

293

"I go to a long and difficult war," Napoleon said, embracing me abruptly, "and I leave you to a long and difficult task."

Then I took Sub-lieutenant Bonaparte in my arms and clung to him for a long moment, unable to utter a single word.

"Say it, Mama, *say it!*" he whispered urgently.

"Remember that honor and duty come before all else," I said, as sternly as I could. "Behave yourself honorably and do your duty."

"So speaks the Spartan mother," Plonplon sneered.

He was going to the battlefield too, as confident as Lebœuf of a speedy victory, but though he did not know it, Napoleon had wisely decided against giving him an important command.

I offered him my hand to kiss. "Please don't run away this time, Plonplon."

His eyes snapped angrily, but he did kiss my hand.

I detained Loulou a moment longer, begging him in my heart to be patient with me while I made the sign of the Cross on his forehead as I always did when he was going on a journey without me or I without him. That old Spanish custom had always comforted me. Now, though comforting me but little, it helped me at least to keep back my tears. Spartan mothers never wept—at all events not in public—and I waved, grim-faced still, as the train drew out of the station.

My third and last Regency had begun.

Later, in Napoleon's study at Saint-Cloud, I gave way to tears. The Empress-Regent. No empty title this time. A special decree two days ago had given me full power during Napoleon's absence. There was a regency council to advise me, of course, but in all matters mine was the final decision. I smiled through my tears. No Plonplon to sour the air of the council chamber with his lumbering presence. How jubilant I felt!

Jubilant!

Dear heaven, what a fool I was! A speedy victory? The idiocy of that vain boast! A long and difficult war? Difficult, yes, but *long?* My pen falters; there are splashes of ink on the paper. I wish with all my heart I were a sober, industrious editor compiling a date-crammed dictionary of events. No emotion, no comments, no explanations. Just a minimum of words, a date, more brief words, another date:

July 3 . . . crisis begins; July 19 . . . France declares war; July 28 . . . Nap. III leaves for battlefield; July 30 . . . Nap. III finds army unprepared at Metz; Aug. 2 . . . Empress receives telegram, first battle, victory suggested.

Victory! An inconclusive skirmish at Sarrebruck, exaggerated out of all proportion in the official bulletins. The people expected good news immediately, Napoleon wrote privately, therefore they must have it. Paris went wild with joy, unaware that the generals, quarreling among themselves, were making real organization difficult.

A separate telegram contained a special reference to Loulou:

He showed no emotion under the baptism of fire. He might well have been strolling in the Bois de Boulogne. His calmness was admirable. In the front line balls and bullets fell at our feet. He picked up a spent bullet to keep as a souvenir. Strong men shed tears on observing his coolness.

Ollivier, who conferred with me several times a day, shed tears himself on reading this telegram and insisted on publishing it. Paris was delighted. Long live the Prince Imperial!

News of the first real disaster reached Saint-Cloud

just before dinner on Saturday, August sixth. An Imperial aide-de-camp, Admiral Gravière, waited with me in the study while the telegram was being decoded. Unsuspicious, he was in very high spirits.

"Paris is in a mood to celebrate, Madame. According to the most persistent rumor, the Crown Prince of Prussia has surrendered with twenty-five thousand men."

It was then that the secretary handed me the first part of the telegram. I read it in disbelief and gave it to Gravière.

"Impossible!" he gasped.

"Read it aloud, Monsieur."

And in a horrified whisper he read: We are in full retreat.

Sentence by sentence the decoded message was placed in my hands. Several generals had suffered a shocking defeat. The provinces of Alsace and Lorraine were indefensible. In the heat of battle, a spasm of pain had caused Napoleon to dismount. The message ended with the words: All may yet be retrieved.

Richard and Pauline Metternich had come out from Paris to dine with me. They listened gravely to my news and assured me with a false heartiness that all was not yet lost. After all, only one section of the army was in retreat.

"Richard," I said, as calmly as I could, "we have already discussed the possibility of Austria joining France . . ."

He shrugged lightly. "The discussions shall continue naturally." His shrug told me all I wanted to know. A French victory would have tempted Austria, but now . . . Oh God! Those five incredible words: We are in full retreat.

My thoughts turned next to the Italian Ambassador, the poet Nigra. Discussions with him had brought up the question of the French garrison in Rome. What if I offered to withdraw it? I knew the futility of that. The promise of Rome would never tempt Victor Emmanuel now. All he need do was wait. I pulled myself up sharply. I must believe in final victory; *not* final defeat.

Later that night Ollivier sent the Prefect of Paris to Saint-Cloud. The news had reached the city. Paris was in turmoil. Ollivier had been surrounded in the street by an angry, menacing mob. There were cries of "Down with the Empire!" and "Down with the Empress!" In a matter of moments the war had become *my* war.

"Monsieur Ollivier urges Your Majesty to return to the Tuileries," the Prefect said.

"As Marie Antoinette did—to face the mob?"

"Your Majesty will be safer at the Tuileries. The guard at Saint-Cloud is a small one."

"Reinforcements could be brought out," Gravière suggested.

"Since this is my war," I said, "my headquarters are naturally at the Tuileries."

I reached Paris after midnight and called a council meeting. One major decision was reached. Parliament, now in recess, must be convened at once. Ollivier objected. He feared a vote of no confidence in his Ministry. So did I, but this was the Spanish woman's war. There was another meeting at seven o'clock that Sunday morning. Measures were discussed for the defense of Paris and a proclamation which I issued the next day, Monday the eighth, was drafted. Oh, such brave, empty words!

"Frenchmen, the beginning of the war is unfavorable. There have been unfavorable beginnings before. Stand firm with me in the face of this reverse. I call for one united party and that party the whole French nation. Here I am in your midst, the first at the post of danger, and here I remain. Defend with me the flag of France, the banner of national honor."

From then on, from August eighth to September fourth, I scarcely slept. Sometimes Pepa undressed me for a brief rest, but whether it was the middle of the day or the middle of the night, I did not know. Often enough I rested in my clothes, then rose for another council meeting, another private interview with this or that minister, another weary argument. The thought of food revolted me, but I must have eaten from time to time, alone in my study. Occasionally I walked in the palace gardens. The gates were locked against the public but behind the railings I sometimes saw clenched fists and heard hoarse cries of rage.

On August ninth, I dismissed Ollivier as the mob demanded. That same day, the Liberal Ministry resigned and Ollivier himself fled to Switzerland.

On the tenth, the lying Lebœuf was dismissed and a new Minister of War appointed. At the same time Napoleon relinquished his post of Commander-in-Chief but remained with the army at Châlons where a stand was being made for the defense of Paris. Fists were still shaken through the palace railings but not quite so violently. The new commander might yet work a miracle.

August eighteenth. Yes, that is another important date. Pepa roused me at two in the morning. General Trochu had arrived from Châlons and requested an immediate interview.

"Madame," he announced, "the Emperor has made me Governor of Paris."

I looked at the man angrily. Ollivier had wanted to make him Minister of War but, not trusting him, knowing him to be closely allied with Plonplon, I had refused to agree. Then my anger faded. For after all Trochu was popular with the people, and that was the reason why Napoleon had made him Governor. I listened while he discussed the coming siege of Paris—a foregone conclusion, it seemed—and the need to send the crown jewels and the treasure of the Louvre to Brest for possible shipment abroad.

"Have you news of my son?" I asked.

"His Imperial Highness has been sent to the Belgian

frontier. Rest assured, Madame, the young man is in no danger."

"Tell me about the Emperor."

"His Majesty is far too ill to sit a horse, but that information is being kept as secret as possible. At a passing glance one would say that his health has improved. A touch of rouge on the cheeks . . ." Trochu laughed as if at a joke and added, "His Majesty is on the point of returning to Paris."

Returning!" I exclaimed. "Does he actually want to return?"

"His Majesty's state of mind is difficult to understand. I myself judge his return essential, as does the Prince Napoleon. His Majesty can do no good by remaining with the army, but he is still the Emperor. I accepted the governorship on the understanding that he would follow me to Paris. Hated as he is, the cloak of my own popularity will shield him. It will shield Your Majesty also."

"My life may be in danger, but I'm not afraid of the mob," I said furiously. "Keep your cloak for yourself."

I wasted no time in sending Napoleon a telegram. Did he want people to say that he was running away from danger? We were on the brink of revolution. His appearance in Paris would bring the mob into the Tuileries. I reminded him of Plonplon and the Crimea, the sneers of the people at that time, and I begged him to return only after a victory. Later, the Council of Regency supported me in this and Napoleon, his health more shattered than I realized, replied briefly: I shall remain with the army.

Then I sent for Trochu. "You came to Paris on one condition, Monsieur. That condition has been removed."

He fell to his knees and kissed my hand. "Madame, I am a Breton, a Catholic and a soldier. I'll serve you to the death!"

A Breton . . . a flowery way of saying that he was an honest man. I felt greater distrust of him than ever. An honest man had no need of a flood of words to express his devotion to duty. I remember rubbing the back of my hand roughly the moment he left my presence.

During the next two weeks I gave as much time as possible to hospital work at the Tuileries, for I'd turned the palace into a hospital for the wounded who were pouring daily into the capital. The suffering I saw wrung my heart, yet the gratitude of the dying, their simple words of praise and thanks, gave me no consolation. Honor and duty . . . The two words embittered my thoughts. Had I really declared with the rest that war was inevitable if French honor was to be saved? A slap in the face which none could sustain, and as a result France was bleeding to death.

Mars-la-Tour— That was another defeat, followed almost at once by Gravelotte, yet another. And then, after a brief respite, an unofficial report claimed that the Emperor was a prisoner in Prussian hands. While waiting for official confirmation, believing but trying not to believe, I sorted out the state documents in Napoleon's study, keeping some, destroying others.

That was September second. On the afternoon of the third, Chevreau, the Minister of the Interior, informed me that many of the palace servants had packed and left the Tuileries. Then he placed in my hand a newly decoded telegram from Napoleon and I steeled myself to read it:

The army is defeated and captive. I myself am a prisoner. Failing to meet death in the midst of my soldiers, I have been forced to surrender in order to save the army.

The little sheet of paper fluttered to the floor. "He should have killed himself first!" I cried hysterically.

Chevreau said: "By 'the army,' the Emperor means the forces at Sedan. Another army is still fighting at Metz."

"How crazy!"

Chevreau bowed. "Madame, we must double the palace guard."

"I won't permit it, Monsieur. No blood shall be shed on my behalf. Have you—have you news of the Prince Imperial?"

"The Emperor ordered him to cross the Belgian frontier. I know no more than that."

"Send for Trochu."

"A wise decision, Madame. He alone can keep order in Paris."

Admiral Gravière sought out Trochu, only to discover that the gallant Governor was somewhat tired after an exhausting inspection of the forts. Moreover, he was hungry and on the point of dining. Chevreau himself went to see the man and reported that he would wait on me after dinner. I spent most of the night destroying private papers and reading newly arrived dispatches from Sedan, each of which stated clearly that the position was hopeless. When I went to bed at four in the morning, Trochu had failed to keep his word.

Pepa roused me at six o'clock. I could hear the church bells ringing. It was Sunday, September fourth. Summer had briefly returned. The morning was bright and clear, with the promise of a day much too hot for that time of the year. I went to my private chapel at seven, chided myself for wasting time on my knees and hurried to the wounded in the Salle des Spectacles. A spectacle, like nothing that had ever been presented there before. At nine o'clock, my last council meeting and there—behold, a bright and chirpy Trochu.

"Either you dine at a peculiar hour, Monsieur, or much too lengthily," I said chillingly.

Trochu laughed gaily and led me to a window. The

Rue de Rivoli was crowded with people but there was no sign of any violent disturbance. He bowed deeply but refrained, thank heaven, from trying to kiss my hand.

"No one can deny that the hour of great danger is at hand, Madame, but I, the Governor, am determined to keep order."

"I pray for your continued success, Monsieur."

"The forces at my disposal are well ordered and ready to obey my instant command. If necessary, the Tuileries shall be surrounded by a band of resolute soldiers. Any man who wishes to harm you must first pass over my dead body."

With that he begged to be excused and hurried away to make another inspection of the forts. I felt a little happier now and even regretted having distrusted him.

The Legislative Body had sat throughout the night and presently a solemn-faced deputation appeared at the council meeting with the request that I should relinquish my Regency powers and place all state affairs in the hands of a council set up by the Body. I refused at once.

"The Emperor made me Regent and the government accepted his will. The Emperor is a prisoner, but *I* am still at liberty. I represent my son, your future Emperor. The dynasty is the concern of the whole of France, not the Legislative Body alone. My concern at this moment is far removed from politics. Paris is in grave danger. I cannot abandon my post. I, the Regent, am not a deserter—"

Before I could say anything more a wild-eyed young man, a complete stranger, burst into the council chamber, shouting, "The mob is in the Place de la Concorde!"

I went to the window. A rapid change was taking place. A solid bank of screaming people was sweeping from the Rue de Rivoli into the Place de la Concorde and as I watched and listened, the leaders reached the palace railings and the locked gates. Then I saw the workmen on top of the ladders. They were hammering at the Imperial Eagles. I turned away wearily as one crashed to the ground. Where was Trochu?

Gravière placed a newly arrived telegram in my hands. Napoleon had refused to treat with Bismarck, had referred him to me, the Regent. I felt faintly heartened. A battle of wits with Bismarck and something saved. Paris itself, perhaps.

The leader of the deputation approached again and repeated his request that I go over to the Legislative Body.

"Have you a decree of abdication in your pocket?" I asked.

He smiled in relief. "That has yet to be drawn up, Madame, but—"

"Draw it up as soon as you can. I still have the strength to tear it to shreds. You may seize my powers but you'll never force me to abdicate."

During the afternoon, somebody told me that Trochu was being detained at the Hôtel de Ville. I think my informant was Richard Metternich—or possibly Nigra. Both had certainly appeared at the time.

"We must have tea," I said. "Nigra shall recite his latest verses."

Nobody laughed. Not even Pauline Metternich.

Nigra led me to the window. The crowd behind the railings was thicker, clamoring more than ever. The pressure on the gates was so violent I expected them to burst open at any moment. We were looking at the scum of Paris, said Nigra, the beasts of prey who were seen only when revolution took the place of ordered government. I stared in horror at the women. There were so many of them. Death at the hands of the mob—I wasn't afraid of that, but I grew hot with shame at the thought of those grimacing viragoes lifting my skirts, tearing at them, screaming lewdly.

Metternich and Gravière joined us at the window.

"The palace guards are still faithful," said Gravière.

"Is it possible to keep back the mob without bloodshed?"

"No, Madame. And even then, without help from Trochu—"

"Not a single shot is to be fired. Is that clearly understood?"

"Clearly, Madame."

"I urge Your Majesty to consider the necessity of flight," Metternich said quickly.

"I'm determined not to run away. You know that, Richard."

He and Nigra pleaded with me for an hour. Others did also. A peculiar lethargy had settled upon me. The faces of those friends who still remained with me grew blurred; even their voices were at times unrecognizable. Suddenly, one face stood out clearly—that of the Prefect of Paris.

"The mob is breaking down the railings. Your Majesty's only hope lies in immediate flight."

"Even if no harm came to you," said Nigra, "the Legislative Body would force you to abdicate."

My mind cleared momentarily. Only my abdication could make a republic legal. That decided me. Flight and *no* abdication. The Empire, my son's Empire, would go into temporary exile.

"Come," said Metternich, "there's barely time." He took my arm. "Hurry, Madame, hurry!"

But what a crazy flight it was, that escape from the Tuileries! Friends crowded about me, weeping and kissing my hands. Vaguely I saw Ferdinand de Lesseps and Baron Haussmann and, turning as Metternich led me from the room, I saw that Nigra was following with Madame Lebreton, the lady-in-waiting who was apparently to be my sole companion. Quickly we passed through the galleries of the Tuileries and reached those of the

304

Louvre where I stopped for a moment, arrested by the fixed, haunting smile of the "Mona Lisa." It seemed to me that Leonardo da Vinci, looking to the future, had created that mysterious smile for me alone.

The smile followed me out to the Place St. Germain l'Auxerrois. It was five o'clock. There were people everywhere. We drew back as small procession of young men with pale fanatical faces pushed through the crowd. "Down with the Spanish woman!" they chanted. How ludicrous! No wonder the "Mona Lisa" smiled mysteriously. There was the Spanish woman in their very midst and nobody recognized her. Nigra summoned a passing cab. Two ladies were off on a sight-seeing jaunt. Madame Lebreton and I clambered into the cab. Metternich closed the shutters over the windows.

"Richard, where are we going?" I asked.

"Monsieur Besson's house, Boulevard Haussmann. He's utterly trustworthy."

"And then?"

"England, by way of Le Havre."

At that moment a ragged little urchin thrust himself between Nigra and Metternich. "It's the Empress!" Nigra kicked him sharply in the ribs and Metternich slammed the cab door.

I sank back in my seat and with my mind clear again, began to take stock of my appearance. A healthy sign that! I wore a black cashmere dress, very crumpled since I hadn't changed it for days. I fingered the white collar, fretting at the thought that it must be filthy. Somebody had placed an unbecoming black felt hat on my head with a black veil attached. Somebody else had hooked a raincoat over my arm. Dear Mr. Worth, thank heaven he hadn't been at the Tuileries to catch a horrified glimpse of the Empress of Fashion! I then discovered that I was grasping a small reticule and, opening it, curiously came upon two handkerchiefs.

Things were not as desperate as they seemed. If it rained, I had a raincoat; if I caught a cold, I had *two* handkerchiefs.

Chapter Twenty-One

MONSIEUR BESSON was not at home when Madame Lebreton and I reached the Boulevard Haussmann. The street was quiet enough. I expect the timid ones were indoors with the curtains drawn while the others were enjoying the fun in the center of Paris. There was even a sleepy Sunday afternoon air about the place, but Madame Lebreton grew frightened after knocking several times and ordered the cabdriver to take us to the Avenue Wagram where my chamberlain lived. That house was deserted too. I don't know what made me think of our American dentist, Dr. Evans; certainly I hadn't a toothache at the time. But in addition to being the court dentist, he was one of Napoleon's old friends, so quite probably that was the reason.

A servant showed us into the reception room. Mrs. Evans was on holiday at Deauville and the doctor was attending to a patient who was anxious to have a hollow tooth capped before the Prussians marched into Paris.

Evans appeared at last, unaware of my identity until I removed my veil.

"Your *Majesty!*"

"Dr. Evans, I'm hungry."

He was a kindly man with a black beard and a handsome profile. "Your Majesty must dine at once," he said, pleasingly practical.

Shortly I was eating heartily. It was my first real meal in weeks. Madame Lebreton merely picked at her food and cast upon me many a look of shocked surprise.

The food was actually smuggled to us in a small back room since Evans himself was entertaining twenty guests at dinner that night. He behaved admirably. His guests discussed my disappearance from the Tuileries. They were well aware of his friendship with Napoleon and looked at him curiously. Betraying himself in no way, he suggested that I was well on my way to Belgium. At midnight he bade the last guest goodnight, and I was able to emerge from my hiding place.

Meanwhile Dr. Evans had made plans for me. It would be foolish to attempt to reach the coast by train. With his assistant, Dr. Crane, he would drive me to Deauville where Mrs. Evans would look after me while he and Crane found a boat in which to make the Channel crossing. Madame Lebreton was to pose as a nurse, I as a patient suffering from a nervous breakdown. Accepting the implication that I had a distracted look, I went to bed, to dream again and again that I was in a lunatic asylum, the maddest creature there. Waking at dawn, I regretted bitterly that the dream was not reality. Madness would have been a fine escape.

At five-thirty, after a cup of coffee and a roll, we were in Dr. Evans' landau—the doctor, Madame Lebreton, young Dr. Crane and the mental patient. Paris had quieted during the night. There'd been no invasion of the Tuileries, no bloodshed. We were at Nantes when Dr. Evans told me this.

"Perhaps I should go back and take them all by surprise," I said.

Evans had found a new carriage and fresh horses. He had also bought a newspaper which he gave me now in silence. TROCHU. The printed name caught my eyes at once. Detained at the Hôtel de Ville indeed! The traitor had been merely waiting there for a call from the Legislative Body. He was now president of the government, and a Republic had been declared. Those oily words of his! And all the time he was planning to betray me!

Soon after this, Dr. Evans discovered that a certain

Sir John Burgoyne was at Trouville aboard his yacht, the *Gazelle*. Sir John agreed to take me across the Channel to the safety of England. There was a dreadful storm and we were in very great danger, but Death remained aloof. At seven o'clock on the morning of September eighth, three days after leaving Paris, I went ashore at Ryde, threw aside my veil and thanked God for England. It was wrong of me, but in the same breath I cursed Trochu.

Loulou was already in England, waiting for me at Hastings where I joined him without a moment's delay. His set face and the troubled, tragic look in his young eyes deprived me momentarily of speech. Tense with emotion, we embraced in silence.

"What a peculiar smell," I ventured presently, my nostrils twitching.

"Boiled cabbage, Mama," he said very seriously. "The English love it, especially when staying at the seaside."

"A strange people."

"But very hospitable."

Then we laughed together and with the emotional tension thus relieved, we fell into each other's arms again, asking question after question without waiting for a single answer.

I remained for a time at Hastings, and while there Pauline Metternich paid me a visit, bringing with her most of my jewelry which she had succeeded in smuggling out of France. Shocked to find me in such miserable circumstances, she urged Dr. Evans to look about for a comfortable country house and so, due to the good doctor's efforts, I was soon able to take possession of Camden Place at Chislehurst, a bare nine miles from London.

My thoughts turned often to Queen Victoria who came at last to see me at Camden Place. The sight of her made me wonder if the old friendship had survived or if she had come merely to pity me. Pity! I wanted none of that and I received her with all the formality I could summon to my aid. Conversation was difficult at first, for I was bitterly conscious of the fact that the Crown Prince of Prussia, the Queen's son-in-law, was now in residence at Versailles and that Bismarck was preparing his bombardment of Paris. Loulou's presence helped a little. He, the man of the house, had received Her Majesty in his father's absence and, unlike me, was betraying neither nervousness nor resentment.

"Do forgive me for being so long in coming to greet you," Victoria said when Loulou had withdrawn. "It would grieve me so very much if you thought I regarded you as an unwelcome guest in my country."

"I came hurriedly and without invitation," I said woodenly.

"But bravely—oh so bravely! Your courage has aroused much admiration. That dreadful storm in the Channel! Sir John Burgoyne told me all about it." Victoria hesitated, dismayed, I can but think, by my unresponsive attitude. "You—you must come and visit me at Windsor and bring the Prince Imperial. Such a nice child."

"He wouldn't relish that description, Madame," I said, as woodenly as before.

"No, of course not! How tactless of me. Having been under fire he naturally regards himself as a man . . . Oh dear, this is indeed one of my tactless days! I had no intention of mentioning that horrible, senseless war. I—" She broke off, much at a loss for further words.

"Shall we talk about clothes instead?" I said, my heart melting a little.

Victoria brightened visibly. "A safer subject, yes!" Then her face fell. "My interest in clothes is not very pronounced these days. No, no, pray don't say how obvious that is!"

The Queen was plainly and severely dressed, but that had been her rule ever since Albert's death and she seemed unlikely to break it. She was in mourning, poor woman, lifelong mourning.

Presently she touched my hand shyly. "Your husband will be welcome in my country. You will, I hope and pray, find some personal happiness in exile—you, your husband, your son."

Personal happiness but in exile. The finality of the word came close to angering me, yet I knew without doubt that Victoria spoke with the utmost kindness.

"You are still very beautiful in spite of all your suffering, but your paleness worries me," she went on, with a pitiful attempt at briskness. "Are you eating proper meals?" And she added when I remained stubbornly silent, "I suspect you are scarcely eating at all. There is, perhaps, a certain constriction in the throat?"

"Yes," I admitted.

"Then, Madame," she said bossily, "I recommend an undoubted tonic—a mixture of rum and warm milk."

I laughed at this suggestion, but hysterically. Queen Victoria, the widow's bonnet bobbing on her head, recommending *rum!* With that she rose to go, leaving me to wonder if my laughter had offended her.

"You will come to Windsor, and soon?"

"If Your Majesty commands it."

Tears sprang to Victoria's eyes. "Dear sister, I do not command, I *invite*. And I speak as a woman, not a queen hedged in by protocol and weighted down by state affairs. I speak, pray do believe me, as a friend, one in need of friendship perhaps even more than you are in need of it yourself."

I knew then that the old friendship had indeed survived and would deepen and strengthen during the years ahead, sustaining and comforting me through whatever trials the future might hold for me.

"Life cannot be everything as we both know," she said gently. "God alone can give us courage and console us."

We embraced, and once again she called me "dear

sister." Small wonder that, because of Victoria, exile grew bearable, even acceptable in the end, and England, Victoria's England, became my permanent home.

Author's Footnote

AND AFTERWARD?

Napoleon III, released when a besieged and starving Paris had capitulated, joined his wife and son in England. He was sixty-two but looked much older and was in very poor health. Eugenie nursed him and a companionship such as they had never known before developed between them. She refused, however, to be influenced by the wild talk of the Bonapartists who plotted and schemed to overthrow the Third Republic which had now replaced the Second Empire, but Napoleon listened eagerly. However, he decided to undergo the operation which he had already delayed too long before attempting a *coup d'état*. This—lithotripsy—taxed his heart severely and brought about his death.

Meanwhile, Loulou, now styled "The Pretender" but regarded by French exiles as Napoleon IV, continued the studies he had taken up at the Royal Military College at Woolwich. He was a soldier intent on learning his profession thoroughly before attempting to establish a new Empire in France. After graduating at Woolwich, he was attached, at Queen Victoria's suggestion, to the Artillery Corps. Restless, yet determined to return to France only if the French nation called him, he went with the British forces to fight the Zulus in South Africa. There he fell in a Zulu ambush, suffering seventeen assegai wounds before he died. The Zulus themselves likened him to a lion, the bravest animal they knew.

It was thought that Eugenie, who had moved from

Chislehurst to a larger country house at Farnborough Hill, would either die of grief or take the veil. Sustained by Queen Victoria's warm friendship, she did neither and, though ignored by France except to be stigmatized as "the Spanish woman," she visited that country *incognita,* bought a yacht and traveled as far afield as Asia Minor, Greece and India. She evinced a lively interest in all that was happening in the world. Modern inventions fascinated her. She was quick to install a telephone at Farnborough and to buy one of the first electric broughams to reach the market. At the age of eighty, she was healthy and energetic enough to climb Mt. Vesuvius. In time she came to forgive her political enemies. She made many friends, including Marconi, who conducted important experiments in wireless telegraphy aboard her yacht. Outliving Queen Victoria, it seemed that the fortune teller might be proved right and that Eugenie would last a hundred years. Unhappily she caught a cold while in Madrid not long after her operation for cataract. That was in 1920. She was ninety-four.

Eugenie's body was taken back to England where *The Times* wrote of her: "Even in the stories of fallen sovereigns there are few so striking and so sad as that of the once brilliant Empress of the French whose bones will lie at Farnborough. She has played her part, and played it with a rare nobleness and dignity."

TOWER NON-FICTION TELLS THE STORY
OF THE REAL WEST

T-125-7 COMPACT HISTORY OF THE
INDIAN WARS by John Tebbel $1.25
Fascinating account of the Indian Wars that raged
in America for 300 years. Fast-paced, readable narra-
tive of uprising and revolt by an acknowledged
American expert.

T-095-13 THE GHOST DANCE MESSIAH
by Paul Bailey   95¢
A Tower original. The story of Wovoka, a Paiute
Indian who became the Messiah of the Indian na-
tions and founded a mystic religion based on the
Ghost Dance.

T-075-17 THE SNAKE DANCE OF THE HOPI
INDIANS by Earle R. Forrest   75¢
An exciting, colorful account of the dance still danced
by the Hopi Indians. Holding deadly rattlesnakes in
their arms and mouths, the Hopis petition the gods
for life-giving rain.

T-095-40 LOS HERMANOS PENITENTES
by Lorayne Horka-Follick   95¢
The story of the secret brotherhood self-exiled in
New Mexico since the 16th century. They practice
flagellation to atone for their sins and crucifixion to
celebrate Christ's death.

T-125-16 BOOK OF INDIAN LIFE CRAFTS
by Oscar E. Norbeck $1.25
Complete handbook of North American Indian crafts,
designs, customs and life styles. 300 unique civiliza-
tions each with its own language and customs. Fully
illustrated.

T-095-59 INDIAN SLAVE TRADE IN THE
SOUTHWEST by L. R. Bailey   95¢
A little-known horror of American history. A barbaric
slave trade in Indians went on until 1935 in the
Southwest United States. Thousands of Indians were
forced to work in mines.

T-095-71 VAST DOMAIN OF BLOOD
by Don Schellie   95¢
Exciting, violent saga of the Camp Grant Massacre
in Arizona. One of the bloodiest incidents in the
history of the American Indian when an Apache
camp was massacred and the whites responsible were
brought to trial.

T-095-66 ON THE BLOODY TRAIL OF
GERONIMO by Lt. John Bigelow, Jr.   95¢
An exciting, first-hand account of the famed Negro
Tenth Cavalry and their relentless pursuit of Geroni-
mo, the most feared Indian in the Southwest.

T-095-76 WHO KILLED CUSTER? by Jack Parks   95¢
Tower Original. More than a historical account of
Custer and his defeat, this is an exciting account of
the parallel lives of Custer and White Bull, the Sioux
who claimed to have killed Custer at the Little Big-
horn.

MEN AT WAR

TOWER HISTORY BOOKS
OF EXCEPTIONAL INTEREST

T-095-7   I WAS THE NUREMBERG JAILER   75¢
     —Col. Burton C. Andrus
The story of the German prisoners held at Nuremberg as told by the American officer who ran the Nuremberg prison. Includes documents and incidents never before revealed.

T-095-14 FABRIC OF TERROR   95¢
     —Bernardo Teixiera
The shocking story of a little known war that raged in West Africa with incredible atrocities and loss of life. With an introduction by Robert Ruark.

T-125-13 THE AVENGERS $1.25
     —Michael Bar-Zohar
The story of the Israeli Brigade, a band of Jews out to revenge the six million dead and who will continue to do so until not a Nazi is left alive.

T-075-16 INCREDIBLE MISSION   75¢
     —Fernande Leboucher
The story of Pere Benoit, a Catholic priest who set up an underground railroad that stretched across Europe and helped thousands of Jews escape the Gestapo.

T-095-53 ACE OF SPIES   95¢
     —Robin Bruce Lockhart
The biography of the most incredible spy in history, Sidney Reilly, who infiltrated the German General Staff, had eleven wives and changed the course of history.

T-125-27 THE YOUNG HITLER I KNEW $1.25
     —August Kubizek
Here is a portrait of Hitler as a young man and student by a man that was his best friend. A revealing insight into the making of a dictator and a madman.

PUBLIC AFFAIRS BOOKS

T-095-38   HELLHOLE by Sara Harris   95¢
           Spell-binding report on life among the prisoners
           in New York's House of Detention for Women.
           By a top-flight reporter.

T-095-63   SKID ROW U.S.A. by Sara Harris   95¢
           A shocking, true account of the men and women
           who populate Skid Row and how they got there.

T-095-70   VOICES FROM SLAVERY   95¢
           by John Harris
           Original. Account of slavery in the old South as
           told in the words of those who were once slaves.

T-150-01   OPERATION OVERFLIGHT $1.50
           by Francis Gary Powers
           The first-hand account of the famous U-2 spy
           plane as told by its pilot who was tried as a spy
           in the Soviet Union.

T-095-78   THE LIVING ROOM WAR   95¢
           by Michael Arlen
           Controlled, sharp, factual account of how tele-
           vision has handled the Vietnam War and Amer-
           ican society in general.

T-125-23   GREAT GUERRILLA WARRIORS $1.25
           by Carleton Beals
           Biographical essays and exploits of the world's
           most famous liberators including Che, Ho Chi
           Minh and Zapata.

T-095-92   SPIRO! by Paul Hoffman   95¢
           Original. A top-flight reporter traces the career
           of Spiro Agnew the most controversial Vice-
           president in American history.

TOWER BOOKS OF EXCEPTIONAL INTEREST

TOWER COOKBOOKS

T-095-12 SINGLE GIRL'S GUIDE TO COOKING &   95¢
          ENTERTAINING—Dixie Dean Trainer
          Original cookbook of tested recipes for the working
          girl. Easy recipes for two or a crowd.

T-095-21 THE BEER COOKBOOK   95¢
          —Berneita Tolson & Edith McCaig
          Over 200 recipes using beer . . . delicious lager . . .
          as the main flavor ingredient.

T-095-28 THE HOUSE OF INDIA COOKBOOK   95¢
          —Syed Abdullah
          The only paperback available on the art of Indian
          cooking. Including how to prepare Indian-style dinner
          parties.

T-095-33 GOURMET COOKING ON A SHOESTRING   95¢
          —Gerri Tully
          How to feed a family of nine and still make ends
          meet. Delicious meals for only pennies a serving.
          Original.

T-095-37 SAVORY STEWS   95¢
          —Mary Savage
          Tasty, easy-to-prepare and delicious recipes for all
          kinds of stews, the budget-minded cook's dream come
          true.

T-095-64 CHINESE COOKING WITH AMERICAN   95¢
          MEALS—Moira Hodgson
          Now! Chinese dishes that are easy to prepare, with
          ingredients that are easy to find, to combine with your
          favorite meals.

T-095-69 HOMEMADE BREAD   95¢
          —Food Editors of Farm Journal Magazine
          All the new short-cuts to making yeast bread. One of
          the most popular cookbooks ever published.

T-125-25 FARM JOURNAL'S PIE COOKBOOK $1.25
          From the pages of Farm Journal Magazine come
          recipes for all kinds of pies, tarts, dumplings and
          desserts.

Tower Publications, Inc., 185 Madison Avenue
New York, New York 10016

Please send me the books listed below.

ORDER BY BOOK NUMBER ONLY.

Quantity	Book No.	Price
....	....	....
....	....	....
....	....	....
....	....	....
....	....	....
....	....	....
....	....	....
....	....	....

In the event we are out of stock of any of the books listed, please list alternate selections below.

....	....	....
....	....	....
....	....	....
....	....	....

I enclose $.............

NAME ....
(please print)

ADDRESS ....

CITY.................... STATE........ ZIP..........

(Send cash, check or money order)
NO STAMPS PLEASE

Add 15¢ for every Canadian dollar order. Please allow 4 weeks for filling orders. No C.O.D.'s please.

Eugénie –
Empress of France –
Empress of Fashion

This is the authentic story of how a dark-haired
Spanish beauty, daughter of a merchant family,
married Louis Napoleon and became Empress of
France. A colorful and intellectually superior woman, Eugénie was admired for her strength of character and her endurance of the embarrassment of
her husband's notorious flings. She was the Queen
of Fashion and held glittering salons attended by
Pauline Metternich, wife of the Austrian Chancel-
lor, and Queen Victoria of England, among others.
Eugénie soon entered into her country's intricate
politics. She handled intrigues, plots and counterplots with incredible political skill, and ruled as
Empress-Regent during her husband's absences
from the country during war. The story of this
fascinating woman is presented along with a splendid recreation of one of the fabulous periods in
history.